Retribution

Vera Morrill

Library of Congress Control Number:		2010903361
ISBN:	Hardcover	978-1-4500-5979-4
	Softcover	978-1-4500-5978-7
	Ebook	978-1-4500-5980-0

This book was printed in the United States of America.

To order additional copies of this book, contact:
Xlibris Corporation
0-800-644-6988
www.xlibrispublishing.co.uk
Orders@xlibrispublishing.co.uk
300219

*For those who are troubled
and those who care for them.*

*'The web of our life is of a mingled yarn,
good and ill together.'
All's Well That Ends Well – Shakespeare*

PROLOGUE

1991

Carefully Susan Hatton unfolded the yellowing newspaper cuttings. The first, she laid to one side. The words there she knew only too well. They had become a part of her life. The second, 'Born Evil?' with its picture of Adolf Hitler, she also discarded. The third and last, was what she needed to read again. It bore the title 'Genius and Madness' and was a report in layman's language about a suggested link between the two characteristics and the fine line which might separate them. The fact that Giles now believed their daughter Gemma, not only clever, but abnormally so, was something she had never wanted to hear.

Was Gemma a bearer of her grandmother's disturbed genes? A genius, bordering on something sinister? How carefully she had watched her own two daughters, until such a time as she had felt it safe to relax and transfer that watchfulness to the newly born Leo.

If she were to approach anyone in the medical sphere about Gemma, there was little doubt that everything would soon be in the public domain. There were few secrets in villages such as theirs. How could she tell Giles, a Vicar, that he'd married the daughter of a murderess? How could she face the villagers, her children's teachers, once they knew her background? How would this affect not only Gemma, but her other children? For years now she had tried to develop a steely resolve which had, she knew carried her through many difficult situations. Sadly, she had sensed that it had nurtured a dislike in some quarters. About that she had been able to do little. Her resolve was a carapace, protecting her from the many trials and tribulations which life seemed determined to throw at her.

The cuttings folded and replaced in their hiding place, she checked her face for signs of tears and went downstairs to pick up, once again, the unpredictable reins of her life.

CHAPTER 1

1985

Within ten minutes of making her brother's acquaintance, Gemma knew she hated him. Everything had been lovely. Everyone had been excited and happy, anticipating his birth. Even big sister Auriol, in bed with a heavy cold, had asked constantly if there was any news. They had waited for what seemed like hours.

Then her father opened the door of the playroom and nodded to Mrs. Biggs. He took Gemma's hand and together they went into her parents' bedroom.

Mummy was propped up against the pillows looking white, but seeing Gemma she opened her arms wide and said, "Here's my darling girl, come and give me a hug, then you can meet your new baby brother, Leo, our Little Prince."

There had been a hint of something different there. Gemma had always been their 'Little Princess' and Auriol, lost in her world of books, hadn't seemed to mind. Now it seemed there was also a prince in the family. Red and wrinkled, he looked more like a doll and Gemma reached out and squeezed his hand to make sure he was real.

Suddenly the doll-like face was even more red and wrinkled and from the tiny mouth there came a cross between a screech and a wail, so loud that Gemma jerked back, almost losing her balance.

In a flash, the peaceful ambience of the room was changed. "What have you done you naughty girl?" This from Mummy, then to Daddy,

"Give Leo to me and take the child away." And as the baby was placed in her mother's arms, "There, there my little Prince, it's alright now, Mummy has you safe and sound. Did your naughty sister give you a fright?" In that moment Gemma knew things were going to be different. Knew that this baby had usurped her own precious place in her mother's love. And, as she retraced her steps to the playroom, she muttered to herself, over and over again, *Just you wait, Leo Hatton, just you wait. I'll get my own back, you'll see.*

And so it began.

Something had gone wrong. Disastrously wrong. This child had left her, bubbling over with excitement, now she moved as if in a trance, unaware of her surroundings.

Eileen Biggs broke the silence, "Gemma, darling, is it a boy, or a girl? Come over here and tell me all about it." No response.

"Have Mummy and Daddy decided on a name yet?"

The child muttered something, just decipherable as 'Leo', then moved to the furthest corner of the room and stared out of the window. Eileen Biggs, so-called Nanny to the Hattons, followed her, and pulling up a chair, tried unsuccessfully to draw Gemma onto her lap. The child remained rigid and silent.

"Leo, that's a nice name. Now you'll have a little brother to play with."

Again, no reply. What on earth could have gone wrong, to have reduced the child to such a dejected state? Surely the Vicar and his wife were well aware of the potential problems, when introducing a new family member? For heaven's sake, they must already have been down that road with Auriol, when Gemma herself was born. It was inconceivable, in this day and age, that they had not gone to great lengths to ensure Gemma felt included in their warmth and happiness at the new birth. Inconceivable perhaps, but . . . ?

At the window, Gemma brooded over the events of the past minutes, the rigid set of her shoulders and the lack of response to Eileen's gentle questions, confirmed that lady's fears.

Inconceivable perhaps, but something *had* gone disastrously wrong, as became very evident in the following days. Once Susan and her new infant became part of the family's daily routine, Eileen saw Gemma never touched, nor spoke to the baby. The girls were often having breakfast whilst Sue Hatton was giving the baby his morning feed. This she did discreetly, half turned towards the warmth of the Aga, but whenever there were gurgles of contentment from the baby, Eileen noticed that Gemma glowered in their direction. Whilst Auriol would often go over and stroke Leo's head or hold his little hand, Gemma acted for the most part as if he was invisible.

Desperately, Eileen tried to redress the balance, but whatever had happened in the bedroom, following the household's new arrival, had deeply upset Gemma, and she showed no signs of recovering from it.

Gemma, cocooned in her own world of misery, knew that her worst fears had come true. Leo had taken over, not only Mummy, but the whole house. Repeatedly, she tried to make things happy, as they had been before,

"Mummy, will you read me a story tonight please? You haven't done that for ages and ages . . ."

"Sorry, darling, I must feed Leo after his bath and then there's Daddy's meal to prepare. Why don't you ask Nanny Biggs?"

"I did ask her and she's much too busy, and Daddy's with Auriol. It's not fair."

Gemma knew from lessons in Sunday school, that it was naughty to hurt other people, but that was probably just for big people. She'd also heard Daddy say that babies were a gift from God, but, as they hadn't had his gift for very long, she felt sure God wouldn't mind at all, if they sent Leo back to him. It was a pity, Gemma thought, that he hadn't dropped Leo into the barn on Mr. Robinson's farm, just across the fields. Mrs. Robinson didn't have any children and would probably have been glad to look after Leo. Then, together, she and Mummy, could have popped across the fields to see him and taken a gift, like the three kings did, and afterwards, come home. That way Leo wouldn't be taking up so much of Mummy's time. Gemma decided that her gift would have been

Johnson's baby powder, because Mummy always said that was the very best thing for babies.

"Are you alright Gemma? Would you like to come and help me fold these sheets?"

As always, Eileen Biggs struggled to keep Gemma involved and occupied.

"No thank you Nanny, I'm busy. I'm drawing Leo and Mummy."

"That's nice. Let me see . . ."

Looking over the child's shoulder, Eileen Biggs felt a stab of concern. The shape meant to be Susan Hatton, was in pastel pink, but the baby was coloured a violent purple. "Surely Leo isn't quite as dark as that, Gemma? It's good of your Mummy, but why isn't the baby the same colour?"

"When he cries and screws his face up, he is quite dark. That's how he looks." Eileen Biggs, returning to the laundry, mulled over for the umpteenth time, the events of the past weeks. Although she had never borne a child herself, years of assisting her sister with a large and lively brood had taught Eileen a great deal about children's emotions and sensitivities. There was still something very wrong, and no-one but herself seemed to be aware of it.

Picking up her black crayon, Gemma stabbed it into her drawing, then sat back, satisfied with the black blob on Leo's arm. Leo didn't like being squeezed. She'd found that out on that first day. She'd try it again. Today, she decided would be a good day. Leo, was probably outside now, in his pram. From the clatter of crockery, Mummy was emptying the washing up machine, and Nanny, she knew, was upstairs. Once outside, she saw that yes, the pram was in the garden and Leo was sound asleep. Carefully, Gemma reached under the safety net, which she knew was to keep out cats, and squeezed his arm. Once again, there was a howl of protest and Gemma hastily disappeared from view, hiding behind the garden shed, and watching as Susan came running out. Soon Leo was quiet again and the coast was clear for Gemma to emerge.

"Gemma where are you? Come and put your colouring things away, there's a good girl," Nanny, alerted by the sudden cry from the garden, called urgently as she came down the stairs.

"Just coming Nanny, I've been watching the rabbits in the field."

"Perhaps Gemma could come with you, Mrs. Hatton? She loves going into the village." This, as Susan was now clearly preparing herself, Leo, and the pram for a shopping expedition.

"Not today, Nanny. Gemma is so slow, and I would prefer to move along as quickly as possible. It's the only way I'm going to get my weight back to normal. Another time."

Gemma, carefully packing away her crayons and drawing, fumed at what she had heard. She was too slow now to go out with Mummy, too small to go anywhere with Daddy and Auriol, and too big to be fussed over, like Leo. But, she now knew, from what had happened in the garden, that Leo would always cry out if he was squeezed or pinched, and when she did it again, she would have to be very, very careful and make sure no-one was around to see her. That night, Leo's crying roused her, as it so often did. She heard Mummy go in to give him his night feed, then all was quiet again. This, she realised, would be her very best time for squeezing him! Once Mummy had gone back to her room, Leo went to sleep again and everyone else would be in bed and asleep.

The next night, waiting patiently, it seemed ages before her mother left Leo, but at last, all was quiet and Gemma tiptoed into his room. By the cot she waited, the dim nightlight telling her what she wanted to know, Leo was sleeping peacefully. Slowly and carefully, she lowered the side of the cot. This time, it wasn't so much as a squeeze as a pinch, lifting his tiny arm, so that she could get a good grip on the thin flesh between her own little fingers. By the time he reacted with a loud cry, she had reinstated the cot-side and was in her own room next door. Hearing Mrs. Biggs's footsteps approaching, she hastily jumped into bed, turning away from the door and drawing the bedclothes over her shoulders.

The next morning, Eileen Biggs, carefully stacking the clean linen in the airing cupboard, wondered again how such a young and presumably intelligent woman like Susan Hatton, could not see for herself that her youngest daughter was grieving over the lack of close contact with her mother. Eileen had decided when being interviewed, that her would-be employer was an authoritarian, who brooked no questioning of her own modus operandi. Now, she was well aware, from the snatches of gossip relayed to her by her sister that the villagers thought it hilarious when Sue Hatton referred to her as the family's 'Nanny'. One of them having apparently, remarked, "That's just one of Mrs. H's high falutin' ideas, Eileen's no more a trained nanny, than I'm a brain surgeon."

With the closure of the care home in the next village, Eileen's job had come to an end and, with it, her ability to rent her small cottage. The offer of a job, living in at the rectory, had proved a godsend and she had accepted, despite anticipating that Sue Hatton could well prove a difficult taskmaster. But this, she hadn't expected. Did no one in this household, other than herself, welcome this child with open arms and show her affection.

Nor did Eileen absolve Giles Hatton from blame. Kind and gentle he might be, but clearly his absorption with all things academic, left little time for the minutiae of family life. On the days when Auriol was not at school, Eileen would see Giles and his eldest daughter slipping out of the side door in the direction of the church. Ostensibly, these were 'sermon writing days' but always Auriol was carrying books bearing no relation to theology and Eileen guessed the two of them were on their way to do what they both most enjoyed, the improvement of Auriol's mind through literature and art. Between Auriol and Gemma, there seemed little contact and even less rapport. This too, she felt could be laid at the Vicar's door. During the week while Auriol was at school, Giles Hatton seemed to ensure his parochial duties were completed. This made it possible, from the time Auriol was at home, for her to be always in his company. The Vicar might do better, she thought wryly, to read some of the many books on bringing up children and how to avoid some of the pitfalls; particularly, she muttered to herself angrily, those which are staring him in the face.

Now, watching Sue Hatton walking proudly up the drive with her pram, she remembered when she had first arrived at the Vicarage that the pram had been a real bone of contention and produced numerous arguments. Giles, having seen the cost of what his wife was angling for, had protested in no uncertain terms.

"It's big, and you can't put it in the car. What is the point?"

"The point is, that I am not having my newly born crunched up in something that looks like a cross between a wheelbarrow, and a case on wheels. I want to show my baby off in style, and bundled up in one of those things, I can't do that. It's not nearly so comfortable for the baby and what about when he, or she, gets bigger? Impossible for a child to sleep in comfort in one of those things." Finally, the pièce de résistance, "You never see the Royals plonking their babies in buggies." So it went on and on, until in desperation, Giles talked to his parents about it. Ruth Hatton, whilst trying to be impartial, said,

"Well I don't always agree with my daughter-in-law, but Sue does have one or two valid points. Remember you're talking to someone from an age when we all had proper prams, but then we weren't required to be as mobile as people are today. I will be more than happy to buy a pram, as a gift for our first grandchild." And, as Giles started to speak,

"No arguments. Just tell Sue to ring me and we'll go and choose a pram together." Laughingly she added, "It won't be quite as good as those the Royals have, I'm not suggesting a Silver Cross, but I'm sure we can find something quite smart for this new little Hatton."

And so it was resolved, with Susan, as usual getting her own way. Whilst a buggy had also been purchased, that was to languish in the loft, until Auriol was old enough to transfer from the stately pram to its more humble successor. 'The posh pram' as Eileen called it, had been carefully cocooned until Gemma's arrival, then, having served its purpose, packed away again, until Susan was able to resume her stately parades through the village, this time showing off to all and sundry her beautiful son.

After several weeks, the pinching and its resultant marks, were enough to send Susan scurrying to the doctor.

"What can it be Doctor? They're not insect bites are they? Tell me it's not leukaemia or haemophilia, please tell me it's neither of those." Sue Hatton was obviously distraught.

"We'll take a blood sample today and I'll be able to give you the result in two days' time, but I really don't think you should worry on that score. The child is a good colour and in every respect looks very healthy."

As Susan left the surgery, Dr. Williams made a note about the visit and the necessity for a blood sample. Had it been anyone else, he pondered, he might even have considered contacting Social Services to query non-accidental injury, but this baby's parents were a Vicar and an excessively devoted mother which certainly made anything suspicious out of the question.

In spite of the doctor's advice, Sue Hatton did worry and her relief in finding later that all things sinister had been ruled out was very obvious. Was she always to be plagued by worries about her children? She had watched over Auriol and Gemma so carefully in those early years, unable, or unwilling, to confide in Giles about her concerns. No-one must know about her own childhood, about her dread that her mother's genes might have skipped a generation and passed to Susan's own children. At last, she had felt all was well. With the arrival of her son, a placid, good-tempered baby, she had started to relax, until now . . . Why did fate continue to deal her one blow after another?

Her marriage had proved, if not a disaster, a serious disappointment. Entering university, secure only in the knowledge that she had a beautiful voice and was a better than average pianist, it was Giles Hatton's innate good manners which had drawn her into a variety of social groups. And, as a diffident teenager, how grateful she had been for that. Not dashingly handsome, his pale blonde hair and academic demeanour, had given him a certain cachet and distinguished appearance which, amongst the usual melée of university students, set him apart. The fact that Giles was reading theology had not appealed to her, but the knowledge that his two older brothers were a senior naval officer and a member of the Foreign Office, hotly tipped to become an Ambassador, had sweetened that particular pill. Surely, she reasoned, with such a family record, his intended career would also result in high office, a bishopric, or even in years to come, the status of Archbishop.

Susan's own background had been blurred into extinction when portrayed to others, "Well actually, I was brought up by my grandparents, you see . . ." a small gulp here to indicate emotion, and add to the dramatic effect, "my parents were both killed in a car crash, when I was very tiny. Apparently, it was a miracle that I wasn't with them."

Murmurs of sympathy from all those around, and people far too polite to ask for further details. Her story had been readily accepted, sufficiently blending lies with elements of truth, to create an acceptable whole.

Now, her life was far from the rosy picture she had imagined, and painted for herself at university. Living in an antiquated rectory, almost impossible to heat, with a husband whose vocabulary didn't seem to include the word 'fun', was not the cosy family existence she had planned. Nor had she been able to establish herself as a vocalist, before the unplanned arrival of their first-born, Auriol, had shattered that ambition. It seemed that for years she had been waiting and watching. First of all, over Auriol, just in case . . . then again, over Gemma, and, when finally convinced her fears had proved groundless, she had delighted in Leo, until now . . . his bruises, something puzzling and inexplicable. Life was so unfair.

Unaware of Sue Hatton's earlier concerns, Eileen Biggs continued her own waiting and watching. She had not forgotten that dreadful night a short while ago, going into Leo's room and finding him, to her horror, lying on his face. He had been quickly turned and revived, but Susan Hatton had had to be told and was, as Eileen had anticipated, almost incandescent with anger and concern.

"He was alright when I put him down after his feed. Surely he's not strong enough to roll over. How on earth could it have happened?"

Eileen Biggs had remained silent. She had her own theories about this and other incidents, but fearing Susan would not even consider them as options, did not voice them.

"Leo's night feeds will be finishing next week, I'm going to have to ask you to go in and check on him during the night, Nanny, but I'll also buy one of those gadgets for his bedroom, so that we can listen to his breathing, either from downstairs or during the night. I'll get one today."

Listening to their conversation, Gemma knew that her nightly visits to Leo's room would have to come to an end. Twice she had met Nanny in the corridor during the night, and her excuses about going to the toilet, or needing a drink, had resulted in a steely glint in Nanny's eyes, which suggested she was not satisfied with the explanation. The pinches could not be so frequent. She would have to wait until she was quite sure that everyone was busily occupied.

There was something else. Gemma could have told her mother exactly how Leo had come to be lying on his face. During that particular night, she had stood by Leo's cot watching his small chest gently moving. That was breathing. When one of their kittens had died, it had been very still and Mrs. Biggs said it had stopped breathing. If Leo stopped breathing, then he would have to be taken away, just as the kitten had been. Carefully, she had rolled him over, so that his face was no longer visible. He now seemed very still. Hearing a sudden sound, she had scurried back to her room. Sure enough, Nanny Biggs was on the move and suddenly there were exclamations of alarm and sounds of activity. The next morning had been really awful. After Mummy had spoken sharply to Nanny, and said she was going out to buy some sort of gadget so they could hear Leo breathing, she did nothing but cuddle Leo, calling him her Precious Boy. He seemed to think it was some sort of game when she hugged him and gurgled back at her when she said,

"Our Little Prince, almost taken from us."

Gemma had been puzzled. She wasn't quite sure who would have done the taking, but the more she thought about it, the more she wished whoever it was, had done it properly.

At the earliest opportunity, Eileen visited her sister and, guardedly, started to pass on some of her fears.

"The trouble is Daphne, the villagers see only one side of the coin. I know they don't think much of Mrs. Hatton, and laugh at her attempts to become what Mrs. Mason calls 'upwardly mobile' and they're a little bit in awe of Mr. H. because, to be honest, his sermons are too high-brow for their taste, but they can't fault him on his duties as a vicar. He's always kind and considerate when it's necessary, but I can't believe he never seems to see what's happening right under his nose."

"Too right, he covers this village as well, and I've never heard a bad word said against him, except, now and again, the complaint that they didn't understand the sermon. From what you say, the eldest girl is a bookworm, just like her dad, takes after him in looks too?"

"Yes, she's tall and slim, with blue eyes, but with her mother's lovely brown hair."

"And Gemma?"

"More her mother's build, brown curly hair, brown eyes and can, as I well know, be a right little madam on occasion. Sharp as a ferret, that one. The boy of course, is lovely, blonde hair, big blue eyes, none of which helps young Gemma. The Vicar and his wife are as different as chalk and cheese, she's quite extrovert . . . though I do sometimes wonder . . ."

"What? What do you wonder?"

"Oh never mind, what I was going to say is she's outgoing, bossy, some would call it, whereas he doesn't seem as if he'd say boo to a goose."

"Well, they do say sometimes opposites attract."

"Between you and me, I always feel there's an uneasiness there. They just don't strike me as a happy contented couple."

"Well, I daresay if you overheard some of the spats me and my Dan have, you'd probably say exactly the same."

Eileen laughed, "Your Dan's an angel. Must be, to have put up with you all these years."

Now Daphne laughed with her. "Isn't it time you were leaving? You might just have outstayed your welcome."

"What does worry me is that everyone makes such a fuss of young Leo, and I agree, he's a lovely child, but few of them seem to realise that young Gemma is pining all the time, both at home and when they go into the village. It might just be acceptable if it was an either/or, situation, but it isn't. In the eyes of that little girl she's lost her mother to an intruder, and it hurts like hell. Then when she goes out, she's ignored again. I'm really concerned, that one day, the balloon will go up and there'll be real repercussions. I'm already suspicious about one or two things that have happened."

"Such as?"

"No, I'd rather not say, it wouldn't be right."

"For heaven's sake Eileen, you're beginning to sound like something out of Inspector Morse. If you had my houseful you wouldn't have time for such imaginings."

Deciding she'd might already have said too much, Eileen's lips were sealed.

Giles Hatton had always been a worrier. His brothers, confident and apparently good at everything, had eclipsed him in the eyes of everyone, except Ruth Hatton, his mother. He was well aware that Susan was dissatisfied with her lot as a vicar's wife.

Knew too, that she was lavishing all her attention on her son, to the exclusion of everyone else in the family. The tentative teenager he had met at university had now evolved into a rather bossy matriarch and, well aware of his own failings, he knew he could not face the endless confrontations, necessary to correct the situation. Teaching Auriol was the joy of his life. Through her, he could realise all his own ambitions. He would make her strong, both intellectually and emotionally, so that she would never have to face up to situations, such as this. He was useless around the house, he knew, but, if Eileen Biggs's giant-sized hints were anything to go by, it was Gemma who was suffering most from Susan's lack of interest in anything or anybody, other than Leo. He really must make an effort to involve Gemma, whenever possible but in what, he wasn't quite sure.

Gemma, watching from the upstairs window, saw her mother once again pushing the pram up the drive, on her way to the village. Before Leo had arrived on the scene, she and Mummy used to stroll through the village together, trying to decide which was the prettiest garden. In the spring, it was always Mr. Cutter's, his fruit trees covered with blossom. In the summer, there was never any doubt about the winner, Mrs. Reed's cottage covered with roses, and the garden knee-deep in flowers, was always the best one of all.

Now, on the rare occasions when she was invited to go with Mummy to the village shops, Leo's presence dominated the outing. Women stopped by his pram and gooed and cooed at him, forever saying what a beautiful baby he was. Occasionally they remembered her presence and commented on how big she had grown. It wasn't enough. Gemma felt like stamping her feet and screaming to the world "What about me?"

Turning away from the window, she took from her own play box her crayons and the drawing of Leo and Mummy. With her black crayon she stabbed Leo's arms with black blobs until hardly any purple remained, then carefully rolled it up and stowed everything away again.

Eileen had to admit it, Gemma was clever. Sometimes several days elapsed before another bruise appeared, and in the ensuing months these would be blamed on Leo's attempts at crawling, then his first staggering, unsure steps. Following a cry of protest from Leo's pram, Gemma was never anywhere to be seen and, try as Eileen might, she found it impossible to keep a check on Gemma's movements. When Gemma was at school, Eileen at least knew where the child was, for a large part of the day. Susan seemed to have made no connection between the lack of bruises during Gemma's school days, but Edith had noted every occurrence, and was pretty sure that her fears had been correct. Worst of all, she herself, was beginning to have nightmares about the situation, waking in the night and wondering whatever Gemma might do next. A few months later, she found out.

"Nanny, I want you to take Leo and Gemma to the village playground for an hour or so this morning. It's dry and bright and they could both do with some fresh air. I have a Mothers' Union meeting at the church, back about mid-day. No school today so there might be some of the other children there – please see Leo doesn't get involved with any of those boisterous boys."

Alleluia! She's actually including Gemma in her plans for once. Eileen was quite pleased to be getting out of the house herself, and anxious to see if she could effect any bridge building between the Hatton's younger siblings. Not that Leo played any part in the antagonism, seeming blissfully unaware of his sister's jealousy.

The playground was relatively quiet on their arrival. Gemma was able to go on the small roundabout, but Susan had been adamant that it was much too dangerous for Leo. The children begged to go on the seesaw and Eileen carefully settled Gemma, then eased the seesaw down so that she could install Leo. For a few minutes Eileen was able to balance the seesaw by holding on to Leo and both children squealed with delight. Until, without warning, as Gemma reached ground level, she let out a loud wail,

"I'm going to be sick Nanny, I'm going to be sick!"

With that, Gemma jumped off the seesaw and Edith, turning towards her, relinquished her hold on Leo. With no weight at the opposite end to hold the seesaw down, Leo's end crashed to the floor and in so doing threw him from his seat. Eileen's heart sank as she turned back to the small boy, seeing him lying still on the concrete surface, but he suddenly rolled over and although his face and one arm were grazed, apart from being tearful, he seemed not, as she had feared, badly hurt. Gathering him up she carried him to one of the seats, then turned to Gemma, who had followed, clutching a handkerchief to her face.

"Have you been sick Gemma? Come here and let me see."

"No, Nanny," Gemma put the handkerchief back in her pocket, "Sorry, I started to feel really giddy and I could taste my breakfast . . . ."

"You do realise that jumping off like that, makes it very dangerous for the person at the other end?"

"Yes, I'm sorry, Nanny. Is Leo alright?"

"Luckily he is, apart from a few scrapes and probably more bruises. I need to get him home and clean him up straight away. Get the push chair please."

The child met her eyes before turning away, and in that moment, as Gemma went to do as she had been told, Eileen knew that this had been no accident. The child had planned it! Worked out in detail what would happen and had, possibly, wanted a more disastrous outcome. If Gemma could be so devious at seven years old, what would she be like in ten years time? Brushing these thoughts to one side, she hurried the children off home. Susan Hatton's wrath would certainly be forthcoming when she learned what had happened, but at least getting Leo cleaned up and a plaster on his arm would help the overall impact. Whatever happens, it will be my fault, there is absolutely no way Mrs. H. will ever accept that her younger daughter might have had a hand in this.

As expected, Sue Hatton was furious.

"For heaven's sake, he might have fractured his skull, whatever were you thinking of?"

"Mummy, it was my fault, I suddenly felt sick and had to jump off . . ."

Gemma's unexpected intervention, was brushed aside with a sharp,

"Nanny was there to hold on to Leo, he's too tiny to look after himself."

Not for Gemma any reassurance from her mother, that she was in no way to blame, or praise that she should be trying to shoulder it. No hug to show, that in any event, she was forgiven for what had happened. The child looked chastened and Eileen saw that after a few moments, during her mother's continuing diatribe, Gemma left the room.

It was two days later, when visiting her sister Daphne, that Eileen was able to offload her anger and concern about the Hatton household, knowing that whatever she said would not be repeated. At first Daphne had been sceptical about Eileen's suspicions, then pragmatic.

"It's quite common for siblings to be jealous of new arrivals in the family, she'll get over it."

"Daphne, Gemma hasn't got over it since he was born, so why should she change now? She's still brooding and jealous and, whilst things stay as they are in that household, I can't see that she ever will. The poor child's sidelined in almost every respect."

"Isn't there something about a middle child syndrome?"

"Yes, but I have a gut feeling that this runs deeper than that. What staggers me is that the child is so clever, amazingly so, for someone so young."

"You can't surely believe, Gemma would go so far as to injure Leo?"

"Well, I've never told anyone this before, so don't breathe a word, not even to Dan, but I'm certain she turned him onto his face during the night, soon after he was born. If that isn't planning to injure him, I don't know what is."

"Oh, come on Eileen, Gemma was only, what, about five then? She couldn't possibly have understood what the outcome might be." Daphne wasn't convinced.

"This isn't your average five year old, this is one small, but extremely intelligent girl. I'll swear Gemma takes on board everything she overhears. I know it's dreadful to say this, but I do believe that she has a real fixation where Leo's concerned and just wants him removed from her orbit." And, as Daphne showed signs of speaking, "Another thing, as soon as that gadget was removed from Leo's room, the one where you could hear his breathing, the bruises started again. Not so often as to create a panic, but still there."

"Can't help feeling you're over-reacting. It's a pity the Hattons don't have a real spat in that household, like my lot do. On rare occasions, we've even had fisticuffs, but it does clear the air and we're all soon back on an even keel. The one rule in this house is we don't go to bed until it's sorted, and if that takes all night, then so be it."

"There's something else I can't get my head round. Mrs. H. at times seems a complete mystery. She's a young mother, a modern mother, who reads the papers and has been to university, she surely knows all the problems about bringing new babies into a family and how it might stir up jealousy, that sort of thing. I did once hear her say she'd been brought up by grandparents and I do sometimes wonder if there's been something lacking there, which might have affected her psychologically. Sometimes it's just as if there's a missing link, things not quite connected . . ."

"For heaven's sake, Eileen, you're beginning to spout medical jargon like an expert. Are you sure you haven't been watching too many detective films on TV? Look, I don't want you to spend all your time off, worrying about the Hattons, I've made some scones and it's time we had a cup of tea."

Eileen sank back into her chair. She'd come for tea and sympathy, and if there hadn't been much of the latter, she could at least enjoy the rest of what was on offer.

Eileen Biggs would have been surprised to learn that her constant digs implying her employer's neglect of Gemma had in fact hit home, so much so, that at bedtime, the following evening, Susan tackled Giles.

"Why couldn't you include Gemma when you read to Auriol at bedtime?"

"Because there's a vast difference in their ages, that's why."

"I wouldn't call a few years, vast. And in any event, don't forget you were reading to Auriol when she was just Gemma's age, that didn't seem to be a problem."

"But Auriol has moved on so much since then . . . They'd be at different levels."

"Always an excuse for doing what you want to do. I'm not stupid you know. I know very well that when you're supposed to be writing your sermons, you and Auriol are all too often reading poetry and looking at pictures of works of art. I know you're trying to improve her mind, but what about the rest of us? I wouldn't mind a bit of slack myself to do some reading or singing. My hands are full. Looking after you and three children, even with Nanny's assistance, is a full time job, especially when you're so often tied up with church work. I get sick of being a general dogsbody and there's never enough money to do anything nice."

"I thought we'd get back to the money eventually. You knew the score when we got married, it's no use whingeing about it now."

"It's just that, when I hear how comfortably off Simon and Charles seem to be, and they haven't any children, I do sometimes think you're in the wrong profession."

"Don't ever say that to me again." Uncharacteristically, Giles exploded, "I'm doing what I've chosen to do and you've been aware of that from the start. Yes, I'll try and include Gemma now and again, but you might also consider just how much time you spend fussing over Leo. Is all that strictly necessary?"

"It most certainly is. You know how easily he bruises, but this conversation is going nowhere and I, for one, have plenty to do." With that Susan flounced out of the room.

Following that encounter Susan would have been surprised to learn that Giles did in fact give a great deal of thought to how he might spend more time with his younger daughter. Gemma couldn't be included in his discussions with Auriol. She was, he kept telling himself, too young. But, had Giles been honest, he would have admitted that he wanted nothing and no-one to intrude on those times. Auriol was for him, a sounding board for his own faith and a link with all that he found beautiful in the arts. With her he could delve into English literature, enjoying poetry and prose again. Often he was able to explore new depths, as Auriol's fresh young mind found new and sometimes, exciting, interpretations. No, those sessions must remain exactly as they were now. It was whilst taking down a book from his shelves for their next meeting, that something caught his eye and gave him an idea.

In the corner, unopened for several years, was his chess set, a birthday gift from his parents whilst away at school. At university he had excelled as a champion and then, as study pressures mounted, the game had had to give way to more important matters. Perhaps he could teach Gemma.

She was a bright child who was doing very well at school. It was worth a try. Auriol had homework for at least an hour each evening, so that would be an ideal time.

Gemma, after her initial surprise, was delighted. Someone had remembered her existence! She listened carefully, as Giles explained the rules of the game. Often he would repeat something, to be met with, "Yes Daddy, I understand that."

It took just four sessions before the house first responded to a joyful cry of 'Checkmate', and the ringing of Gemma's laughter. Auriol, raised her head from her books and smiled, a delighted Eileen Biggs paused at the kitchen sink and Susan laughed with Leo, at the unexpected sound.

Susan's pleasure was short-lived, when, after a few short weeks of a pleasing calm in the household, Giles's comments set alarm bells ringing in her head once again.

"It's quite phenomenal. I mean, we know the child is bright, but to master the game in such a short time . . . I mean . . ."He stopped, lost for words.

"Perhaps her beating you was a fluke, beginner's luck. It does happen."

"Not in this game, or very rarely. I know I'm a bit rusty, but for heaven's sake, I was considered the best at uni., and here a child of ten is wiping the floor with me. I thought Auriol was clever and she is, in a different way. Gemma's attention to detail is, for a child, amazing, quite amazing . . . ." As Giles walked away, he was still muttering to himself, leaving Susan to her own worries.

She watched as Giles went into his study and then went straight to their bedroom. From under the base of the box which housed her few pieces of jewellery, she took out three newspaper cuttings. The first was headed 'Couple die in car crash murder mystery'.

Mr. Geoffrey White and his wife Mary, of Kettering, have both died following a serious car crash two days ago. Their car struck a wall in Ward Lane and Mrs. White was killed on impact. Alive when police reached the scene, Mr. White died on the way to hospital. Some of Mr. White's injuries were unrelated to the crash and police are investigating the possibility that he was seriously injured before the car went out of control. They leave a thirteen year old daughter, Susan, who is being cared for by her grandparents.

There was more about the necessity for a Post Mortem and that an inquest would be held at a later date, details with which Susan was all too familiar. What hadn't been revealed until the inquest was the fact that Susan's mother, noted for her violent mood swings, had never confessed to the fact that her doctor had told her she was schizophrenic and should receive treatment. Finally, the truth surfaced. Her mother had repeatedly stabbed her father at the wheel of the car, until he collapsed and everything spiralled out of control. For years the whole nightmarish episode had left the orphaned, teenager Susan, terrified about the possibility of inheriting those genes.

That fear remained with her still.

Carefully Susan unfolded the two other cuttings. One was headed 'Born Evil?' with a picture of Adolf Hitler and the second 'Genius and Madness', the latter suggesting the possible link between genius and madness. Giles's statement that Gemma was highly intelligent had struck a very sensitive chord and was for Susan, the worst possible news. Her teachers had said Gemma was bright, but there had been no indication of it being an unusual brilliance. Giles, who was not easily surprised, had quite clearly been rocked back on his heels by Gemma's outstanding ability on the chess board.

What to do next? If she were to discuss this with a doctor, Susan had little doubt that in the village any confidentiality clause would very soon be broken. And if Giles and his family were to learn that Susan was the daughter of a mentally sick woman who had murdered her husband, then all their lives would be torn apart.

Susan was conscious of the fact that her ongoing anxieties and way of dealing with them had left her isolated. She had no close female friends. Her in-laws were kind, but she had kept them at a distance. And in the village the whispering as she approached or left other women, underscored the knowledge that she was, if not disliked, very unpopular.

A wave of self-pity threatened to engulf her and she struggled for composure.

The years of analysing her own behaviour, watching her daughters for signs of abnormality, had left her, in spite of what onlookers might see, vulnerable. Leo's bruises had been a worry, but apparently unconnected with her main problem. Where could she turn now, if Gemma was to show signs of inheriting her grandmother's genes?

Sounds of voices close by and Susan hurriedly folded the cuttings and placed them out of sight. Her eyes dried, façade in place, she moved to the staircase.

CHAPTER 2

Driving through the village of Moordean, Simon Hatton saw little had changed since his last visit, several years earlier. Typical in having a church, a pub, a sub-post office and a small school, it was English in character, but to live here was, probably, boring in the extreme. From what he had gathered from his parents, there was gossip and goodwill here in about equal amounts, and whilst some youngsters would have willingly dragged Moordean into the 20th century, there was sufficient resistance from older residents to prevent that happening and maintain such traditions as existed.

One such tradition was the annual fete, held in mid-July, and Guy Hatton, Simon's father, had been invited to perform the opening ceremony. By a fortunate coincidence, his ship just having docked in Portsmouth Harbour, Simon had phoned to say he would be spending a few days with his parents and, hearing about the fair, had expressed his intention of joining the whole family for that occasion.

Simon, dashing in his newly acquired Captain's uniform and Susan's in-laws, elderly but supremely elegant, heightened Susan's sensitivity about her own family's necessity for economy. Her navy and white dress had been smart enough when first purchased, but now was beginning to look somewhat passé, at least two inches too long, and an outfit with which the villagers were all too familiar. She thought how wonderful it must be to be able to afford a really smart new outfit now and again, without having to worry about which child needed new shoes, or any other apparel. However, the warmth of Simon's greeting and his obvious delight in seeing the children, helped in some way to ease the pain.

Embracing her, Simon smiled and commented,

"Sue, my dear, impossible to believe you're a mother of three. You grow lovelier with the years."

"I can see you've learned that flattery will get you everywhere, Simon."

"Fact, not flattery, I assure you. Now . . ." turning to the children, "Auriol, I can't believe how you've grown. Quite the young lady now and Gemma, you're, what seven, eight? That's naughty of me, you're my god-daughter, and I ought to know."

"I'm seven, nearly eight."

"Seven, and another young lady in the making. And," as Gemma preened herself, "this is Leo. Do you know who I am?"

"You're Uncle Simon and I like your cap and that gold stuff," pointing to the gold braid.

"Nice isn't it? I think it's time to make tracks, we mustn't be late for Granddad's speech and seeing him cut the ribbon. Gemma, do you know the way?"

"Yes, it's right next to our school."

"Then you shall be my guide" and taking her small hand, Simon led the way.

"I hear there's a coconut shy and a shooting gallery. I might even be able to win something for my nephew and nieces."

Watching her brother in law, Susan compared him again with Giles. Simon's fair hair was bleached almost white by the Mediterranean sun and his skin the colour of dark honey. By contrast, his blue eyes and white teeth were highlighted and this coupled with the crisp white collar at his neckline and dark blue and gold of his uniform made a very impressive whole. No wonder the local females, once having admired Mrs. Hatton Senior's dress, swiftly turned their attention to Simon and there it remained. There was something else, another quality which Giles certainly didn't possess; both his brothers were tactile. On arrival, Simon had hugged and kissed her and his arm had remained across her shoulders, even as he had greeted the children. Long after it was removed, she could feel the comforting warmth and strength in that embrace.

Whilst at university, Giles had seemed reasonably outgoing, but he now seemed to have developed a tunnel vision which covered only theology and Auriol's education. Of course, he went through the motions of visiting sick people and greeting people at church and in the village, but his manner could in no way be compared with the urbane charm of Simon, who was obviously used to entertaining at the highest level and giving orders, which he expected to be obeyed. There was an edge to Simon's character, which was both thrilling and charming. His brother, Ambassador Charles, had also had that effect on her. Both were, amazingly, unmarried. If only she had crossed the paths of Giles's brothers before she had settled for quiet, and to be honest, rather dull Giles, her life could have been so different. Now, as Simon looked down at her, she felt something not experienced for years, a rush of raw, sexual passion. For heaven's sake, Susan remonstrated with herself, get a grip, you're not a teenager and this is your brother-in-law. Ignoring the note of warning, she smiled warmly in return. Perhaps it wasn't too late?

Noting that look, and well aware of his dashing brother's appearance and obvious success, Giles Hatton, standing in the shadow of a marquee, scowled uncharacteristically. *What on earth was Susan up to? Simpering wasn't usually her style and that the recipient should be his brother! What was it about his elder siblings that seemed to attract success and adulation wherever they went? It had always been the same, they had been the lively, smiling, contented ones, whereas he had always seemed to carry emotional baggage throughout his life. Going away to school had been delayed because he was still bed-wetting, then his obsessive desire to do well in examination, had resulted in the most violent of migraine attacks. New ventures always made him nervous and the fact that he was regarded as the sickly one in the family, only compounded the problem. Now Susan, who could be so sharp-tongued, was fluttering her eyelashes at Simon, like some love-sick teenager. The sooner it was time to go home and put an end to this charade, the better.*

Fastidious in appearance, Susan's father-in-law, Guy Hatton, oozed goodwill. And she knew from experience that this was not a facade, he really was the most generous spirited man she had ever met. Ruth Hatton, her mother-in-law, Susan saw in a different light. To the outside world a gentle soul, Sue was always aware that behind that smiling exterior was a steely resolve; if not quite the iron fist in a velvet glove, then something very close to that. Today, Ruth carried her seventy years well, her silver-grey two piece in a delicate georgette receiving many admiring glances from both men and women and reminding Susan yet again of their own fragile economic circumstances.

"I'm afraid you'll find this rather dull." Susan apologised to Simon, as they entered the fairground.

"On the contrary, I love the quintessentially English village feel about it. It's probably what I miss most about being abroad such a great deal."

"Perhaps you wouldn't love it quite so much if you were here all the time. This is one day out of the year, life is not always as *exciting* as this."

Simon didn't miss the heavy sarcasm in her voice and looked at her sharply. "No, I can imagine on a day-to-day basis, it might seem rather dull. But Susan, you surely find plenty with which to occupy yourself?"

She laughed, "I certainly could, if I didn't have four other people to look after.

Although, I do have one evening when I actually let my hair down and that's Thursdays, when I go to an aerobics class."

"So that's how you managed to keep your figure."

Sue laughed. "I doubt it, it's probably because I never have much opportunity to sit and read, or just watch the world go by."

"And have you got friends at this class?"

"Not really. We're such a small village, only about a dozen attend. Mostly young ones, who would have nothing to do, otherwise. I think most of the mums of my age are far too busy attending to their kids. I'm at least lucky enough to have Eileen Biggs to see to the young ones, and Giles, of course, always sees to Auriol."

Was it his imagination that there was an edge to her voice on that last comment, he wondered? Surely she wasn't implying anything sinister? Quickly he dismissed the thought as unworthy and downright nasty. His brother was many things, but not that. He was in fact, too saintly for his own good. Now, scratching noises from the tannoy, suggested announcements were imminent.

Their discussion came to an abrupt halt, as they listened to the opening speeches, argued as to whether the judges had been correct in their selection of winners for the flower arranging, and cake making competitions, and watched the children take part in a variety of games. At last they were summoned to the tea tent, where Simon's charm had ensured that the ladies there had put together two tables, so that all eight of them could sit down together for a cream tea.

Not until they were all back in the vicarage and Susan upstairs, overseeing the children being put to bed, and attending to Leo in particular, were the seeds first sown in Giles's mind, that Susan might be correct in her assessment, that he had been less than diligent as a father. Simon's queries about the children's schooling, jolted Giles into the realisation that, with the exception of Auriol, he had given no thought whatsoever, into provision for his other children. He was well aware that Susan had a penchant for social climbing and to date had ignored this, as one of her more foolish foibles. However, realistically, he knew that his children must receive the best of educations, if they were to succeed in a world which was increasingly commercial. His father, he decided, was a wise old bird and might be able to offer words of advice.

And advise, Guy Hatton did.

"We needn't worry about Leo for the time being, I think he should probably start in the village, get himself acclimatized to school routine, and then you should consider a move. From what I hear the Moordean School is better than average, Auriol has certainly done well there and Gemma shows every indication of doing so. A bonus is that the school's close to home so there are no worries about transport. Auriol will be leaving soon and I think she'll probably sail through Common Entrance and go to the Chichester Academy for Girls. If she's awarded a scholarship, then expenses there will be minimal, but your mother and I will always be happy to make up any shortfall. With luck, Gemma will follow in her footsteps and," a quick glance at Simon, "her godfather, I know would be happy to help. As soon as Leo's old enough, I'd certainly like to see him go away to school, even if he returns home at weekends. Good for him to get away from the feminine environment. I know that's a long time ahead, but don't forget your brother Charles, he is after all, Leo's godfather." And as Giles pulled a face,

"I know, I know. It's a matter of pride, but I think in this case it's important enough to shelve that. Again, your mother and I would always help, but I actually think your brother would like to be asked. With no family of his own and no marital prospects on the horizon, I'm sure doing something towards his godson's education would give him real pleasure."

Giles, as always, went through the motions and said all the right things, but his high-domed forehead was still furrowed as he contemplated the unpleasant task of having to go with a begging bowl to his two elder brothers. Pinning his hopes on Auriol winning a scholarship, he consoled himself with the knowledge that no decisions needed to be made about the other two for a very long time.

But the subject was not closed. As soon as Simon and his parents had left, Susan rounded on him.

"What was all that about?"

"What? What do you mean?"

"Whilst I was upstairs you were all deep in conversation, which seemed to stop rather suddenly when I joined you. What was such a secret, that I couldn't be included?"

"Susan, there was nothing secret, I assure you, we were discussing the children's education."

"I see, you were discussing *our* children's education and I wasn't a party to it."

"Only because you weren't in the room when the subject came up."

"How very convenient and what did the four of you decide, about *our* children's education."

"Dad said he and Mum had always promised to help with the eldest one's education and Simon said he knew he could speak for Charles, and that as godparents to Gemma and Leo, they would both be happy to contribute when necessary."

"I see, so we have to go cap in hand to your brothers, in order to give our offspring a decent education."

"I don't like it any more than you do, but there's no alternative." Guy stood up, "And before you say any more, I might ask why, when talking to my brother you were all sweetness and light, acting as if butter wouldn't melt in your mouth, you saw that as acceptable behaviour. Now, suddenly, when I had the rare opportunity to discuss something serious with him, I'm in the wrong. It's been a long day and I'm not prepared to discuss it further. I have to take early communion, so I'm retiring. Good-night."

Prompted by his parents, Charles Hatton, Ambassador to Greece, on his next visit to England, announced his intention of visiting not only them, but his youngest brother and his family. From the beginning, he had had an uneasy feeling about Giles's marriage. Meeting Susan before the wedding, he had found her to be the very opposite of Giles, her apparent worldliness in direct contrast to his brother's permanent air of detachment. A shrewd judge of character, Charles felt something did not quite ring true in Susan's story about the loss of her parents, but admonished himself that if this was a family secret she preferred not to divulge, then that was her prerogative.

At Grafton House, his parents were not only delighted to see him, but anxious to put him in the picture, with regard to Susan and Giles and their children.

"She's besotted with her little boy, is in danger of forgetting she has two lovely girls." This, from his mother.

Guy Hatton, as always the mediator, "Ruth, you're exaggerating. They're all lovely children, doing well at school too. Auriol's a charming girl, now at Chichester Girls', Gemma's top of her class at the village school with a brilliant report and Leo, who's only just started there, has settled in well."

"I'm not exaggerating, and I agree they are all lovely children. But when did Susan bring them round here for a meal, for instance? It's not for want of being asked, the reply is always the same, it will be too late, and past Leo's bedtime. As if we couldn't ensure we worked round that, or that they came for lunch, which I've also suggested.

There's something else. Her behaviour with those children has been repetitive. During Auriol's first years, she hardly let the child out of her sight, then when Gemma came along, Auriol was pushed towards Giles, so that Susan could spend all her time with baby Gemma. Now, we're seeing the same thing with Leo. It's as if she doesn't want anyone else to get to know them. Everything and everyone else seems to be excluded. There's always some excuse, as to why the children can't come and see us and now it's invariably centred on Leo."

"Well, I expect she has her hands full," Guy still anxious to pour oil on troubled waters.

"That's no excuse, Susan has Eileen Biggs to help her and Eileen's a good worker. With the children now at school, I can't believe Sue is rushed off her feet, all day and every day. And why hasn't she mentioned Gemma's wonderful school report? If Leo had come first at anything, we'd never have heard the last of it."

"Well . . ." Charles, trying to act as mediator and break up the discussion, "I doubt if Susan gets much help from brother Giles, I can't imagine him being much use about the house."

An explosion from Guy, "That boy lives on another planet, always has, and always will. But you're not here to listen to moans and groans about Giles and his family. You haven't seen your godson since the christening, and there's no doubt about it, he's a real little charmer. But I have a feeling, the sun's over the yardarm and it's time for a stiff drink and to hear some of your news."

The next day, seeing for the first time the Vicarage with its high-ceilinged cold rooms and draughty corridors, Charles felt some sympathy with Susan. She had now developed into what the Americans called 'a feisty lady' and, he suspected, this new Susan was a direct result of dissatisfaction with the life she was now forced to lead. In a strange way, he found this Sue Hatton more attractive. When her curly brown hair was tossed and those dark brown eyes flashed in anyone's direction, it was a sign that Susan was about to signal her disapproval. They might have three children, but having met her again, he was even more convinced, that Giles was not the man to handle this small human dynamo.

Susan found Charles's presence exciting. Repeatedly, she tortured herself with the knowledge that her gorgeous brother-in-law was an Ambassador and lived in an Embassy, in a beautiful warm country. No problems with cold rooms there. Large and broad shouldered, he dominated any room, but it was his voice which thrilled her. He never seemed to raise it, yet the timbre was such that people listened, when he spoke. No wonder he had achieved such high rank. Charles and Simon were both not only intelligent, but had such charisma, they would always surface as leaders in any group. Not so Giles, whilst at university, she had thought him to have a certain aura of gentility and, yes, even glamour, now against the backdrop of everyday life, that impression of him had totally disappeared. In the village he was liked, but not loved, and, Susan had to admit, she was beginning to feel that way about him, herself.

"Sometime Susan, you must all come and visit me in Greece. I'm sure I could give you a really lovely holiday. There's plenty of room at the Embassy and of course, a vast amount of sightseeing right on the doorstep. What do you think?" Charles smiled down at her.

"Charles, need you ask? I'd absolutely adore it."

"Then that's agreed, we'll see what can be arranged before I'm moved to Outer Mongolia, or somewhere equally unattractive."

Susan, shooting a quick glance at Giles added, "That will be something to keep me going in the cold winter months and the humdrum days ahead."

To her amazement, in bed that night Giles suddenly drew her to him and said,

"Perhaps we can find something else to keep you going during those humdrum days."

They both went through the motions, but their coupling was a faint imitation of the passion they had known. Each knew as they attempted to sleep, that it had been an unsuccessful attempt to right what was now seriously wrong.

The visits of her brothers-in-law had proved a double-edged sword for Sue Hatton. Loving their company and basking in their success, she inevitably, made sharp contrasts between their successful careers and that of her husband. More frequently now, Sue tackled Giles about family matters and held her ground, until she had got her way. The onset of Auriol's menstruation had been one such example.

"Things will have to change now, Auriol's periods have started."

"What do you mean, things will have to change? What are you talking about?" Giles was genuinely puzzled.

"You've filled that girl's head to the brim with so much knowledge about different cultures and civilizations, made her au fait with every conceivable art form, many of them nudes, that she's in danger of thinking nudity is the norm, rather than the exception."

"Don't be ridiculous!"

"I know it, for a fact. She's quite unperturbed when I go into her room and she's stark naked. As her mother, that's acceptable, though I still think she might perhaps reach for a towel, or her dressing gown. What concerns me more, is the fact that *you* often go into her room and, presumably, find her in the same state?" Susan's eyebrows arched in query.

"She's my daughter for heaven's sake," Giles bridled, "I can't help it, if now and again, I catch her unawares."

"I'm sorry, but it's got to stop. I'm going to tell her that in future we must all knock on her door, and she must cover herself, before she opens it."

"This sounds like much ado about nothing."

"For goodness' sake, Giles, get into the real world. Supposing, just supposing it was to get out, that the Vicar is used to going into his teenage daughter's bedroom, when she's starkers."

"I would hope that, if it did 'get out' as you put it, people would realise that, as a Vicar, I'd have no ulterior motive."

"You really don't live on this planet, do you? Parents have been questioned by the police for having pictures of their *own* small children in the bath. And as for that, 'as a Vicar' nonsense, don't you ever read the papers? You've surely seen that clergy of every denomination are often accused and sometimes jailed, for unacceptable behaviour."

"But that wasn't with their own children."

"There you go again, forever burying your head in the sand, like a blasted ostrich. Not knowing, or not wanting to know, what goes on around you. Fathers, and sometimes mothers, have been known to assault their own children, of both sexes. I'm afraid, Giles, we're back to that famous line, and like Caesar's wife, you must be 'above suspicion'. Anyway, Auriol can't carry on like that, now we know she's going away to school and then university. People would start to talk about her, you must see that?"

"You've made your point," Giles's reply was grudging, but he knew she was right.

The last time he'd walked into Auriol's room and found her naked, he had been startled to see she now had the body of a young woman, fully formed breasts, and a mass of pubic hair. It had been disconcerting to say the least of it and he'd been determined to put that image to the back of his mind, and forget about it. Now, the conversation with Susan had troubled him, more than she could ever know.

Meeting Sue all those years ago, he had thought, in her, to have found his soulmate, but the ensuing years had well and truly quashed that idea and with that, the physical side of their marriage seemed to have died a death. Perhaps Sue was afraid of another pregnancy, but in this day and age, that shouldn't be a problem. There was no doubt that it was with Auriol, he was now most comfortable. With her, he could discuss and analyse not only literary topics, but questions about a wide variety of doctrines. He had never thought of her as a young woman, until now . . .

Auriol's reaction to Sue Hatton's dictat about her nudity, was first surprise and then some serious contemplation. Judging by the repeated barrage of raised voices, her parents seemed to be constantly at odds with each other. Her lovely, gentle, father seemed so often to be unsure of himself, questioning his own beliefs, asking her for opinions to bolster his flagging commitment. She knew of no other family like her own. These days, her mother alternated between a nervous edginess when dealing with her family and Nanny, and an overt show of affection for young Leo. Gemma no longer laughed and skipped around, as she used to, instead, she seemed morose.

As part of her Common Entrance exam, Auriol had been required to read an article on psychology and comment on it. Two words from that, which now sprang to mind were 'introverted', which certainly summed up Gemma's current behaviour. And 'dysfunctional'. The latter, she'd learned, meant 'disjointed, not a cohesive whole'. That, she decided, exactly summed up her family, they were a collection of separate units and the only thing which apparently unified them, was their genes. At one time theirs had seemed a happy home, but not any more.

Hearing the sobs, and finding Auriol in floods of tears, Eileen Biggs hastened to comfort her.

"What is it, my darling? Can I help?" Auriol shook her head.

"Nothing can be this bad, my love. You've got a mum and dad, a little sister and brother and me, and we all love you to bits." For some reason, the tears now flowed more freely.

There could be only one reason, Eileen decided. Hormones!

CHAPTER 3

Leo was just five years old, when some of the strange happenings in his life started to fit together, like the pieces of a jigsaw. Marks, which so often appeared on his arms and feet, were noted again by Mrs. Biggs, but now, surprisingly, summarily dismissed by his mother.

"He bruises easily," she commented and to Leo, "Darling boy, you must be more careful, look where you're going. Little princes should not be covered with nasty black marks."

Leo had listened, been more careful and was always amazed at the appearance of yet another red, quickly turning to black, mark. Sometimes he thought he'd dreamed that someone came into his bedroom and pinched him, but Mrs. Biggs said that must have been a bad dream and he should forget it. Leo had, of course, no recollection of almost dying, when he was only a few months' old, but sometimes his mother would cuddle him and in the process of hugging and squeezing, say things like, "My precious boy, almost lost to us."

He'd asked Mrs. Biggs about it, who told him parents did watch over babies in cots, in case they rolled over and couldn't breathe properly. She said she'd been horrified, on one of her nightly check-ups, to find Leo almost on his face. She had quickly revived him of course, but had had to tell his mother. It was obvious to Leo, from the way Mrs. Biggs had bridled with indignation and pursed her lips whilst relaying the story, that his mother had been very displeased indeed. Not until he went away to school, did everything suddenly become clearer.

Eileen Biggs felt herself, to be permanently on the horns of a dilemma. Ninety nine per cent certain that Gemma was at the bottom of all the problems related to Leo, she was equally certain, that Susan Hatton would not even consider such a possibility. Small Gemma might be, but she was quick and intelligent and would perhaps soon find other ways in which to show her disapproval of Leo's existence. She was older now and surely realised that what she had done earlier to Leo was very wrong. Would that prove a deterrent in the future? Trying to stop him breathing as a baby, when she herself was so young, was one thing. She could not have realised the seriousness of her actions. But if Gemma was to continue her vendetta, with added strength and more knowledge, just how dangerous might that prove?

All Susan's energies continued to be channelled into ensuring Leo's life ran smoothly and where possible was enhanced. Contacts made in the village invariably reflected this. By the time Leo was almost six, Susan had, conveniently, become very friendly with the owner of a riding school, Nora Leeson, a friendship which had resulted in a number of raised eyebrows in the village. At the weekly meeting of the Women's Institute it had been the central topic of conversation.

"It's perfectly obvious what she's up to now. First 'Nannies' and now wants that child to join the upper crust and become a rider."

"Bit of a waste of time surely, I mean, the whole thing about hunting is under discussion. By the time he's old enough to take part, there probably won't be anything to join."

"And pretending they're bosom pals all of a sudden, I mean that woman Leeson, has only one subject – horses. She's boring, boring, boring. And, without being too catty, she's starting to look like one of them."

There were chuckles all round and then, "Seriously, I can't imagine they have a thing in common. I think Mrs. H. is just hoping that she'll soon be in a position to get young Leo some cut price riding lessons." There was agreement all round and at that point their Chairwoman's gavel rapped smartly, to bring them all to order.

Within a few short weeks, it was agreed that Leo have lessons on one of Nora Leeson's ponies, at a reduced rate of course, and each Saturday morning the small chestnut mare was brought to the Vicarage, escorted by Claire, one of Nora's young assistants. Gemma was beside herself with rage. Her younger brother was to have the pleasure of something she had been asking for, for years. Her mother's reply was, "It's more important for Leo to learn now. After all, he will eventually want to ride with the local hunt."

"But Mummy, ladies take part in the hunt. I've seen them. And they look so lovely in their bowler hats."

"I'm sorry, Gemma, they may look attractive, but I've personally never thought riding to be a suitable occupation for ladies." Susan's tone said there was to be no further discussion on the subject.

A few weeks after Leo's birthday, the pony and its escort, arrived as usual. As she often did, Gemma came out to walk around and check the tethers and the reins. Claire smiled as she watched Gemma pretend to busy herself, ensuring everything was in order. Leo, excited as always, was quickly mounted. The pony moved off, but almost immediately reared slightly, tossing its head in distress. Then it started to canter, the terrified child clinging to its reins. Again the pony stopped and bucked, this time managing to dislodge the child, who cowered on the ground crying and terrified. By the time Claire got to the pony, the mare was reasonably quiet and Claire was able to seize her bridle and lead her back to the Vicarage courtyard, with a tearstained Leo bringing up the rear. Not until the pony's saddle was removed was the problem solved. Under it were several small, but sharp, pieces of stone which, whilst annoying, were not ultra painful until the weight of Leo's body pressed them into the mare's flesh. Claire knew the saddle had been perfectly clean, when placed on the pony's back, and was immediately suspicious, Gemma having been the only other person present. Tentatively, Claire broached the subject to Mrs. Hatton, who was hugging Leo and drying his tears, "I wonder Mrs. Hatton, if Gemma might have done this, as some sort of joke?"

Susan Hatton erupted, "I hope you are not for one moment suggesting my little girl did something to harm her brother, who might have been killed. I think, young lady, you are merely trying to cover the tracks of your own incompetence. I shall tell Mrs. Leeson that I do not expect to see you here again . . . ever, and that she should be very careful of putting too much trust in you, in the future. Now, be on your way, I must examine my child to see just how much harm has been done." With that she swept away, almost dragging Leo in her wake.

This proved to be not only the last visit of young Claire, but Leo's last riding lesson. Much to Gemma's carefully concealed delight, her mother decided that preparing Leo for membership of the local Hunt, was not worth running the risk of her precious boy being injured, or even, perish the thought, killed. In any event, it now seemed that the days of riding to hounds were to be numbered.

"I know how much you were enjoying the riding lessons, Darling Boy, so don't you worry, Mummy will think of something to cheer you up." The cheering up came in the form of a baby rabbit, snow white, fluffy and quite adorable. Leo loved her and Gemma was green with envy. Giles had organised a hutch and explained that Snowy was now Leo's responsibility. He was told what Snowy should have to eat, where to gather it and that her hutch must be cleaned out at least once each week. Thrilled to be in charge Leo set about his duties with enthusiasm.

"You've done it again, Leo." Gemma said reprovingly a few weeks later.

"What has he done, Gemma? Explain yourself." Susan rushed to his defence.

"I don't think Snowy's been cleaned out for ages and I can't see any sign of her having had any food today. She smells too . . ." Gemma pulled a face.

Leo flushed scarlet. "She has been fed, I did it this morning. And she's due to be cleaned out tomorrow."

Gemma knew Leo's routine, he always gathered Snowy's leaves together and put them in the hutch just before he left for school. Susan still walked Leo to the school gates because, as she said, "There are so many road hogs who tear through the village and our pavements are so narrow." Whilst Susan was away, Mrs. Biggs attended to the children's bedrooms, sorted out their washing etc. Carefully checking Mrs. B.'s whereabouts, it was all too easy for Gemma to go to the hutch, remove the food, stuff it into her little satchel, and then scatter the leaves in the hedgerows as she made her own way to school. After ten days, Snowy was found dead in the bottom of the hutch and it was patently obvious that she had died from malnutrition.

"It was asking too much of such a young child," Susan protested, "I blame myself for buying the wretched animal. Now the dear boy is heartbroken again, just as he was after the riding episode."

"There has to be a funeral, Mummy. Daddy always has a funeral when somebody dies." Leo looked suitably pitiful.

"Yes, darling, we'll ask him."

But 'Daddy' was less than enamoured with the idea, finally agreeing to dig a small grave, and say a few words at the grave-side. On the question of wearing his cassock and providing a headstone, he was adamant.

"Absolutely not, Susan, don't even go there." And, more gently to Leo, "I'll say a few words, and we'll thank God for filling the world with beautiful creatures which we can all enjoy and then, if you wish, we'll sing a few verses of "All things bright and beautiful." Before Leo could once again raise the question of a headstone, Susan added, "Later, dear boy, we'll make a small wooden cross with Snowy's name on it."

The 'dear boy' was heartbroken and very, very confused. Useless for him to protest over and over again, that he had fed Snowy every single day, no-one believed him and yes, the rabbit had looked all skin and bone. It was all very peculiar.

But the most careful of criminals often leave behind important clues and so it was with Gemma. Two days after Snowy's demise, Mrs. Biggs retrieved Gemma's satchel from the hook behind her bedroom door, intent on ensuring there were no letters from school, or work waiting to be completed. Lifting out the contents, she saw two rather shrivelled dandelion leaves flutter to the floor. She was just retrieving them, when Gemma burst into the room. No words were necessary. Eileen pondered as to whether she should tell Susan Hatton about her discovery, having heard her employer's brusque rejection of the young groom's suspicion,. Would Susan accept that Gemma had wanted to belittle Leo in his mother's eyes, so that she might receive some of the loving attention he currently received? The knowledge of what had happened, hung between Gemma and Eileen Biggs, for twenty four hours. But before she could come to a decision and act, Eileen met her own coup de grace.

At breakfast, carrying a newly poured cup of tea to her seat, she was thrown off balance as Gemma leapt up, colliding with her just behind Leo's chair. Hot tea hit the back of his neck and soaked his shirt. In a flash Mrs. Biggs had removed the latter and laid a clean table napkin across his shoulders, so that only a small area looked red and uncomfortable. Soothing cream was immediately applied and the child seemed relatively unperturbed by the incident. Not so Sue Hatton.

"This is the last straw Mrs. Biggs. The child could have been marked for life. How could you have been so careless?"

"It was a pure accident Mrs. Hatton. Gemma chose that moment to leave her seat and knocked the cup from my hand".

"Enough! This is not the first time I have had to question your competence, but it is the last. Please pack your belongings and be ready to leave as soon as possible."

And so for Eileen, years of agonising over Gemma and trying to provide her with the love she felt the child needed, came to an end. In some ways it had been a burden and this was a relief, but Eileen knew that, whilst removed from the scene, wherever work next took her, she would, through her sister, be keeping an eye on the Hatton family.

It was going to be a case of 'Watch this space'.

Gemma had mixed feelings about Eileen Biggs' departure. It was obvious that she had worked out exactly what Gemma had been up to on several occasions and so it had been necessary, but . . . From Nanny Biggs she had received nothing but affection and the feeling that she alone, understood what Gemma had suffered since Leo's birth. But with the arrival of her replacement, Gemma's concern turned to one of delight. Nanny Bright, Gemma quickly decided, bore quite the wrong name on two counts, the lady being neither bright by nature, or endowed with common sense. There was little doubt in Gemma's mind that the Not-so Bright One had secured the post by her immediate show of devotion to the blonde-haired, blue-eyed Leo. A reaction, she knew, was always guaranteed to score a great number of Brownie points with his besotted mama.

Giles's parents, all too aware, of Susan's absorption with her son, finally prodded Giles to make a move, to curtail this.

"Get the boy away from home, as quickly as possible," this from Ruth Hatton.

"It might sound cruel, but all that 'Little Prince' and 'dear boy' stuff will not help him to hold his own in the big wide world."

And so, bracing himself, Giles tackled Susan.

" I'm not happy about the boy attending school here in the village."

"Why ever not? It was good enough for the girls." Sue's retort was sharp.

"It was *adequate* for the girls, but both teachers there are female, and I feel it is time the boy was placed in an environment where there are also male teachers, and a stricter discipline. It will make him more socially at ease and broaden his horizons."

Giles, knew only too well, that the only way to prise Leo from Susan's over-protective attitude, was to stress the social advantages. His assumption was correct and Susan, weighed down by the self sacrifice of saying goodbye to her 'darling boy', but accepting it was for his own good, set about making the necessary arrangements.

At last, his suitcase packed with every conceivable requirement, Leo left with his parents, on what was for him a great adventure.

In spite of Giles's protestations, Susan insisted on accompanying them, in order that, however tearful, she could ensure that 'her boy' would be comfortable and that the school's accommodation met with her own rigorous standards for Leo.

Living at school for five days each week, resulted in an important discovery for Leo. During those days there were no further bruises and no more unpleasant events. Only when bruises reappeared at the weekends, did Leo begin to realise that his bruises and the other incidents, might not have been accidents. Gemma had been present when the pony had suddenly taken fright and nearly thrown him; could she perhaps also have been responsible for the bruises? On the weekend following this idea, he forced himself to stay awake on the Friday night and, after midnight, heard a small creak as his bedroom door was opened. Just as Gemma approached the bed, Leo sat up.

"What do you want?"

Gemma was startled, then recovered. "Leo, you cried out and I thought you were having a bad dream. As I was closer than Nanny, I thought I'd come and see what was wrong." Leo knew he had made no sound and his suspicions were confirmed. Hard as it was to believe, Gemma seemed determined to hurt him in some way. But why? As he had expected, the night-time bruising now stopped and Leo decided that Gemma, guessing he was suspicious, would give up her attempts to hurt him. Lulled into a false sense of security by the incident-free weekends which followed, he was unprepared for what happened next.

On an Autumnal Saturday afternoon glowing with sunshine and colour, Gemma and Leo were told to accompany Nanny Bright on a country walk and, at Mrs. Hatton's suggestion, gather blackberries. Armed with small baskets, they set out until Nanny, tiring of the children's energetic forays into areas, where Gemma assured her were 'the very best bushes', found a grassy knoll from which she could see their movements and sat down, leaving them to their picking.

"Here's a good one, with lots of berries," Gemma called to Leo. He came across to inspect it.

"They're a funny shape. Don't look like the others to me."

"Don't be silly, blackberries come in all shapes. They're not as sweet as the others, but Mummy will mix them all up in a pie. I've just had some, they're O.K. Try some, but eat them with the others, then they don't taste sour". She held out her palm covered with an assortment of both. Leo dutifully placed a few of the blue-black berries in his mouth together with the more usual blackberries. He pulled a face,

"Ugh, they're *very* sour."

"Don't be such a baby. Come on, it looks as if the Bright One is ready to go." As Leo looked in Nanny's direction, Gemma dropped the remaining berries from her palm and crushed them underfoot.

It was not until they reached home that Leo started to feel unwell and Nanny bustled him off to bed. Then he started to be sick and the doctor was called. The violence of the vomiting, made Doctor Sims immediately suspicious that this was some form of poisoning and Nanny and Gemma were questioned. Both insisted that Leo had been warned to only pick blackberries and not touch any of the other bushes around. The doctor administered an emetic and at last the sickness subsided and Leo was able to sleep.

"I regard this, as sheer carelessness on your part Nanny, a carelessness, which could have had a very serious outcome." Receiving the rough edge of her employer's tongue, Nanny Bright had long ago decided, was an unfortunate part of her job and she had soon learned that the quieter she remained the sooner it would evaporate.

Once recovered, it was Leo, who, having told no-one about Gemma's part in all this, now had his worst fears confirmed. Nonplussed, he puzzled over how he could avoid his sister's obvious intent to cause him harm. An invitation from one of his school friends, to stay with his family one weekend, led to a further development.

"I'm going to be a full-time boarder next term," James said. "My Dad's work takes him abroad a lot and Mum would like to go with him sometimes. Like you, I'll be nearly eight then. I wasn't too keen at first, but if you could stay as well, Leo it would be great. There's rugby every Saturday morning and lots of time for cricket and football, we could have a lot of fun."

"I'm not sure," Leo hesitated. "It's not that I don't agree it would be great, it's just that I'm not sure if my parents can afford it. My sister Auriol's pretty clever and I know they want her to go to university."

"Oh . . ." James sounded deflated. "Well try them, you never know, you might have some rich relations somewhere."

"I think we've got those, but whether they'd want to cough up for my school fees is another matter." Leo pulled a face. "Anyway, I'll try."

And try he did, knowing that this would solve his other problem of getting away from Gemma for considerable periods. The suggestion that poisoned berries might have resulted in his sickness was attributed to the fact that innocent little Leo had eaten them unawares. Whilst Leo had not divulged the truth of the matter, he felt Gemma would realise that from now on, he would be watching her every move. He still could not understand her motive. She was behaving like something out of one of his, now discarded, children's books – a wicked witch. From what Nanny Biggs had told him, it sounded possible that Gemma had tried to kill him as a baby, then there was the pony business and finally the berries. If only he could get away to school, perhaps when he came back she would have grown out of whatever it was that was bothering her.

In the event there wasn't a problem. Much as she dreaded the thought of him leaving home, anything Leo wanted meant that for Susan, no stone should be left unturned until he got it.

"Leo is their only grandson, I'm sure your parents would be glad to help," this from Susan, rather plaintively. Giles agreed. He too, had been giving the matter a great deal of thought, recalling the conversation he had had some years ago, after the summer fete. Never by any stretch of the imagination a 'hands-on parent', he was aware that his own absorption in his clerical work, the needs of his parishioners and the necessity to produce regular sermons, left Leo very much in the company of the females of the household.

His own upbringing, with two lively elder brothers, had been boisterous and fun and if, like his elder daughter, he had sometimes slipped away to read, then that had been of his own choosing. There was too, another consideration. Susan was an excellent mother to their brood, but there was no doubt that the boy received the maximum of her attention and, it had to be said, overt affection. Clearly Leo was keen to enjoy the company of other boys and would probably benefit from it socially. With these factors in mind, he approached his parents.

"No problem," his father boomed, "delighted to help in any way. Just what the boy needs. With respect, it's time he got away from all the petticoats in your house. Needs a lot more rough and tumble, to help him grow up. It might mean you get a little less out of the pot, when we shed 'this mortal coil', but you won't mind that, I know."

"But can you afford it?" Giles was anxious.

The Hattons came from a long line of gentlemen farmers and lived close to the Glyndebourne Estate in Sussex. The last fifty years had seen all the farming and part of the land handed over to farmers in the area, but Giles's parents had retained the elegant Georgian house close to the outskirts of Chichester and the fields, which Mr. Hatton senior referred to as his 'nest egg'. Their three sons were each in settled careers of their own choosing. Charles, the eldest, now British Ambassador to Greece, Simon a Commander in the Royal Navy and if Giles's calling had taken him into a less lucrative position than the others, he had one huge advantage over them, being the only one of the three to have married and produced children. His parents delighted in the fact that they had grandchildren, over which, Susan permitting, they could dote in their old age. With a smile, Guy Hatton patted Giles on the back and said,

"No problem, as we've always said, delighted to help. Auriol's scholarship meant we haven't had to contribute very much so far and we'd always bargained on doing that. We'll probably get rid of another couple of fields, the developers are always on our backs wanting to buy land."

"But . . ."

"No more 'buts' . . . You let me know what it'll cost, from now until he's eighteen, and we'll arrange to provide the finance. What about other things, uniform, sports gear, that sort of thing?"

"He's already got those and anyway, I'm sure we can manage all that."

"Just don't forget Leo has a godfather, who's single and certainly not short of money. I know Charles would love to chip in."

Giles pulled a face, "I'm sure he would. I just hate the thought of running to big brother and . . ."

"And saying you can't manage?"

"Well, something like that."

The subject, as Giles thought, was closed. Two weeks later a letter arrived from Charles, who, having been acquainted of the situation by his father, informed them that he had set up a bank account in Leo's name and would be paying into it a monthly deposit of £300 to cover such incidentals as school trips abroad, sports equipment etc.

And so it was settled, to the delight of both Leo and his friend James, that Leo would become a full-time boarder. Now, Leo thought, Gemma would have fewer occasions on which to do spiteful things and as he got bigger and stronger, he could ensure she didn't get away with them.

Gemma torn between delight at his imminent departure, fury at the mournful expression her mother now seemed to wear permanently and teeth-clenching rage at the comments from villagers, saying how sad they were to see 'their little angel' going away for long periods, worried away at the problem.

"Perhaps I'm invisible," she thought "obviously brown hair and brown eyes don't mark you out as an angel, but my hair's curly and I'm not bad looking, if anybody ever took the trouble to examine me."

When Susan had, finally, resigned herself to the fact that Leo was now going to be away for some time, nametapes were sewn onto every conceivable garment, instructions about cleaning teeth and attention to hygiene were given for the umpteenth time, and at last he was ready.

On the morning of his departure, Sue descended the stairs in her smartest dress. A dismayed Giles moved forward.

"I know you said I shouldn't go, it would be too upsetting, but can't you understand I must see where he's going to sleep, get him settled in and talk to the Matron, that sort of thing?" In the background Leo shuddered, but Giles had decided that having won the major battle, it was now advisable to let her win this relatively small skirmish. "Of course my dear, I do understand."

The return of her parents from the school, with Susan still muted and tearful, was almost more than Gemma could stand. *Anyone would think there'd been a death in the family. It's like that expression in the Bible when people are mourning . . . Sackcloth and something or other . . . Yes that's it, sackcloth and ashes. It's enough to make anyone sick. He's only gone away to school for goodness sake, and that's not a million miles away.*

But it was not until the following morning in the empty house, that a more composed Susan was able to consider her changed life. Again she mourned the fact that Giles's choice of career, had deposited her in this rural backwater. Her own musical talent, both as a singer and pianist, had become non-existent as a vicar's wife with three fast-growing children and limited funds. Now, Susan decided was the time to take stock, to look more closely at her two daughters and her own position in the village, and to see how she could most usefully utilise, what she felt to be her own, considerable, talents.

In the adjacent village, Eileen Biggs had heard all about the poisoned berries and now knew that her suspicions had been confirmed. Useless to go to the Vicarage and try and talk to Mrs.Hatton. Her response would be exactly as it had been when the stones were found under the pony's saddle. She decided to write a letter, which Mrs. Hatton couldn't ignore and even if she tore it up after reading it, perhaps Eileen would have alerted her to a serious problem in her family. After much deliberation she wrote,

Dear Mrs. Hatton,

I feel I must write to you about a matter, which has been troubling me for some time. I have a great concern for Gemma, who ever since Leo was born, has seemed to me to be very disturbed. No longer can I accept it as a coincidence that Gemma has been present whenever there has been an accident of any sort involving Leo. Before you react to this, I must tell you that I saw the proof of the fact that it was Gemma, who ensured the rabbit died for lack of food. She was present when Leo ate the berries, when the stable girl was blamed about the saddle and certainly when she jumped off the seesaw and Leo was flung off. Were you not aware that on the weekdays when Leo was away overnight, the bruising didn't occur? I also noticed that the bruising only started again, after the baby monitor was removed from Leo's bedroom. You must draw your own conclusions from that.

I have a real concern about Gemma, and about Leo's safety. Since I left you, I have been working at a small nursery, and am studying for an Attendant's Certificate. This has meant reading a great deal about children and the symptoms they display. Whilst Gemma was certainly jealous of her new baby brother, I am concerned that the problem might run deeper. My readings suggest children displaying similar signs are in need of a great deal of love and affection. Perhaps she should be seen by a doctor?

Whilst I am sorry to lay this problem at your door, I would blame myself for not telling you all this, if any other 'accidents' should occur. Please give my love to the children and my regards to you and your husband.

Eileen Biggs

P.S. Please be assured I have discussed this matter with no-one else.

It was a few minutes before Sue Hatton's initial anger gave way to horror. Eileen had put into words, her very worst fears. Eileen had also pinpointed some things of which she herself, had been unaware and had, tactfully perhaps, not mentioned the fact that Leo when very tiny, had been found on his stomach. Surely at barely five, Gemma had been too young to plan anything so horrendous? Her past had not gone away. Her worst fears had come out of the closet and might now engulf her, again. The Biggs woman had tried to soften the blow. All that business about love and affection was double speak for 'You have neglected her'. Going to the doctor was not an option. Here in this small village, where everyone knew just about everything about everyone, the word would be on the street in no time, and if Gemma had to see a psychiatrist . . . ! She would ignore the letter.

There might be a solution. With Auriol and Leo, both now weekly boarders, Gemma and I will be together a great deal. If the problem is just jealousy, then that surely will go away in their absence? If I make sure that Gemma and I spend as much time together as possible, then I'll be able to make up for neglecting her in the past, and keep an eye on her at the same time.

The following morning in the empty house, a more composed Susan was able to consider her changed life. Her own musical talent, both as a singer and pianist had become non-existent as a vicar's wife with three children and limited funds. Now, was the time to take stock, to look at her position in the village, and to see how she could most usefully utilise what she felt to be her own, considerable, talents. Confident that she could both watch over Gemma and spread her own wings, she started to give it some thought.

CHAPTER 4

Giles found his wife's sudden interest in the church daunting. In the past, she had adequately fulfilled her role, visiting sick or troubled parishioners, attending at least one service each Sunday, and being present on all special occasions. These searching enquiries as to how often the church was cleaned, how much the choir boys received at weddings, who was on the flower rota etc., were way beyond her expected duties and puzzling.

There had been just three occasions when Susan had been asked to sing in church, twice at weddings, and once at a Christmas service, subsequently receiving many plaudits. Other invitations had not been forthcoming, possibly Giles felt, because of her insistence upon the highest standard of accompaniment. It had taken Giles's considerable diplomacy and a struggle with his conscience about white lies, to explain to the Moordean church organist, that the musician imported for Susan's solos, was a close and dear friend.

As always, Susan, unable or unwilling to react to the vibes emanating from those around her, continued in her exploration of what made the church tick; its Deacons and Wardens, the Sexton and of course its parishioners. The knowledge that Mr. Fisher, the ageing choirmaster, was finding it increasingly difficult to handle the boys in his charge and that choir numbers had dropped dramatically, was grist to her mill.

The following Sunday, Susan saw her opportunity, carefully cornering Mrs. Fisher as she was leaving after the morning service.

"Mrs. Fisher, my dear, you're looking well, but I'm afraid Mr. Fisher . . ."

"What do you mean Mrs. Hatton? Is something wrong?"

"Not exactly, it's just that . . . well, I feel he doesn't look one hundred per cent fit these days. Don't you agree?" Mrs. Fisher hesitated.

"Well, he's been rather quieter than usual I suppose, but he hasn't said anything's wrong. He sleeps a lot of course, dozes in the armchair, but then we're both getting on a bit."

"Yes, but you see my dear, that's his body telling him to rest, in fact, insisting he does so. Perhaps he's doing too much."

"Well, I know some of the boys are a bit of a handful and he has to watch them or goodness knows what they'd be up to. Not that I'm complaining, Mrs. Hatton and neither would Fred, after all boys will be boys."

"I know that *neither* of you are the sort to complain Mrs. Fisher, but haven't you thought it might just be the time for your husband to curtail his commitments? After all, he's been a good servant to the church and you wouldn't want to lose him, through his clinging on to something which has become a worry."

"Oh my goodness no, I hadn't thought about it like that. Perhaps I should have a word with him."

"Yes, but tactfully, my dear. You know how stubborn men can be. My Giles is just the same. It's probably better to just drop a pebble now and again, then he'll gradually come round to the idea and think it was his in the first place."

And Susan, who was an expert on the subject of dropping pebbles, discreet or otherwise, was confident that very soon she would have the new challenge she wanted. Within two weeks, Mr. Fisher had resigned and in the absence of any other volunteers, and with the obvious advantages of Susan's considerable musical expertise, the Church Deacons were happy to appoint Mrs. Hatton as their new Choir Mistress. 'Happy' is not perhaps the correct word. Susan's statement that she would be opening the choir to admission for girls, was controversial, but her categorical statement, that this was a non-negotiable decision, and would determine her acceptance or refusal of the post, created considerable concern.

As one irate farmer said "We can't have the woman dictating her terms, before she's even got the job."

"But we don't want to upset the Vicar." This from the local solicitor, totally unaware that the Vicar was, in fact, as disenchanted with the idea of his wife taking over the choir, as were some of the Deacons. Voting was not unanimous, but with two 'No's' and one dissension, the 'Ayes' won the day.

Once Susan was installed, the three boys, who had been the instigators of previous trouble, were sent packing at the first hint of disobedience and speedily replaced by three biddable, nice looking girls who, fortunately, were able to sing in tune.

Throughout all this, Gemma had her own hidden agenda. Delighted that she now had periods when she and her mother were alone, she started to blossom in the new warmth which surrounded her. There was just one problem. Uninvited as yet, by her mother to join the choir, Gemma now made it her business to sing around the house and garden, at every available opportunity.

At school, she begged her music teacher to let her sing a solo at the end of term concert, thus ensuring her parents would have to sit and listen without the usual household distractions. It was there, finally, that Susan's attention was suddenly alerted, her musical knowledge taking over. The child's voice was pitch-perfect, she could sing! Even at twelve years, Gemma had quite a stage presence and as her sweet, bell-like soprano soared to the rafters of the school gymnasium, the audience showed that they loved it.

Once again, Gemma was her mother's 'darling girl'. Joining the church choir was now obligatory, and, joy of joys, Gemma must learn to sing in tandem, with her mother's beautiful contralto. Villagers stopped to congratulate her in the street and life was wonderful.

Invited to sing a duet with her mother, at the induction of a new Bishop in Chichester Cathedral, proved to be the icing on the cake. Giles's brother, Charles, a friend of the Bishop Elect, expressed his wish to attend.

"After all, I must hear my niece sing. This could be the first of many such important occasions. It would be nice if Leo could be there too, an opportunity for me to get to know my godson. I'm conscious of the fact that I've neglected all your children over the years."

Gemma, preening herself at her uncle's comments, was less than pleased to learn that Leo had been given leave from school. Trust him to muscle in on the act. The ensuing conversation between her parents left her seething.

"We can't possibly provide Charles with the style to which he's now accustomed," grumbled Susan.

"He's my brother, for goodness' sake, and he hasn't always lived the grand life. He'll fit in with anything we have to offer."

"I've kept saying we ought to rejig the playroom, it would make a lovely big bedroom, and what was Nanny's little room could be turned into a dressing room with a washbasin and shower."

"I know it would be an asset, but there's not enough time and certainly not enough money, to consider it now. What about putting him in Leo's room?"

"No, I don't want that disturbed, after all it's such a treat for him and us, to have him home for the weekend. Auriol will be home for the weekend, the girls can share her room." Susan's mind was made up.

Life for Gemma was no longer wonderful. 'The darling boy' was about to come home and his mother was ready to 'kill the fatted calf', or do whatever she felt appropriate in the circumstances. Leo must not be inconvenienced on any account, it seemed, but it didn't matter that Gemma was to be uprooted and on the eve of such a special performance, when she'd be finding it difficult to sleep anyway. Nothing had changed. Leo, was still his mother's angel, and everyone else had to take a back seat.

Gemma went through the motions of course, kissed Leo warmly on his arrival and if he stiffened and looked ill at ease during her embrace, no-one but she noticed.

For her godfather, Gemma's greeting was unreserved. Tall and distinguished looking, he exuded success. Charles's comment,

"My dear Gemma, you've grown into a little beauty, with your pretty curls and those eyes, they're just about the colour of my very favourite, plain chocolate." At that moment, Gemma knew herself to be his slave for life.

The induction service, within the ancient Chichester Cathedral, proved a wealth of pageantry, with the stone walls providing a perfect foil for the blazing colours of the clerical garments. Gemma loved it all, the soaring stained glass windows, the magnificent floral arrangements and the sweet voices of the choristers, which sent shivers down her spine. But it was the sea of pink faces, which fascinated her most of all. So many people and they would hear her sing. She would see that she gave those choristers a run for their money! And she did. Mother and daughter, voices beautifully blended, delighted the congregation and when at the last the service came to a conclusion, people flooded to congratulate the two soloists. Gemma basked in the euphoria of success. They liked her. It was a lovely, lovely day.

Emerging from the cathedral, they found there had been a heavy shower during the service, but now the sky was blue again and the sun shining. It was Charles's idea . . . smiling at Susan and Gemma, he said, "You've both done us proud, your singing was truly superb. Now let us enjoy the rest of this wonderful day. What I would really love is a walk near the sea. Any suggestions, Giles?"

"Well . . . discounting the seaside towns, difficulty with parking etc., I'd say Beachy Head is our best bet. It's about an hour's run from here."

"Perfect! It's now 11.15, so we'd be there by mid-day, a brisk walk on the top of the cliffs, plenty of good sea air, then back to civilisation for lunch. Where's the nearest possibility for that?"

"Eastbourne I'd say, but it will be after one o'clock and it is Sunday, might prove difficult to get in anywhere." Giles sounded decidedly dubious.

"No problem. I'll ring the Embassy, they've got lists for just about everywhere. I'll ask them to find something suitable, book a table and ring me back later."

Susan thought how simple life was when there were always people at the ready, to do your bidding and iron out any possible problems. Listening as Charles telephoned his instructions, she sat back in the people carrier borrowed from the Embassy pool, relaxing in the glow of the success of the morning.

Arriving at their destination, Leo and Gemma were first out of the car, with Giles following, glad to stretch his long legs after the journey. He laughed as Leo and Gemma started hurrying from the roadway up the steep incline. At twelve years Gemma pretended to be so grown up, he thought, but in a situation like this, she and Leo were like a couple of puppies, ready to run wild when let off their leads.

At what point Giles became alarmed, no-one knew. Suddenly the hard line of the cliff top was starkly outlined against the blue of the sky, and a shock wave went through him. There was no fence! Shouting to the children to stop, Giles started to run. Oblivious to his urgent calls, carried away on the wind, the children hurtled forward, until Leo himself, sensed danger of a different kind. They were close to the edge and his sister was just an arm's length away on his left. On the instant that Gemma turned towards him, Leo veered sharply to the right, and it was at this moment that Giles arrived between them. Attempting to seize Gemma's hand and pull her backwards to safety, he missed his footing, slipped on the wet grass and, like a scene in slow motion, slid relentlessly forward, over the cliff's edge and out of sight.

Gemma's mouth was open, but emitted no sound. Leo turning, white-faced and disbelieving, to the space which had been his father, hurled himself at her, screaming and pummelling her with his fists. From behind them, came a second scream and a clamour of exclamations. Then Charles was there, dragging the distraught Leo off his sister, hauling them both backwards to safety and, at last, peering carefully, very carefully, over the edge. On the rocks at the base, he could just make out what appeared to be a bundle of clothes, with one sleeve extended. Clearly, Giles had made a desperate attempt to save himself. There was no movement and in that instant, Charles knew his brother to be dead.

CHAPTER 5

Auriol, though ashen-faced, appeared to be the only one in control. Taking out his car keys Charles handed them to her.

"Take everyone to the car. I'll make some calls." And, as an after-thought, "You'll find a small brandy flask in the glove compartment, give everyone a mouthful – just a mouthful, mind."

Quickly, Charles rang the police and asked for assistance, then phoned his parents, requesting that they go to Giles's home at once, and be prepared to stay for several days. That he believed Giles to be dead, he omitted to say, merely that there had been a bad accident, his brother was hurt and the family very distressed. He then phoned the Embassy, asking them to make contact with Moordean village and ask to speak to one of the Church Deacons. Ministerial cover had been provided for Giles's attendance at the cathedral; not only would this need to be extended, but there would now be other duties for a minister to perform. He asked that the Deacon alert the women of the church to the fact that the Vicar's family would be in desperate need of assistance, during the coming days. Having covered as many eventualities as he could think of, he waited for the police to arrive.

The death of their comparatively young vicar sent shock-waves through the village and as Charles had anticipated, the women came forward immediately to assist his bereaved family. Whole meals arrived as if by magic, laundry was whisked away and reappeared in neatly ironed pristine piles. Charles obtained special dispensation, so that he could remain during the period of the post mortem and inquest and made contact via the Admiralty with his brother, whose ship was somewhere in the Far East.

His next suggestion was not so well received. "I think the children should return to their respective schools on Thursday,"and, as Susan started to protest, "I feel it's important that, for the moment, they should move within the parameters of a regular routine. Once the funeral arrangements are made, they will have further disruption."

The children protested, and uncharacteristically, Susan seemed unable to make a decision, finally leaving it to Charles and her father-in-law to discuss all aspects of the necessary arrangements and come to their own conclusions.

Initially, Leo had seemed the most disturbed, his outbreak and attack on Gemma on the fateful day, being attributed to his extreme trauma and distress. In spite of being constantly told that it had just been a terrible accident and no-one was to blame, to the surprise of the others, he still refused to speak to Gemma, as if he felt she was the root cause.

"He's still in shock," Charles said to Susan, "I really feel he will be better amongst his friends for the time being. Once the funeral has taken place, he might be able to bring the matter to a conclusion, if not, we'll have to seek professional help."

The more her mother and uncle fussed over Leo, the more Gemma fumed. She and her father had had little in common. By the time Gemma was born, he and Auriol had already developed a shared love of books, and from this close liaison Gemma had always felt excluded. Her own bedtime stories had been read by the Nanny of the day, whilst her father continued his habit of reading nightly to his elder daughter. Gemma would miss his presence of course. A presence, she had often felt, helped to offset the overbearing evidence of Susan's love for her youngest child. On occasions Giles's quiet words or manner, had made Gemma wonder if he too, found her mother's fussing over Leo, whilst seeming to ignore her daughters or himself, unacceptable.

But the rage which really gripped her, driving her to hot tears and misinterpreted by the others, was one of frustration. Leo, the object of her hatred, was still here, his pretty little face now pale and drawn and still, being fussed over by the other members of her family. Ironically, she had not intended to kill him on that day . . . it would have been stupid to even attempt it on the cliff-top. Other members of their family, she knew, would be following them up the hill, and watching. No, that was not her way. Every detail had to be carefully planned, and there must be no onlookers. No suspicious viewers able to relate afterwards, exactly what had happened, or her part in it. Had Leo been the one to fall without her assistance, it would have been an unexpected bonus, but now he was benefiting from the incident and she was once again being ignored.

Each member of the family struggled to come to terms with their own grief, and in some cases, guilt. Guy Hatton recalled how he had so often berated Giles for not 'being a man' and standing up for himself. How he had argued with his wife, Ruth, who had always protected her youngest son, and said Giles must be allowed to follow his own instincts. Now, Giles was dead, and he, his father, was overwhelmed with regret that their relationship had not been closer and more loving.

Charles, remembering the little brother, always with his head in a book, knew Giles to be gentle and kind, but, when confronted with hard decisions, unable to face the realities of life. The church had seemed for him, to be the ideal career. There, he could submerge himself in theories and ideologies, rather than fact; but to what cost, within a family environment? His wife had not seemed content and his children not enjoying the close bond Charles recalled having had, with at least one of his brothers.

Susan had managed to contain her own emotions, which vacillated between shock and frustration. Long ago, she had realised that her feelings for Giles, during those first passionate months at university, had resolved themselves into what one might feel for a dear friend. Furious now at the futility of such an unnecessary accident, she wallowed in her own sense of guilt, grieved at the sudden parting, but was not heart-broken. Like Gemma, she raged inwardly. Her own plans, to do something worthwhile with her life, were now shattered. With three children to support and no man around, life was going to be very different indeed.

Leo was reliving once again every moment of what had happened at Beachy Head, blaming both Gemma and himself for his father's death. If only he had seen the danger earlier. Had realised that he and Gemma were alone on the cliff-top. Freed from the confines of the car, it had seemed so natural to run and run, upwards, towards the sky. Only at the very last moment had he become aware, sensed what might happen, and as Gemma put her hand out, he had swerved from her contact. In that split second he saw his father, already sliding on the wet grass, and then the vacuum as he vanished from their view. Impossible to believe that in those few seconds he was gone. Impossible to forgive Gemma for her part in his death.

Gemma knew from Leo's reactions that he had thought she intended to kill him on Beachy Head. That merely confirmed to her his stupidity. How did she imagine she would have attempted that, with the whole family coming up the hill behind them? Didn't the stupid boy realise that everything required planning to the last detail and that was something at which she was very good? Hearing her father's shouts hadn't she put out her hand to stop Leo going further, only to find him moving away and leaving the gap through which her father slid to his death.

Why hadn't they died, she and Leo? If anyone ever got around to asking her, she would be quick to point out that their body weight was so much lighter than their father's. By the time he started his slide on the wet grass, his weight and the fact that he was still running, would have carried him forward with greater momentum. She would miss him. Her father was one of the few people who treated her like an adult and that was only since he discovered she could beat him at chess.

On the day Leo returned to school, Gemma, hiding her relief, shed false tears and mentally warned him, 'Out of sight you might be, but certainly not out of *my* mind. You've been lucky so far, but there'll come a time . . . '

Later, Gemma and Auriol having also been returned to school, Charles and his father sat down with Susan to discuss immediate problems, the major one being the loss of Giles's income, and the tenancy of the Vicarage. Susan, horrified at the thought of leaving her home and the village where they were now established and reasonably content, was forced to realise that this might prove a necessity. Once preliminary funeral arrangements had been discussed, Charles left, ostensibly to make a business call, returning later to say he had been to see the Bishop, whose see included the village of Moordean.

"The Bishop tells me changes for this area are already afoot. The Church can't afford to finance a vicar for every rural parish, some of them very small indeed. He feels now would be the appropriate time to unite Moordean and Oakdean under one priest, and proposes that the young man who has been covering for Giles, the Rev. Finlay, should do just that. Finlay's already installed in the Vicarage in Oakdean, so there'll be no question of your vacating the house for some time."

Hearing these words sent shockwaves through Susan. Of course, she couldn't stay here indefinitely, the house came with the job, but . . . Seeing her alarm Charles added,

"Susan, my dear, you must not concern yourself with this now. It's not imminent, no decisions have to be made and you're not to worry about it."

As expected, the inquest on the following Friday, recorded a verdict of Accidental Death, with recommendations to the relevant council, that fencing should be erected and warning signs prominently displayed. The will revealed nothing unusual, as Susan said wryly, "Poor Giles had nothing much to leave."

The females who felt Giles's death most keenly, were separated by two generations. His mother, Ruth, was never to recover from losing her youngest son, her presence in Giles's home proving to be one of

Charles's rare miscalculations. Badly traumatised, Ruth was unable to assist him in the administration of Giles's household, proving, on the contrary, to be yet another person requiring care and attention.

Reality did not strike her eldest grand-daughter, Auriol, until 48 hours after the event. Her father, Auriol told herself, would soon walk in, bruised but alive, having been saved by landing on a shrub, or falling into the sea. All would then be well, and back to normal. When this failed to happen, and policemen and women came to the house with doleful faces, Auriol was, at last faced with the irrefutable fact that her father was no more. How to carry on without him? He had been her soul-mate, loving tutor and mentor. Now, she was on her own. Unable to form friendships easily, the hurdles of future examinations and entrance to university seemed insurmountable.

She remembered the day when she had been so upset at the realisation that the word 'dysfunctional' described her own family and how Eileen Biggs in trying to make things better, had talked of love, and somehow made it worse. At her new school, she'd heard theories bandied about, that the middle child in a family was often the one out on a limb, and she knew too, that this very much applied to Gemma. It was probably the reason for her peculiar attitude at times, and her ambivalent moods. Now, she herself would be out on a limb; how could she cope without her father?

"Auriol, I need your help." This from her uncle. "Could you please go and see your grandma? Her doctor's not very happy about her, thinks she's already had a very minor stroke and is suggesting that as soon as possible she returns home, to a more tranquil environment. It's essential that she has something to drink, even if food is out of the question. Try to persuade her to have fruit juice, tea, coffee, anything you think might tempt her. I know you're suffering too . . . Can you do that?"

"Of course, Uncle Charles, I'll go up right away."

"Good girl. Oh, something else. I've been in touch with your godfather and they're flying him home, so he should be here in a few days."

Uncle Simon, somewhere on an aircraft carrier in the Pacific. An accident such as this, Auriol thought, was like a giant net spreading out in all directions, dragging people to its grieving core. Fifteen minutes later, precariously balancing a tray laden with assorted drinks and a covered dish of buttered toast, she was tapping on her grandmother's door. There was no response. Manipulating the tray with difficulty, she entered the room, setting her burden down on the edge of the dressing table. Ruth Hatton was curled in a foetal position with the clothes up to her chin.

"Grandma wake up, I've brought you a drink." There was a muffled 'No' from under the bedclothes.

"Please Grandma, I've been told that I must have some breakfast and you know I hate eating on my own."

There were sounds which might have indicated agreement and then Ruth's tousled head appeared, peering over the edge of the eiderdown.

"Never liked eating on your own, did you, Auriol? Reading, writing, even walking, but when it came to food, you always wanted company."

Auriol almost choked, as she swallowed her anxiety, and tried very hard to smile.

"Too right, I don't know why, but there . . . Now, there's apple and orange juice, tea, coffee or neat milk. What's it to be?"

"What are you having darling?"

"I thought perhaps coffee would be best, help me to wake up . . ."

"Then coffee it is, nice and milky . . . You know how I like it."

Before Ruth could change her mind, Auriol had the coffee poured, set it down on the bedside table, then assisted her in sitting up against her pillows. Ruth was ashen-faced and her eyes darkly ringed. For the first time Auriol noticed how prominent the lacing of dark blue veins was on the back of each hand. Still, Grandma was sipping her coffee and Auriol felt that she herself was beginning to think more clearly. Having laced both cups with honey, now at her first mouthful she felt the hot liquid coursing through her body, and was grateful for it. Gingerly, she bit into a piece of toast. It tasted good. How could anything taste good, she chastised herself, when her father was dead and she would never see him again?

"Grandma . . . ?" she held out the plate of toast.

"No, my darling, thank you . . . perhaps later. I will try . . ."

And so they drank their coffee, the strained silence giving way intermittently to trivial comments as, striving for normality, they waited to see what developments the next few hours would bring.

The funeral was to take place on the Tuesday, following the inquest. Simon was being flown back from the Pacific and would arrive on the Saturday. Following her doctor's recommendation, it was decided that Ruth and her husband should return home on Friday evening, accompanied by Auriol. A phone call arranged that the two senior Hattons' regular lady helper would go into the house and ensure beds were made up etc., She was also prepared to make herself available to assist with food, throughout the days before the funeral.

Auriol, uneasy about the arrangement, protested, "Why me? I can help out far more here, and this is where I ought to be."

"Darling, Simon is your uncle and it is a few years since you saw him. That apart, you're so good with Grandma. I know you'll make sure she rests for a few days. She'll need help sorting out what she's going to wear on Tuesday, there are lots of things you can help with, which we can't really expect someone outside the family to do." Susan hadn't expected resistance from this source for Auriol was usually so biddable, but, she reminded herself, these were difficult days for everyone and Auriol too wanted the reassurance of being at home, surrounded by everything familiar, in a suddenly unfamiliar world.

But it was Charles's comments which provided the balm to soothe Auriol's feelings of rejection.

"Auriol, we're asking you to go because you are the eldest, and the most responsible. We know we can rely on you to do and say the right thing, whatever arises, and we'll see that you're returned here on Monday evening, so that you can make your own preparations, decide what to wear etc. Meanwhile if there's a problem, just give us a ring and between us your Mother and I will sort it out. O.K.?"

His warm embrace reduced her again to tears. This was what had always been missing in her own family, why did they rarely hug and kiss, as other families seemed to do?

"I'll go and pack my bag", she said and turning to her mother, "I'll need a new pair of black tights, most of mine have runs."

As expected, the church was packed, its bells tolling mournfully for the loss from their village community of someone who, whilst not loved, was highly respected. Assisted by the new incumbent, the Bishop conducted the service and Susan's choir did her proud. Children from the Sunday school had brought their own small posies, which were placed on the altar. Simon read the lesson and Charles delivered the eulogy, with the polish anticipated from someone in his profession. Finally, as the clock struck mid-day, Giles was laid to rest in the small cemetery behind the church.

Ladies from the village had arrived at the Vicarage at 10. a.m., laden with food, exclaiming at their good fortune that for early May the weather was both sunny and unseasonably warm. The invitation to the wake had been extended to anyone who wished to attend, and by the time people arrived, extra chairs had appeared in the garden as if by magic, trestle tables set up, urns bubbled away and, in a discreet corner, there was alcohol for those who felt the need of something stronger. Rarely was Susan overwhelmed, but the sight of what the ladies had achieved, and the effort clearly involved by everyone concerned, reduced her to a flood of tears.

Auriol felt it somewhat distasteful that everyone should be standing around chatting in the sunshine, smiling even, as if it was just another social event. Her father was dead for heaven's sake, this was not a time for being sociable.

Gemma noted only the fuss the ladies made of Leo, "Growing so quickly", "And so handsome, no wonder he's the apple of his mother's eye", the latter comment causing her to almost choke over her chocolate éclair. This would not be a good day to attempt anything foolish she decided. Tomorrow, Leo would be returning to school, but during the summer break . . .

Deciding not to take up the open invitation to the wake, in case it proved awkward, Eileen Biggs, had managed to squeeze into the church, and watched Gemma with interest. The family, seated at right angles to the main arrangement of pews and parallel to the coffin, were in full view. The twelve year old had grown up. She looked pale, but Eileen saw that her eyes darted here and there, as she took careful note of who was present, and what was said. This was a different Gemma, from the one she had seen singing at the Moordean School Concert. There, she had exuded a glow of confidence, and, receiving congratulations afterwards from her parents, had looked ready to burst with happiness. What a difference from the introverted child of a few years ago, who had been so sullen and morose when being ignored.

If only Susan Hatton would wake up to the realisation that Gemma's character was being formed now, and just how it developed might be entirely dependent upon her own behaviour towards the child. Gemma was going to be a beauty, and, what was more, a talented beauty, who might just prove difficult to handle. Eileen had received no reply to her letter, nor had she expected one, but perhaps now Mrs. H. would make even more of an effort. Losing her husband, and with her other two children away at school, would surely leave her with ample time to devote to Gemma, which could be to the advantage of them both.

Anxious to give Susan and the children a future target, something to which they could look forward during their sadness, Charles spoke to them that evening, concerning the summer break.

"I wondered if you would like to come over and stay with me in Greece for three weeks. I'll arrange to keep some days as free as possible and hire a yacht, so that we can visit some of the islands." He smiled at their surprised faces. Gemma spoke first, "But we don't know anything about sailing . . ."

"Then it's just as well I do," Charles laughed. "But these yachts for hire do have a crew, there'll be a skipper and his assistant and, you'll be glad to hear, a cook. When I'm busy at the Embassy, you can take yourselves off sight-seeing, or if it's too hot, we do have a swimming pool, so you can be either very active or very lazy, as the mood takes you." Charles had noted the gleeful expression on young Leo's face when the trip was first mentioned, but was at a loss to understand why, after a quick look in Gemma's direction, the look of delight had given way to one of abject misery.

Charles was further surprised, when Leo spoke up,

"I'm sorry Uncle Charles . . . I was going to tell you, Mummy, this evening, before my return to school . . . you see my friend James has already asked me if I could go away with them, during the summer break. His mother says it would be lovely if I could, because when the family goes abroad, James is usually on his own. So, if Mummy agrees," looking at her, "I hope you won't think I'm very rude, if I don't come with you, but go to Portugal instead."

"No problem, old chap. It would have been nice to have you with us, but I can quite see that with someone your own age, you'll have a great time. I'll leave you others to mull it over, just in case you'd prefer to do something different."

Susan was grateful to Charles for his invitation. He had already explained that on the Bishop's instructions, rent for the Vicarage would be waived for the next six months, because of the very exceptional circumstances. During that time, she would be able to consider what her next move should be. A period abroad, free gratis, would assist with financial problems and give them all a complete break. She was sad that Leo would not be with them, already feeling keenly his long absences at school, but as her father-in-law and Charles kept assuring her, it was good that he should be in a more masculine environment during this period of growing up.

The more time she spent in Charles's company, the more Susan saw that, whilst possessing Giles's intellectual ability, his courteous manner and attention to detail, Charles at all times had an air of authority. Gentlemanly yes, but by no stretch of the imagination would he have been described, as Giles had been frequently, 'a gentle man'. Six feet tall with dark hair flecked with a distinguished grey, and blue-grey eyes, he had kept himself slim and fit, in spite of what must surely be endless hours spent at this desk.

Wryly she thought, that having a private pool in your back garden, must help a great deal in this respect. His lack of a wife or partner, was intriguing. Was he gay? Or did the very nature of his office, encourage women to faun over him, and share his bed. With a retinue of servants to look after him, and society women ready for whatever was on offer, he perhaps felt a wife would be an unnecessary appendage. Life was so unfair, she decided. Now if she had met either Charles or Simon first . . . ?

Gemma had felt quite excited at the prospect of swimming with Leo, sailing with Leo, surely these would present ample opportunities for her to do what was necessary, and get him out of her life. She knew of course, what this talk of another invitation was all about, if there hadn't already been one, Leo would no doubt wheedle his way in, to make sure he spent the summer break with James and co. The only upside of this holiday business was that he would not be a thorn in her flesh; she would have her mother and Uncle Charles all to herself, apart from Auriol, who didn't count.

Leo, obviously, now knew the score, and was as determined to thwart her, as she was to get rid of him. Stupid boy, he hasn't yet realised, he's dealing with someone of superior intelligence . . . but he will, eventually.

CHAPTER 6

The holiday in Greece was proving everything Susan had hoped for. Heeding Charles's warnings about sunstroke, she and the girls swam in the pool, then relaxed in the shade of umbrellas, or the orange trees, which were dotted here and there. On these occasions, Auriol made the most of the time by doing preparatory reading for her A Levels, whilst Gemma, to Susan's amazement, also seemed to be permanently immersed in a book.

"You've suddenly developed into a bookworm, Gemma, what are you reading?"

"Well, this is an Agatha Christie . . ."

"Goodness, I'd have though that was a tad dated for your generation."

"Well yes, but I like mysteries. I've found quite a selection on Uncle Charles's shelves, Dick Francis, Ruth Rendell. One writer I like's even more dated than Christie, not the author himself, but what he's writing about, if you see what I mean.

His books are set in medieval times, and he tells them, as if he's a monk of that period. They're very clever." Gemma was careful not to stress the murder element in what she was reading, only that they were mysteries.

"I'm amazed, I'd have thought a thirteen year old would be more inclined to light-hearted material about pop stars, footballers' wives, that sort of thing."

"Ugh, no way", Gemma said smiling, "you obviously don't know me very well."

The barb passed unnoticed, as Susan laughed, "Obviously not."

After dinner on their third evening Charles, determined to use the holiday to develop a closer relationship with his brother's wife and children, asked Auriol, "How are the studies coming along?"

She pulled a face, "Well, I'm knee deep in 'Othello' at the moment and finding it beyond belief that jealousy could drive him to kill someone so close to him, someone he professed to love."

"My dear, it happens all the time. When someone regards something, or somebody as their own territory, another person moving in and taking over, is asking for trouble."

"But in this case, no-one else has moved in . . ."

"Ah, the point is, Othello thinks they have."

"In that case, why kill Desdemona, and not the so called invader?" Auriol sounded puzzled.

"Because, to begin with, he thinks she has been complicit in the taking over and then, well I'm afraid it's rather like the small child and his toys syndrome."

"What do you mean?"

"If a mother suggests to her child, that he shares his favourite toy with another child, he may be so attached to it, that he'll destroy the toy, rather than comply with her wishes."

"That's terrible." Auriol was genuinely shocked

"Terrible it may be my dear, but sadly it's true. Human beings and many other animals are very territorial indeed and we reveal the worst sides of our nature, when anything or anyone invades the area we regard as our own. The mother/child bond is particularly strong and a mother will fight to the death to protect her offspring. It's even been suggested that because of this, marriage might become a thing of the past whilst the strongest bond of all, mother and child will continue to hold firm."

"So a woman might have several children, by different fathers?" Gemma pulled a face.

"That already happens in some cases, as you probably know. But what is also happening, is that more and more young people are cohabiting, without getting married. In a way, the number of single mothers proves the point that the mother/child bond is the strongest of all, and will survive, whatever else goes to the wall. In the 'Othello' pairing of course, there are many other factors, his colour for instance . . . but I think Gemma's trying to say something else, am I right?"

"Yes," with a quick glance at her mother, "if there is, as we've already agreed, one mother bonded with several children, would she, in that case, defend them all equally?" No comment from Susan, but she had noted Gemma's glance, and was aware of the reason for the question.

"That's quite a shrewd observation for a thirteen year old. Not being a parent, it's quite a tricky one for me to answer. Logic says she should defend them all, because she would care for each of them impartially, but emotions are not always logical and like it or not, I'm sure that in some families there are favourites, who might get priority treatment . . . not in yours of course!" His warm smile included them all and they smiled back. "But that's enough literary analysis for one evening. Now, can you all play table tennis?"

A 'Yes' from both the girls, hesitation from Susan, "Well, I used to at university but haven't played for years so . . ."

"That's good enough, it'll soon come back to you. Let's go down to the games room and see if we're ready for the Olympics."

Later that night, Charles ruminated on the conversation and Gemma's part in it. There was something about the girl he couldn't quite fathom. She didn't seem particularly close to Auriol, and certainly not to young Leo when he was around. In fact, Charles sensed an antipathy between them, and had not forgotten Leo's violent outburst, as he struck out at his sister following Giles's death. Very curious. Could be hormonal of course, she was at a tricky age. He'd never thought Susan would be the easiest person to live with, too many highs and lows in her nature, and prepared to move heaven and earth to get her own way. Perhaps Sue had been too hard on the girl about something, and Gemma was still brooding about it. It would be interesting to see what happened in the next few weeks.

It was whilst lazing on deck as they sailed round the islands that Charles broached another difficult topic. He had been in daily touch with his father in the U.K. and knew that his mother, Ruth, was far from well. Her doctor was sure there had been another minor stroke, sufficient to make her confused and forgetful. His own suspicion was that this was the beginning of Alzheimer's, and he had warned his father that he must be prepared for this.

"I've got a proposition to put to you, Susan." Charles knew this was not going to be easy. "You know that your stay at the Vicarage will soon have to come to an end, and we have to consider alternative accommodation for you and the children. I've been talking to Dad about Mum, and the news is not good. You're aware that their house is far too big for two old people, would you consider . . . ?" He stopped, seeing the look of horror on her face.

"I hope you're not going to suggest that I move in and become some sort of carer or nursemaid, and run that household, just to avoid paying rent anywhere else? I'm fond of Ruth, but with the children growing up, I did think I might be able to consider doing something worthwhile, something I would enjoy."

"No, hear me out, and think about this sensibly. Mum already has a carer and this sort of help will be increased, as it is needed. Should her condition deteriorate so that it becomes necessary, then she will go into a home. Leo is away at school, Auriol will soon be going to university and Gemma, well we don't know just yet about her future, but for much of the year, it would only be you and Gemma at the house. You talk about paying rent for accommodation, but decent places to rent are not easy to come by. The parents are not short of money, someone comes in to do the cleaning, laundry etc., so you would have no outgoings on the house. We could also look at the possibility of turning one of the wings into your own domain that way you could see as much or as little of them as you wish."

Susan sighed. "Oh dear, I feel I must have sounded like some awful ogre, and you have all been so kind. I know it's selfish, but it's just that I would like to get back to my music. You and Guy have obviously given this a lot of thought, and I'm grateful for that. If we did have an area of our own, I think it might work . . . the children are not little I know, but they play their own type of music, rather too loudly for the grandparents' taste I think, they're often on the phone, or watching television, and it would completely shatter the tranquillity of Guy and Ruth's home."

After her first, sharp reaction, Charles was pleased she was now thinking logically.

"I confess it would be a load off my mind, if I thought you were able to keep me posted about what was happening. Dad's no chicken, and whilst I try to speak to him daily, there could be times when a decision has to be made fairly quickly. Having said all that, let's consider you personally. Do you want to sing professionally or to be involved with music?"

"Oh the latter, I'm much too old to try and break into the former."

"I do have a contact at the London Academy of Music and Dramatic Art. Would you like me to have a word with him about the possibilities of employment?"

"Charles, would you? That would be wonderful. I feel so out of touch. But supposing I got some sort of a job, what about Gemma?"

"Ah, now that's where this arrangement would be helpful to you on another account. Whilst she's still at school locally, there would always be a home for Gemma to go to and, whilst Dad's still around, a sensible adult if she had a problem. She could always eat with him too, when necessary. Later she'll probably go on to university so the amount of time at home would be reduced. In any event you might find that your working year could in some way work round school and university vacations. What do you think?"

"I think as always, dear Charles, you have done your homework very thoroughly, and covered just about every eventuality. Gemma's a good girl and I know she would never willingly cause any trouble so, yes, I will start looking at work possibilities and yes, I will also start packing up our things at the Vicarage, trying very hard to be as ruthless as possible. By the time I've finished, the charity shops should have a field day."

Charles laughed, "Just don't try to do it all on your own. I know some of it will be very personal, but where possible, do get some help from the village. I'm happy to fund that, and all your removal costs, so don't overdo things. You should also go and have a look at Grafton House and the rooms which will be yours. At the moment they're furnished, just decide what you want left, and what removed, and we'll organise it."

"It's such a beautiful house, I've always loved it, but it's a while since I went into the wings. I'm sure some of the things there, are far superior to anything Giles and I were able to afford, so it's unlikely I'll want to jettison much."

"Don't forget a lot of it would have come to you anyway, when the parents pass on. In that event, there might be things Simon and I would like to keep, but at the moment, neither of us is in need of furniture. Although . . . come to think of it, Simon will probably descend on Grafton sometimes, when he's on leave. He does have a flat in London, but I know he likes to get into the country, and of course he enjoys it when there's a shoot down there."

"Goodness, does that still happen?"

"Yes, but it's all out to franchise. If you remember, some distance from the house there are two cottages. All the shoot business is transacted there, and there are sufficient rooms for an overnight stay for eight guests, plus the organisers. A local man breeds the pheasants, and when they're mature enough they're released into the valley, which you've probably seen—it's about a mile from the house."

"Yes, I have seen it, but absolutely ages ago. So these young pheasants are bred, just so that someone can go out and kill them?"

"'Fraid so. But it is big business, and none of it should in any way impinge upon your life in Grafton."

"I'm glad you warned me. If I'd seen a man carrying a gun bearing down upon me, I might just have been somewhat alarmed."

"My dear Susan, I find it difficult to think of any situation, which you would find alarming." Charles smiled, "I'm quite sure, you would be able to cope with just about anything which comes your way."

She smiled back, "You're just saying that, because you know it's true."

As with everything which Charles handled, their transference from the vicarage to Grafton House was smoothly effected and, once installed, Susan had to admit that Charles had been absolutely right . . . again. The house was beautiful. Of Georgian origin, it had an elegant portico and tall windows which, at the front, faced a rather imposing drive and, at the rear, looked out beyond the gardens over the fields. Seeing the exquisite pieces of furniture in the west wing of the house had left no doubts in Susan's mind that they should remain in situ. Giles's desk was kept, and placed in Auriol's room, and Susan retained her own bureau, various items which had been wedding gifts, her china and kitchen tools.

An extra bathroom and shower room had been installed upstairs, and downstairs rooms, which would have been occupied by servants, had been beautifully converted into a kitchen, housing all the necessary modern equipment, but in units which retained the style of the property. Another section of these downstairs rooms included a utility room and a double garage, because as Charles had said, Susan's family would very soon be of an age when they would expect to drive. An access corridor, upstairs, was not sealed off, in case of an overnight emergency with Susan's in-laws, and there was one access door downstairs, to which just she, and her father-in-law, had keys.

"Come at look at this Mummy," Gemma, excited, had found the garden, created under Charles's instructions, for their private use.

"It's absolutely lovely," Susan too, was overwhelmed, seeing what lengths her brother-in-law had gone to, to ensure their comfort. One section at the rear had been closed off with mature shrubs and garden furniture was already installed.

"We can sit out here in the sun . . . and have tea. It's perfect." Gemma was ecstatic.

Susan's phone call to Charles in Athens was fulsome in her praise at what had been achieved in such a short time. Very soon, Susan and Gemma felt comfortable at Grafton and totally at home.

Because of the upheaval of the move and the necessity for Auriol to prepare for A levels, it had been agreed that she should board full-time at her school until the examinations were over, and for Gemma this period when she had Susan to herself was idyllic.

It was Susan who first gave Gemma the idea. The two of them were on their own, but Leo was due to arrive for the weekend, as it was his birthday. Susan mentioned that the pheasant shoots had just started and Gemma, immediately interested, started to ask questions.

"Are the men already here then?"

"Yes, they arrived whilst you were sound asleep, at about 6.a.m. Not that they came up to the house, they take that left-hand turning to their cottages, but I heard several cars close by. They're probably already out by now, we'll hear the shots soon."

Thinking Gemma might be alarmed at this, Susan quickly added,

"The shoot takes place on the side of the valley, quite a distance from here, so there's no danger."

"And what happens exactly?" Gemma was now showing a real interest.

"Well, the beaters will have come in from the village, together with the people who own and train the dogs. Here, it's mostly black Labradors, but a lot of people use large setters, they're all gun dogs."

"Then what?"

"Well the gamekeeper will know exactly where the pheasants are. The beaters will form a circle behind them and the guns, that is the men with the guns, will be lined up ready. Then, at a signal, the circle will start to close in, making a lot of noise and beating on the ground. As the birds fly up to escape the commotion, the 'guns' will shoot at them."

"And the dogs?"

"They will have been held by their trainers, behind the line of fire and at a signal, they will move forward and collect a dead pheasant and bring it back to the person who shot it. The dogs have very soft mouths, so that they don't in any way damage the bird."

"Which is already dead?"

"Well yes, but if it's to be sold for cooking, it mustn't look as if it's been mauled in any way."

Gemma picked at a thread in her skirt, so that her mother could not see that her eyes were gleaming. She shuddered. "It sounds absolutely barbaric."

Susan smiled sympathetically. "Well at least it's a quick death and I suppose we all hope for that." Gemma bit her tongue, to prevent herself from smiling. It had been perfect here, with just herself and Mummy, but once again darling little brother Leo was about to descend on them and spoil it all. Perhaps it was now time for her to have another attempt.

CHAPTER 7

At Grafton House, Ruth's condition had deteriorated, and Alzheimer's had been confirmed. She now had two carers, who came in daily and, following pressure from both Charles and Simon, Guy employed a Cook/Housekeeper. Susan's own life had now improved dramatically, Charles's 'word' to the Professor he knew at L.A.M.D.A. having paid dividends. A study of Susan's impressive report from university, followed by a challenging interview, and then a month's briefing on examination technique, had resulted in her appointment as an external examiner. It was ideal. There were periods when life was rather hectic and she was travelling around the country, and then weeks when she might have just two appointments at HQ, and the other days were free. This was just such a week. Auriol was away studying and Leo were just returning for the weekend, because it was his birthday.

Gemma had made up her mind. Grandpa was the one to tackle first.

"Grandpa, could you do me a really big favour?"

Gemma was very good at putting on her innocent little girl act.

"Darling, if it's possible, of course. What is it you want?"

"Well you know Leo's coming home tonight for his birthday tomorrow?"

"Yes, I'm looking forward to seeing him."

"Well, I would like to give him a surprise, something he'd really love, but I'm not sure if it would be possible to organise it." This because, as Gemma knew full well, Guy always loved a challenge.

Guy bridled and hurrumphed. "If it's at all possible, I'm sure I can arrange it. But what is it?"

"It's just that Leo's always loved hunts and shoots and things, and I wondered if it would be possible, as a birthday treat for him, to go on one of your shoots?" Gemma sounded plausible, whilst knowing full well, that Leo loved animals and would hate seeing them killed.

Guy was surprised. "I didn't know he was interested in that sort of thing, but, to begin with, they're not 'my shoots', in fact they are really nothing to do with me."

"But they're on your land."

"Ah yes but . . . Look you'll have to leave it with me. They don't usually allow children anywhere near the shoots, but they owe me a few favours. I'll need to make some phone calls, leave it with me, come back in an hour."

"Thank you so much Grandpa, I know how good you are at fixing things. Don't tell Mummy will you? She can't keep secrets, especially anything to do with Leo."

With that, Gemma disappeared into the west wing, and Guy Hatton reached for the phone.

Gemma was back promptly and Guy was waiting for her.

"Well I've arranged something for you, hope it meets your requirements. Finlay was quite adamant that he couldn't have you and Leo anywhere near the guns, but you can walk with the beaters, as long as you keep behind their line. You mustn't ever get in front of them. Do you understand?"

"Of course, Grandpa, it sounds wonderful, just what I wanted. Leo will be so pleased. Thank you so much and please, I'd still rather you didn't tell Mummy, I'll just say we're going for a walk after lunch."

"I don't know what all the secrecy's about."

"Well she'll have planned her own surprise and I want this to be my very own."

He laughed, "Right you are, Mum's the word. Now . . ." turning back, to his newspaper.

"Grandpa, I'm ever so hungry, could I have a biscuit or something please?"

"Of course, dear girl. Just help yourself to whatever you want, I don't think Mrs. Beale is here yet, but you know where everything's kept."

She had worked it all out, revised her earlier plan. It was going to be impossible to get Leo anywhere near the guns, but there was another way. Something she had recalled, about the bottom of the valley. That could be even better. In the kitchen, she went straight to the giant chill cabinet in which the day's shoot of pheasants was always kept overnight. Sure enough, there they were. It took just a minute, and some tugging, to extract a handful of the longest tail feathers. Wrapping them in a piece of paper towel, Gemma went out of the front door, calling "Bye Grandpa."

Quickly, she hurried to where she could get cover from the trees. It wouldn't do for Grandpa, or her mother, to catch sight of her. Too many questions would be asked, all difficult to answer. At last, she saw the cottages to her right and now moved in a large arc, to ensure she wasn't spotted by any of the 'guns' or beaters, late returning to base.

Now she was at the valley, and it was just as she remembered it, from all those years ago, when Nanny had taken Auriol and herself for a walk, during a visit to the grandparents. The shoot was to be on the incline, mostly covered with shrubs and trees and nearest to the cottages, but here at last was what she had been hoping to find.

Gemma came to a halt in front of an area covered with long grasses and reeds, and cordoned off by rope, and a rather battered sign, saying 'Danger'. The whole patch was screened from the incline on one side, by several very large bushes. Nanny's words came back to her very clearly. "It was a terrible accident . . . such a young man. He was walking with his girl friend, stumbled to one side, and suddenly found his feet were held fast and the mud was sucking him down. She tried to keep hold of him, but he knew that she too, would be pulled down with him, if he didn't let go, so he did, and just disappeared into the mud."

Auriol had asked why this quite small patch would be so dangerous, and Nanny said local people believed that long ago, there was some sort of pit there, which now always filled with water, but looked innocent enough, because of the greenery on the surface. Then, she obviously felt she'd said too much and closed the subject.

Yes, it would serve her purpose very well. Grasping the signpost, Gemma tugged, then, failing to move it, searched around, until she found a large stone. Now she struck the post backwards and forwards, until it finally became looser at the base, then with a great effort, managed to pull it free. Quickly, Gemma hid it in the bushes and then ran round the perimeter of the swamp, pulling out the smaller posts to which the rope had been attached, until she had completely dismantled the roped enclosure. Now, everything was in one pile and she dragged that too, out of sight, behind the bushes.

There was just one more task. Carefully, Gemma removed the pheasant feathers from their wrapping, securing them together with a rubber band. Then, breaking a branch from the nearest bush, she patiently used it to push the cluster of feathers, until the quill-like ends were embedded in the mud, and couldn't easily be blown away. It was difficult and took longer than she had expected, but at last the feathers were in position and reasonably upright. Surveying her handiwork, she decided the cluster looked as realistic, as she could hope for. The swamp area was well screened from where the shoot would take place, and hopefully, all those involved would be too far too occupied with their own activities, to see what was happening in the distance. She could do no more.

Just how dear little Leo, who loved animals and hated the killing of all wild creatures, would react when he saw what was intended, she couldn't imagine. But he was so polite, he couldn't refuse a carefully planned birthday surprise, could he? Wiping her hands on the paper towel which had held the feathers, she put it in her pocket, made a final check that all was ready, and set out for home.

The birthday boy duly arrived and was fussed over by a delighted Susan. Cards and presents were opened the next morning, and Gemma left mother and son to talk about what was happening at his school. Gemma had given Leo a smart pen and pencil set and he seemed delighted with them. Grandad Hatton joined them for lunch and discreetly tipped Gemma a wink, confirming that all was organised.

After lunch, Gemma suggested that she and Leo should go for a walk, so that Susan could 'put her feet up'. Laughingly she added, "I'm sure Grandpa will want to go back and do the same." Leo's agreement to the walk was somewhat guarded, what was she up to now, he wondered?

Once in the valley, she waved a greeting to the assembled beaters and started moving towards them. "Where are you going?" Leo asked.

"I've got a surprise for you Leo, Grandpa's arranged it for your birthday. We're going to watch the shoot."

Before he could respond, they had reached the beaters and one of the men came forward to greet them. "You must be Gemma and Leo. I'm Fred, welcome, and a happy birthday to you, young man." He shook hands with them both and then continued, "Now, your Grandad's told you the drill, keep behind our line and you'll be fine. O.K., let's go and take up our positions."

So the arc of beaters formed and a reluctant Leo, pulled along by Gemma, took up their positions about three yards behind Fred. Looking up the valley's slope, they could see where the ground cover of bushes and shrubs reached the trees and that beyond that, there was a clearing. They could not see the 'guns'. Suddenly it was very quiet and the signal when it came, was unseen by the children.

Without warning, the silence was shattered, and then the noise was deafening. Each beater carried a stick and some of them held clappers as well. They moved forward beating the ground, and there was a sudden flurry of beating wings, as the large birds rocketed into the sky. Shots rang out and, bird after bird, dropped like a stone.

Leo pulled away from Gemma's hand, recoiling in horror. "It's horrible, horrible, I hate it, why did you bring me here? I'm going home." He started to cry and moved to the right.

"For heavens' sake, Leo, stop acting like a baby, you're ten years old. Grandpa's going to be really disappointed that you didn't like his surprise. We'll go home, if that's what you want, but it's no use going back the way we came, they'll still be retrieving the dead birds and Grandpa said we mustn't go anywhere near the 'guns', or where the dogs are working. We have to go back down the valley."

With that, Gemma strode off and Leo thankful to have started the journey home, hurried after her. At first, when she stopped, he couldn't see what she was pointing at, then she called,

"Leo, hurry up and come and see, I think one of the birds is down here, it must have been injured." Joining her, they moved forward together and now he could see the brightly coloured feathers on the ground, partly obscured by the long grasses.

"Oh Leo, the poor thing. It's probably in agony. Perhaps it's been hit and can't fly. I'd go and get it, but I'm so stupid, you know I feel faint at the sight of blood."

Leo, anxious to recoup his grown-up status as a ten year old, moved forward.

"I'll get it, Gemma, perhaps if it's still alive, we could take it to the RSPCA, or something." With that, Leo moved quickly towards the feathers. There was no reaction to his first few steps, but then the ground became softer, and he was suddenly aware that the area was muddier than he'd thought, then, that his feet were sinking, and suddenly, Leo knew he was in danger.

"Gemma, it's a swamp, I'm sinking. Help."

"It's only mud, Leo, come back here if you're scared."

"No, no! It's a real bog, the sort that pulls you down . . . it's doing it now, it's going to swallow me up." He screamed.

She didn't move. Then said slowly, "It's probably better if you keep still Leo, the more you thrash around, the worse it will be."

"Help me, get help, do something! It's pulling at my legs." He screamed again.

She didn't move. "Gemma, please, please do something quickly, it's going to kill me . . ." His voice died to a whisper.

Someone was approaching. Without turning Gemma called, loud enough to be heard by whoever it was, "Leo, I don't know what to do . . ."

On Fred's exclamation, "Oh my God!", Gemma turned.

"Where are the ropes and the warning?" he asked, already on his knees and laying his beater's stick on the swamp. It was not long enough!

"Quick girl, I need your help, look for the ropes, they must be here somewhere." For a moment she was immobile and he guessed she was in shock. He called to the boy,

"Leo, don't move, we're going to get you out of there." The boy was whimpering with fright. Brushing Gemma to one side, Fred moved towards the bushes and immediately saw the pile of rope behind them.

"Quick girl, help me with this." At last Gemma moved, and he pulled a long length from the pile, thrusting one end into her hand and taking a clasp knife from his pocket. Within seconds, he had cut off a substantial piece, then tied one end into a lasso-like noose. The boy was now immersed to just above his waist.

"Leo, I'm going to throw this to you. Put it over your head and arms – it must be round your middle, *not* your neck. Here it comes."

It didn't work. Fred's throw was not accurate enough, and Leo far too frightened to reach out for the noose, but the second attempt was successful. Leo managed to slide the rope over his head and arms, so that it was under his armpits, and Fred started to pull. Slowly, very slowly Leo's body surfaced from the swamp, until at last he lay at their feet, covered with mud and shaking violently. Fred wrapped him in his jacket and they now heard others running towards them.

Gemma, tears streaming down her face, turned to the approaching beaters. "It was awful, awful. If it hadn't been for Fred, Leo would have died and I couldn't do anything to help him." She collapsed into the arms of one of the beaters.

"Good grief, Fred, what the devil's been going on?" This, from the man holding Gemma.

"Good thing you said you couldn't see the kids and were going to look for them. When you didn't come back . . ." He looked round in dismay, "Where on earth are the ropes and the sign?"

"Vandals, I expect," this tersely from Fred, "but no time for that now. Some of you take the children to the drive, the boy will have to be carried." Taking out his mobile phone, "I'm going to ring his mother and ask her to bring the car down to meet us and phone for a doctor. The boy's traumatised and I think the girl's in shock. We won't worry the old boy yet, don't want him ill as a result of this."

The tears still wet on her face, Gemma was inwardly fuming. What was it with this brother of hers? He was like a cat with nine lives. Whatever she did, he seemed to come out of it safe and sound. Now, she had to face both her mother and Grandpa, although hopefully with the latter's involvement she'd covered her tracks.

Seeing her children in a state of distress, Susan was too frightened to be angry. Her priority must be to care for them, until they were recovered. One of the men helped her to run a warm bath for Leo and once the mud had been removed, he was wrapped in a large towel and rubbed vigorously to get the blood flowing again. The boy's eyes were glazed over and he had not spoken, since he was removed from the swamp. The man suggested an old fashioned remedy of massaging his limbs and chest with brandy might help, and Susan was only too pleased to try anything which would bring colour back to his face and recognition of his surroundings, into his eyes. At last, the pallor receded and cocooned in blankets, he seemed to focus on the two people with him. Then he spoke, "I'm so sorry Mummy. I know it was meant to be a treat, but I hated it, and I didn't know about the swamp . . ."

"Darling boy, there's nothing for you to apologise for. Don't try and talk now. I think the doctor has just arrived, and I'm sure he'll be pleased that you're looking so much better."

Downstairs, Gemma was being fussed over by Fred, and the other beater. They heated milk, found some brandy, added a small amount and then insisted on her drinking it, "To counteract the shock," because as one said, "You've had a fright Missy, and no mistake."

When her grandfather suddenly appeared, Gemma, conveniently, burst into tears again. Guy Hatton, distraught that he'd unwittingly placed the children in danger, angrily wanted to know whatever had happened to the roped-off enclosure, but as Fred pointed out, anyone could walk into the driveway and main entrance, and from there into the valley. "Mindless vandals," he fumed, "the boy could have died."

"I thank God, Fred, your quick thinking prevented that. I think we're going to have to completely enclose that area in such a way that no-one will venture in. Perhaps barbed wire is the only answer."

The doctor complimented them on Leo's treatment, suggesting he should now have a hot drink and with it take the tablet he prescribed, which would help the boy to sleep.

"It's almost the end of term, Mrs. Hatton, perhaps it would be as well to let him stay at home for the next few days, just to ensure there's no delayed shock reaction."

Finally, they all left, Grandpa back to his own rooms, the doctor, the beaters and Fred to their homes. Susan and Gemma, having thanked the latter profusely, were at last alone. To Gemma's surprise, there were no recriminations forthcoming from her mother, rather she seemed concerned about Gemma's own state.

"Have you had a hot drink, darling?" and, at Gemma's nod, "right then. I know it's early, but you do look pretty wiped out. Supposing you go and get tucked up in bed and read one of your books for a while. I'll bring you some supper on a tray later and another hot drink, then perhaps you can put all this behind you, and go to sleep."

Gemma, delighted to be the centre of Susan's attention, happily agreed and disappeared, leaving Susan alone with her thoughts.

And Susan had a great deal to think about. The absence of any connection with her own family had, in the early days, been a subject for discussion, but gradually, questions ceased to be asked. On meeting Giles, she had explained that her parents had died in a motor accident. The information that whilst her father was at the wheel, her mother had produced a kitchen knife and stabbed him repeatedly, she had not divulged. With her father's collapse, the car had gone out of control and smashed into a wall, killing his wife Ivy instantly. When rescuers got to the scene, her father had been on the point of death. It was left to the forensic scientists to determine from the knife, and the angle of the stab wounds, what had happened. There was more. At the inquest, her mother's doctor had come forward to say that Ivy was schizophrenic. He had repeatedly asked her to seek further treatment, fearing that the condition was worsening, but she would not listen to his advice.

Susan, twelve years old when this happened, had always been aware that her mother had occasional violent mood swings, which affected the whole household. Always the anger had been directed towards her father. His late arrival at the meal table had once resulted in china being smashed against the wall, and plates full of food being consigned to the waste bin.

The young Susan had been brought up by her paternal grandparents, who acted as if her mother had not existed, never allowing her name to be mentioned. It was a relief when she finally left their home and went to university, determined in future to look after herself and live elsewhere. At that point, every connection with her own family was severed, the money from the sale of the family home enabling her to meet her living and tuition expenses, and still have a nest egg in the bank. Meeting Giles had proved a godsend, they were comfortable together and he had, importantly, a gentle disposition. His proposal was accepted with enthusiasm.

For a time, Susan had become obsessed with her own persona, examining her own actions for signs of abnormality. How she had reacted in a given situation, or how she should behave in another, became of primary importance. Paranoiacs, she had learned, had low boredom thresholds and with Auriol's arrival, she had watched the child carefully for any untoward signs. The girl's bonding with her father had proved a real bonus. With gentle Giles as a father, there could be no problems. Then Gemma was born and Susan doted on her, delighted that Gemma, too, showed no signs of odd, or volatile behaviour. At last, Susan had stopped looking for problems where, she convinced herself, none existed and so when Leo came on the scene, it seemed she had a totally healthy family and could relax. Until now . . .

Eileen Biggs had not exaggerated. Leo's accidents were too frequent to be coincidences, and in all of them, Gemma had been present, if not directly involved. Gemma, at the difficult adolescent age, might find it hard to relate to a ten year old, but occasionally, she had seen Leo glance at his sister, almost as if he was afraid of her. And, dear God, all those years ago, Nanny finding the baby unable to breathe . . . . But Gemma was only four years old then, it wasn't possible, surely? Why had Leo refused the promise of a holiday, the thought of which had obviously excited him? Her thoughts, haphazard and fragmenting, so alarmed her, that opening her clenched fists, Susan found her nails had pierced the skin of her palms. Now, she recalled the terrifying moment surrounding Giles's death and young Leo pounding his sister with his fists. Disbelieving, shocked beyond reason, yes, but why Gemma? Gemma had not pushed her father over the cliff, so why would Leo think she was in some way responsible?

And today's episode . . . Could Gemma feasibly have planned it? It would have meant the removal of a signpost embedded in the ground, and the poles and ropes around the site. Gemma was of average height and build, surely not strong enough to do all that, and how would she have persuaded Leo onto the precise area, which was highly dangerous? Then surfaced the most frightening question of all. Was Gemma trying to kill her brother?

Following the deaths of her parents, Susan had read a great deal about paranoia and schizophrenia and it seemed that in both cases the sufferer's animosity was centred on certain people, and that they invariably felt themselves to be victimised. Often the sickness was caused by loneliness, a feeling of isolation, but for heaven's sake Gemma was a member of a family, she couldn't possibly be lonely. Now, Eileen's frequent hints came back to her. "Perhaps Gemma could come with you to the village Mrs. Hatton . . ." "I'll happily bath Leo, if you'd like to read Gemma a story." And then the comment in the letter, which had made Susan see red, suggesting that she should show Gemma more love and affection.

Did Gemma feel victimised, because of Leo's presence? And if so, had she herself constantly aggravated the situation, by devoting so much time to the boy and excluding her youngest daughter?

Repeatedly, Susan told herself it was all nonsense. After all, Grandfather Hatton had had a hand in organising today's outing. Nanny had been present when the children were picking berries and Leo, only little, had put in some of the wrong shape by mistake; there *had* been the bruising and that nasty incident when Leo was a baby, but cot problems happened to dozens of babies. The stable girl had been very angry about the stones under the saddle and had even suggested that Gemma was responsible . . .

And yet? Wearily Susan made her way upstairs. She checked that Leo was sleeping peacefully and then went into Gemma's room. Staring down at her daughter, brown curls spilling over the pillow, her pretty face relaxed and innocent, Susan decided she herself, must be having delusions. It was not possible that this young girl, who looked and sang like an angel, could have master minded some of the things which had happened. Telling herself that she was letting past events in her own childhood cast doubts on her present existence, and that it must stop right now, Susan retired for the night.

The next morning Gemma was eating her breakfast when the phone rang, and as Susan turned from the sink, she jumped up quickly, "It's O.K. Mum, I'll answer it." Returning she said, "It was Grandpa, saying if I was well enough, he's going to church and would I like to accompany him, he's bringing the car round in half an hour. I said yes."

"You're sure you feel up to it?"

"Absolutely, anyway I'm sure he'd like the company, I think he misses Grandma not being able to go out and about with him."

"Good girl."

Susan watched as Gemma drained her teacup, then heard her running up the stairs. Clearing the table Susan decided that her thoughts last night had been a result of her own state of shock, she really must not allow herself to imagine things, which could not possibly have happened.

Upstairs, Gemma smiled at herself in the mirror. *Just right*, she thought. *Grandpa to myself for a time, and I can make quite sure that he's aware of his part in yesterday's mishap, and suggest he really must do something about vandals coming onto his property and creating a danger to others. I'll start by saying we ought to say a little prayer for them, so that they might stop their evil ways, that should do it!*

Susan let Leo sleep on, so that the effects of the sleeping pill would have run their course, and it was eleven o'clock when he emerged bleary-eyed but smiling.

"Darling, how do you feel? Sit down and I'll get you some breakfast."

"I'm fine now, Mummy, but a bit sleepy still. Just cornflakes and fruit please."

She picked up the frying pan, looking at him questioningly, he shook his head, "No, definitely no, thank you." Once his needs had been catered for, she sat down with him.

"You know Doctor Ramsey said it might be better if you stayed at home now, as it's almost the end of term. I don't want you feeling ill when I'm not there to look after you. It is possible you know, to have a sort of delayed shock after a nasty experience like yours." Leo was alarmed.

"I really would rather go back tomorrow, as planned, Mummy. You see it's at the end of term, when the exams are over, that all the fun things start to happen." He became animated. "There's a special cricket match where they form two teams, each one a mixture of Junior and Senior boys. I'm quite good at cricket, you know, and I think I stand a chance of getting into one of the teams. There are concerts put on by the Drama group and the Musicians, oh and yes, there are chess and Scrabble competitions and . . ."

"Stop darling, I think I've got the picture. I wouldn't want you to miss out on the fun, when I know you've been working really hard and your teachers are pleased with you. But promise me, you will go and see someone straight away, if you feel unwell? I'll give you a note to explain what's happened."

"Oh . . ." Leo hesitated, "I don't want you to make a big thing of it, Mummy. The seniors will think I'm a bit daft, that I couldn't see the difference between solid ground and a swamp."

"No, I won't as you say, 'make a big thing of it', but I think Matron should know what happened and that you've seen our doctor." Susan was not to be swayed on this.

"O.K."

"But, as we missed your birthday tea yesterday, we'll have it today. I've got a lovely cake and all your favourites, scones and jam and lashings of cream. We'll ask Grandpa to join us again, then, if you have another early night, you should be well rested, before you get back to all those jollifications at school."

Leo knew better than to question Susan's forward planning and thoughtfully returned to his banana and cornflakes. She could not, or would not, accept that, far from finding the school regime rigorous, he had from the start, enjoyed having a daily time-table. He liked knowing exactly where he should be, at any given time, loved the horseplay in the showers and the ordered, quiet discipline of mealtimes at the long refectory tables. In assembly, the masters with their gowns and colourful hoods were a joy and the only females around were Matron who never, ever embraced anyone, as his mother did, and the school secretary who, with one glance over her steel-rimmed spectacles, could stop a senior form, six footer in his tracks.

There was another thing, even more important. Staying at home, would have added another ten days or so, to the already interminable six weeks of summer holidays, to be spent in Gemma's company.

He couldn't think how she'd arranged what happened yesterday, but was in little doubt that she had. He remembered, that when he had first called for help she had not moved, until Fred appeared on the scene, and then suddenly she was all tearful and concerned. Gemma really did want him dead. But why? What had he ever done to her, to produce such hatred? Should he tell someone, his mother perhaps? No, he recalled his mother's furious reaction when the stable girl had suggested Gemma might have put the stones under the saddle. There was no way his mother would believe him. Who then? Grandpa? He was too old to be worried about this, especially with Grandma so poorly. Auriol? She was rarely at home these days, and when she was, her head was full of getting to university and making new friends. His best friend James would listen, but he'd probably think Leo was bonkers to even think of such a thing. No, he would just have to put up with it, the good thing was that he was growing all the time, and soon, perhaps sooner than she thought, Gemma might find him a force to be reckoned with. Meanwhile, he must be watchful and wary, particularly during the summer break. *Just you wait Gemma Hatton, there'll come a time when I'm bigger and stronger than you and you'd better look out because I'll be getting my own back on you!*

CHAPTER 8

At her school in Chichester, Auriol, her exams over, and no further lessons to attend, packed up her personal belongings, ready for going home. Her interview at Oxford was imminent and, deciding there were several items she needed before making that journey, she walked into the city to do some shopping.

"Auriol!" Turning, on hearing her name, she saw Eileen Biggs, hurrying towards her.

"Auriol, it's so nice to see you. Have you finished school yet?"

"Well yes, and no. Mrs. Biggs, it's been ages . . . how are you?"

"I'm well, thanks. Look, my dear, have you got time for a cup of coffee? I'd love to hear your news."

"That would be great. It's such a lovely day. What about the Cathedral café? We could sit outside there."

Within a few minutes, they were doing just that. Any uneasiness Eileen might have had, about the fact that she'd left the Vicarage under a cloud, was soon dispelled by Auriol's relaxed manner.

"I was saddened to hear about your father's death. What a dreadful thing to happen."

"Yes, we were for a long time, all shell-shocked. I couldn't imagine how I was going to manage without Dad's advice, especially with entrance to uni., that sort of thing. But . . . . well, you've probably heard we've moved house, had to of course, and we're now living in one wing of the grandparents' house. I think that's helped all of us, because there was a lot to think about, which took our minds off other things."

"And your mother? Is she coping alright?"

"Yes, the good thing that's come out of all this, is that she now has a job, which I think she really enjoys. She always wanted to use her musical talent and now she's an examiner with LAMDA," and seeing Eileen's puzzled expression, "the London Academy of Music and Dramatic Art. It's fairly flexible, not a nine to five, five day week job, and with all of us away at school, it works very well."

"You're all away at school now? Even the young ones?"

"Well, I've just finished here at Chichester, before going to uni., Leo's a full-time boarder at his school, Gemma's the only one who goes home nightly, her school's fairly close. It seems to work quite well. Grandpa's there, if there's a problem and Mum is going to be late home, or whatever."

Eileen, hesitantly, "How is Gemma these days?"

"Gemma? Oh, she's OK, I think. You never quite know with Gemma, one day she's on top of the world and the next she seems weighed down with misery. Oh, and of course, you won't have heard, that those two young ones had a nasty accident, just recently."

Eileen tried not to show too much alarm, "No, I haven't heard, what sort of accident?"

"Well, it was at that place you once showed us, years ago before Leo was born, the swamp on Grandfather's land. Do you remember?"

Eileen remembered only too well. "What happened?"

"Well, it seems someone had removed the Danger sign, and all the poles and ropes which stopped people going onto that area. Leo thought he could see one of the pheasants from the shoot, lying there, as if it was injured. He went to try and save it and was dragged down into the swamp. Fortunately, just as it was getting really nasty, one of the beaters arrived and got him out."

Oh my God! The girl remembered, after all those years. I told the children it was very dangerous and that someone had died there. Gemma knew where the patch was. Nothing's changed. She's still behaving exactly the same.

"And they were alright afterwards . . . both of them?"

"Well, they were both very shocked, of course. The beaters were brilliant, seemed to know exactly what to do and by the time the doctor arrived, Leo was starting to show signs of improvement . . ." Auriol grimaced, "We do seem, as a family, to be accident prone. And Leo in particular, look what's happened to him in his short life."

Eileen, well aware of those happenings, sent up a silent prayer that Susan Hatton would reread her letter and, in the light of this recent event, take her middle daughter to see a doctor, at once. Draining her coffee, she prepared to leave, "And you, Auriol, where next?"

"Well, I have a firm offer from another uni., Durham, which is very good, but I have an interview at Oxford on Friday, and I'd love to get in there and read English. It was always Dad's wish that that would happen."

"And I'm sure it will. You're a good girl and I know how hard you work. Give my regards to your mother and love to Gemma and Leo. Remember, I'll be wishing you success, every step of the way."

A quick embrace, and Eileen was on her way, her heart heavy with the knowledge that Gemma was still a serious threat to Leo. It was not over.

A nervous Auriol set out for her interview at Oxford. Constantly she reassured herself that, having already been promised a place elsewhere, it would not be the end of the world if she was not successful. But always she remembered that this was what her father wished for her. This, for him, would have been the reward for his dedicated tuition over the years.

It was, as she had anticipated, a painful and nerve-wracking ordeal. She was for a few moments tongue-tied at the breadth of the questions posed.

"How would you set about producing 'Hamlet', Miss Hatton?" This, to someone who had never been in a play, let alone visited the theatre very often. She gulped, bit the inside of her mouth and desperately tried to focus on all the things her father had taught her. Characterisation, the key to all English Literature!

"I would read the play several times and study the characters, making notes on any idiosyncrasies and clues as to appearance and behaviour." Murmurs of approval.

"In one word sum up the essence of Jane Austen's novels."

"Gentility".

A 'Very good' from someone, and by the time the session was concluded, Auriol in a bath of perspiration, felt she had done reasonably well.

Studying at Oxford, 'the city of dreaming spires' would be for her a wish come true. In her imagination, the joys of further exploration of literature had always been foremost in her mind. Only rarely had she considered fellow students and the experience of living miles away from home.

The excitement of her acceptance, and the bustle of packing and leaving home over, she was at last established in a hall of residence. Now, she was in a city thronging with people of her own age, desperately trying to come to terms with the major change in their lives. She found to her joy, that there were others who also revelled in England's heritage of literature and that another amazing offshoot of her long periods with Giles, was that she knew all about sex. She had of course, often seen young Leo in his bath, but when Auriol was twelve, Giles had brought her human biology books to study, explaining the whole reproduction process. Next, he came laden with art books and showed her pictures of the most famous nude statues and paintings in the world.

Giles's words to her had been, "It's impossible to study English literature without a knowledge of sexual love and its down-side, lust. The majority of classical novels turn on an incident created by one or the other, and," handing her a copy of Shakespeare's Sonnets, "the best of all poetry centres on it. Do not be prissy or squeamish about discussing sex, it's a fact of life and must be dealt with."

She quickly realised, just how wise his counsel had been. In tutorials, she joined in free-ranging discussions and to the amazement of fellow students, suggested points of interest and eroticism of which they had been unaware. Often the females were embarrassed, whilst the males surveyed Auriol in a new light. She had seemed so quiet, a bit of a country bumpkin you would think, but goodness, she knew her stuff and then some! After a few short weeks, Auriol had taken careful note of what the other girls wore, and paid more attention to her own attire. A visit to the hairdresser produced a short, more stylish cut and on that lady's advice, a few auburn highlights were added to improve the appearance of Auriol's rich brown hair. Now for the first time, Auriol loitered around make-up counters, asking salesgirls questions, until she had acquired suitable moisturisers and cosmetics.

Her metamorphosis did not happen overnight and it was, with quite a shock, that her fellow students, male and female, suddenly realised, that far from standing out as nondescript, amongst a bevy of bright young things, Auriol was not only articulate, but good looking, with a rather gamine appearance. Casual invitations to join groups at their evening sessions in the pubs, now became more frequent. Giles's tutorials had not included lessons on alcohol, and, with the exception of a glass of champagne at Christmas, which she had hated, Auriol was unfamiliar with the wide variety of drinks on offer, or their effects. She discovered cider, and found that just two large glasses of that, was enough to make her feel relaxed and very sociable.

Now, instead of spending a lonely evening in her room at the Hall of Residence, she was often to be found enjoying the company of people she could call her friends, and realised with some surprise, that as a rule, she was more comfortable with men than women. Their approach to the work in hand seemed more analytical than that of the females, whilst she, having been schooled by a man, felt on that same wavelength. The conversation of some males was dominated by sport, of no interest to her, but with others, she found she could have satisfying discussions about politics, and what was happening in the world in general.

Her realisation that she herself had led a rather rarefied life, and knew very little of what went on in other households, came as a shock. School friends had not been invited to the Vicarage for tea, except on very rare occasions, so she knew little about the backgrounds of other families. Intelligence had told her that some would be wealthier and some poorer;

now she found that often the dialects of their counties separated people from those with the cut glass vowels, a fact marking them out as having spent the whole of their young lives in private tuition.

The first young man of the latter breed she met had been equally shocked to learn of her own limited education; his expression and lacklustre conversation resulted in the encounter being swiftly terminated. He was not typical. And here another lesson was learned. She must not generalise, but judge each person on his or her, own merits.

It was in those early weeks, that two very different individuals began to form a large part of Auriol's life. Diane proved the exception to Auriol's decision that she was more comfortable in the company of males, rather than females. Whilst not studying English Literature, Diane was in residence at the same college, St. Hilda's, she was reading History and came from the Cotswolds. Diane had, to her parents' pride and joy, won a scholarship to Westonbirt, a single sex school and from there, it was always anticipated, she would have little difficulty getting into Oxford. Auriol's first encounter with Diane had been in the Bodleian Library, where they found themselves each reaching for the same book. A smile and, of necessity, a silent introduction, and they became aware they were in the same Hall of Residence.

If Auriol was gamine in appearance, Diane was just the opposite. She was, Auriol thought, your typical English beauty, small and blonde with blue-green eyes and cheeks as Diane herself said, 'like little Worcestershire apples'. Dissimilar in appearance, they were both quick witted, enjoyed the same type of humour, subtle and with doubles entendres, a fact which from the start saw them invariably functioning on the same wave-length.

Diane was an only child, and had, from an early age, been used to adult company. Like Auriol, she had been forced to adapt to mixing at school, but both girls had retained a need in their lives for periods of solitude. Each recognised this in the other and respected it, so that their times together were the more rewarding and enjoyable. When their non-tutorial periods coincided, they would agree to meet and strolled along the river banks, watching the relentless practice necessary for the rowing eights.

On very hot afternoons, they would take out a punt and head for a spot shaded by overhanging trees, enjoying the sheer bliss of doing absolutely nothing.

"What do your parents do, Diane?" This, at one of their early meetings.

"They have an antique shop and small art gallery in the Cotswolds. We live over the shop," she laughed, "I suppose that's where my love of history started. It's very busy in high summer, less so at other times, although if the forecasters promise a spell of good weather for a few days, it's surprising how it affects trade. These days, people are far more likely to drop everything and go away for a short break. What about yours?"

"My Father's dead, died a few years ago in an accident. He was the vicar of the village church and our home was in the Vicarage close by. Now we live in one wing of my Grandparents' house. Mum's an examiner for the London Academy of Music and Dramatic Art, she sings and plays the piano. And I have a sister Gemma, who's fourteen and a brother Leo, who's ten."

"I can't imagine life without my Dad. How on earth did you cope when he died?"

"It wasn't easy for any of us. He was the one who taught me so much about English and I suppose about life in general. I'm eternally grateful for that, it's made everything here so much easier. Sometimes when we're analysing a passage in tutorials, I can almost hear him saying "Now come on Auriol, the clues are there, what does it mean? What is the writer trying to say?" He was a kind, gentle man and yes, I do miss him terribly."

Clearly Diane's parents, whilst not affluent, had allocated sufficient money for her to live comfortably at university and Auriol's Uncle Simon had ensured the same, so the girls were not, as some of their contemporaries, constantly having to count their pennies and could afford the occasional evening meal out together or afternoon tea after a walk by the river.

Auriol had developed another close friendship, with a young man in her teaching group, Colin. He was from Yorkshire and his parents had had a struggle to fund his time at university, but by dint of determination and hard work, had managed it. Colin was deeply grateful for the sacrifices they had made on his behalf and equally determined to see that they were recompensed in some way.

"Dad's a teacher at a high school, where there are about 1500 pupils which sounds nightmarish to me. He's a Year Head and, surprise, surprise, teaches English. Mum works in a travel agent's, but sometimes does a stint on a Sunday at a care home to make a bit of extra cash."

Auriol kept quiet, feeling guilty that her own path to university had been relatively smooth, with both Grandad and her godfather, Uncle Simon, helping out.

"Is it just you and your parents at home?"

Colin laughed, "I think things would have been easier if that had been the case. I've got two sisters, Jo's fourteen, hasn't been well lately, and missed a lot of schooling and Lynne, the baby, is just seven."

"I've got siblings as well. Gemma's fifteen and Leo just ten. I think Gemma wants to go to uni. and study music; Mum did that, they're both really good singers. As for Leo, well he's too young to think what he wants to do."

"He's outgrown the space man syndrome, I take it?"

"Good heavens yes, if he was ever in it. That sounds far too adventurous for Leo, he's young for his age. I'm afraid Mum babies him rather, but he now boards at school, so I think that will help him to untie the apron strings."

Colin smiled, "One thing's for sure, once you start at uni. you can forget the sort of cosseting we any of us got at home. Here, it's every man for himself and at times, dog eat dog."

"Not that bad surely?"

"No, but from what I've been told, you have to be prepared to stand on your own two feet. Even in discussion, people will talk you down and make you look small, if you're prepared to let them get away with it."

If Diane was Auriol's soulmate, then Colin was her sounding board. He it was to whom she turned for explanations about student unrest, the shortage of money amongst her contemporaries, and the necessity for so many committees and in-house clubs and societies.

"Of course they're unhappy, Auriol. They've come here prepared to work their socks off and suddenly find that when they want to unwind over a few beers, they have to count their pennies. By the second year, they can see the overdrafts in their bank accounts building up and know the likelihood of being able to repay them for some years is receding fast. Then there's the competition . . . With the best will in the world, it can't be ignored that some students play the learning game better than others and therefore are more popular with their tutors."

"What on earth do you mean?"

"If you don't hand in work on time and turn up for tutorials looking as if you've been up all night, then you'll not be popular with your tutor. If, on the other hand, you arrive looking all bright-eyed and bushy tailed and say 'I'm really sorry sir (or madam), but I didn't quite get the hang of this and my research doesn't seem to have taken me any further forward', he, or she, will feel you are making a genuine effort at progress and give you a second chance." He grinned, "Not that any of this is something you need to worry about. From what I've seen and heard, you'll never have that problem. Yes, there are a lot of student organisations here and yes, it is necessary in order to give us a voice. If we do have complaints, the governing body is far more likely to listen to what a representative committee has to say, than an individual."

When Colin was in full spate, Auriol could not help but compare him to her father.

It was certainly not a physical likeness, and his voice could not have been more different, but there was an earnestness about Colin, a desire to be understood and, when his reading glasses slipped to the end of his nose, she could imagine herself, for a few brief moments, back in her father's company. Perhaps, she decided it was this that endeared him to her. Unlike some of the other males, his language was not full of sexual innuendo, nor was he constantly trying to score points and appear superior. Auriol was, she decided, very fortunate in having two such good and supportive friends.

In common with many of her peers, Auriol vacillated between enjoying her studies to the full, and wondering if reading Law might have offered her more career opportunities. Discussions with Diane about this resulted in them signing up for computer lessons. Whilst they had both had some IT instruction at school, they decided that technology was moving so fast, they must try and keep abreast of it. They were pleased to find that the two evenings they spent each week, were giving them the sort of detailed instruction, which hadn't been on offer at school.

As Diane said, "At least if we can't get a job for ages, or we're between jobs, we'll have something else to fall back on."

"Quite apart from that, you've only got to look around to see that computers are now used in just about every type of work, banks, shops, surgeries . . . it's going to be impossible soon to exist without some knowledge of them."

And so, busily occupied, meeting essay deadlines, researching projects, the weeks were fully occupied until examination time was upon them and the end of their first year loomed on the horizon. During those last weeks Diane had a proposition for Auriol.

"Next year we'll be out on our ears, as far as the Hall of Residence is concerned. Why don't we double up and look for a flat together? We get on well, both have the same sort of work ethic. What do you think? Say if you hate the idea, I won't be offended."

"Diane, I think it would be great. We both like being on our own sometimes, but it's very different from being on your own for acres of time and having no-one to talk to when you want to discuss problems, that sort of thing."

Diane laughed "Plus the time when you get a much lower grade than you'd hoped for and you want a shoulder to cry on."

"Too right, let's start looking right away".

"Hang about, first we need to get some of the local papers and visit agents and then, and this might be our best bet of all, we need to target those who are due to leave in the next few weeks, they might be leaving a suitable des. res."

"Good thinking. I knew there was an excellent reason I needed you as a partner.

We'll start today."

And start they did, fired with enthusiasm. An enthusiasm which lasted all of three weeks. They soon found that, whilst there were plenty of houses to let, flats were in very short supply. Finding a clean, reasonably well furnished semi, they thought they had struck oil until they asked the price and then realised that the three bedroomed property was way ahead of what they could afford. Until . . .

"Auriol, don't bite my head off but what about asking Colin to join us? He's a good friend of yours and a really nice lad. Like us, he'll be looking for somewhere to live next year. Why don't we ask him if he would be interested?"

Auriol hesitated, "It's not quite what we had in mind, is it? I mean, we wouldn't be able to pad around in our undies and I hope he can cook for himself, because neither of us is any great shakes at that. But . . . well, yes, I suppose it might be an advantage to have a man about the house. When a fuse blows for instance. Can you mend those?"

"No way."

Auriol grinned, "Then I guess that settles it. I'm seeing him later, to discuss our project, I'll sound him out and if he's interested, we ought to take him round to the house ASAP."

And so it was determined. The three of them would share the house and all the finances involved, the girls to have the first choice of bedrooms and, the landlord permitting, they would share the cost of an extra table, so that each bedroom had its own desk facility.

Next came an invitation from Diane's parents, to stay with them in the Cotswolds for a couple of weeks during the summer vacation.

"I know it's not as exciting as going abroad," Diane said, "but the area is beautiful, especially in the summer and there are lots of things to do and see. Mum and Dad will be busy of course, but since I passed my driving test I'm much more of a free agent and we can go as far afield as you would like."

"Scotland?"

Diane laughed, "Well perhaps not quite that far."

"Please thank your Mum and Dad, I'd love to come, but ought to just check at home that there's nothing I'm expected to do. They might have made plans that I don't know about."

"Sure. Just let me know as soon as poss., and we'll start making arrangements."

Susan was torn, between relief that her brood each had some commitments for the long vacation, and, at first, sadness that they would have little time together as a family. But there was one bright spark, for this year, Simon, Leo's godfather, had stepped into the breach, with an invitation to them to spend a period in London, using his flat. As his letter said,

I shall be away I'm afraid, but it's a shame for the flat to stand empty, if you can make use of it. There are 3 bedrooms, one quite small, but on the whole, the accommodation should be adequate for your requirements, I'm sure the girls will be happy to double up. There's so much on offer in London. Once you've made your plans, and dates are fixed, why don't you book up for one or two shows? I know they're horrendously expensive, so have included a contribution towards your running costs. I have a 'Mrs. Mop', who looks after me whilst I'm in residence, I can contact her and she'll have beds made up and put basic essentials in the fridge for your arrival. If you leave her a list, she'll do any routine shopping for you and I also have an arrangement with her that when I'm home, she'll prepare a meal for me, two or three times each week. I'm sure she'd be happy to do the same for you. Her expenses are on me, so don't worry about that.

You should visit some of the great London museums and art galleries, walk down Bond Street and along the Embankment. Then of course, there are the famous churches, St. Paul's and Westminster Abbey; Hyde

Park, Buckingham Palace and the Changing of the Guard and what about a trip down the river? Really the list is endless.

Your family is growing up fast, Susan, soon some of them might have to work and live in London, now's the time for them to become familiar with some of its aspects, it's an education in itself.

Now Susan thought, they would have some time together as a family and, grateful for the invitation, mused on how generous Guy's family had been to her and to his grandchildren. She couldn't imagine how they would have managed without their ongoing thoughtfulness and assistance.

And so it was resolved. They would all be at home for one week together at the beginning of the vacation, then, spend two weeks in London. Following that, Leo would take up James's invitation to go with his family to the Italian Lakes, Auriol would go to the Cotswolds and Gemma, much to Susan's surprise, expressed a wish to accept an invitation from Fran, a school friend who lived close to Bournemouth.

"She's quite a character, Mummy. Just pipped me to the post as top of the form *and* won the music prize, plays the violin like a dream. They have their own swimming pool and Fran's been having some lessons to improve her butterfly stroke. I think she fancies herself as a future Olympic champion."

Susan would be alone. At first, slightly disconcerted by this, in retrospect, she was delighted. Two whole weeks, without demands being placed upon her time. As expected, Ruth Hatton's condition had deteriorated and it had been necessary to put her in a home. Grandpa Hatton was just recovering from the trauma of this, and agreed, after urgent advice from his doctor, to check himself into a quiet hotel in the Lake District for a few weeks, where food and service according to the doctor, were 'second to none'. Susan had just two commitments during this period, both in Chichester, just a few miles away. She decided that, following the Conference she had to attend, she would treat herself to a visit to the Chichester Festival Theatre. For their London visit, following Simon's suggestion, she had already booked seats at the Albert Hall for

'Carmen' and at the Palace Theatre for 'Les Mis.' Such a lot of things to look forward to.

The first week 'en famille' passed without a hitch. Her children seemed both glad to see each other and to see their mother, only Gemma having been at home for some weeks. Auriol was a changed girl. Her new haircut, a touch of make-up, a growing interest in clothes, together with a stimulating environment and the input of many new faces, had worked wonders. She was, as Susan knew her own generation would describe it, 'switched on' and amazingly witty at times. No longer the quiet bluestocking whose only interests lay between the pages of books, Auriol was now aware of the world as a whole, and her own place in it.

Leo too was changed, bubbling with enthusiasm about school activities. Eleven years old, he was taller and the charming air of 'little boy lost' had disappeared forever. Handsome as ever, with his blonde hair and startlingly blue eyes, Leo was now more positive in his approach to everything, almost as if he were saying to the world at large 'Don't mess with me, I'm tougher than you might think.' Changed in his appearance and his demeanour yes, but to Gemma's disgust, his mother's affection for him was still overt and tactile.

Living with her, Susan was aware of the physical changes in Gemma. Now at fifteen, she was a very attractive young woman; discovering a bust, and the onset of menstruation, having been taken in their stride. Tall for her age, she had now tamed the riot of brown curls and, whether tied back in a ponytail or, on special occasions, more elaborately styled, Gemma's brilliant smile was guaranteed to act as a magnet to any young, or even older men in the vicinity. Susan had always known Gemma loved to be the centre of attention and now watched with some concern just how readily she flirted and drew people to her side.

I have an awful feeling that she'll be at risk at university, Susan thought, *she seems to be sending out the sort of signals that a lot of men will misinterpret. I can only advise and hope that she listens, and pray two more years at school will see her settling down. Auriol, bless her, has been quite the reverse, now suddenly emerging like a butterfly out of her chrysalis. Giles would have been so proud of her and rightly, but she'd be the first to say he played a large part in giving her the confidence she now exudes.*

Happy, as Susan now knew she would be, to see them go their different ways during the holidays, she also realised she desperately needed this time to take stock of her own situation and feelings. Sex with Giles had been routine and lacking in passion. How she regretted that now. Perhaps she should have made more of an effort, showed more enthusiasm. No longer did Susan miss his presence, but she did feel keenly the absence of physical love. Surely she couldn't be expected to live like a nun for the rest of her days? For heavens' sake, she was only forty two and not unattractive. There had to be more to life than celibacy and watching her children grow up.

Their London visit had proved happy and informative, as Simon had said, there was so much to do and see, too much by far to fit into two weeks. Only one incident had marred the holiday and looking back, it seemed relatively trivial. A trip to Harrod's had been a must, on their second day. They had drunk coffee on the restaurant's balcony, made small purchases in order to obtain the store's distinctive green and gold bags, and then set out to find Hyde Park. The crowds at the traffic lights outside Harrod's were quite dense and, whilst Auriol and Sybil managed to stay together, the other two were split up. Waiting for the lights to change, there was suddenly a concerted gasp of horror as Leo half stumbled, half fell into the path of the oncoming traffic. Massive screeching of brakes was followed by gasps of relief, as a man's long arm shot out and dragged the boy into the gutter, a bus missing him by inches. The lights changed and Leo was hauled onto the pavement, surrounded by his family.

"What on earth were you doing Leo? Too near the edge I suppose. This isn't Moordean you know, you can't take chances here." Shock and anxiety gave an edge to Susan's words.

"I wasn't too near the edge, someone pushed me from behind."

"I know they were all jockeying for position, anxious to get across, but most people here are well aware, that you really have to keep your wits about you when crossing London roads. Are you hurt at all?"

"No, just a scrape on my knee, nothing much." Leo looked round and met Gemma's gaze.

So . . . it wasn't over. Was he, whilst in her company, destined always to be on the alert for danger, watching every step? He would have to tell someone about it, soon. But who? Who would listen to a boy of his age, accusing his teenage sister of all sorts of wicked crimes? They'd probably say he'd been watching too much TV, or reading too many thrillers. But it was Gemma who read the thrillers. Nowadays she seemed to go out of her way to conceal what she was reading, unless it was something to do with school, but one day, when her holdall was downstairs and open, he'd seen the covers of the books inside . . . Rankin, Dick Francis, Ruth Rendell, she had them all. Somehow he had to get through this problem. But, for the moment, he would, in a few short days thank goodness, be saying good-bye to her, his darling wicked sister.

On their return to Grafton House, the massive sorting out of clothes to be laundered and repacked, proved hectic, but within a few short days the house, and Susan, heaved a sigh of relief, as the three children left for their various destinations. Susan's relief would have been short-lived, had she been aware of another dramatic change in Gemma's psyche.

With the onslaught of puberty, had come the Voices. Gemma was not surprised; her father's teaching had told her she must listen for God's voice, telling her what to do. At first, when she was not the centre of attention and receiving compliments, a single voice urged her to do something to rectify the situation. This must be God. Even when two others joined in, pressing her to take more and more drastic action, she was not dismayed. Hadn't Giles continually preached about God being three in one? But at times, the Voices increased to such a number and the volume was so deafening, that she wanted to cover her ears and scream at them to stop. Soon she found their suggestions would tumble into her mind telling her what to do and once she started to carry out their wishes, the concerted cries of "Yes! Yes!" told her of their approval. Today, Gemma departing for a holiday with her talented friend Fran, the Voices had already started their murmuring. She knew now, that their plans coincided with her own.

CHAPTER 9

Susan had gone to her Musicians' Conference, prepared for her evening at the theatre, believing that such occasions required something more feminine than the outfit she had worn all day. In her large briefcase, was a carefully folded gold satin blouse, a toothbrush, make-up and large ear-rings, and on arriving at the theatre, her first port of call was to the Ladies Cloakroom. There, she repaired the ravages of the day spent in a stuffy room, changed from a business-like shirt to her blouse, dabbed herself liberally with perfume and then deposited everything, except her handbag, with the cloakroom staff. From there, to the bar, where she bought a large glass of white wine and ordered a gin and tonic for the interval. The barman pointed out the area where ordered drinks would be placed and gave her a number to identify her own.

At the end of the first half of 'She Stoops to Conquer', Susan was still smiling at the antics on stage, when she reached out for her interval drink. Surprised, she saw that there were two drinks with the number seventeen on them, and was just wondering if she was at the wrong site, when a voice said,

"You *are* in the right place, the other drink is mine." The owner of the voice, a handsome, smartly dressed man in his middle years, smiled at her.

"But . . . ?" Susan was still puzzled.

"Well you see, I was behind you, when you ordered your gin and tonic, so I asked the steward to order one for me also and put it on the same number."

"I see, that is, I don't think I do. Why?"

"You looked charming, were obviously on your own, and I realised that I knew you."

Now Susan was really surprised. "You knew me, but . . . ?"

"I believe Mrs. Hatton, that I heard you sing a few years ago, in the cathedral here, am I right?"

She laughed, "Oh that, well you are right, but it was ages ago."

"Nevertheless, I enjoyed it tremendously. Also, I wanted to say how sorry I was to learn of your husband's death on that same day. I can't even begin to imagine how devastating that must have been for you."

"Devastating just about sums it up. But I don't remember too much about the service, were you with the clergy?"

"No, I was with the civic dignitaries. In fact, that was during my year as Chairman of the Council."

"Oh Lord, I have dropped a clanger haven't I? I was probably introduced to you at some point."

He smiled, "Yes, you were, but as it took all of about ten seconds, don't lose any sleep about the fact you didn't recognise me, especially as you later had a great deal more to concern yourself with. Look, I'd love it if we could talk some more, but I think the five minute bell will be going soon, so we'd better drink up. Why don't we meet up at the bar after the show, and continue our conversation . . . if you would like to, that is?"

"I'd love it, but whilst you seem to know my name, I certainly don't know yours."

"I'm Mark Fleming and you are Susan, if I remember rightly."

She drained her glass and picked up her handbag, "Right, Mr. Mark Fleming, I'll see you later, at the bar."

"I'll look forward to it with delight," he said, as if he meant it. They were both well aware where it was leading and, by the time they parted that evening, backgrounds had been discussed and another meeting arranged. Mark Fleming was divorced, his wife having left him, as he laughingly pointed out.

"She didn't actually leave me for the milkman, but someone very close to that. He was in fact, the Divisional Managing Director for a nationwide milk delivery company. Fortunately we have no children. I'm sure she was probably bored out of her skull by my endless City Council commitments and was looking for someone with money and sufficient leisure time to enjoy life. And what about you, Susan? I know you have a daughter. She sang with you quite delightfully, at the cathedral that day."

"That was Gemma, she's now fifteen, going on twenty five! I have another daughter, Auriol, studying at Oxford, she's just nineteen and my baby, Leo, he'll soon be twelve. He's at a boarding school and with Auriol away as well, there's just Gemma and me at home for much of the time."

"I suppose after Giles died, you had to leave your home in Moordean?"

"Yes, we were living in the Vicarage, so that couldn't continue. Giles's parents and his brothers were brilliant, I don't know how I would have coped without them. We're now living in a wing of the grandparents' home, Grafton House, about three miles to the east of the city."

"I know it, of course, part of my constituency, a few years ago. A beautiful old Georgian house with, as I recall, a lot of land."

"It is beautiful and the arrangement works quite well. We're as self-contained as we wish, and all careful not to step over boundaries and invade each other's privacy. Although having said that, my mother-in-law has dementia and has now been put in a home, so there's really only Guy, my father-in-law, to worry about and he's an absolute sweetie, who wouldn't willingly hurt anyone. He's just delighted to see his grandchildren now and again."

"So, with only Gemma living at home and she's at school during the day, do I assume you're a lady of leisure?"

"Absolutely not! I'm an examiner for LAMDA, and travel around quite a lot in the course of my duties. I cover the Southern Counties, but there are regular trips to HQ to deal with paper work and for meetings, although I have to say, that the former is diminishing. I've had, reluctantly I must say, to get to grips with the computer, and do find now, that being able to send results in via e-mail, has made life so much easier."

"Well . . . I've got to hand it to you. In a relatively short time, you've obviously got your life sorted, and brought up a family."

"It hasn't been easy and I couldn't have managed without help from father-in-law Guy, and Charles, my brother-in-law. At all levels, emotional and financial, they've been my bedrock. But that's quite enough about me. What are you up to now? Still a councillor?"

"No, I decided that after ten years I'd had enough. My father was in the property business and I was left well provided for, when he died. It was the one subject about which I knew quite a lot, having worked with him since I left school, so I took over from where he left off. This city and its environs are ripe for development, close to the coast and to the South Downs, accessible to Gatwick and Heathrow, it's got such a lot going for it . . ."

"And the culture . . . ?"

"Yes of course, our stunning cathedral and the theatre, which has such an excellent reputation. I'm sure you know that stars will play here for a pittance, compared to what they could claim elsewhere. Long may it continue."

"You're not going to spoil the area are you?" Susan's question was somewhat tongue in cheek.

Mark smiled. "Everyone asks me that. The last thing I want to do is to spoil such a beautiful area, but I'm also a business man and . . ."

"Not one of those hard-hearted types, who bulldozes everybody and everything in his path?"

He laughed, "I hope not, but I never make promises."

"What never?"

"Well, hardly ever."

On the Wednesday of the second week, while the children were away Susan invited Mark to lunch at Grafton House. Both knew it was a turning point and, having made desultory conversation over their chicken salad,

Mark picked up his glass of wine and smiling broadly said, "Here's to us, no strings, except those we wish to tie, and no recriminations if anything goes wrong." Smiling, Sue raised her glass to his, then with a wry smile took the phone off its rest.

"Better make sure we're not disturbed" she said and taking his hand, she led him upstairs. Seated on the edge of the bed, he put his arms round her. She shivered, as he kissed her and started to undo her blouse.

"It's been a long time," she said haltingly.

"For me also," he replied, "But, if we're out of practice, we'll just have to keep trying 'til we get it right." Together they laughed, and from that point onwards, it was a joyful mating. She, impressed by the muscular solidity of his body and he equally impressed by her firm breasts and abdomen." Minutes later, they lay on the bed, hand in hand, in a state of post-coital bliss.

"I'm sorry it was too quick, difficult after so long, to . . ."

"Mark darling, you managed to wait long enough for me to join you, it was wonderful."

"Next time will be even better," he said.

Later, on their way downstairs he added "Your stomach's so firm, it's amazing after three children."

"It's all to do with my diaphragm."

He looked at her in astonishment, "You're not wearing a diaphragm . . . I would have known surely?"

"Idiot, not that sort of diaphragm. Part of me, my own built in one. Years of singing and breathing techniques have, I think, helped me to use my abdomen properly and that's probably kept me in reasonable shape."

"I love your shape," he said and kissed her.

Together they made tea, taking the tray out into the small enclosed rose-garden. The sun was warm, the bench comfortable and Guy's roses, chosen for their scent, lent an exotic flavour to their afternoon. Mark carried the tray indoors and returned, kissing her on the nape of the neck, so that once again she shivered with delight and expectancy. Suddenly, they both became aware that they were not alone. At the small, gated entrance stood Gemma, surveying the scene.

"Gemma darling," Susan leapt up. "What on earth . . . ? I wasn't expecting you until Saturday." Her embarrassment was patently evident.

"Obviously . . . and this is?" It might have been an adult speaking.

"My good friend, Mark Fleming."

Equally embarrassed, Mark stepped forward, extending his hand.

"How do you do, Gemma, we have met before, but it was a few years ago."

Her eyebrows arched in query.

"At the Cathedral when you sang so charmingly with Susan . . . your mother. I was with the civic party and we were introduced to you both."

"Mark was Chairman of the Council then, do you remember?" Both knew they were talking too quickly, in order to calm the tension in the atmosphere. Now Susan moved forward and embraced her daughter. "Darling, you haven't said why you're here, is something wrong?"

Gemma burst into tears. "It's Fran, there's been an accident . . . in the pool."

Mark took the girl's elbow and led her to the garden bench.

"Oh my dear, how awful, how bad?"

"She's dead. Drowned in their own pool."

Fear coursed through Susan's veins. Quietly she asked "And you, Gemma, are you alright? Were you there? What happened?"

"Fran went to do her daily practice swim and I stayed on the patio outside. I must have fallen asleep in the sunshine, and woke up, thinking she was a long time," her voice broke, "when I went to find her . . . I saw her at the bottom of the pool."

She broke down again.

Mark interjected quietly, "You said 'outside', is this an indoor pool?"

"Yes, but one side can be opened right up onto a patio area."

"Why didn't you phone, Gemma? I'd have come to get you?"

"I did try a couple of times, Mummy, but couldn't get any reply and the answer phone wasn't switched on." Gemma was aware of the quick guilty look, which passed between them.

"Anyway it wasn't necessary, Mr. Sinclair was going to drive me, but I could tell he and his wife wanted to be together, and on their own, so he hired a car." She sobbed again, "Fran was an only child you see and so successful at everything, she'll be really missed at school, everyone thought she'd be Head Girl next year, but now . . ."

"We didn't hear the car drive up," this from Mark.

"No, I saw the cars, so I knew someone was here, and asked the man to drop me in the drive."

Gemma refrained from adding that she had looked through the sitting room window, and seeing a man's jacket on a chair, had drawn her own conclusions, biding her time until she knew her entrance would create the maximum disturbance and embarrassment as possible. *People were so gullible! A few tears and they were all sympathy, trying to 'make it better', as if she were about three years old.*

The Voices had started the day Fran beat her to the 'top of the form' slot. They had been insistent and persistent in their urgency, telling Gemma to remove this person who threatened her status, both musically and academically. Days of flattery and enthusiasm on her part, about matters which left her cold and Gemma at last received the coveted invitation to stay with Fran's family. The Voices' reproaches for a time had been almost deafening, but now Gemma had done what they wished, and they were silenced. No longer would Gemma be in the humiliating position of second best. If it had proved more complicated than she had expected, Gemma preened herself, that her attention to detail had paid off, as it always did, and now at last, the Voices were satisfied.

Everything which Fran possessed screamed of wealth and Gemma had not been surprised at the elegance of the Sinclair home, with its manicured lawns and private pool house, the latter having been designed specifically to encourage and assist Fran in her aim to be a champion swimmer. On their second day in the pool, Gemma made mental notes. The shallowest end was four feet deep, enabling Fran to make the turns in her daily practice sessions, without a break. Observing Fran's procedure carefully, Gemma saw that sixty lengths of her speciality, the butterfly stroke, left her tired and noted, that Fran's parents admonished her on several occasions not to exceed this amount, as it was too exhausting. When the session was completed, Mrs. Sinclair was quickly at hand, with Fran's energy drink and something to eat.

Mr. Sinclair said laughingly, to Gemma, "This girl of ours, always wanting to be the best and constantly pushing herself to the very limit. Twice she's felt quite exhausted after doing just that, so we keep warning her not to stretch herself too far."

Wonderful, Gemma thought, *it is then that I must make my move. That fits in very nicely with what I have in mind, thank you,* and the Voices tittered.

Access to the water was by two flights of steps, one at the corner of the deep end and the other diagonally opposite, at the shallower level. Gemma noted that the butterfly stroke involved keeping the head well down, and that Fran always wore goggles. Gradually, her plan evolved and, the morning that the Sinclairs said they had an invitation to a lunchtime business reception, Gemma knew the time had come. Mrs. Sinclair was anxious that the girls should have everything they needed,

"Jenny will be in at mid-day and prepare your lunch. She'll bring it out to the patio at 1.15p.m." then laughing, "Gemma, see this girl of ours rests for at least an hour after her practice. We do have to watch her, she's a stickler for punishment!"

The pool was housed in an extension of the main building, the side facing the garden consisting of glass sliding doors, which opened onto a large patio and BBQ area. At one end of the pool were changing rooms, showers and toilets, well stocked towel shelves and a drying cupboard, while the other opened onto a bar and seating area.

Following the Sinclairs' departure, the two girls sat outside in the sun and looked at the newspaper headlines.

"I can't decide which would be the most amazing, being a violinist like Vanessa Mae, or a swimming champion, and taking part in the Olympics. Imagine standing on the rostrum with a gold medal round your neck and everyone standing to sing the National Anthem . . . What do you think, Gemma?"

"I'd definitely prefer the violinist idea. After all, that sort of stardom goes on and on, whereas with the Olympics, when it's over, it's over."

"Well not quite, the gold medallists become household names and they're invited to open fairs, speak on TV, that sort of thing."

"Still think the other has more substance. You might go on being famous for years, there's no limit as to how long you play the violin, whilst there could well be a limit on the other, age wise. There'd always be younger and fitter people challenging you."

"O.K. you've convinced me. Not that either is likely to happen, but it's nice to dream isn't it? Now, I'd better *stop* dreaming and do something about it." And with that, Fran got up and moved towards the pool area.

"I'm going to stay out here and sunbathe, I'll come in when you're finishing." Gemma lay back on the sunbed.

"O.K.", with that Fran donned her hat and goggles, took a swig of her vitamin drink, and dived into the water.

Now Gemma moved to a garden seat, from which she could observe Fran through the sides of the pool, and immediately the Voices started counting the lengths. When Fran reached 55, Gemma went into the changing rooms and picked up one of the large folded towels. The Voices continued their counting and Gemma waited. At the 58th length, she moved towards the pool bearing the towel, as if to ensure the instructions of Fran's parents were being carried out. But, as Gemma had anticipated, the sight of an audience, spurred Fran on for a further two lengths and it was as she approached the shallower end, on her final lap, that Gemma made her move, and stepped into the water. Starting her turn, Fran suddenly found her head enveloped in the towel and strong arms pushing her downwards. Blinded by the towel, she struck out wildly, but now the energy expended on her long swim, began to tell and she found herself losing ground to her opponent. Held under the water, the towel still around her head and upper arms, her legs became weaker, until at last her strength gave way and she sank to the bottom of the pool.

Quickly, Gemma removed the towel and standing in the shallows held it aloft, squeezing as much water as possible out of it, whilst keeping a watchful eye on Fran's body, ready for any sign of revival. Once sure that this wasn't going to happen, Gemma climbed out of the pool and spread the towel out in the sun to dry off the excess moisture. After fifteen minutes, ensuring her own costume was relatively dry, she took the towel into the drying room, using another towel to mop up, where she had entered and left the water. At five minutes past twelve exactly, she ran screaming into the kitchen to tell Jenny that Fran was at the bottom of the pool.

CHAPTER 10

Mark's farewell had been, of necessity, brief and formal. To the white-faced Susan, he said, "Let the girl talk about what's happened and cry, she'll need to get it out of her system." Then he was gone and what had been an idyllic few hours were suddenly soured, immeasurably. But worrying about that would have to wait, as Susan considered the fact that she now had a much more serious situation on her hands.

"Gemma," Susan pointed to the recliner, "I want you to sit here, and relax. I'm going to make you some coffee and I'm adding some brandy to make you feel better."

Unaware, that Gemma had left the recliner and was listening at the open window, Susan then rang Fran's father.

"Mr. Sinclair, I can't begin to tell you how distressed I was to hear about Fran. I'm not going to intrude on you now, but I just wanted to thank you for arranging transport for Gemma to come home and to say that I will be in touch with you in a few days' time."

There would be an inquest of course, Gemma would have to give evidence and much would depend on how she replied to the questions then, and on her behaviour. How, Susan wondered, would Gemma deal with that? If she really had had a hand in Fran's death, would she fall apart, under questioning? Or, would she, in some way, reveal that she had a medical problem which required examination? As always, Susan underestimated her daughter's ability to detach herself from situations, and Gemma's innate acting skill, which enabled her to present the appropriate façade as and when it was required.

Within three short weeks, the matter was resolved. Fran's doctor, who had signed the death certificate, and the forensics expert who examined the body, concluded that it was 'Death by drowning'. Fran had not been hurt in any way, but the body showed signs of anaphylactic shock and it was felt that she might have swum too far and for too long, so that her system had finally collapsed under the exertion. Sympathy was extended to her parents and the young girl who had found her, and was still clearly very distressed, and then it was over. Gemma's Voices were silenced, but for how long?

Someone who had read with interest, the report of the inquest into the death of the schoolgirl by drowning, and the account given by the only other person present, Gemma Hatton, was Eileen Biggs. She had, as she'd intended, watched from a distance, the events in the Hatton household, and been saddened by the death of Giles Hatton. Rumours circulated in the village, about young Leo's behaviour, striking his sister after his father's fall, and refusing to speak to Gemma for some time afterwards, had intrigued her. Obviously the girl had not pushed her father, which would have been revealed at the inquest, but had this accident been in some way connected with Gemma's bizarre attempts to hurt Leo? And why would she kill a friend? Immediately, Eileen knew the answer. If the friend was upstaging Gemma in any way, whether at school or elsewhere, then Gemma would have dealt with it in her own way.

Eileen had been fortunate in finding another job almost immediately, at a new nursery set up in the next village, Oakdean. The fact that she had been with the Hattons for over ten years, had, without a reference, spoken for itself. This, coupled with her reputation locally as a reliable and committed worker, good with children, ensured that the nursery manager was delighted to have her. Her sister had insisted that Eileen must come and live with them. Daphne's eldest son had just left to join the army and, as she said,

"His room's not much more than a box room, but Jenny will be the next to go, she wants to train as a nurse, so there'll be another larger room for you to move into when that happens. She shares with Sophie

at the moment, but when she goes, we'll swap you and Sophie over."
And as Eileen started to protest, "Makes sense, another couple of years
and she too will fly the nest. Mind you, that's one I'll miss, she really
does pull her weight. Lovely little cook. Dan says I'm not to take 'No'
for an answer. Besides, an extra bit of cash coming into our house will
be very useful."

Whilst Eileen's life was now comfortable, enjoying her contact with
the little ones at the nursery and living in the relaxed, undemanding
atmosphere of Daphne's home, she still often worried about Gemma.
Surely, the girl's fixation with Leo was abnormal, even allowing
for a jealous reaction to Sue Hatton's cosseting of the boy? Eileen,
remembering the inventiveness of the small girl and her attention to
detail, shuddered at what this older Gemma might next attempt.

Someone else who was very intrigued by the swimming pool incident
was Leo. Constantly, he asked for more details about the accident.

"Was Fran floating on the pool when you found her, Gemma, or
could you see her lying at the bottom?"

Auriol was at last driven to say to him, "That's enough, Leo, can't
you see it's too upsetting for Gemma to have to keep on discussing it?"

But Leo knew, not only exactly what he was doing, but also, that
for the first time, he was tormenting Gemma, rather than the other way
round. To his delight, some of the more penetrating questions seemed to
have caught her off balance, and her answers were hesitant, a new and
welcome experience for him. Always, he noticed, when this happened,
she immediately became tearful and produced her handkerchief.

One thing which did surprise and worry him was that if, as he
suspected, she had engineered this death, then she was spreading her
net further than just himself. Why Gemma hated him so much, he had
never been able to fathom, but what possible reason could she have for
killing her best friend? Although, come to think of it, he couldn't recall
a single occasion when the girl Fran had been mentioned, prior to the
holiday invitation.

These were all much on a par with the thoughts which Susan could
not get out of her own mind. The incidents with Leo, and now this.

Why would Gemma want to harm a school friend? And if jealousy was the root of her antagonism towards Leo, what reason had she to be jealous of Fran? And then, loud and clear came the answer, as she recalled Gemma's own words. "She pipped me to the top of the form", "She's a wonderful violinist, won the music prize" and, perhaps most important of all, "It was expected she would be Head Girl next term." Once again, Gemma had escaped censure, but what next, and perhaps more importantly, what should she, Susan, be doing about it?

Her worst fears were confirmed two weeks later when Gemma came in from school bursting with enthusiasm, "Mummy, you'll never guess . . . I'm to be Head Girl. Mrs. Jacobs called me into her study this morning . . . Don't cry Mummy, I mean, I know they're only tears of happiness but . . . I told the girls at school, when I tell my mother, she'll be so proud and happy she'll burst into tears and you've done just that." Putting her arms round Susan, "I'm so pleased, not only for myself, but for you as well, I knew just how you'd feel. Suppose I go and put the kettle on, and then we can have a cuppa and I'll tell you what Mrs. Jacobs said my duties would be. So many things . . . I'll have to be there when all sorts of dignitaries arrive, and help show them round the school. Isn't that an honour? Then there's Speech Day, handing the prize books and trophies over to the guest speaker, so that she can present them and I have to wear a special gown for that. Just imagine . . ." Still prattling she disappeared into the kitchen leaving Susan to dry her tears and again confront her fears.

She would tell Mark. He was kind and loving and would understand, be able to give her sound advice and the burden would be shared. Twice Susan attempted it, getting no further than "Supposing Fran's death wasn't an accident?" Twice she got as far as hinting that Gemma's role in the matter might have been not as stated. Each time he had answers.

"The doctor and the forensic team have said what happened and even if Gemma got her story slightly wrong, that's understandable, isn't it? Perhaps she was in the pool when Fran collapsed and was panic-stricken and unable to act, again quite understandable in a sixteen year old. If that happened, she's probably now too ashamed to admit it, and who can blame her?" And, at Susan's second attempt,

"Darling, Gemma might look very grown up, but she's only a child, and at an age when her hormones are all over the place. They might have been skylarking in the pool and she's too frightened to say, but whatever it was, the people who know about these things have given their verdict, so it's better to leave well alone, and stop worrying about it. After all, the girl's not traumatised, seems to have got over it very well I would say, and thrilled to bits that she's now Head Girl, such an honour for both of you."

Susan gave up, but decided that in any future attempt to confide in anyone else, she would have to start at the beginning, with her own mother's sickness and the resultant deaths of both her parents. Only then could she expect someone to take what she was saying seriously and hear her out.

Gemma's next piece of news from school gave Susan more food for thought.

"I had to go and see the Careers teacher today, Miss Burns, she asked if I'd ever considered becoming a professional singer. When I said no, but I was planning to read Music at uni., she said she'd like me to think about an alternative. She explained that, if I left school early, I'd be able to concentrate for the next two years on languages and singing. I'd need German, Italian and French which could be taught privately and of course, ongoing singing lessons, learning opera scores etc., but I don't have to tell you that, you know all about it."

Susan's mind was racing. The thought of Gemma going to university had tormented her. Supposing Gemma felt she was being upstaged there by someone . . . anyone, would the outcome be the same, as had happened with Fran? Perhaps, Susan thought, this could be the way out of her own dilemma. Tuition could be arranged from home on a one to one basis, so that no competition would be involved with others. That would certainly apply with the languages, and by pulling a number of strings, she herself, could probably arrange that any musical coaching was on the same basis . . . in fact, quite a large amount, she was sufficiently qualified to do herself. There was something else, something she recalled from the medical books she had read. The composer, Beethoven, was apparently described as sullen, morose and driven, and doctors felt that he might have become a dangerous psychopath, if he hadn't written music. That had, they suggested, been his salvation. If Gemma's life became steeped in music, perhaps she too, would be sufficiently motivated to overcome any other disturbing tendencies. This must be the way forward.

Carefully Susan chose her words, not wishing to sound too enthusiastic,

"We'll certainly look into it, darling. It would mean you'd be at home a good deal. Are you sure you wouldn't feel you'd missed out, by not going to university?"

"Definitely not." Gemma grinned. "I think you could be my teacher for quite a lot of what's needed, wouldn't that be fun?"

"Don't think you'll be able to get away with . . ." Susan had been going to say 'murder' but quickly corrected herself, "things, just because I'm your mother. I shall be very strict. Are you sure Gemma, this is the sort of career you want? Once trained, you'd have to apply to various well-established choirs to try and get a foot in the door, and do as much solo work as possible, both paid and unpaid, so that you become reasonably well-known. Hopefully then, someone will spot you, write something nice about you in the papers and your career would take off. But an awful lot of people try to do just that and spend a great deal of time 'resting'. You know what that means don't you?"

"Yes, it's a polite way of saying they're out of work."

"Exactly. Could you handle that?"

"I think it's worth the risk. I loved it when I sang at school and everyone was listening to just me. And when we sang together in the cathedral, it was just magical."

"It will be a long hard road, Gemma, it's not all just standing on a stage and hearing the applause and kind comments."

"I know, I know, but Mummy, please do let me have a go, I'm sure I can make a success of it," then with her little girl innocent look, "especially with you to help me."

"Well if you're quite sure . . ." Susan's tone was measured. "You can tell Miss Burns we're going to look into the logistics of finding language coaches in the area and I'll also find out if there's anyone connected with the opera scene, currently or retired, who could back up the tuition I can give you."

Gemma rushed off with her mobile, clearly anxious to spread the information about her change of career direction, to as many friends as possible, leaving Susan once again to reflect on the situation. No longer surrounded by competition in her studies, with Leo at school, and a further source of irritation removed, perhaps Gemma would bring to a halt the desire to eradicate from her orbit, anyone who got in her way. She could only hope and pray that through the creativity Gemma brought to her singing, the unpleasant elements which had surfaced from time to time, would disappear for ever. Perhaps Mark had been right after all, and much of this could be attributed to hormones, and then again, perhaps she herself was clutching at straws! Shattered by once again having to make a major decision about her middle daughter, Susan sank back in the armchair and closed her eyes.

CHAPTER 11

In Oxford, the house sharing was working well. If there were times when Auriol and Diane longed for space in which to have a girly chat, equally there were times when the presence of Colin in their shared house was very reassuring. A plus point was that he could cook!

"I think I've got the solution to that." Diane was constantly trying to get them organised. "Supposing Colin makes dinner say, three times a week, we girls could do all the shopping and clean the bath and the loo, weekly. We'll all keep our own rooms clean, that goes without saying, and perhaps every two weeks we could together have a blitz on the sitting room and kitchen. What we could also do is treat Colin to a meal at Brown's now and again, as a break from cooking and our way of saying thank you." This the girls had agreed they must do, knowing that Colin's budget didn't run to such extravagances.

Getting washing dry proved to be one of the biggest problems, especially during wet spells and they soon found to their cost that these were fairly frequent in the Oxford basin. Often, they were reduced to taking a bag full of clean but wet garments to the launderette, in order to get them ready for ironing. They soon learned that Colin was a down-to-earth Yorkshire man, who called a spade a spade.

"For goodness' sake, you two, can't you find somewhere else to hang your tights and those other unmentionable bits hanging around the bathroom? Smalls they may be and small they certainly are, but it comes to something, when I can't find somewhere to hang my towel." For a time they conformed, but after a while, back came the underwear and another caustic reminder from Colin, that he found them distracting.

Auriol found Colin hard working and with a dry sense of humour. Frequently, they got their heads together to discuss pieces of literature, prior to the next tutorial. To Auriol's eternal gratitude, Colin never once referred to her gaffe on one such group occasion. Discussing one of the classical love poems, which referred to 'milk above and cream below', Auriol said, to everyone in general, "I can understand the milk reference, but what's this about cream?" Someone kicked her under the table and Colin quickly interjected another comment about the structure of the poem, so that the moment passed, with Auriol stunned into silence, but scarlet with embarrassment when she, belatedly realised that the reference was to semen.

Having been approached by one of the Drama groups to assist with creating an evening of entertainment, Colin and Auriol put together a 'spoof' based on 'Romeo and Juliet'. Juliet was seen fluttering around in her nightdress, clutching a mobile phone and asking repeatedly "Romeo, Romeo, wherefore art thou, Romeo?" Two girls as telephone operators with imitation phone mikes, were seated at each side of the stage, at the front of the apron, and one immediately responded, "Thank you for calling the Verona helpline. You are currently held in a queue . . ." etc., etc. At the next "Wherefore art thou?" the second operator answered with an equally typical, but unhelpful reply. After several minutes of this from the two operators, realising she was getting nowhere fast, Juliet fainted and was removed by her Nurse.

The audience loved it and Auriol and Colin were asked if they would be prepared to provide more material for future performances. They found that the classics and even the Bible, in which Auriol was very well versed, were all rich in material they could use. The realisation that, together, they formed a highly compatible working team was slow in coming to fruition, but once acknowledged, they resolved that as soon as their workloads permitted, they would get their heads together and write a play.

Diane's input was also of value.

"Don't forget, you two, that there's a whole raft of situations, which are both historical and hysterical." They looked at her quizzically. "What about the pope who turned out to be a female? After that discovery, any potential incumbent had to sit on a throne, like a commode, so that his/her sex could be checked, before he took office."

They looked at her in disbelief.

"It's true . . . well, I think it is. It would make a great story line anyway."

During sessions like this, they found release from their studies and usually ended collapsing in giggles.

Surprisingly, Diane's religious background was much stricter than Auriol's had ever been. Also surprising, was that away from home and her parents, she still adhered to her regular Sunday habits and always, on Sunday mornings, set out for St. Bartholomew's, the church nearest to their house. But it was on a weekday evening soon after their return from the summer break, that she suddenly announced that she was going to the park to hear a Gospel Speaker, who was in Oxford.

"Why don't you come with me, Auriol? It's a lovely evening."

"But won't it be too dark?"

"No, this chap's quite well known, there's going to be floodlights and a rostrum, all that sort of thing. We could stop somewhere for a drink on the way home."

"Sorry, no, I don't think it sounds quite me." Auriol was very mindful of what her father's opinion of some such speakers had been.

That was how it started. Diane returned full of enthusiasm for the young preacher who had been "Absolutely wonderful," adding, "Paul's such a charismatic young man. And of course they do such a lot of good work for charities."

"Who are 'they' exactly?" Auriol wanted to know.

"Well, they call themselves the 'Friends of Jesus' and 'friends' is just the right word for all of them, I can't begin to tell you how welcome they made me feel."

"I thought it was a sort of public address, how did anyone come to speak to you personally?"

"Well, Paul talked to everyone about his beliefs and how we could all help to make the world a better place and then, people who wanted to ask any further questions, were asked to stay behind."

"So you did, and asked what?"

"Well, there seemed to be quite a few young people with Paul. He is, I suppose, thirtyish, and when I asked where they all came from, they explained they lived in a sort of commune. Then of course, they wanted to know all about me."

"And you told them?"

"Auriol, of course I told them, what is this, a third degree or something?"

"Of course not, it's just that you seem very impressed and I'm trying to find out why."

"Yes, I was impressed. If you want to know any more, you'd better come with me tomorrow night, then you can see for yourself."

"Tomorrow night? Whatever happened to that essay on the birth of Russian democracy you have to finish?"

"It'll just have to wait," Diane said airily, "I happen to think this is more important."

Later, Auriol and Colin blamed themselves bitterly for not reading the signals before it was too late. They should have realised earlier that this was more than just a temporary blip in Diane's orderly life. All too soon, Diane had joined the organisation and was attending meetings four or five times each week. Often now at the weekends she would be missing, her only explanation being, that she had been assisting with 'a mission'. As far as Auriol could gather, Diane's telephone calls home were becoming more and more sporadic, and there were incoming calls from her parents, asking if Diane was well, as she hadn't been in touch for some time. Auriol, who had to field these calls, tentatively explained that Diane was at Bible Class, or whatever reason she had that day left with her housemates. Her work in the History Department was suffering.

Twice she was called before her tutor to explain why work had not been handed in on time, or not handed in at all.

Then came the awful day when Auriol and Colin arrived home to find Diane's bedroom empty and her belongings gone. There was a hastily scrawled message for them, '*Sorry, I have to go where I am most needed and most loved.*' Sick at heart, Auriol phoned Diane's parents, who literally dropped everything and arrived very late that evening. The police were asked to help. Did they know the whereabouts of this Rev. Paul Rule, who seemed to have been based in Oxford for at least six weeks?

The answer was not encouraging,

"The problem is, the young lady in question is twenty years of age, an adult, and is therefore quite at liberty to go with anyone, and to anywhere she might choose. We do know of this Rev. Rule, he comes into Oxford to speak now and again, but he doesn't live in this area and from what we can gather, he lives in a commune somewhere in the north. We could try and find him, but as I said, unless the young lady is being kept against her will, there's nothing we can do."

Diane's parents were distraught. How could this have happened to a loving daughter and why, if she had wanted to make a drastic change in her life, did Diane not feel that she could at least discuss it with them and not acted without giving them any warning whatsoever? Clearly concerned about her safety, they spent hours making enquiries in, and around the city.

The organisation, Friends of Jesus, was familiar to some of the people questioned, and their answers were not what Mr. and Mrs. Slater wanted to hear. Somewhere these people had a group of houses, occupied mostly by young women. It was said, and here the voices were lowered, that the so-called Reverend had the girls so brain-washed, that they seemed oblivious to the fact that he was running the whole complex as a harem. The more babies produced were, Paul insisted, 'More followers for Jesus'.

Mrs. Slater wept, Diane's father fumed, all to no avail. What the police had said was true. As an adult, Diane was at liberty to choose when and where she went, and with whom. Explanations were made at the university and a provisional agreement drawn up, that her place would be kept open until the end of the next year, the following June.

"I should have seen what was happening," Auriol said for the umpteenth time, "it was so unlike her, neglecting her studies, being ticked off by her tutors."

"It's no use blaming yourself, I was here too." Colin, sounding genuinely surprised, added, "I just never, ever could have imagined her doing anything as stupid as this."

"The thing was she always seemed to so happy, absolutely glowing."

"Yes, but with hindsight, that's probably how this bloke works, it wasn't so much that she'd suddenly 'seen the light', but that she was totally infatuated with the chap himself."

"Still . . ."

"For heaven's sake, Diane was already a clean-living, sensible hard-working girl, going to church every week, what more did these people want?" Colin stormed on one occasion.

"It depends what they're looking for, she's a very handsome young lady with a gorgeous figure *and* money in the bank. Probably that scored highly on Brownie points with that Paul fellow." Auriol was at her most cynical.

"Don't joke about it!" Colin's tone was sharp, "It's much too serious for that, she could be anywhere and, for all we know, she could be in danger."

"Sorry . . . Her parents have decided they can't do anything else here. Once home they're going to hire a private detective to try and track Diane down. After all, if what we've heard is true, that Paul & Co. have a base somewhere with babies on the agenda, then that must mean registering with the NHS."

"Probably we'd find that's all classified information and they're not prepared to help. These days, we're all so hemmed in by those damned Human Rights and Civil Liberties, that no-one's prepared to infringe them, even when we think someone might be in need of support."

They tried to act normally, but the dynamics of their household had changed. Auriol shopped alone, Colin cooked for two and daily they were bombarded with jocular remarks from their peers, about their 'little love-nest'. These constant references to their new situation started to leave their mark, highlighting their reactions to each other.

Colin, although straight talking and masculine in his life-style, was reticent and lacking in confidence about his studies, and Auriol repeatedly found herself encouraging him, assuring him that a particular piece of work was of a good standard. The more focused of the two, and with the advantage of having had expert coaching since she was small, Auriol consistently obtained better than average grades, with apparently little effort. Matters came to a head one evening. Diane had been gone for over three months and Colin and Auriol returned from a tutorial, having had their submissions for the previous week returned. A quick look, told Auriol she had an A grade and hastily, she started putting her work away, before Colin saw it. Too late.

"You might as well tell me . . . I'll hear it from someone, in due course. Not another A?" Auriol hesitated.

He exploded, "It is, isn't it? Another bloody A. Do you know what I've got? A miserable C. All that damned hard work for a C. It's just a waste of time, and I'm a waste of space. What's the point in going on? I'll never get a degree at this rate. I might just as well pack it in and go home."

"Colin, calm down. Of course you'll get your degree. The tutors are often harder on some students than others," she grinned wryly, "I think Professor Arnold just likes girls."

"Don't give me all that soft soap Auriol. You sail through everything without breaking sweat. No, I'll have to do some serious thinking about my own way forward. I just can't afford to waste my parents' hard-earned cash with nothing to show for it."

To Auriol's horror she saw that his eyes were full of tears, she flopped into a chair and covered his face with his hands.

"Colin darling, don't upset yourself." She put her arms round him. "Remember, I've been very lucky, with a father coaching me since I was small. Perhaps we could work together more, discuss points of interest, that sort of thing, that's certainly how Dad got me never to take anything at face value. And don't forget, when we're writing those sketches, we're a good team. But please, please, don't talk about giving up, I couldn't go on without you here."

Raising his head, he looked at her directly.

"Do you mean it?"

"Of course I mean it. You're very important to me, "she laughed, "I daresay the Psychology Department would have plenty to say about that. Probably along the lines that I'm desperately in need of a father figure, that sort of thing . . ." Her voice faltered as she felt him staring at her intently.

"Auriol, I don't want to be your father figure. I want to be something very, very different. Do you understand? It's just that, I've never felt I could say this before. You see . . . well, what I mean is, we're worlds apart . . ." He hesitated.

"For God's sake, Colin, you're not going to go all wishey-washey on me and start spouting a lot of nonsense about class, I thought that went out with the Dark Ages."

Auriol was standing now.

"You mean . . . ?"

"You great mutt, I love being with you. I love sharing this house and I might add, some of my innermost thoughts with you. What more do you want?"

"What about love?" Colin looked at her quizzically.

"Darling, we can't have it all, well not all at once. Let's just live for the day and see what happens."

"Does that mean . . . ?"

"Oh yes, my darling, it most certainly does." And together, they mounted the stairs.

Auriol, articulate when discussing sex within the confines of the tutorial group, soon learned that she was less knowledgeable about the subject, than she had previously thought. Paintings of nude men had in no way prepared her for her surprise at seeing a male erection, and whilst the love poetry with its whimsical comments, about 'rosebud nipples' and 'milky-white skin' sounded charming in its context, what seemed to have been lost along the way, was the fact of having to peel off all one's clothes first, or expect the other participant to do it for you. It all seemed so undignified. Then, there was the matter of the gyrations with the condom, when she had to try hard not to giggle. Auriol couldn't help feeling it was all rather primitive and, trying desperately not to hurt Colin's feelings, she attempted to get this across to him, after they lay back exhausted. Slight correction needed there, he was exhausted, she had felt that things were just getting started and it might after all be quite a pleasurable experience, when suddenly it was apparent that it was all over. Why did the expression 'bloodied but unbowed' keep popping into her mind?

At first, Colin laughed too at her reaction, said her analytical brain was coming to the fore again, then scowled, and suddenly Auriol realised she was in dangerous territory. It was quite the wrong time to infer that Colin, just recovering from the impact of a C grade, had not been a spectacular lover. As her father had warned, sex could be the root of a multitude of problems. Matters improved gradually, but some months were to elapse, before Auriol rid herself of the feeling of being cheated by the arts, with their mouth-watering hints about sexual bliss being something spectacular, which as far as Auriol was concerned had to date never quite materialised.

CHAPTER 12

Overwhelmed by Paul Rule's quite beautiful face, his mesmeric blue-green eyes and ardent declarations of true love, Diane knew that she had at last found her soul mate. Together, they would bring many more people into the circle of the arms of Jesus and the world would become a much better place because of that. Travelling with him in his car to start her new life, studying his profile, and listening to him talk about the many influential people he had met on his travels, she knew that she had been right to join him. This was Life with a capital 'L', not the boredom of endless discussions about military coups and monarchies being deposed. On entry into Paul's county, Durham, she read the sign 'Land of the Prince Bishops' and felt how appropriate it was, that it was from here this wonderful young man had originated.

Just over the border, Paul exclaimed, "Here we are" and turned into a small cul de sac with five houses. As the car came to a standstill, two small children emerged from one and came running over. Quickly, Paul jumped out of the car, picking each child up in turn, and swinging them round, to the children's obvious delight. Then, turning to Diane, he said,

"There's something I must do, if you'll excuse me. Go to No.3 and tell whoever answers the door, that you've come to join us, I'll bring your things across later."

Obeying instructions, Diane tapped on the door. It was opened by a young woman, Diane recalled seeing at Oxford.

"Oh good, you're here, do come in and make yourself comfortable, Paul will come and join us in a moment. A cup of tea?"

"Thank you, that would be lovely." Diane looked around her curiously. The girl, who she remembered was called Bryony, seemed at ease. Perhaps she was some sort of housekeeper. The room into which Diane was led, was adequately if not plushly furnished, but there were flowers and pretty cushions, so obviously Bryony was something of a needlewoman. Excusing herself to go and make the tea, Bryony went into the corridor and called up the stairs, "She's arrived, come and be introduced."

There was a flurry of movement on the stairs and then two young women appeared, hands extended, and smiling a welcome.

"You're Diane aren't you? We do hope you'll be happy with us."

Introducing themselves as Anna and Isla, they jumped up to help Bryony with the tea and then settled into the armchairs.

Diane was puzzled. One of these girls she recognised, but who were the others? They seemed to lounge around as if they lived here, but Paul had given her the impression the two of them would be living on their own.

"Do you live in the other houses here?" she asked, trying to sound as casual as possible. There was an awkward silence. Then Isla said "She doesn't know yet."

"What do you mean? What don't I know?" Diane's tone was sharp.

Now Anna spoke, "We all live here. That's what a commune is, we thought you knew that."

"You live here in this house? I thought Paul lived here?"

"Indeed he does, he *lives* with all of us."

With the stressing of the word 'lives' and the expressions on the faces of the three girls in front of her, Diane suddenly began to appreciate the enormity of what they were intimating.

"You mean each one of you . . . ?"

"Yes, that's exactly what we mean, and with the others."

"What others?"

"In the other houses. Paul has just gone to see the new baby, born yesterday and to say hello to the children."

"The children?"

"Yes, Cathy and Drusilla came out to the car, but Maureen is always too nervous to let her little ones run out in case there's an accident. Paul will be glad this one's a boy, we only have two boys so far"

"Are their fathers away somewhere?"

There was a stunned silence. Then Bryony spoke,

"Paul *is* their father, we thought you knew. He should have told you earlier. Surely you've heard him talk about having babies for Jesus?"

For a few moments, Diane was too shocked to speak then, "Well yes, of course, but I thought he meant within the context of a home with a Mum and Dad, not like this.

I mean you're not Mormons are you? Living in the UK, Paul can't have married you all?"

"Diane, we're not married to Paul, any of us, but we all love him and those who have his children find he is a wonderful father."

Diane started to cry. "Don't upset yourself. I know the idea takes some getting used to, but lots of people cohabit these days and don't bother to get married, and we've all found that living like this has many advantages."

"Such as . . . ?" Diane choked out the words through her tears.

"Well, we all keep house together, taking it in turns to go on the road with Paul and if there are children, everyone helps out in looking after them."

"But what about the usual sort of life that married people lead?"

Anna spoke up, "I think you mean sex . . . ?" Diane nodded.

"That isn't a problem either. Paul has his own room and invites us in there, as and when, he wishes. It works well, because obviously there are times of the month when we're not available, or we just don't want to be bothered."

"So you're like concubines, just on tap, when the lord and master feels like it?"

All three of them seemed to find this amusing.

"If you put it like that Diane, yes I suppose we are, but it's been working well for quite a few years now, I've been here four years."

"Four years, you could have only been . . . ?"

Isla grinned, "I was sixteen and a half, but you have to admit Paul is one gorgeous male and I've never had any regrets. From what I've read, these other lords and masters to whom you refer, were often fat and ugly."

"So . . . are there no other males here?" Diane was still trying to get the total picture.

"Oh yes." said Anna, "The end house is where our menfolk live. We would find it difficult to manage without them. We grow all our own vegetables and fruit here and keep a few cows and chickens, and the men look after all that. They take turns to go away with Paul on his missions and they also help out with the children. They're very good."

"But they don't live with the other girls?"

"I take it you're referring to sex again? No, they don't live with them and wouldn't be interested in doing so. They're all homosexuals and were chosen because of that."

Bryony now intervened. "I think it's probably best if I show you your room, Diane. You might want to have some time to yourself, to think about things. No-one will keep you here, you're not a prisoner. Everything will depend on how much you want to be with Paul." With that, she led the way and Diane, still sobbing quietly, meekly followed.

Opening the door to a small, almost cell-like room Bryony said,

"This is yours, there's not a lot of room for storage, I'm afraid, but then none of us has very much. For the next few days you'll be with Paul." and moving down the corridor, she ushered Diane into a very different room. It was ornately furnished with draped curtains at the head of the king-size bed. There were two armchairs, a television set, a small table with two upright chairs and built in wardrobes along one wall. Diane gasped at the impact of the colour, palest green with splashes of gold and royal blue. Large windows looked out over green fields. It was gorgeous.

Bryony smiled at her stunned expression. "It's quite lovely, isn't it? You see we all love Paul, and we know how hard he works whilst he's away, so we do like to make him as comfortable as possible. I know it possibly reinforces your idea about the concubines and their lord and master, but we don't object to that. Sexual pleasure to be fully enjoyed, should be with the person you love in truly beautiful surroundings, so we all work to keep this a very special place." Bryony waited, then seeing that Diane was still reeling under the impact of what she had learned in the last hour or so, she continued,

"Through that door is the bathroom. Why don't you freshen up? Change if you wish, there are various clothes in the wardrobe, then sit here by the window and relax. Paul will be back very soon and today as a special treat, we'll be serving your meal up here." She was gone, and Diane sat on the edge of the bed, trying to take in everything that had been said.

She'd read about communes of course, but had never imagined there would be this freedom of approach to sex. Whatever the girls said, it was very much the same as a harem. Here, instead of eunuchs watching over the girls, it was homosexuals who, whilst unlike the eunuchs, who were incapable of sex, these men were capable, but not interested. And the little ones . . . ? Yes they were with their mothers, but what sort of a future did they have? On a personal level, she would be expected to share Paul with a collection of women, her dreams of a cosy little love nest, now being well and truly shattered.

And what of the alternative? How could she return home like a dog with its tail between its legs? She, who had been so enthusiastic, so sure that she truly loved and was loved in return. What a fool she would look to her parents and to Auriol and Colin, who knew her so well. Yet everything Paul had said and done had convinced her of his love; it would be stupid not to put it to the test. Yes, the other girls were pretty, but were they as intelligent as herself? Paul was clever and needed someone of a comparable intellect, to keep him abreast of people's reactions to his speeches. Perhaps this was her role, personal adviser and assistant; secretary too, if necessary. Surely, it would be worth all that, just to be with him?

As for his sex life, perhaps there, she could also have an important role to play. To do so she must ensure that, with her, he was totally fulfilled, requiring no stimulation from a variety of other pairings.

That was the answer. She must be everything to Paul, his aide in everything to do with his ministry, and a loving partner in his bed. Then, in time he would find that Diane was all he needed and abandon this strange, unnatural life-style.

She had decided. Quickly, she made her way to the wardrobe. There she found a selection of somewhat revealing nightwear and negligees and, selecting two of the more modest, she retired to the bathroom, had a quick shower and returned to the armchair.

He was not surprised to find her still in the commune, or at her attire. Many others had travelled the same road, had come to the same conclusion and always it had worked in his favour. Having burned their boats on the home front, not one had been prepared to suffer the embarrassment of failure and return home with the loss of face it would entail. Securing this one had been a matter of pride. She was an Oxford student, one who had been a scholar at a famous school; people would see now that his ladies were not pathetic creatures, with little else to offer in their lives. Now, they would realise that even the most intelligent and attractive could be drawn to his cause. Diane was pretty and bright and would be very companionable – for the time being.

Paul Rule was an accomplished and experienced lover. Used to approaching virgins with the gently, gently approach, he gradually coaxed them, until they were ready to explore their fantasies and indulge his. Repeatedly, Diane felt she would drown in ecstasy. Soon at the merest loving touch, she was anxiously awaiting the next and then longing for the moment of orgasm. For forty eight hours they lived cocooned in fragrant and beautiful isolation. There were no phone calls, just a periodic tap on the door to indicate that a tray of food had been placed outside. By the end of the two days, Diane knew there could never, ever, be any other man in her life.

She knew her time with him was over when, the next morning, there was a tap on the door and Bryony called, "Diane, do you need a hand to move your things into your own room?"

A quick reply from her to the negative, then Paul, glowing from his shower, said "I'm afraid it's time, my darling, but you'll only be just across the way. You know I'd like you here as often as possible, but . . ."

"Yes, they explained." Diane looked miserable.

"Good. I have to go over and see the children. Would you like to come? I think you should meet the others."

"Yes, just give me another five minutes."

The three nearest houses each contained a young woman and two children, whilst one girl, Sophie, was obviously in an advanced stage of pregnancy. The girls were all pretty, which worried Diane. Had this just been personal preference on Paul's part, or was there a hidden agenda here, was he aiming to produce a handsome good-looking brood of his own? Unbidden, thoughts of Hitler's supreme race of Aryan children sprang to mind. The girls welcomed Diane and introduced their children. It was as if, she thought, a new neighbour had come to call. Only Diane appeared to find the situation in any way embarrassing.

In the other house she met Liam, Jason and Grant, and they too were polite and welcoming. In addition to their gardening chores and accompanying Paul on his speaking travels, Grant explained that Liam was a qualified plumber and Jason experienced with computers, which meant they could earn extra cash in those areas. Diane had been curious as to how the group managed financially; now some of the questions were being answered.

Yes, they also helped with the children, took them out, gave their mothers a break, that sort of thing. "And even," Liam laughed, "we have been known to cook, but the fact that we aren't asked very often speaks for itself."

It all sounded very cosy and precious and Diane couldn't help thinking, too good to be true. There must be times when the girls fell out, or the boys had a spat. Anything else would be abnormal. She admonished herself, '*Come on, Diane, the whole situation is abnormal. What have you let yourself in for?*'

In her nun-like room that night, the sound of Isla's light footsteps as she tripped along the corridor to Paul's room gave Diane a great deal more to think about.

CHAPTER 13

Ruth Hatton's death in the autumn had had little impact on all their lives. As her husband Guy had said,

"She left me three years ago with the onset of Alzheimer's. Once your loved one no longer knows who you are, it is for both of you and all your family a living death. Death itself is a happy release."

Leo, struck down with a vicious attack of chicken pox, had been unable to attend her funeral. Now, returning to school after the sudden death and burial of his grandfather, he had much to think about. Every member of Leo's family had been shocked by Guy Hatton's unexpected death, in his sleep. For so many years, Leo now saw, his grandfather had been a constant in all their lives, gently guiding and advising, listening to their problems, generous with both his time and money. Now he was gone and, without exception, they all realised how sorely he would be missed, as a reference point and confidante.

That Guy Hatton had also been a much respected and popular person, both in and around the Chichester area and beyond, was also obvious from the large number of people who attended the service in the cathedral, in celebration of his life. People Leo had never seen before stood up and said they had been proud to be Guy Hatton's friend. Representatives from a whole raft of charities said that without his benevolence they would not have been able to continue. And, listening to the reading of his grandfather's will, Leo had been amazed, not just by the generosity of the bequests, but by the detailed way Guy had considered the needs of everyone around him.

To my beloved sons Charles and Simon Hatton, I leave Grafton House, its contents and the grounds, as shown on the plan; that is, the land which extends beyond and includes the 'Shoot' cottages and the 'Shoot' valley. Both sons are now in employment and currently own no permanent residences but on retirement, they may choose to live in the house, which has afforded their mother and me so much pleasure and happiness. Organisation of the shooting is in the capable hands of an agent and will remain so, overseen by my solicitor, for as long as they wish to retain it. In leaving them the house, I am hopeful that they will continue to allow their deceased brother's wife, Susan Hatton, and her children, to remain in the wing she presently occupies.

To Susan, I bequeath the tract of land beyond the 'Shoot' cottages, which I believe will appreciate in value. If sold, it should provide her with ample capital with which to build another home for herself elsewhere; if retained, it will prove a 'nest-egg' for the future.

To my very dear grandchildren I bequeath as follows:—Auriol's educational expenses are already catered for and trust funds have been set up to cover the further education of Gemma and Leo. To each of them, I leave the sum of £20,000, aware of the fact that they will soon be of an age, when purchasing their own living accommodation and a means of transport will become necessary. Further trust funds have been set up to cover the eventuality of my sons marrying and having issue of their marriages.

Leo had watched his uncles and his mother weep at the love and care with which Guy had ensured all their needs were cared for, in the most appropriate way. There were gifts to all those who had served him both at home and on the estate, and to those who had cared for his wife, both at Grafton House and in the hospice. Nor had the many charities Guy Hatton supported been forgotten. Too late, Leo realised that his grandfather had been a role model of the highest order, a pillar in the community and a loving member of his family.

His Uncle Simon, on compassionate leave, had endeavoured to turn the boy's mind to other matters, and inevitably the subject of school and

Leo's progress had arisen. To Simon's surprise, Leo started to enquire about entry into the Royal Navy.

"How old would I have to be before I could join, and do I have to go to university first?"

"You're now thirteen?"

"Yes, just."

"Some years ago you could have been admitted as a boy seaman at the age of fifteen, but not any more. But, no, you don't have to go to university and you would be eligible at sixteen. If you're really keen, I can tell you what will be your best way forward. Do you have a Combined Cadet Force at your school?"

"Yes."

"Join it straight away! Those CCF's are regarded as recruitment for officer material. In fact, at one point, their title was something like Officer Recruitment Force; that's all changed now, I suspect because it smacks of privilege and isn't politically correct. There you'll not only get a good grounding in seamanship and what life is like in the Navy, but you'll also be sent to Dartmouth for work experience, several weeks per year, and that is invaluable."

"And someone at the Cadet Force will keep me informed as to how I apply for all this, and what happens next?"

"Of course, that's what they're there for. Once a year, at HMS Sultan in Gosport, the Admiralty Board meets, they're known to us as the AIB, Admiralty Interview Board. If they accept you for officer training, you'll be sent from there to the RN College at Dartmouth, and . . . . well, then you're up and running."

"So, I could leave school at sixteen?"

"Yes, but Leo, it's not all sunshine and roses you know, it can be really hard graft. You'll be assessed every so often and must get decent to good results. You'll have education tests, as well as seamanship, so don't think you're in for an easy ride. Once in, if you're overseen by one of the old school mariners, he's likely to give you a very rough ride, especially, if he thinks you've been to a posh school and had a relatively easy life." And, surveying Leo's slight frame and innocent looks, Simon asked, "Do you think you're up to it? Are you sure this is what you want?"

"Absolutely, Uncle, I know I'd love it."

"Well then, the very best of luck and keep me posted as to how it's going. Who knows, I might see you on one of my ships, in a few years' time."

Gazing out of the train windows, Leo grinned to himself. School for just three more years, when he would be away for much of the time, and then life on the high seas. Just let his dear sister Gemma, see what she could make of that!

A variety of foreign language tutors had been found for Gemma, all within convenient striking distance of Chichester, and her studies had now begun. Only when Leo was present did her hatred surface, and, she now realised at seventeen, that it really was for her a case of 'out of sight, out of mind'. The one to one relationships with her tutors, her desire and determination to build a successful career as a professional singer, Susan all to herself at home, and Gemma was in her element. Except for one thing . . . Mark Fleming was still on the scene. Susan had adjusted all her own commitments to ensure she was not away overnight, leaving Gemma alone in the house. This presented Susan with another problem, as to how she could enjoy a full relationship with Mark, when Gemma was so often at home. Accordingly, Susan arranged her meetings with Mark at Grafton House, choosing times when she knew Gemma would be at her lessons. It was very noticeable, however, that on those occasions when Gemma returned early, to find Mark and her mother enjoying a cosy cup of tea together, the girl had been barely civil.

Was she never, Gemma thought, to have Susan's attention without Darling Leo or someone else, diverting it to themselves? Somehow, Gemma decided, Mark must be dealt with, but how? One day, whilst ostensibly reading, she listened with interest to the two of them discussing Guy's will.

"It's a huge piece of land, Susan, and worth a great deal of money. There have to be seven or eight fields, which would each hold at least eight houses. Could be turned into a really nice little complex."

"No way, Mark, I'm not interested. Perhaps in the future, when the children are all settled in jobs and probably living elsewhere, but definitely not now. I love this area and I certainly don't want to be the one who spoils it."

"And you're assuming that it would be spoiled. That's a large assumption!"

"Can we drop the subject?" Then, laughing, Susan added, "I know only too well what you entrepreneurs are like once you get the bit between your teeth."

"O.K., but I hope whenever you do decide to do something about it, you'll at least talk to me and let me have first refusal."

"Goodness, you are keen! Now can we talk about something else please? They're doing a revival of 'Perchance to Dream' at the theatre and," looking across at her daughter, "that's something you ought to see, Gemma. Perhaps we could all go?"

"Excellent idea. Let me have the dates you two ladies can manage, and I'll get some tickets."

Gemma, smiling her agreement, thought how pathetic they both were, with their childish attempts at placating her and drawing her into the fold. She was, however, delighted at what she had heard about the land. His entrepreneurial instinct was clearly Mark's Achilles' heel and she must somehow make the most of it. Alone one day, Gemma went through Susan's papers and found the plan showing the marked tract of land Guy had bequeathed to Susan. 'Borrowing' it for a day was an easy matter, as was photo-copying it and replacing the original in Susan's desk. Carefully, Gemma drafted out, and then typed a letter to the Reporters' Office at the Chichester Gazette.

Following the death of Mr. Guy Hatton of Grafton House, a very desirable piece of land has now come onto the market. Competition between would-be purchasers is expected to be fierce, as the land has building potential for some 60 or more houses of quality.

Already prospective buyers have been to see the land, the most notable being Mr. Mark Fleming, former Chairman of the Chichester and District Council.

Although the source had been anonymous, the Gazette Editor was obviously aware that the news would generate considerable local interest and, together with Gemma's copied outline plan of the area, the article as she had written it was printed in full.

Susan was incandescent with rage. A delighted Gemma, listening to her mother berating Mark on the phone, hid her self-satisfied smile. It had worked!

"How could you Mark? I made my feelings about that land absolutely clear. I can't believe you would do such a thing." A pause.

"Well of course, you would say that. Obviously, someone saw you there and others . . .

"How dare anyone, even set foot on it without my permission? It's trespassing, as you well know, and if anyone is seen anywhere near it in the future, I shall give the gamekeeper instructions to shoot at them . . . No, don't say any more. I just can't begin to say how disappointed I am in you." And the phone was slammed down.

Messages on the answer phone from Mark, received no reply. Flowers arrived and were discarded, as were letters protesting his innocence. Feeling very pleased with herself, Gemma had her mother all to herself again.

CHAPTER 14

Diane's decision to escape the confines of the commune, was made exactly ten weeks after her arrival. Early misgivings had been allayed, if not entirely quashed, each time she was welcomed into Paul's bed, but she had taken careful note of the group's activities, whilst deliberately giving the impression of being contented with her lot.

On arrival, Diane had been asked to give what money she had to the communal pool, and she had handed over all that was in the account used for her expenses at university. Instinct had prevailed, and Diane made no mention of the 'backstop' account her parents had insisted on opening for her, to cope, as they said, with any emergency which might arise.

Casual enquiries about the commune's finances had proved enlightening. Collections made at the meetings, the money the men earned from gardening and plumbing, family allowances, social security cheques, everything went into the common fund.

"What about the houses, Bryony," Diane asked innocently, "are they owned by the commune, or rented?"

"Oh they're rented, they could never have been bought by us. When Sadie, in the first house, met Paul in the early days, she was an orphan and a loner, but she'd just received a large bequest on her grandfather's death, so that was put in the bank and makes quite a substantial amount of interest and helps pay the rent. It certainly enabled Paul to get his ideas off the ground." *How very convenient for Paul, Diane thought, that Sadie should prove an early conquest and, surprise, surprise, a very well-heeled one.* But none of what she had learned could explain Paul's lifestyle. He ran a car, his tastes in food and wine were expensive. How were these financed?

One evening in November, she noticed the lights of a car pulling up outside the house and Anna came running down the stairs, wearing a very smart blue velvet dress and beautifully made up. Before Diane could comment, Anna called 'Cheerio', the door closed behind her and they heard the car drive away.

"I've never seen Anna look so smart. Where's she going?"

Bryony's reply was terse, "To meet an old friend, who's staying in the area."

Before Christmas, there were two other such incidents, this time involving Isla and Anna. On a third occasion, they left the house together. Each time, Diane listened for, or was aroused by a car returning, heard their footsteps on the stairs and saw that the time was about 5:00 a.m.

Christmas proved difficult for Diane, missing the family atmosphere of her own home terribly. Try as she may, she couldn't rid herself of the feeling that she was watching some surreal film, where people were playing parts and not always very well. The children had been brought over and, for their benefit, everyone went through the motions of donning paper hats and helping them play games.

But there was now something else, which was gnawing away at Diane. Both Sadie and Ellie from the other houses had blue eyes, and Paul's eyes were also a brilliant blue. *Surely she thought, it was not possible for such parents to produce children with brown eyes?* The little girl Drusilla, who had run to the car on Diane's arrival, had chocolate brown eyes and dark hair, whilst one of the boys in the third house, whose mother was a blonde, with dark eyes, had the greenest eyes and reddest hair Diane had ever seen. Observing Paul closely at the Christmas get-together, Diane saw that Paul paid particular attention to the new baby and those children who, like himself, had blue eyes and dark hair. It seemed fairly obvious these were his children and the others were not, but if that was the case, what of the others? Who had fathered those children?

It was not until Isla and Anna simultaneously announced that they were pregnant, that everything began to fall into place. In order to finance his lifestyle, Paul was running something comparable to a stud farm! These girls had been sent out to be 'served' by other men and for that, they would have received payment. Later, the tear-stained young women would return to the men saying something had gone wrong, they were pregnant, and would need substantial funding for their babies, if they were not to disclose this to wives, sweethearts etc. In this way, Paul's number of 'Babies for Jesus' increased and also his income from the Child Allowance and other support groups.

And, Diane now realised, seeing Anna and Isla's woeful faces, they, like others before them, would soon be farmed out to the other houses, leaving room in Paul's domain for new recruits. Only Bryony remained a constant in his life and Diane began to wonder now, if that was what she had always been, his sister perhaps, or even, the thought almost beyond belief, his wife. Certainly, she was someone who was so close to him, that she was prepared to countenance everything that he did, however ignominious or illegal.

Diane was still puzzled. Whilst what she had learned would provide extra monies, in order to keep this establishment, its occupants and Paul's lifestyle up and running, there would surely be a shortfall. And then, overhearing a chance remark from one of the men, all became clear, and she cursed her own stupidity. Picking a few flowers for the vase in Paul's room, she heard Grant call to Liam,

"Don't forget we're on duty tonight."

"What us? Or the girls?"

"It's the girls' night, so all the kids will be with us. But for the record, it's our turn on Friday, some who've been before and one or two new ones."

Diane thought she would faint. So this was where all the money came from! Regular open house, either for gay men, or for men wanting women. Paul's so called Friends for Jesus was nothing more than a highly profitable bordello.

On her arrival, Diane had been told she was not a prisoner, but she continued to sense that her moves were watched and to a certain extent, controlled. Her mobile had been removed, on the premise that she must cut herself off from her old life and form a new one. To her request that she send a letter to her college friend, Paul had replied, smiling,

"I'd prefer to see it before it's posted, as I'd hate you to give clues as to where we are to anyone. We don't want people coming to stare at us, as if we're some rare species, which we are of course!"

Diane's letter to Auriol was carefully worded. Paul would be returning to Oxford at the end of January for a daytime meeting in the park and although Diane herself would not be able to attend, she did hope that Auriol and Colin too, would be able to go and hear him. They would then realise, what an inspiration he had been to so many people. She hoped they were both well and progressing with their studies, and that they would convey the message to her parents, that she was well and happy.

Paul approved. "Good girl," then added "you don't want to go and see them?"

"I think it's better not. I don't want arguments, if they try and persuade me to return."

"That's sensible. Now go and post your letter, there's a box just down the road. The fresh air will do you good, you're looking a bit peaky."

Sliding the biro into her pocket was easy and, positioning herself at the reverse side of the box as if studying collection times, she had, in a matter of seconds, written on the back of the envelope. *Help me please. Be there.*

As arranged, two weeks later, Paul and Grant made an early start for Oxford and Diane put her own plan into action. "Do you need anything from the shops Bryony? I'm going down to the village."

"No, everything we need is delivered. What are you going for?"

"Well I need more pants and tights and one or two personal bits, the sort of things I'd rather not ask the boys to get."

Picking up her handbag and a shopping bag, Diane set out. She had checked the times buses left the village, knew she would have to change, and that the journey would take about an hour. She had enough money to get her to the first stop and, quickly finding a cash machine and using her undisclosed credit card, Diane drew sufficient for her journey.

Seeing Oxford again with its domes and towers, a wave of nostalgia hit her, but this was not the time for weakness. From the safety of the bus station booth, she phoned Auriol, praying she had received the scrawled message and would be in. Hearing her familiar voice, Diane almost wept with relief.

"It's me, Diane . . ." she couldn't go on.

"Thank God. We've got your letter. Where are you?"

"The bus station but . . ."

"Stay right there, we're coming to get you."

Within ten minutes, Auriol and Colin spilled out of a taxi and she was in their warm embrace. At last, they all drew breath, the girls dried their tears and Auriol asked,

"Where, now? Back home?"

"No, there's something I need to do . . ."

In the small café at the station, Diane gave them a brief outline of her experiences and what she planned. They drank coffee, tried unsuccessfully to eat, then Colin hailed a taxi to take them to the entrance to the park. Diane knew that Paul always started his daytime meetings at about mid-day, 'To catch the lunch-time crowds' and sure enough, they could see in the distance, the striped awning which backed and partially covered the small stage. The microphone was in place and the loudspeakers were already inviting people to "Come and hear the well-known and much admired Reverend Paul Rule, who will tell you about his organisation 'Friends of Jesus'. I know you will be impressed by what he has done, and is doing, for the welfare of our children. Listen, whilst he invites you all to be part of creating a better world for the future. Rev. Paul . . ."

The day was dry and bright and by the time Paul Rule walked onto the stage, about 100 curious people hearing the loudspeakers, had gathered in front of the stage. Carefully, Auriol and Colin moved forward, shielding Diane, close behind them, from view. They remained on the perimeter of the crowd. It was not until Paul's speech reached its climax, with the section Diane knew so well about having 'Babies for Jesus' and making sacrifices for the underprivileged, that she moved swiftly forward. Suddenly she was beside him on the stage, and pushing him away from the mike.

The crowd perked up. There was a ripple of excitement. This was much more interesting. Paul Rule, at first nonplussed by Diane's appearance, stood uncertain as to what was happening, and in that moment, Colin and Auriol positioned themselves between Paul and Diane, who was now clutching the mike.

Diane stared straight ahead at the people gathered, and spoke confidently.

"This man," pointing at Paul, "is a fraud and a hypocrite. He calls himself a Reverend, but he has never qualified for that title and certainly does not deserve it. He takes your money, in fact he takes anybody's money, and uses it to satisfy his own pleasures and to meet his own ends. Silly, stupid girls, such as me, who fall for his good looks and are sweet-talked by him into joining his organisation, soon find themselves living in a brothel. His 'Babies for Jesus' campaign suits him very well. It allows him not only to fulfil his own lusts, but to use the child support money to buy his champagne and fine food."

There was a groan of disbelief from the crowd and here Grant stepped forward, only to find his way blocked by a policeman, who having seen the crowd gathered had called for help. Now, he placed a restraining hand on Grant's arm, making it quite clear that the girl was to be allowed to continue. As Paul started to make a quick exit from the other side of the stage, another policeman arrived, his stance and expression, also telling Paul that he was not going anywhere.

Diane continued. "My advice to you all, is to go away and tell everyone that this man is an egotistical cheat and a liar, and that the best we can hope is that very soon he will be behind bars."

For a moment, there was a stunned silence, then a ripple of applause interspersed with calls of 'Good on yer girl, well done!" and "Very brave."

One or two people came up and tried to shake Diane's hand, but Auriol could see she was now emotionally exhausted and on the point of collapse. Quickly she took her to one side, just as two familiar figures detached themselves from the crowd and ran towards the stage. Auriol and Colin looked on, as Diane was locked in her parents' embrace, cried with them, and then smiled with relief, on seeing that she was once again surrounded by people she loved and trusted. They watched as Paul and Grant were taken away by the police. As the crowd dispersed, with people shaking their heads in disbelief at the wickedness of the world, together, they all left the park and made for home.

Whilst Diane sat and talked with her parents, Auriol and Colin prepared tea and then made themselves scarce, knowing their own turn to learn the details would come in due course. All were in agreement, that what Diane had done, had taken a great deal of courage, and that what she needed now, more than anything else, was a period of complete rest, so that she might come to terms with what had happened to her over the past weeks.

It was decided that Diane should go back with her parents to their hotel and then, if she felt up to it, spend a few hours the next day with her friends, before returning home. Ecstatic at the reunion with their daughter, the Slaters were just grateful that Diane appeared to have come out of her ordeal exhausted, but, otherwise, apparently unscathed.

The Diane who duly arrived the following day was, Auriol and Colin decided later, a different girl from the one who had left them several short months earlier. This girl was resilient, determined, and much more worldly-wise and if, from time to time she chastised herself for being 'such an unutterable, gullible fool', who could blame her?

"Why didn't you try and make the break earlier, as soon as you suspected that something very odd was happening?"

"Because, Auriol, I was stupid and still thought I might be misjudging him. He was so loving towards me and I couldn't really for some time believe some of the things I was suspecting. I suppose in a way, I was hoping my fears would be proved wrong."

"And the children . . . ? What about the children?"

"The children *were* happy . . . they were after all living with their mothers and had sibling playmates or others, close by. They were well fed and as far as I could see they were never ill-treated. But . . ."

"Yes, but.?"

"What sort of an environment was it otherwise? Their mothers selling their bodies on a regular basis, and think of the risks that implies, both from a physical and risk of infection point of view."

"Some, you said, were quite definitely Paul's?"

"Yes. Of course, I had no proof, other than their appearance. Now that I have realised how arrogant and self-satisfied he was, I believe he thought he *was* propagating some sort of superior class, a bit like Hitler's ideas about the Aryans. In a way this bears out what he kept talking to me about . . ." Diane hesitated.

"Go on . . ."

"Auriol, it sounds immodest to even repeat it, but he was constantly referring to how intelligent I was, and how our children would have the benefit of brains and beauty."

"But you're not . . . ?"

"No, and I thank God for it."

"If charges are brought against him, you do know you'll probably have to give evidence?" This, from Colin.

"Of course, and I'll do so willingly, before any other lovesick young fool like me gets sucked into his clutches."

"Right, let's change the subject." Auriol's tone was brisk. "What are your plans?"

"Well I'm going to spend at least a month with Mum and Dad, first of all. That's the least I can do, after the heartache I've caused them. They're suggesting we might have a couple of weeks away, somewhere in the sun, which would be great. But, before I leave Oxford, I'm going to make an application to see if I can resume my studies next September. I know you'll probably have gone long before then, which I'm sad about, but I agree with Mum and Dad, that I mustn't let this man spoil what I intended to do with my life, so . . ."

"Diane, that's absolutely great. We'll keep in touch about it, but perhaps you'd like us to keep the lease on this place open, until you know exactly what's happening."

And so it was decided. Complete again at last, the Slater family made their farewells, leaving Auriol and Colin a great deal to think about. Auriol's fears about Diane, had not been allayed by the only letter she had previously received from her. Clearly, Diane was living in a commune with other men and women and there were children there too. Diane had not gone into details about their parentage, but Auriol was convinced from what she had read about communes, that sex was just one of the many functions shared between the inmates. She had shuddered, at the thought of the shock this must have been to the well-brought-up Diane. Whilst her own relationship with Colin was quietly satisfying, Auriol had none of the illusions which Diane must have had about Paul, that it was a 'til death us do part' romance. To this end, she periodically dropped small pebbles into her conversation with Colin, to make him realise that when their degrees were completed, they would probably be going their separate ways.

Now at last, Auriol could see a way to bring their co-habiting to a conclusion. She would stay on and work towards her M.A. degree and, by opting for the period 1900 to the present day, she could further explore her own talent at script-writing. Whilst she and Colin had had considerable success in that area, he would probably be the first to acknowledge that her input had in fact been greater than his. Perhaps this was the way forward for her, career-wise.

Sharing the house with Diane would be brilliant and, whether they invited someone else to join them, or could manage financially without doing so, could be decided later. There was no possibility that Colin would spend another year in Oxford. Realistically, his degree would probably not warrant further qualifications, but in any event, he would be needed in Yorkshire and anxious to get a job to supplement the family income. She sighed with relief; in this way she could not only let Colin down gently and ease him out of her life, but could assess her own talent in other areas, and judge just where her future lay.

What a joy it had been to welcome Diane back into the fold. Auriol hadn't realised just how much she had missed having another young woman around, nor, how much she had been plagued by the nagging worry about her safety. That single guarded letter they had received, had told them nothing concrete, except that something was wrong. Why was there no address? Why did she not extol Paul's virtues, as she had done initially? Then the long silence and, just at the time when both she and Colin had felt there would be no further communication from Diane, their mixture of delight and alarm, at receiving her letter saying she needed help. Her bravery, during the resultant denouemént in the park, had filled both of them with admiration and respect.

Auriol was surprised too, at how moved she had been to see the rapture with which the Slaters had greeted their daughter. Mother and daughter had sat holding hands as if determined that nothing would separate them again. She was both surprised and rather disturbed, at what she now realised. Never could Auriol recall having such rapport with Susan. A kiss on arrivals and departures, but not this loving closeness. Nor, could she remember seeing such demonstrations between Susan and Gemma. Only with Leo was her mother overtly affectionate, both in speech and gesture. When her father was alive, Auriol had not been aware of this, but now, seeing how others lived and reacted to each other, she recognised that, as she had suspected soon after Giles's death, theirs really was a dysfunctional family.

CHAPTER 15

Leo lost no time in taking his uncle's advice, and found that the master in charge of the Cadet corps, Mr. Brooke, was only too delighted, not only to have a new recruit, but one whose uncle was a naval Captain. Richard Brooke felt certain that in the not too distant future, he would be able to persuade Captain Hatton to come and talk to the boys. How much more stimulating it would be for them to hear at first hand, what it was like to be on the bridge directing operations, and outlining some of the many duties, pleasant and unpleasant, which the Navy had to perform. The boy was intelligent, and would in any event, probably have been selected as officer material, but this connection would undoubtedly clinch it. The Headmaster would be pleased and any reservations he might have had about the Combined Cadet Force would be put on hold.

Having never previously felt the need to discuss his family with the other boys, with the exception of his friend James, Leo now found he had acquired a great deal of kudos with both the naval connection and the fact that, as everyone now seemed to know, his other uncle was the Ambassador to Greece. Suddenly, he was everyone's favourite, even to the extent of being selected for matches, which would otherwise have been out of his reach.

Almost fourteen, Leo had developed from an angelic looking child, into an extremely handsome young man. He had decided he hated rugby, it was both dangerous and dirty. What pleasure could one possibly find he thought, in being knocked about and covered in mud at the end of it? Cricket, Leo felt, was a much more civilised game. He knew already that his cricketing whites showed off his blonde hair, blue eyes and handsome profile to best advantage. When there was the added plus of a healthy looking tan, he quickly learned that sisters of any of the other players were quite anxious to make his acquaintance.

Not that Leo was very keen on girls. The remoteness of his sister Auriol, and the peculiar and often dangerous escapades of Gemma, had persuaded him that girls were not to be trusted. Even his mother could at times prove very irritating, forever wanting to hug and kiss him, as if he was still a toddler. No, with the approach of puberty, he had already decided that females were unpredictable and not nearly such good company as boys and men. With the male of the species you knew from the start exactly where you stood.

His lessons at Thaxton were going well. Mr. Brooke had warned his naval cadets that they would need good grades in both Maths and English, to be accepted as officer material, and Leo had already shown he had an aptitude for both. Surprisingly, he had found the new addition of Latin to his syllabus, at 13 years, fairly easy, and Leo's art teacher was delighted at his ability at painting, in both oil and watercolour.

The visit of Simon Hatton to Thaxton, during the Spring term, was an important event, not only for his nephew Leo and the Headmaster, but most of all, for Mr. Brooke and his naval cadets.

Like his brother, Simon was an accomplished speaker and Leo made a mental note that this was another important facet of an officer's duties, which would need to be mastered. Now Captain of an aircraft carrier, the boys listened in awe to Simon Hatton's accounts of rapid deployments to areas in the world, where there might be trouble. He showed them slides of 'the calm blue waters of the Med' with waves towering above the decks of the carrier. To their amazement he told them that there were some members of the Royal Navy who were always sick as soon as their ships left the calm waters of the harbour and entered oceanic waters.

"How do they manage, Sir? What do they do?" one boy looked very puzzled.

"Well, sea-sickness could prove to be very serious if allowed to go completely unattended, but there are several golden rules. If the sufferers live on a mess deck, that is, with perhaps, 20 or more other sailors, there is a standard practice. The 'sickies' as we will call them, go up on deck armed with oilskins, and tuck themselves between storage lockers and parts of the super structure, anywhere they can find shelter."

"Sir, why don't they just stay in their bunk or whatever?"

"Because it is always better to be in the open air, rather than in a confined space. With them, they always take a bottle of water and a packet of dry biscuits."

"But Sir, what's the point, if they keep on being sick, they'll just throw up again?"

"Exactly. The point is, that the stomach must have something to reject. If it doesn't, then there's the risk that the lining of the stomach will be damaged in the process of vomiting. Do you see?"

There was a chorus of approval as the boys saw!

Simon continued, "Don't think being sea-sick rules out the possibility of a naval career, I know one sea captain who is always sick as soon as his ship leaves the harbour, but he knows what to do. He, and other officers, would of course, always have someone watching over them, whilst they're being ill."

"How do you know if a harbour is deep enough for a big ship like a carrier?"

"We don't always, but the local harbour pilots do, they know the different channels and any hazards, for which they must make provision. As a general rule, a local pilot comes out in a small boat, boards the ship and then takes charge of getting her into harbour."

"That must be an exciting job, Sir, going onto all those different ships from all over the world."

"Yes, but don't be under any illusions, it can also be quite frightening."

The boys registered surprise.

"Yes, frightening. I have a friend who's a Trinity House Pilot, the British pilots who bring our ships into harbour. He once said that the electrical hoist, which is supposed to lift him from pilot boat to the upper deck, is often out of service and if he's called out, we'll say at

Southampton, at two o'clock in the morning, and there's a Gale Force 6 or 7 blowing, having to climb the rope ladder up the side of a ship, which is as high, and in some cases higher than a house, can be a very terrifying experience. Don't think that grown-ups are never frightened, it's not so. When the pilot has to bring in a container ship which is at least a quarter of a mile long, the sight-line from the bridge to the water," and here he demonstrated on the blackboard, "is so distant, that if there's a small yacht out there and you lose sight of it, it can be a serious problem."

"So what happens, Sir, about that rule that steam should always give way to sail?"

"Well, realistically in those circumstances, it just can't happen. The big ship would never be able to stop in time, if a small vessel cuts across its bows. Remember that. I know some of you sail dinghies and it does mean that, if you're in a small boat you must keep your wits about you and always be on the alert for big ships in the shipping line, which might not be able to stop in time."

The boys were very impressed. Leo, basking in his uncle's glory was also astonished. Who would have thought that Uncle Simon, who usually seemed fairly quiet and, Leo thought, not very adventurous, was for much of his life on a big ship, where clearly there was always a great deal happening.

Simon told them about misjudged landings on deck, when the only thing which saved the plane and its occupants from 'ditching' in the sea and possibly drowning, had been the trip wires.

"Have you ever been on board when there's been a serious accident, Sir?"

Simon hesitated, "No, I haven't personally, but my uncle was on an aircraft carrier some years ago when there was a bad accident, not far from Malta. The planes were on deck being re-fuelled. When that happens, the pipe carrying the fuel has to run from the bowels of the ship where the fuel's stored, right up through at least three decks, until it reaches the planes. On that day, it passed the wireless rooms where one of the radio operators was tapping out a message on his machine, when a spark flew off it. What no-one had noticed was that there was a split in the pipe, and it had been pumping out fuel on its journey up through the ship. The spark touched the fuel and the fire erupted through all the decks."

There was a gasp from the boys. "Did the ship blow up, Sir?"

"No it didn't blow up, but it was a tragic accident, nine young men were killed and many were injured. There is something else you should know about accidents on board. As soon as the alarm bells ring, everyone must immediately report to his designated emergency station. At the same time, other officers, in order to contain the fire or whatever is the problem, and save as many personnel as possible, have their own duties, which are first and foremost to close the hatches and seal off the spread of fire, or any part of the ship which might have been holed.

"Try to imagine yourself in this position. You are in a lower deck, hear the alarm and start to make for your own emergency station, only to find that as you climb each ladder upwards, suddenly the hatch above you is slammed down, and you have to try and find somewhere else."

The boys' faces said it all, this was the real thing, not learning how to read maps, what the various instruments were called and how to use them, or how to march.

"However, we no longer use the Morse Code tappers, and I can assure you that on board there are the most stringent anti-fire regulations. Remember what I've said and don't *ever* be tempted to disregard them. Now, I think we should talk about something more cheerful, lining the decks when we enter and leave harbour for instance, and of course if you're lucky, the monarch's Fleet Review."

All in all, it was such a success that Mr. Brooke couldn't wait to ask Simon Hatton if he would come back again sometime, and give them a second instalment.

"I'd be glad to do so, but you'll appreciate that I am of necessity, away a great deal. What we could perhaps consider is the possibility of a visit by your boys, when my ship's next in Portsmouth. They could be given a tour of inspection, see the planes on deck, that sort of thing. I'm sure they'd be interested to see what a mess deck looks like and the officers' quarters. We might even run to a glass of squash and a few cakes."

Richard Brooke was ecstatic, "That would be wonderful, Captain Hatton, and I can't thank you enough for this afternoon. It's so kind of you to take the time out, I know you lead a very busy life."

"My pleasure, now if I could just have a quick word with young Leo, before I leave?"

"Of course, Sir. Cadet Hatton, here please, the rest of you dismiss."

As Mr. Brooke and the cadets disappeared, Leo, all smiles, came forward and sat beside his uncle. "That was amazing, Uncle Simon, I know they all enjoyed it. I certainly did."

"Good, now I want to talk to you about something completely different. Next summer's holidays . . . have you got any plans?"

"No, it's too early for that, nothing's been arranged."

"Good. I wanted to suggest this before you had all made other arrangements. An Italian lady-friend of mine," Leo grinned, "I can assure you, young man, we are just that, good friends. Sofia, has a very large and rather plush apartment in Venice. I've told her I won't be able to visit her this summer, as I'll be at sea during July and August and she's suggested I invite some of my family to make use of it, for perhaps a couple of weeks. Once Sofia has our dates, she would then let her apartment to other people during the free weeks. What do you think?"

"Well, none of us have been to Venice, and it looks amazing in the films and on TV."

"It's certainly one of those places you ought to try and see at some point in your life. Look, I've spoken to you, before you get fixed up with your friend, James, isn't it? I'll phone your mother and she can ask the girls. The sooner we can clinch the offer the better. I've got to make tracks now, Leo, I've enjoyed seeing your school and I've heard nothing but good reports about you, from the staff. Your father would have been proud of you. Well done, and keep up the good work."

With that, Captain Hatton, slim and elegant in his beautiful uniform, started his car's engine, a quick wave and he was gone. Leo was still smiling, as he turned back to the school's imposing entrance; then, the smile gone from his face, he stopped in his tracks. Two weeks in Venice, it sounded idyllic but on reflection there were just two major problems. Number one, Gemma. She was also to be invited and would probably be present, and two . . . all those canals! The combination of those two factors sounded no longer idyllic, but rather terrifying.

Gemma had decided that Dominic Letang was an idiot. He was supposed to be teaching her French, so that she could sing in that language, but he seemed to dismiss, as of no account, the fact that she had covered the basic stuff at school, and just wanted to make sure her accent was correct. So, what on earth was M. Letang doing, constantly banging on about declensions of verbs and sentence structure? There was another thing, he never appeared in the least impressed with her appearance, even when she had made a special effort to dress as smartly as she imagined he was used to seeing in Paris. And she did often make an effort, because in spite of the fact that he seemed a bit slow on the uptake, he was rather dishy

Of course, he was getting on a bit, probably in his late thirties. He was married to an English woman and had left his native country, France, to live in Arundel, his wife's birthplace. There, he taught French four days a week at Lancing College and gave private tuition at home on other days. The Letangs had a charming cottage on the outskirts of the town, with a stunning view across the valley of the castle and the college, silhouetted against the backdrop of the Southern Downs. Having decided one day to take the bull by the horns, Gemma said in her forthright way,

"Do I really need to know all this, M. Dominic? Surely the lyrics will already be determined whatever the piece and I only have to sing them?"

"It is necessary, Mlle, that you fully understand, in order to act through the music and interpret to an audience what the composer and lyricist wishes."

"But I do understand, at least most of it, so why do I have to know how the verbs are put together, that sort of thing?"

"Because the French sentence structure is not necessarily the same as English and to express it correctly, you must also understand how the French speak."

Gemma was not convinced and told her mother so, in no uncertain terms.

"Gemma I really do think you should afford M. Letang the courtesy of allowing him to teach you the way he wishes. And don't forget, it isn't only the singing which is involved. Supposing you got the opportunity to sing at, let's say, the wonderful Paris Opera House, you would need to converse with people setting up your contract, with officials there and with other members of the presentation. Then there are menus, just think how many menus today are in French. You surely don't want to be made to look an idiot, because you don't understand what's on offer?"

No, one thing Gemma never wanted, was to be made to look an idiot. So she listened carefully to M. Letang, forgave him for not commenting on the pretty dress or blouse she happened to be wearing, and started to make progress.

With her Italian tutor Carlotta, Gemma was from the start on good terms. A year before she had left school, Miss Burns had suggested that Gemma took some extra tuition in Latin. That had proved invaluable, underscoring the root forms of so many different words and enabling her to race ahead with her study of Italian. Whilst Carlotta was herself a retired teacher of Italian, she introduced Gemma to members of her own family, insisting that Gemma spoke only Italian in their presence.

Carlotta was bubbly and extrovert with blue-black hair and skin which at times appeared almost translucent, but her figure was certainly not that of an Italian lady in her middle years, being amazingly svelte-like. One evening, as Gemma watched Carlotta and her daughter Maria, happily tucking into huge platefuls of spaghetti, she asked with her usual outspoken approach, "How on earth do you two manage to remain so slim, when you eat all the wrong things?" Whilst her Italian phrasing left much to be desired, the whole family quickly got the message and there was a great deal of laughter and good humoured discussion. In a few short weeks, Gemma and Maria were able to chatter away discussing make up, TV, and anything and everything that was in the news.

Describing her coaching as her membership of the League of Nations, Gemma encouraged Susan to dredge up from the past some of her own foreign language skills, so that they might converse together. Delighted that Gemma seemed to have settled down and was at last prepared to accept that her tutors knew best, Susan refreshed her own, by now rusty, knowledge of French, Italian and German. Gemma was in her element, for not only was she making headway on the language front, but she was now her mother's superior when they conversed, and repeatedly able to correct her on phrasing and pronunciation. *It's still there,* Susan thought, *she still wants always to be on top and in control, even with me. What have I done? What have I produced? What should I do about it?*

Gemma knew that an unexpected by-product of her language tuition had been the fact that all her tutors had much to tell her about their native country and, in some cases, the last war. Lessons at school about the latter, had left her relatively unaffected by that period of history and all its implications, but her acquaintance with her German tutor and his family quickly altered that.

She decided on first meeting them, that Rudi and Margaret Derix were an oddly matched couple. Rudi was the child of an Austrian Jew, Wilhelm, who had managed to leave the developing holocaust of Europe with his fiancée, just one week before Hitler had closed the borders of Nazi Germany. Brought up steeped in the Jewish tradition, Rudi had, at the age of twenty-five, married a very English girl, a Christian. They had no children and whilst Rudi was an avid reader, constantly studying some new project, his wife Sandra, seemed to be part of the local upper class set, rode to hounds, and loved to party. *Well, they say opposites attract,* Gemma thought, *and I suppose they seem happy enough, but whatever do they find to talk about?*

Sometimes Rudi would bring his father, Wilhelm, into her lesson and ask him to relate to Gemma some of his experiences. His parents had owned a book shop and he told her matters had come to a head in Germany, when the SS men had set fire to some of the shops in the Jewish ghetto. She was intrigued when Wilhelm said that, as a teenager walking on his way to school, he would sometimes stop and cut a cabbage in a field and eat chunks of it on his journey.

"Were you very poor then?" Gemma asked in her hesitant German.

"Far from it, my dear. We were in fact, quite wealthy. The business had been in our family for several generations and," here a note of sadness crept into his voice, "I knew that one day I would inherit it." Then, smiling, "but we Germans, and in spite of what Hitler said, we did and still do regard ourselves as German, rarely ate much at breakfast. That is why today, I so much enjoy what you call 'the full English'".

Rudi explained to Gemma later, that his mother had died of a broken heart just three years after their arrival in England. She was a Polish Jew and her parents and three brothers had all disappeared in the nightmare of Hitler's Europe. These discussions, the struggle sometimes to understand, then the patient explanations, were a delight to Gemma. Susan had already introduced her to German Lieder and Gemma loved them. Whilst at the moment she felt that church music was going to be her forte, Gemma knew that at eighteen, there was still much ground to be covered and it was essential she keep her options open.

The news about next summer's holiday in Venice had at first delighted her and then filled her with horror. Auriol had declined the invitation saying that she was staying in Oxford with Colin during the break, as they had decided to enter the Edinburgh Festival and had a great deal of writing to do. Leo had already accepted and then, to Gemma's dismay, Susan asked Simon if Mark could be invited in Auriol's place. Learning that her mother and Mark were once again an item had been a bitter blow to Gemma. Mark had finally convinced Susan that he had really not surveyed that precious land of hers and someone had been mischief-making in even suggesting it. Now, not only was her pet aversion Pretty Boy Leo going to be present, but also dear Mark.

The holiday had suddenly taken on a totally different and unpleasant aspect. On the other hand . . . both her pet hates were to be closeted under one roof for two whole weeks, perhaps . . . ? Who knows? There would after all be no shortage of lovely canals! The Voices chuckled and Gemma smiled.

Their arrival in Venice was not auspicious. A slate-coloured canopy shrouded the city and the grey waters of the Lagoon slapped thirstily against the steps of the Piazza. Susan, who had been to Venice before, assured the other three, "It will be gorgeous tomorrow, just wait."

Their spirits were lifted on arrival at the apartment which was to be theirs for two weeks. Simon's friend, Signora Sofia was waiting to greet them and show them round.

Set behind the tourist area of the city were many private buildings, enclosed behind high walls which hid from view the delights behind. Sofia's house was no exception. Once through the covered entrance, they were confronted with a riot of flowering shrubs and the pleasant sound of fountains. Inside, they found a large salon with windows along one side, overlooking the rear garden and pool. The latter had been cleverly created to blend in with the other ancient stonework. Here and there were pieces of statuary and the pool itself, whilst not huge, was certainly adequate for the needs of their small group.

The four bedrooms, the salon and dining room were all beautifully furnished and the kitchen had been modernised, so that as Gemma remarked, it was almost 'state of the art'. They were all in agreement that this was a very lovely place in which to relax and enjoy some sightseeing.

The next day, as Susan had forecast, was brilliant, with the sun bathing Venice in its own peculiar golden light. Together, they watched the gondolieri plying their trade and promised themselves a ride later in the week. They drank a very expensive cup of coffee in St. Mark's Square and laughed when, on receiving the bill, Mark said he thought he'd just bought one of the gondolas. Splitting up, they visited the palaces and churches until exhausted, then returned to their flat and enjoyed a leisurely swim before going out to eat. Here, Sofia proved very helpful, in recommending that for much of the time they go to cafes and bistros where the locals ate, and 'save your money for other treats'.

Four days passed in this leisurely way, then one morning Susan announced that she and Mark were going to take the boat across to the island of Murano and asked if the others would like to come, too.

"I'd rather just poodle around St. Mark's Square again if you don't mind, I feel there's so much more that I didn't really see." All this was Leo's double speak for '*I would really rather not be in a water taxi, or any other moving vehicle, with sister Gemma, if that can possibly be avoided.*'

"Leo, darling, please do exactly what you wish, that's what holidays are all about."

"What about you Gemma?" Mark sounded concerned that she might be the odd one out.

"Well, if you don't mind, I thought I'd have a totally idle day lounging by the pool. I've got some language lessons to look at, but I'm not sure yet whether I'll have the energy for those."

In fact, Gemma had discovered that her Italian could now be put to very good use. She had seen in their walks around the city, a poster outside the Londra Palace Hotel announcing that, in addition to the Pharmaceutical Convention which was due to be held there in two days′ time, there would be a display of items representing Venetian history. Items on show would reflect the city's history which was steeped in intrigue, tragedy and alchemy. It was the latter word which caught her eye. Alchemy conjured up pictures of poison and witchcraft, it could well be worth a visit.

Gemma was not disappointed. There was a whole section devoted to the Borgias, another to the very short life-span of so many Roman rulers and how this was probably achieved and, finally, a whole section on poisons. Here, the lecturer explained the workings of a small gilt button, about half an inch in diameter.

"If sufficient pressure is put on the outer rim, the centre opens, you can just see the mark where that happens. Then, a needle-like point appears from the recessed well inside. Ancient records show that poison would be housed in the tiny enclosure, a trace of which, if introduced into the blood stream, would kill in seconds. The nature of the poison has never been determined and because of that no antidote has been found. What the records do tell us, is that no-one has ever survived. Any questions?"

"But after all these years, surely it can't still be functional and the poison will have lost its potency?" One young man was clearly unimpressed.

The lecturer smiled, "We know that no poison has been put into the button for years, but there's probably enough in a crystalline form both on, and around the needle to prove lethal. It's never been put to the test however, if you Sir . . . ?"

There was a great deal of laughter and the group listening moved on to the next exhibit. Gemma waited until the loudspeaker announcing that Convention members should assemble for coffee attracted everyone's attention, and in that moment she acted. Whilst Gemma was in the Ladies Cloakroom carefully, so carefully, swathing the button in layer after layer of tissue, everyone searched for it. Assuming it had rolled off the table, the edges of carpets were raised with caution, vacuum cleaners were brought in and emptied tentatively, until it was finally decided that the search should be abandoned. As the lecturer said, "The poison was probably no longer active and the button could well have been kicked several times and is now lying somewhere at the bottom of the Lagoon."

The button was not in the Lagoon. It was in fact safely stored in a small jewellery box, which Gemma had bought and with it was a pair of rubber gloves purloined from the kitchen. The Voices murmured and chuckled their approval. Now she had to bide her time. Three days later, that time arrived. It was very hot and the acid-yellow sunlight so strong that Susan said she must get into the shade. Hearing Mark and Leo announce that as soon as their lunch had settled, they were going to swim, it being the only way to keep cool, she admonished them, "I'll probably have a siesta, so don't make a lot of noise in the pool."

Gemma said she too, would have to stay in the shade and had decided to read on the balcony outside her room, which was covered by an awning and pleasantly cool. She also added, laughingly, "No noise in the pool please, I might just have a siesta myself."

Seated on her balcony, Gemma had a clear overview of the pool and watched as Mark and Leo swam and dived and enjoyed the water. Then Mark climbed out, dripping and said "That's me done, a quick shower and forty winks and then I'll be ready for another delicious Italian meal, just as the sun goes down. Bye . . ."

He was gone. Gemma waited on the landing, listening for the shower to be switched off and keeping well out of sight, as he came up the stairs. Then she moved. Gloves on and holding the tiny box, she made her way to the cloakroom and shower area behind the pool. There were Leo's clothes and his shoes. Carefully, she extracted the button and placed it inside the right shoe, ensuring it was out of sight. There, it was done. Removing the gloves and screwing them up into a ball in the palm of her hand Gemma started to climb the stairs and it was there she met Mark.

"Forgotten my shoes," he said with a rueful smile. In that moment she knew what she had done. Remembered, how often Leo padded around bare-footed. The shoe into which she had placed the poisoned button was Mark's! Turning, she took two steps down, then stopped . . . How to stop Mark from putting the shoes on and explain why?

If Leo heard anything suspicious and she was in the vicinity, he would certainly suspect her involvement but . . . if all went according to plan, the removal of Mark could also work in her favour. In the turn of the stairs, she waited . . .

Hearing the crump as his body hit the floor, Gemma looked quickly across to see if Leo had been alerted by it. No, he seemed to be having a breather, at the far end. With a quick movement she was in the cloakroom. Mark lay on the floor, showing no sign of life. In a flash she removed his shoes. Yes, the button was in the sole of his foot, with the point at its centre clearly embedded and holding it in place. Using the ball of rubber gloves as a shield, she pulled it away, snatched a towel from the rack and with that over her hand and arm, once again made her way up the stairs. Within seconds the button was replaced in its box, wrapped in a handkerchief and pushed to the bottom of one of her drawers. Time enough to dispose of that later. Now she must be ready.

Slipping into a cotton wrap Gemma lay on her bed. Perhaps it hadn't gone *quite* according to plan. On the other hand, with a bit of luck, one of her pet hates would have been removed from the frame, *if* the poison had really done its work. There had been no time to see if Mark was dead, but no doubt all would be revealed in due course. Meanwhile, she must appear to be totally shocked and totally innocent. She closed her eyes and waited.

Leo's shout of alarm from below was followed by the sound of Susan's footsteps on the stairs. Then came a banging on Gemma's door and it was thrown open, Leo's voice urging, "Gemma, come quickly, Mark's collapsed." Slowly she sat up, as if trying to rouse herself from sleep.

"What do you mean, collapsed? Has he fainted?"

"No, no, it's worse than that, we don't know what it is, come and see."

Mark wasn't dead. Her mother was trying to raise his head, at the same time shouting to Sofia's maid to phone for the water ambulance. Leo helped in turning Mark onto his side, in what he assured Susan was 'the recovery position' and oxygen was administered as soon as the paramedics arrived, but after ten minutes, they shook their heads and said "Hospital", clearly not holding out much hope for vital signs. It was decided that Leo and Gemma should follow the ambulance in a water taxi. Implicit in this decision was the unspoken awareness, that should the worst happen, Susan already shocked and traumatised, would need to be escorted back to the villa. Mark's death was pronounced just minutes after their arrival at the hospital.

The children, stunned and silent, and Susan, apparently unable to comprehend what had happened, followed the instructions of the policeman who travelled back to the villa with them. Next on the scene was Sofia, with her doctor close behind her. He, accepting no opposition, insisted that Susan take the sleeping pill he prescribed and retire.

Sofia was now in charge, relaying messages to and from the police and the hospital and, two weeks later, escorting them to the airport from which the three of them and Mark's body were to be flown home. About this Susan had been adamant. Suggestions of cremation in Venice were dismissed out of hand.

"Mark held a very important role in Chichester for some years, and he cannot be cremated in a foreign country. It's right and proper that he has a full-scale funeral and is buried with a certain amount of pomp and ceremony and I'm going to see that it happens," and choking back her tears, "he also has many friends there, who will want to say their own farewells."

The Post Mortem had revealed only a small puncture, rather like a pin prick on the sole of his right foot. Accepting the possibility of this being caused by some obscure but deadly insect, the blood was tested and retested, revealing nothing untoward. In every other respect, Mark Fleming appeared to have been a man of relatively good health for his age. There were no sinister circumstances, no suggestion of discord between himself and the other three members in the apartment, all of whom could account in detail for their movements that afternoon. The Coroner decided that the only verdict could be one of Misadventure.

Sinking into the plane's seat, Gemma thought back over the events of the past days.

Even if it was a different scenario from the one planned, it's still quite a satisfying result. That very useful little button really is now at the bottom of the Lagoon. Unfortunately, that still leaves just one, very hard to get rid of, thorn in my flesh . . . Leo.

Leaning forward across her mother, Gemma flashed the young man in question, a brilliant smile.

Mark's funeral met fully Susan's requirement for pomp and ceremony. He had been an affable and efficient Councillor and his term, as Chairman of the Council, was remembered with both affection and admiration. Condolences were extended to Susan by many of his fellow Council and business associates and, to her surprise, by Gemma's former headteacher, Mrs. Chapman.

"I did want to find out from you Mrs. Hatton, how Gemma is doing in her new venture?"

"She seems to be progressing well. I've been rather surprised at how quickly she has become quite fluent in all three of the languages she's studying."

"I can assure you Mrs. Hatton, I would have expected nothing less, nor would the members of my staff. You see we always had her earmarked as an extremely intelligent girl. Her ability to pick up new theories never ceased to amaze us. I think she is one of the few girls we have had through the system, who would have scored very highly on the Mensa register. I wish now, that we had had her tested. I think the results would have been startling. Gemma was not interested in sport, but academically, she was very quick at assessing situations and her attention to detail was second to none."

Once again, the confirmation that Gemma was outstandingly intelligent. Susan tried to register a surprise she didn't feel, "I knew she always did well in her studies, but I don't think I was quite aware that you all thought so highly of her . . ."

"Then we were at fault and I apologise. It sometimes happens, with exceptionally bright pupils, that they never really find their niche during schooldays and I think Gemma comes into that category. I feel now, that through her music and the acquisition of different languages, she may at last be reaching her true potential. I think she will go far in her new career and I wish her every success."

Susan murmured her thanks and moved on to the next person wishing to sympathise with her. And with that, Mrs. Chapman was gone.

Later Susan found the headteacher's words coming back to her. Yes, Gemma had always done well at school, but how had she, her mother, not been aware that she was outstandingly clever. *Too busy looking out for other things,* she admonished herself. *Now the girl was romping through three different languages like there was no tomorrow, and talking about learning Spanish and Russian. Five years on, and puberty dealt with, Gemma's voice was greatly improved, rounded in tone and with a rich mellow quality to the lower notes. And yet . . . ?*

Why do I always come back to a query, when I'm thinking about Gemma. I try not to think the unthinkable, but she was in the house when Mark died. Yes, she said she was asleep and Leo said he had to rouse her, but why, oh why, does Gemma always seem to be somewhere in the vicinity, when something seriously unpleasant happens? And, if she had a hand in it, how and why? As to the why, yes she probably resented Mark, just as she's always been jealous of her younger brother, but we're not talking about child's play here, we're talking about murder. Now, her headmistress is telling me, as Giles believed, that Gemma has an outstandingly brilliant mind. I know the medics make some connection between genius and madness, which in its most common form is schizophrenia. Certainly my mother was clever, in a cunning, crafty, devious way. Oh God, I think I'll go mad worrying about all this, I might have discussed it with Mark, bless him, he was always a good shoulder to cry on, now even he, is removed from my orbit. I miss him so much.

To Susan's amazement Mark had remembered her in his will. Leaving her his very pleasant town house in Chichester, he had said,

I think Grafton House will soon be too large to maintain. Neither of your brothers-in-law are there often enough to take advantage of it. When that happens, you will need somewhere to lay your head. I know you love Chichester and I was hopeful that one day we would live there together, but if you are reading this, then it is not to be. When your land is sold you will be quite a rich lady. I'm glad about that, I feel you still have much untapped energy to offer, what about a Council post? Finally, just for the record, I did not set foot on your land, someone making trouble I think, perhaps one day you'll find out who that was. Think of me often and enjoy my lovely home.

You have been my special lady for some time. I have loved every minute of it, and I have loved you.
Mark

CHAPTER 16

It was not until Leo's third year at school, that he became aware, not only of his own separateness with regard to the other boys, but of the possible reasons for it. Even James, with whom he had been friends since the beginning, seemed so often not to be on the same wave length as himself. James loved contact sports, which Leo hated, enjoyed tinkering about with all things mechanical, as opposed to Leo's interest in flora and fauna and the creative arts.

During one of the English Literature lessons, the word 'homosexual' occurred in the text and immediately titters and mutterings rippled around the classroom. Mr. Stock put down his book and surveyed the boys over the rims of his spectacles.

"As you obviously find this word amusing, can we assume that you all know exactly what it means? Hands up and tell me please." For a moment, there was a stunned silence, then a tentative hand was raised.

"Dorley, be so good as to tell the rest of the class, please."

The boy flushing scarlet hesitated, then "It's when two men . . ."

"Yes, Dorley, when two men what?"

The boy searched for the word, "When they . . . copulate."

"Well done, obviously the biology lessons have rubbed off, on at least one of our number."

Another hand went up.

"Please sir?"

"Yes, Grant?"

Another scarlet face. "It's just that, we've been told what happens during intercourse between a man and a woman, but a woman has, well the birth canal . . . the . . ."

"Yes, the vagina. Good, continue."

"It's just that men don't have that, so how can they . . . ?"

"Conjoin. A good point, anyone any ideas?"

"Sir, do they use the anal passages?" Grimaces all round and shuffling of feet.

"Exactly Woodruffe, that is what happens."

"But sir . . . ?" Another voice.

"Yes Simpson?"

"Surely the birth canal is quite wide, but the anus . . . how can it be possible?"

"The anus will stretch on occasions and this can be facilitated by lubrication."

Smothered groans and exclamations of disgust around the classroom.

Mr. Stock picked up his book, "Right boys, you now know the basics of what occurs. The next time we come across the situation during our reading, I want you to be able to discuss it sensibly. Throughout history, there have been periods when this behaviour has been considered acceptable, as it is by many today, at other times it has been ruled illegal. Down the years, aristocrats have often been bisexual, in other words, kings have had queens to produce heirs to the throne, whilst at the same time not only having mistresses, but also male lovers. In religious communities where priests are required to be celibate . . . which means?"

"They mustn't marry, sir."

"Good, Dorley."

"Where celibacy is required, other relationships have sometimes developed. It is most rife, as you might expect, in single sex communities . . ." he paused, looking at them, over his spectacles, "such as this. And indeed, also, amongst the female of the species, but more of that on another occasion. Just remember, that poetry and prose will often refer to such liaisons and it would be difficult to appreciate a whole raft of English Literature and indeed any literature, without being aware of that. In future, I will expect you to deal with such references, in a reasoned and mature way."

Suddenly a number of rather odd occurrences started to make sense to Leo. The childish endearments to which he had been exposed at home, had given way at school to 'handsome young chap', and even rather jocularly, 'the lovely Leo'. Senior boys had smiled at him without apparent reason, asked him to run errands, made excuses for keeping him in their rooms. Nothing untoward had happened, but he had felt there was something unspoken, something which had left him with a feeling of unease.

There was something else. He was conscious of the fact that the combination of his mother's cloying affection, Auriol's bookish detachment and the undoubted hostility of Gemma, had left him highly wary of the female species, and whilst some of his peers boasted of having girl friends and dates, he was not the slightest bit interested.

Not attracted by the rough and tumble of many of the school sports, Leo excelled at tennis, swimming and cricket and loved the male company, which these provided. Now, Mr. Stock had made it obvious, that men could bond together in the same way that men and women did. It didn't have to include that sex business of course, that wasn't necessary and sounded both unpleasant and weird. But men could become really close friends. It made sense. Males thought in the same way, liked the same sort of things, weren't always wittering on about clothes and shopping. If there had been any doubts at all in his mind, they were now dispelled. He would join the Navy and the fact that it was largely a single sex community, as Mr. Stock had put it, would suit him down to the ground.

His mind made up, Leo wasted no time. At every available opportunity, he was at the Cadet Officer's side with offers of help. Mr. Brooke, whilst quite bemused by his persistence, attributed it to the fact that the boy was very anxious to emulate his uncle's success, with the result that at the earliest possible date, just 15 years and 9 months, Leo's application was submitted to the Royal Navy for consideration for entry.

"It won't be activated of course, until you are almost sixteen."

"And then, Sir?"

"Then we hopefully move on to the next stage. You must have five GCEs under your belt of good standard and two of these must be Maths. and English Language. You already have the latter, plus Geography, all taken a year early, that's right, isn't it?"

"Yes, Sir."

"Then we'll put the application in and say you are due to take several others in June. At the same time, we'll submit some of the excellent course marks you've received for those subjects, that should help. If all goes well, you'll be called at the next interview date, which is three weeks after your exams, and just a week after your birthday."

"Where will I have to go for the interview, Sir?"

"HMS Sultan, just outside Portsmouth. There'll be other applicants of course, all anxious to get on the officers' course and into the Royal Naval College at Dartmouth. That's why this interview is very important. You would be there for two and a half days and don't be under any illusions, even when people, probably officers, are just chatting to you as we are doing now, this is in fact, part of your interview, and you will be being assessed on how articulate you are and whether you can easily discuss a whole raft of subjects. Boys who talk about nothing but football, or are single minded to the exclusion of other topics, are definitely marked down."

"It all sounds pretty formidable, Sir."

"It is, but you'll agree that the rewards are immense. You are fortunate that you have in your uncle an excellent role model."

"If I did get in, Sir, what comes next?"

"Well, all new recruits do a broad-based training for about a year, then move on to training for their own particular trade. By then, you'll have been given a choice between warfare, logistics and engineering."

"It definitely won't be the latter Sir. That's not even in the frame. I'm useless at anything mechanical."

Mr. Brooke laughed, "Well you might have to overcome that. It could be quite difficult to be in the Navy, without some knowledge of that. You're OK with IT work I take it?"

"Yes Sir, did very well in my course work in that. It's something I enjoy."

"Good. If you pass everything required of you, you'll be admitted as a Midshipman or Sub Lieutenant, and very soon sent to sea. You're lucky that these days the periods of overseas service have been drastically reduced. It used to be something like two and a half years, now it's less than a year."

"It still sounds as if I'll be away from home a great deal, Sir?"

"Yes you will, Leo, does that worry you?"

"Not at all, Sir", and Leo turned away to hide his smile. The relief was overwhelming. Another four or five years hardly seeing anything of Gemma would suit him very well. He was already five feet seven inches and with luck, he'd soon be a six footer. Just let her try any more of her nonsense and he'd be more than capable of dealing with her. Roll on 'A life on the ocean wave', as far as he was concerned, it couldn't come quickly enough.

There was never any doubt about Leo's acceptance into the Royal Naval College at Dartmouth. Product of a good boarding school, academically well above average, with an impeccable background and, discreetly emphasised, an uncle, who was a Royal Naval Captain, Leo was almost fast-tracked on his journey to the Senior Service. By the time he was eighteen, he was established as a Sub Lieutenant on the destroyer HMS Wayfarer, and had served several weeks at sea. A letter from his Ambassador uncle, Charles, expressing his approval at Leo's progress, reached him whilst on board.

Dear Leo,

Delighted to hear you are now a fully-fledged Naval officer. Well done. Why don't you come and see me when you next have some time free? As you can see, I am still in Athens. A move would have been nice, but as yet it's not on the cards.

Whilst I'm sure you enjoyed a few bevvies with your friends on your 18th, you were at sea and probably deprived of a full-blown celebration. Come and stay here and we'll crack open the champagne!

Rooms are always ready, so twenty four hours' notice would be ample and should you wish to bring a friend with you, that would be fine and provide company for you when I have to be otherwise engaged.

Do give it some thought. My input, as a godfather and uncle, has been pretty limited to date and it would be nice to feel I was putting that right, and getting to know the grown-up Leo.

My love and good wishes. Charles

Several months passed before Charles's invitation could be accepted and, answering Leo's phone call, Charles exclaimed with pleasure.

"Wonderful! We really will crack open that champagne. Now, are you bringing a friend?"

"No. Sorry, Sir, but my close friends wanted to go home to see their families."

"And you didn't?"

"Well, Sir, it's just that Mother's always so busy with her council work, Auriol's at Oxford of course . . ."

"And Gemma?"

"Oh, she's all over the place, performing and so on, never likely to be at home."

"Right, so you're coming alone. Well, I'm sure we can give you a good holiday. I'll see what I can arrange and Leo . . . ?"

"Sir?"

"Not so much of the Sir."

Leo laughed, "Sorry, Uncle Charles. Force of habit."

"I quite understand. Now give me your flight arrival time and I'll send my driver Andreas to meet you."

And so it was arranged and the next part of Leo's jigsaw puzzle began to take shape.

Since Leo's birth and the shock of the discovery that she was no longer the centre of her mother's world, Gemma had been preoccupied with her own image. As a small girl, she started to sit for long periods in front of the mirror in her bedroom, trying to work out if, in some mysterious way she had become very ugly overnight, and as the years passed, Gemma continued the habit of closeting herself away and examining her reflection. Repeatedly, she asked herself, how she was perceived by others. Was her hair too curly, too brown, her nose too snub, her eyebrows too thick?

Now fully grown, the self analysis continued. Perhaps she was too tall, too short, too thin, too fat? The people she met seemed friendly and polite enough, but she had no close friends, no one in whom she could confide. She smiled wryly, not that she would ever want to bare her soul to anyone. How could anyone else possibly understand her ongoing feelings of rejection? How could they understand how necessary it had been for her to do what she had done?

She knew all about the church's teaching of course, but all that 'Thou shalt not kill' stuff was directed at ancient people with swords and axes, and if God wanted to lay down some rules and regulations, then he should have added that there were always some extenuating circumstances, which required drastic action.

Gemma knew she should feel happy. Her career was going well, with as many requests to sing at private functions as she could handle and an increasing portfolio of regular short term contracts, one of which was a six week period as soloist with the Bournemouth Sinfonietta, touring the region. An invitation to play the lead in an amateur production of 'Carousel' was turned down on her agent, Robert Craven's suggestion.

Robert was in his fifties, but anxious to be taken for thirty, and on this occasion, was amazed at Gemma's ready acceptance of his advice. To date, he had found her feisty and, as he frequently said to his male partner, "She's too clever by half, thinks she knows everything, about everything." In this instance, listening to the reasons for refusing the offer, Gemma had known him to be right.

"You have no experience in this genre and in addition to the singing, there would certainly be a great deal of acting, and some dance routines. However low key these might seem to you, if you want to go down that road, then you must have some tuition and a lot more practice, before you consider accepting something of this nature. A choreographer would expect you, as a professional, to understand the names of the steps he or she, wants you to do and to pick up on the sequences very quickly. You don't want to appear inexperienced and foolish in front of an amateur cast, who will be expecting great things of you, as a professional."

The last comment persuaded her. Gemma's self-image was far too precious to her to take any such risk, and her first port of call, after her conversation with Robert Craven, was at a dance school, where she registered for a series of private lessons in tap and modern dance. Within several weeks, she knew the names of a whole raft of different steps and routines and was tolerably proficient in both genres. The opportunity to play in Carousel might have passed, but should others occur, Gemma would be ready.

Gemma knew there was still something wrong with her life, but even whilst she was considering this, Susan's phone call from Charles, saying that he and Simon were on their way to visit them, came as quite a shock.

"What on earth is going on?" Susan exclaimed. "They only seem to manage to appear together when something really serious is afoot and latterly, that's usually been a funeral!"

"Perhaps one of them is going to get married and they want us to be the first to know." Gemma looked thoughtful.

"Married? Those two? I doubt it," Susan laughed. "They both live the life of Riley as far as I can see, and love it. I suppose Simon might have been re-routed to the Admiralty or something like that, and could commute and spend more time at Grafton . . ." then, more brusquely, "No, it can't be that, he's much too young to be reduced to pen-pushing."

The reasons for the visit were made apparent immediately and showed that Mark had been quite correct in thinking the uncles might soon wish to off-load Grafton House.

"I think, learning of your bequest from Mark Fleming, has focused our own feelings about our current situation." This, from Charles. "Grafton is such a large property, expensive to maintain and realistically, we've decided we can't either of us imagine a time when we would be likely to take up permanent residence here. We feel the time has come to sell it." Anxious that Susan should be aware that they had given it a great deal of thought, Simon added, "There would have been no question of our doing so if we hadn't been sure there was now ample provision for you and your family. I suppose the next question ought to be, do you like the house Mark has left you and do you think you could be happy there?"

Susan smiled, "I absolutely love it. I've always liked Chichester, it's a city that isn't in the least overwhelming, not daunting in any way. I know I'll be comfortable there. I've been somewhat on the horns of a dilemma for a few weeks, knowing Mark's wishes and wondering if I should let the house, until such a time as either I, or the children were ready to occupy it. And I confess, thinking how soon it would be polite for me to say to you, that I would like to move there."

"So," Charles laughed, "dilemma solved. We're all agreed, and you may be quite sure we'll soon be descending on you for hospitality, in fact you'll probably be sick of the sight of us in no time at all."

"Never!" Susan protested.

"That settled can we now get down to specifics – dates, furniture etc., that sort of thing?"

"Yes, Sir. At once, Captain." Charles grinned, as he saluted Simon.

Watching Susan bustle about making coffee, he reflected on what seemed to be a personality change in her. He recalled meeting Mark on that fateful day of Giles's death and having been impressed by his easy charm. He had sensed later, from telephone calls and letters from Susan that this had been for both of them, a serious and committed relationship. Losing him must have been for her, a devastating blow. Now he sensed that the previously sharp tongued and rather hyper-critical Susan, was no more. In her place was a mellower, more satisfied lady. One who no longer rushed into situations with all guns blazing, could it be that, having lost two men very close to her, she now realised life was too short, to be always on the defensive or the attack?

But, underlying that satisfaction, there was something else, something he couldn't quite identify. He dismissed financial problems as a possibility. She was now quite a wealthy lady, owned a substantial property in Chichester and the educational futures of her children were all well provided for. Clearly, she found her LAMDA work fulfilling. Perhaps it was the loss of Giles and Mark which had left her with a lack of stability, the feeling that at any moment things might change. Or perhaps, he was just imagining things.

Details of the move were speedily determined, the three of them each selecting personal items and Simon and Charles arranging to store their own pieces, until such a time as needed. Moving into a fully furnished and, as she readily acknowledged, beautifully equipped home, Susan's needs were reduced to those items which held for herself and the children sentimental value. The land bequeathed to Susan by her father-in-law was sold for a more than satisfactory price, and Susan and Gemma took up residence in the Chichester house, which had been Mark's pride and joy. Susan was now a very wealthy woman, reflected in her new stylish appearance and an increasing confidence in her own ability.

Gemma reluctantly admitted to herself that Mark had been quite a shrewd cookie. His suggestion that Susan would make an effective councillor had certainly sown seed and very soon, her mother had given up her musical career and become a well-established and highly regarded member of the City Council. Gemma now found something else to be unhappy about. Council work had taken over Susan's life and her involvement in it occupied about 80% of her time, something unequalled by even Mark's part in her life.

Clearly, Susan thrived on the challenges presented, the usage of her administrative skills, the speechmaking. She was now a free agent and able to afford to have regular help in cleaning the house. Linen was sent to the laundry and someone regularly arrived to cut the grass and tend the garden. Gemma spent many hours alone and somehow even her musical successes could not compensate for the fact that the person she most cared about seemed once again to be always pre-occupied, poised for flight between meetings, or ploughing through the volume of paperwork on her desk.

Alone on one such occasion, Gemma looked around her. Mark's home was lovely, no doubt about that. And her mother, thank goodness, had stopped her weeping and wailing and at last, seemed content. Which was just as it should be, considering she'd come out of the whole business so well. Who could have imagined, when they were living in that dreary Vicarage, not so very long ago, that since then they would have lived in not one, but two gorgeous houses. And it was of course, all thanks to her, Gemma.

What a shame it was that she couldn't take the credit for it all and shout from the rooftops and, in particular, to her mother, "I did it. I got you here." It was at times like this, when she felt Mark's presence everywhere. The framed photograph, which had stared back at her accusingly, was gone. Its 'accidental' breakage, which had left her mother regarding her suspiciously for several days, might have left a space on the wall, but always she felt he was still there, watching. Her arch enemy Leo was of course out of reach, and likely to be so for some time. She pulled a face.

Perhaps his warship or whatever he was on would become involved in some unpleasant international incident and Leo would come to a nasty end. Gemma smiled; There was no harm in wishful thinking . . . *A regular boy friend might help*, she thought ruefully. *Now in her twenties, and no-one permanently in the picture. Why was that? They'd seemed keen enough for several weeks and then just melted away. And she'd felt sure the sex had been O.K.* She laughed aloud. *She didn't have B.O. She'd asked her mother to confirm that. Perhaps she'd been a bit over-exuberant. Men might not like that. Something to do with that macho thing, about always wanting to instigate, and be in control. Hard luck chaps! There's one here who is never going to lose control. Dream on, the lot of you.*

The Speed Dating session she'd secretly attended, had proved a disaster. Men twice her age mostly, and the few younger ones, stinking of cigarette smoke or beer. And even worse, the morons with whom it was impossible to carry on a conversation. Fancy having to spend an evening with that!

No, none of that was for her, because, if she was perfectly honest with herself, which she always tried to be, whilst loving being centre stage during singing engagements, at other times she preferred her own company. After all, it was patently obvious that she was always a jump ahead of the people who crossed her path. Men were often such nerds and so many of the girls and the women she met either bimbos obsessed with shoes and bling, or older ones anxious to talk about dribbling infants and how well they were proceeding with their bodily functions. Yuk!

There were throaty chuckles from the Voices, as grimacing, she snuggled down into the armchair and turned to her latest purchase, a murder thriller by Moira Venables, entitled "Attention to Detail."

Colin's hopes for a shared future, in which he and Auriol lived and worked together, writing material for TV and films, were shattered on hearing Auriol's discussions with Diane over the phone. Quite clearly, he did not feature in her plans for the future. His own news from Yorkshire was bleak, his sister's cancer was spreading and it was clear that he was needed at home, to give support both financially and emotionally. Once their exams were over, he must be ready to leave for home as soon as possible.

Auriol tried to make it easier, "Colin darling, of course I'll try to come and see you as and when it's possible, and you must come back here."

They both went through the motions, uttering empty words, knowing that it was over. He, the more devastated, having expected so much, Auriol always aware that theirs was a temporary relationship, born of convenience. Her subsequent viva voce for a First merely underscored the gulf between them, as he accepted his own Second Class Degree and said his goodbyes.

Diane had confirmed her intention of returning to her studies at the university and arrived in time to meet Susan, who was attending the Degree ceremony. The girls then enrolled for their respective courses and stayed on for ten days to relax and, as they laughingly said, 'Wander down memory lane'. Diane's acerbic comment that there was one lane she had no wish to traverse, reduced them both to giggles and Auriol felt that Diane was at last ready to put the whole unhappy business of Paul and his 'babies for Jesus' behind her.

Now having 'wheels', courtesy of her grandfather's bequest, Auriol waited until she had seen Diane safely en route for home and set out to visit, for the first time, her mother's new home, thinking as she left behind the 'dreaming spires' how lovely it would be to return to Oxford without any encumbrances. An invitation to stay with Diane's family and enjoy the Cotswolds and then join them for two weeks in Madeira, added to a great deal of pleasurable anticipation.

Auriol had seen little of her mother since the death of Mark, and the subsequent move, from Grafton House to Chichester. She had noted Susan's smart appearance at the Degree ceremony, but it had been a day of great excitement and celebration with little time for lengthy, personal discussion. Now, without those distractions, she found Susan's new persona amazing. Clearly, just returned from a meeting, on hearing the car arrive, she rushed out to meet Auriol, looking every inch the successful business woman. The smart terracotta suit, perfect with her brown hair, now sleekly styled with highlights of blonde.

"Darling, welcome to your new home . . . good journey?"

"Absolutely fine. Mummy, you look amazing."

"And you look better than when I last saw you."

"Oh that was the aftermath of the exams and that horrendous viva voce, I felt exhausted."

"And looked it, but never mind, it's behind you and results like that will probably open a great many doors in the future. Come along, let's get inside and make ourselves comfortable." Together they carried in Auriol's cases and assorted bags and at last, Auriol sank thankfully into one of the large comfortable armchairs.

"Mummy, it's beautiful. What a lovely room!" Auriol drank in the restful colours of palest green and ivory.

"It is beautiful. I know I'm very lucky, not only because of Mark's generosity, but because he had such excellent taste. Let's face it, I could have been left a monstrosity with hideous furniture and colours I hated."

"Well, I haven't yet seen the rest of it, but to me it looks exquisite and so peaceful."

"Yes, and that's amazing, because we're so close to the heart of the city and to a road."

"But this is an old house and they have very thick walls, as to the road, it's very much a subsidiary and doesn't appear to carry much traffic." Auriol looked searchingly at her mother, "You look wonderful, not working too hard?"

"Good heavens no, I love it. The cut and thrust of the Council chamber is right up my street, the admin., all of it, suits me very well indeed. I've just been appointed Chair of the Planning Committee and that's the biggest sub-committee there is, so it's quite a challenge."

"Well, congratulations to you too. Where's Gemma?"

Susan hesitated. Why was it that whenever Gemma's name was mentioned anywhere, anytime, it immediately put a constraint on the conversation?

"Oh, she's rehearsing for a lieder concert at St. Mark's . . . Said to expect her about seven, so if it's OK with you we'll have dinner then."

"That's fine, and what about Leo, what's he up to now?"

"He's probably on his way to Athens. Charles invited him there ages ago and it's only now that he was entitled to some leave and asked if I would mind if he went there for a holiday, instead of coming here. Your uncles have been so good to us all in so many ways that I felt I must say yes. I do think that perhaps sometimes, Charles misses the contact with his family, particularly now that both his parents are gone."

"And what about you? Any boy friends in the offing?"

"Boy friends? For heaven's sake, Auriol, I'm a bit passé for that."

"Mummy, the way you look today, I would think they'd be beating a path to your door." Then deciding she had said quite enough on that subject, Auriol jumped up and headed towards what she thought might be the kitchen, turning at the door and grinning at her mother, "Right, let's change the subject. A cup of tea?"

CHAPTER 17

Leo's first evening in Athens was, as Charles had promised, one of celebration. Dinner was set for the two of them, in Charles's small private dining room. French doors opened out onto one of the numerous patio and garden areas and Leo was never to forget the heady perfume of the flowers on his introduction to Greece.

As befitted the Ambassador's status, even dining 'en famille' was special.

In whichever direction Leo looked the view was a collage of carefully selected objects, all pleasing to the eye. Before they sat down, there was champagne first of all, on the patio, where Charles drank a toast to his nephew's new status in the Royal Navy. Then, relays of delicious food were served at the exquisitely appointed table by a smiling maidservant.

Later, over coffee Charles said, "I have an engagement tomorrow evening, so if you agree, I'm going to suggest that Andreas takes you into the city. He has a son, Stavros, about your age and he'll drop you at a taverna where Stavros and his friends usually meet."

"Won't there be a language problem? My Greek isn't very good!"

"Good heavens no, everyone speaks English nowadays. There's just one thing you should be aware of . . ." Charles hesitated.

"What's that?"

"Well, there's still one faction here that doesn't like, or welcome the Brits."

"Why?"

"Oh, it's really ancient history now, dates back to the 1950's when we . . . let's just say, there was a lot of trouble then and people were killed. The Greek Cypriots even formed an underground movement EOKA – have you heard of it?"

"No, never . . . what was their problem? I mean . . . what did they do?"

"They were fighting for the union of Cyprus with Greece."

"A terrorist group?"

"In a way, yes, but it's a long time ago and now probably only the generation which was heavily involved, might bear grudges. At that time, they were very anti-British, so you might just, now and again, get the feeling of a slight undercurrent, I certainly do, even here at the Embassy."

Leo grinned, "I wouldn't have thought youngsters would be too much concerned with what happened in the 50's. As you say, it's almost ancient history to them. I guess today they'll be far more concerned with how much red wine they can put away in the course of the evening."

Charles chuckled, "You're right there, and on that subject be careful. Remember this lot are trained to drink from the cradle, which we are not. Their capacity can be formidable."

"Oh, I'll be careful, Sir, sorry . . . Charles. I am improving in that respect, having been trained in a hard school at Dartmouth and now on board."

Charles rose, "I think we should call it a day, you've been travelling and must need some shut eye. Just get up when you're ready. Have breakfast outside in the cool and that's another thing, with your colouring be very careful, the sun here is fierce. Ask one of the staff, they'll always provide you with sunscreen. I'm hoping to be able to join you for a mid-morning coffee and a swim. Then we'll get Andreas to drive us round the city, so that I can point out landmarks and so on, and help you to get your bearings."

"It sounds great and thanks for a lovely evening. I think I might have chosen the wrong career. All this seems somewhat superior to living on board a ship!"

Leaving Charles chuckling, Leo made his way up the impressive Embassy staircase, reflecting on the evening. His uncle had certainly gone through the motions of treating him like an adult, but just how would he have reacted if he'd been told that Leo was not only grown-up, but sexually active, and not in the way his uncle might prefer? Towards the end of his time at Dartmouth, his developing relationship with Grant Somers had seemed innocent enough. They were good friends, who enjoyed and never tired of each other's company, with physical contact never progressing more than a masculine type bear hug. But Leo sensed the change within himself, and knew that in any company, he was now very quickly aware of those who were, as he was, different.

Soon after his arrival on board Wayfarer, he had found that amongst the young lieutenants, Richard Doyle was frequently at his side. His presence, it could be argued was essential in an advisory capacity, but Leo from the start, recognised something more. A brush of hand against hand, their ensuing mutual startled expressions when this occurred, signalled to both of them that it was a matter of time before the next stage. And, when shore leave was available in Gibraltar, Richard's suggestion they share a taxi, so that he could show Leo round the naval base was readily accepted and known for what it was. A few hours later in the depths of a hotel bedroom, Leo recalled how he and his class mates had shuddered at the thought of the male sex act. He himself, had thought then that it sounded abhorrent, but now realised it was not so.

Now, months later, miles away from home, he had some hard thinking to do. Having come to terms with his own sexuality, the problem to be faced was would others be prepared to accept it? Sleep for Leo was that night long in coming.

At the taverna the next evening, Leo was grateful for Charles's warning words. Glances, not so much from the group which included Andreas's son, Stavros, but from others drinking in the bar, ranged from the discreetly wary to, occasionally, downright hostile. The young men he was with were, as Leo had anticipated, more anxious to enjoy their evening drinks than to discuss matters political, but clearly some of the characters in the room had quickly realised when he arrived with Andreas, Charles's driver, that Leo had some connection with the British Embassy.

Now, Leo tried to dismiss the undercurrent of hostility and listened to one of the more dominant members of his own group. Philip, a young man Leo had already sensed to be 'like himself', was quite unperturbed by sidelong glances and quite specific in his invitation, "Meet me at the harbour in the morning, Leo, and we'll go for a sail. There'll be another couple on board, keen sailors like myself. Don't expect anything palatial, my yacht's very basic . . . although it can sleep four at a pinch. Mostly, I just use it to take friends out for the day, around the harbour and beyond. Don't forget the sunscreen, or you'll be cooked to a frazzle by the time we get back. There are hats on board. Oh, and bring swimming gear of course, unless you're into skinny dipping."

Sunshine and a stiff breeze made the next day perfect for sailing and Leo soon spotted Philip on his yacht at one of the jetties. The 'Ariadne' was, as Philip had warned, very basic. About 30 feet long with dark sails, its outstanding feature was the beautiful wood used in its construction, with the woodwork of the deck and cabin, all obviously lovingly cared for. Philip's friends, Gregor and Alexis, were already there unloading supplies of bread and cheese, lager and ouzo. Leo had brought along a large bag of fruit and some honeyed pastries from the Embassy kitchen and, introductions made, Philip detailed each of them off to carry out various chores. In no time at all they were under way, and Leo, himself now quite expert at reading maps and compasses, was interested to see how competent Philip was both in his handling of the yacht and his knowledge of the parameters and depth of the harbour, the tide and the prevailing winds.

"Shouldn't you all be at work?" Leo asked innocently, and then he laughed with them as realisation dawned. It was a Saturday.

They were quick to point out that in any event, Gregor and Alexis, as students, were now on their vacation, whilst always in the market for earning a little on the side. Inevitably, their interest in Leo's uncle and the importance of his status in Greece surfaced.

Gregor said "I've never quite been able to get my head round the fact that an Embassy is regarded as a piece of the country it represents."

Leo laughed, "Me neither. To be honest, the Embassy here might be a part of the United Kingdom, but it doesn't look like any part of the UK with which I'm familiar. I've got some questions of my own, though. What on earth went wrong all those years ago, to cause such bitterness between the Brits and the Greeks?"

"To put it in a nutshell the Brits countenanced the annexing of part of Cyprus, which is, after all, part of Greece, and handed it over to Turkey. We, Greeks, felt the Brits let us down badly. Underground organisations sprung up, you've probably heard of EOKA, and they struggled to reverse the decision. A lot of Greeks were killed and the bitterness has been handed down through the generations, especially where a father died and left a widow with young children. Those children were then indoctrinated with a deep resentment at what had happened."

"And it's still there, that resentment? To be honest, I could feel the vibes from the other side of the bar as soon as they guessed I had some connection with the Embassy." Leo's face registered his astonishment.

"Oh, you'd feel the vibes alright and I wouldn't walk alone in that area on a dark night if I were you."

"Surely they wouldn't be violent . . . to me . . . after all these years?"

"Don't be under any illusions, Leo." This from Gregor, "Those who are the most bitter about this, will not let it go . . . ever. They are constantly seeking out ways in which they can get their own back for what happened."

Alexis now chipped in. "Have you met Jason yet, Leo?"

"No, who's he?"

"Well if, and when, you meet Jason, you'll understand more about this saga. His grandfather was killed during fighting in 1958. His grandmother was one of the women who sent an appeal to the press, the mayors, and local politicians saying that their husbands were not criminals, but honest patriots working for the solution of all the problems which beset their country. Jason's father, Nicolas, became a member of ANE, which EOKA formed to bring younger children under its control, so he was indoctrinated from an early age into the beliefs that the Brits had let our country down. As the eldest of five, Nicolas always felt responsible for the family and he passed on this intense hatred to his eldest, Jason.

"You will meet Jason, eventually", Alexis added, and the three of them laughed.

"What's so funny?" Leo asked.

"It's funny, because you might have seen him already, from a distance." Gregor chuckled.

"What? What are you talking about?"

"Jason, dear Leo, works at your uncle's Embassy."

"But . . . I thought you said he hated the Brits. I don't understand, why on earth would he work *for* them and *with* them, if that's so."

Philip shrugged, "Because, dear friend, he likes to keep his ear to the ground, know what's going on, that sort of thing. Make no mistake about it, he's a very shrewd chap and the hatred is still there, whilst when it suits him, carefully concealed. He studied English at uni., together with political history and well, some of us think all that was part of a structured plan, to get in on the ground floor, to always know what's going on."

"But, surely it's all so much in the past . . ."

"Try telling that to his grandmother Jocasta, she's been wearing black for most of her life and the one aim in her life seems to be getting justice for her dead husband and his friends. Her grandchildren have always been brought up in an atmosphere of seeking retribution." Philip was now deadly serious.

"Have a good look around whilst you're in Cyprus. Yes, there are lots of Brits here now. When they first came, living was cheap here and the climate good, the former no longer applies. They were accepted then because they were helping our economy."

Alexis also anxious to make sure Leo understood the bitter feeling in some quarters, added, "Go to where our borders are with that slice given to Turkey and you'll see just how fortified it is. Don't try to cross that without a visa or you'll never get back. We don't have Turkish Delight, because the name itself annoys us. Here we have Cyprus something or other. There are whole empty deserted villages where the Turks have been driven out."

"But the British didn't do that," Leo protested, "they were never involved in the fighting."

"They countenanced the annexation, handing over our land to the Turks, and for Jason and his family, that is enough to shoulder the blame and consider them always our enemies."

Now Philip, "Just one thing, Leo, if you should meet Jason in the Embassy, it would be better if you didn't acknowledge him in any way. He's a loner and likes to remain that way. I wouldn't want him to think we'd been talking about him."

Pondering on this conversation at a later date, Leo was still puzzled. He wondered about asking Charles for more details about the Cypriot revolt, then decided against it. Instead, he told his uncle about their picnic on the beach, the old, but beautiful condition of Philip's boat and the studies of Gregor and Alexis. Charles, obviously interested, said Leo was to invite any, or all of them to the Embassy for a swim, or a meal, and seemed delighted that he had so quickly made some new, young friends.

Coming down the main staircase five days later, Leo saw a young man leaving Charles's office and crossing the entrance hall to the administration section of the Embassy. He was very handsome, slim and dark and obviously intent on the paperwork he was carrying. *So that's Jason! What a shame to waste a face and body like that on a heavy load of hatred dredged up from the past, whilst his peers are all out enjoying themselves in their beautiful country.*

Because it was beautiful. He and Philip had visited ancient amphitheatres and museums, walked around amazing historical buildings, swum in the warm sea and sailed out to quiet beaches. The latter had once again been Leo's undoing. The relaxation of their bodies in the aftermath of swimming, their closeness on the warm sand and the seclusion, had encouraged them in a coupling, which they both knew was merely one of self-gratification.

It was this same hedonistic approach which caused Leo, on an evening when Charles had an appointment, to invite Philip to have dinner with him. They ate in style and drank deeply of the wine offered, before retiring to Leo's room. It was there in Leo's bed, that Charles found them some two hours later. His appointment having been concluded earlier than expected, he decided to ask Leo how his evening had progressed. Tapping on the door, and finding the two young men in bed together, left Charles, white with shock. He left the room, slamming the door behind him and shouted, "Downstairs the pair of you, in two minutes."

Sheepishly, they arrived in his study. Philip was summarily dismissed,

"The pair of you disgust me. I want *you* out of here now and I don't want to see you again." Then, turning to Leo,

"I'm shocked beyond belief, at you. I know the modern trend is to countenance this sort of thing and what you do in your own time, under your own roof, is entirely your own business, but for people of my generation, this is still unacceptable. And for you to carry out such behaviour in the building for which I am responsible, is unforgivable. You may stay in the Embassy for the period of time we agreed, but no-one else is to be invited here and I think I shall find myself rather too busy to spend time with you, during the next few days. You may go."

Leo, still reeling under the impact of his uncle's displeasure, knew that he had made a serious mistake. Charles and Simon were the two people, he had always felt he could rely on to assist him financially if necessary, and certainly, to help him through any emotional crisis, such as the business with Gemma. Now he had burned his boats. He and Charles would never again be comfortable together, no doubt Simon would be told and eventually his mother, and such family life as he had, would be torn to shreds.

Once he'd calmed down, Leo decided Charles had been very much over the top about what happened, after all, in today's climate, male and female partnerships were considered acceptable. Steeped too much in

Embassy life, I suppose, all that pomp and ceremony associated with Ambassadors, very fuddy-duddy and old hat. What a pain! Back to bed now and another lesson learned. He grinned to himself ruefully. Had it been worth the hassle? Probably not.

Charles Hatton sat at his desk, head bowed, fingers interlaced across his forehead. Had he been too brutal? His words, too harsh? He was still trembling from the shock at what he had seen. But, and this was, he knew, the crux of the matter, had his reaction been normal? Or was it the outcome of his own uncertainties, his carefully concealed feelings of guilt?

He straightened up, placing his hands palms down on the desk and stared into the darkness beyond the uncurtained window. For as long as he could remember, he had tried desperately to bury those feelings, forced himself to entertain females, who were all too willing to share his bed. There had been an occasional temporary satisfaction and a physical sense of relief. And that was all. Denying himself experimentation with other relationships, had not been easy. Many were the young, handsome men, anxious to please the Ambassador, whether by nature, or with a view to promoting their own interests, not always obvious. There was one such on his payroll, right now. A young Greek Adonis, always at hand, smiling, subservient. He, Charles knew, would at the first sign from himself, have been ready and willing to meet any requirements outside his remit, as a clerk.

Over the years, Charles had forced himself to resist all such temptations, had known that the merest suspicion of scandal attached to his ambassadorial status would have put an end to his career. A career, which provided him with a life-style, of which most people could only dream. He had considered taking a wife, a hostess for the many social occasions. Doing so could have provided 'cover' for other activities. But, unless such a partnership, with all that it entailed, was agreed from the start, it would be both cruel and unfair to involve another. There was something else. Much as he enjoyed female company from time to time, the thought of having one living under the same roof, fussing about clothes and furnishings, sharing his space, would he felt, be intolerable.

Before Susan met Mark, he had been aware that she was from time to time, sending him the sort of signal which suggested she would be quite willing to take their relationship to a different level. That certainly had been a non-starter. Fond as he was of Susan, he saw her as unpredictable and certainly not one to take a back seat when he was on official duties.

He sighed deeply. Was it his own shortcomings, regrets, and to some extent, bitterness, which had exploded into anger towards the boys? If that was so, it was done now and couldn't be undone. Hopefully, they would see his anger as natural for someone in his position, and the fact that they had been under his roof, might put the incident, and ensuing outburst into perspective, as far as they were concerned.

Charles stood up. Now he must pick up the pieces. Some of the staff would know of course. The flirtatious Jason, would certainly be aware of it, having it seemed, a sixth sense for everything which happened at the Embassy. It would be advisable to stick to what he had said to the boys. The Greek boy was already on his way home and there was no necessity for him to see Leo in the morning. He would make sure of that, by having his own breakfast served here in his study, claiming pressure of paper-work.

Why was nothing straight forward? He had looked forward to spending these few days with his nephew and now all the pleasure of the visit had been drained away, because of this one incident. There would always now be tension between them, a tension which could have repercussions throughout the family. Life was so difficult. Wearily, Charles Hatton climbed the stairs to bed.

It was just twenty four hours later that Leo met Jason. A note pushed under his bedroom door, suggested that they meet at a taverna on the outskirts of the city and that if they should bump into each other in the Embassy itself, Leo should not attempt to make any contact.

"You know who I am?" Jason asked as they shook hands, then found a quiet table.

"Well yes, I saw you once in the Embassy, and Philip and his friends did explain that they knew you and where you worked."

Jason laughed "And no doubt gave you all the family history about why I am, like I am, etc., etc."

"Well . . ."

"Say no more! You and I are going to be good friends . . . and perhaps more." And looking at the perfect, almost golden, skin of Jason's face and the penetrating blue-green eyes, Leo knew there was no possibility of him denying it

The parting with his godfather was, as expected, strained. Impossible now to restore the camaraderie of those early days in Athens, but equally impossible to curtail the furtherance of his relationship with Jason. Back on board ship, his friendship with Lieutenant Richard Doyle was speedily terminated and a prolific and increasingly ardent correspondence begun with Jason.

When Jason's despatch to the London Foreign Office for a short course on Embassy security coincided with Leo's own shore leave, he quickly called his Uncle Simon. Simon, apparently unaware of the Athens incident, was quite happy to give Leo and an unspecified friend, the use of his London flat for a week. Whilst in Athens, there had merely been time for Leo and Jason to send out signals, indicating to each other that they would like to take the matter further. In London, with no censure and recriminations, they soon became a devoted couple.

Daily, Leo was exposed to the drip feed of the poison, which had Jason in its thrall. At first, Leo questioned how such hatred could have continued down the years, but listening to the difficulties which the women in Jason's family had encountered throughout those years, through the loss of their menfolk, he began to sympathise, gradually becoming indoctrinated. To date, he himself had felt a growing bitterness, always directed towards figures in authority. There had already been one discreet reprimand about his life-style, from a senior Naval officer. Whilst not ultra serious, the warning had rankled. Who were these people to make decisions which had such impact on other people's lives? What right did they have to tell others how to behave or live? Politicians, senior service personnel, all were only too anxious to throw their weight about.

For the first time, he realised that he and Gemma did have something in common, something, which had evolved from those early years. Each, in their turn, had been the centre of attention and, whilst at times, he might had been irritated by his mother's cosseting, he had felt loved and wanted, as Gemma must have been before his arrival. Now, the only time he felt like that was in Jason's company. Suddenly, the whole world seemed to be against young people enjoying life, having fun. His anger, at what he considered to be Charles's old-fashioned attitude to homosexuality, burned the more fiercely when in Jason's company.

"I can't believe, in this day and age, Charles reacted the way he did. Anyone would think we were in the Middle Ages, although come to think of it, there was a much more laissez faire attitude to people enjoying life in their own way, then. I really thought that, in Charles's position, he would have interacted with dozens of people . . ."he hesitated, "like us."

"I know from experience, that he has. The trouble is, Leo, the British hierarchy and, from what I've seen, that of many other countries, function all the time on double standards. What is acceptable when meeting people socially, especially if they are trying to obtain favours, is totally unacceptable at other times, if, and when, the occasions suits them."

Jason had so many stories to relate about the hypocrisy of the British, during the Cypriot crisis and Leo, to date inexperienced in the world of politics, listened and accepted unquestioningly Jason's version of events. He believed that his uncle was now, however belatedly, the political symbol of what had gone so horribly wrong, fifty years ago. Yes, Charles had a wonderful lifestyle, but surely an honourable man would not be prepared to live in such circumstances?

And so it was a very different Leo who eventually went to see his mother at Chichester. This young man was the product of his early years, which had vacillated between overbearing demonstrations of motherly love and frightening, often dangerous incidents, engineered at the hands of his sister. Added to this was now another dimension. Beneath his handsome charming exterior, this Leo had developed a huge reservoir of hatred for those in authority who had in any way attempted to discredit his own lifestyle. One day, he determined, the Do-gooders sitting in judgement on him, and others like himself, would be called to account, and he would be happy to be a part of that. But Leo knew that before that, there was something else he had to do. One day, his ever-present steely resolve must find an outlet to ensure that somehow, somewhere, he would wreak revenge on his sister.

There had been no mention of the Athens affair in Susan's letters and phone calls, and Leo could detect no change in her manner towards him, so assumed that there had been no report from Charles. When Leo's visits home became less frequent, and trips to Greece more regular, Susan, busily steeped in her own world of urban politics, at first accepted his reasons for wishing to spend time with young friends he had made out there, as perfectly plausible.

Soon, her invitations became more pressing, pointing out that he was after all, only based in Portsmouth, which was a relatively short distance from Chichester, and that she and Gemma were longing to see him again. He took the latter part of the statement with a large pinch of salt. If Gemma was anxious to see him again, it probably meant that she had cooked up some other nasty surprise for him. At last, he could stall his mother no longer and arrived one evening, having promised a stay of five days. (Mentally saying to himself, *if I live that long!*) As Auriol had been, he was astonished at his mother's changed image. Even her method of speaking seemed to have undergone a change. The absence of all those cloying 'darling boy' and 'my baby' epithets was a relief, and he began to feel relaxed and comfortable in the new surroundings he was being encouraged to call home. Or he was, until Gemma arrived.

She, too, had changed tremendously from a rather flamboyant teenager to a smart self-confident young woman, who clearly enjoyed her new career. She embraced him warmly and he went through the motions of being equally pleased to see her. It was not until Gemma produced an invitation, which was addressed to both Leo and herself, that he began to feel edgy.

"I can't possibly go and leave Mum on her own, when I've come specifically to see her . . . and you too of course," he added hastily.

Susan said, rather too quickly, Leo thought, "I'm afraid I'm already committed to a reception at the Guildhall, so you two young things go by all means and enjoy yourselves."

"Wear your uniform, please, Leo, it's so smart, and I want to show off my handsome young brother."

"Well, if you both insist. Tomorrow night isn't it, where and what time?" *Why did he always feel suspicious when Gemma was supposedly being pleasant?*

"It's only a short distance from here by car. It's the twenty-first of a friend I met at one of the drama groups, there'll be plenty of people our age there."

"At his home?" Susan asked

"No, at a local restaurant. That place called "Cassie's" on the corner of Piatkus St."

Susan smiled, "Should be OK, I haven't had a meal there, but it looks really nice from the windows."

"And we're asked to arrive about 8:30 p.m. There's a meal and then a disco."

Leo pulled a face. "I'm not much of a one for dancing."

"Then it's high time you were. I'd be grateful if you'd drive, Leo, I know it means watching what you drink, but I'm a relatively new driver and I don't think I'd trust myself, after even one glass of wine." *No,* Leo thought, *and I don't trust you whether drinking or not.* But, politely he answered, that of course, he would be happy to drive his sister.

The evening was pleasant enough and Leo carefully, had only one drink at dinner with which to toast his host, and then agreed to have one other, whilst watching the dancing. When the evening was drawing to a close, it was at Gemma's insistence that he went onto the floor with a young woman she knew. Other guests were far too busily occupied to notice that in Leo's absence, Gemma added a little something to his drink. A few minutes later, she took Leo on one side and said, "I hate to do this to you, but someone has just offered to take me home and I'd love to take him up on it, if you wouldn't mind. Can you find your own way back?"

"Of course. It's no distance. You go and enjoy yourself. I've got a key and I'll see you in the morning."

Leo did see Gemma in the morning . . . from his hospital bed. Three minutes into his journey, he suddenly became so dizzy and faint, that he couldn't see or think clearly, finally passing out at the wheel, striking a central reservation, and bringing the car to a halt on the pavement, inches from a shop frontage. It was a lucky escape, severe whiplash and bruised ribs, a cut on his forehead, but otherwise unscathed. The police were of necessity, involved. Early assumptions that Leo had been drunk, were denied by those who had sat next to him at dinner, and during the dancing. Then the results of his blood test were received and there was clear evidence there that his drink had been spiked, by whom they could not say. Leo of course *could*, but would not.

Did he imagine it, or were his mother's searching looks evidence that she might at last be growing suspicious of Gemma? In any event, the sooner he left Chichester the better. It was clear that Gemma's vendetta was by no means over. She still wanted him out of her life, by any means within her power.

Susan was not only suspicious, she was beginning to feel desperate. Everything which went wrong in their family had Gemma at its root. That could no longer be considered coincidental. She now knew beyond doubt that her younger daughter was sick, but how to get Gemma to admit to it, and more importantly, how to persuade her that she needed treatment to deal with her sickness? Shades of Susan's own mother refusing help from the medics came rushing back, and the subsequent, horrifying result. Leo could have been killed, which is presumably what Gemma had wanted. Susan had never thought she would be in a position to say it, but it was a relief when Leo came out of hospital and reported back to his ship. Perhaps now, she would somehow find a way to sort out the problem, which was becoming more ominous as the years went by.

CHAPTER 18

Whilst seeing the logic behind her decision, Susan was disappointed when Auriol decided to return to Oxford, earlier than tutorials required. Full of enthusiasm for taking her Master's degree, Auriol wanted to get herself established in situ before the new influx of students arrived. What Auriol hadn't said, was that with Susan so often away on Council business and Gemma's frequent absences, she had found the Chichester house rather too quiet after the vibrant, social atmosphere of Oxford.

Diane was on a cruise with her parents, who had had to wait until the tourist trade in the Cotswolds slowed at the end of the summer season, and Auriol was anxious to reorganise the house before her return. They had agreed that following Colin's departure, no third party should be invited to join them. Inevitably, this would have resulted in questions as to why Diane hadn't proceeded with her degree the previous year and this could have proved embarrassing for them all. Financially, the girls could manage and although it would mean extra input from both of them on the cooking and housekeeping front, they decided it would be worth it to have the place to themselves.

Susan had insisted that she wanted to contribute something to help with this.

"I want to chip in with making it more homely, and more feminine, for you both. I thought perhaps new bedspreads and cushions and, probably the thing you need more than anything else, a tumble drier."

This warmer-natured, more understanding Susan had smiled when she announced this. "I don't want you to be constantly taking things to the launderette to dry them off. It's rained every time I've been to Oxford, so I can imagine that that particular part of your survival there was a nightmare."

Now as Auriol excitedly watched the new machine being installed and realised what a difference it would make, she wondered again at the change in her mother. It was as if Susan had shed a carapace of resentment towards the world, and was now happier and more confident than she had ever been. Which, Auriol decided, was quite peculiar, considering that she had lost both her husband and more recently her lover.

On the other hand Susan had, following Giles's death, and with the help of the uncles, managed to pick up the threads of a career and now, similarly, she was actively employed and obviously enjoying life. I suppose we all find ourselves fulfilled in different ways. For some women having children is enough, but in today's climate more and more women need more out of life. *Realistically, the money probably helped too. People say it doesn't bring happiness*, Auriol thought, *but it does cushion you in all sorts of ways, and that provides its own contentment.*

Her mother had been caring and loving towards her throughout her Chichester visit. In fact, in retrospect, she realised that there had been only one instance, when her mother had seemed rattled. That was the evening when Gemma had arrived home late from a recital engagement and said there had been an accident. Immediately Susan was on her feet, asking, "An accident? What sort of accident?"

"One of the soloists fell, backstage. It was about mid-way into the second act. Several of us were making our way to the wings for one of the big numbers, when she stumbled and fell."

"Did you see her fall?"

"Of course I did, Mummy. I was right behind her. The rest of us were all due on stage, so we had to leave her. The show must go on, that sort of thing. Obviously the paramedics were called and she was carted off to hospital. Later, we heard her leg was broken."

"Was she one of the lead singers?" Susan hardly dared to ask.

"Oh yes, I had to cover and do an extra number. That wasn't a problem. I always make sure I rehearse one with the orchestra, in case of emergencies, or as an encore. It does mean though, that she can't take part in next week's concert, so I'll have to do some extra numbers, but that's easy enough, in fact I'll enjoy it. I'm going to make a coffee, anyone else interested?"

Once in the kitchen, Gemma enjoyed replaying to herself, the events of the evening. The production was a concert version of 'The Mikado' and, whilst she was singing the part of one of the 'three little maids', Gemma was not playing the coveted lead role of Yum Yum. The Voices were sarcastic, telling her the Director must have thought she wasn't good enough, although her training and singing were far superior to that of Janet, the girl chosen.

The dressing room for the 'three little maids', was on a mezzanine floor, and to approach the stage, the young women had to go down a flight of eight stairs. In their stiff Japanese garments and with the flat padded shoes necessary for their roles, this was never easy. When the five minute call came for them to move down, and into the wings, Gemma, behind Janet, in the line up, slipped and fell slightly forward. The movement caused Janet to lose her balance. Her fall to the bottom of the stairs, was almost predictable. It was, as someone later remarked, an accident waiting to happen. The Voices, loud in their approval, joked about 'elf 'n safety, and Gemma bravely dried her tears, and prepared to go on and sing the principal soprano role.

There had been some delicious moments. For the first time, Gemma had heard the famous words over the Assembly Hall's loudspeaker system, 'Is there a doctor in the house?'

And when one did appear, the doctor was able to say that one of Janet's legs was broken and, he suspected, two ribs were cracked. Obviously, she was badly shocked and in a lot of pain and would be out of action for some time. (Titters of delight from the Voices.)

At last, from the Director, came the words Gemma had been waiting to hear. She was to sing the lead role for the remainder of the run. Her joy at this was only eclipsed by the resounding applause from the audience for the young lady, who had so bravely stepped into the breach, and sung like an angel.

As Gemma went into the kitchen, Auriol saw that her mother's face had suddenly changed colour and she looked very strained. Gemma, re-emerging, made some comment about accidents happening frequently backstage during shows because, of necessity, the lights were dimmed there, and at last Susan had seemed to relax.

In fact, covertly watching Gemma's animated expression, Susan's mind was again in turmoil. Another accident, to add to the whole raft of nasty things which happened whenever her youngest daughter was present. And so soon after the recent incident with Leo and the car. Was Gemma spreading her net wider? Was her sickness, if that's what it was, worsening? Where would it end? As Gemma's mother she must do something. Now they were well away from the gossip of the village, perhaps she could persuade Gemma to see a doctor . . .

Unaware of Susan's predicament, Auriol had drawn her own conclusions. Her mother had of course been shocked, because Gemma was now the one remaining chick in her nest, and Susan must often fear for her safety, particularly as Gemma's work took her to strange towns and unfamiliar buildings, often at night-time. Yes, that must have been the problem, and why Susan had suddenly looked so worried. Dismissing it from her mind, she decided it was time to experiment with the new, very welcome addition to the Oxford house.

Delighted with its performance, she felt she'd earned a break from house cleaning and set out for the Students' Union to see if any of her friends had yet touched base. Sure enough, there were several about to start their final year and a few who like herself were staying on for their Master's Degree. Joanna, reading Law, bounced over to say hello. Jo was bubbling over with enthusiasm about a new Professor on the legal team.

"He's a Canadian, early thirties I'd say. Was here at Magdalen some years ago, took his Masters, and since then has been in Europe with the European Parliament, getting himself abreast of all things European . . . in law I mean. Although I don't doubt the girls were beating a path to his door. Auriol, he's absolutely gorgeous, tall and rather hunky, an Oxford Blue for cricket, would you believe? Dark hair, but not black, and grey-green eyes. I warn you, you'll be pig sick you're not in the legal department when you see him."

And she was! Auriol had smiled at Jo's ramblings, but had to admit that in this instance, she had it absolutely right. Rarely did an Oxford professor fit into the category of gorgeous, but Neil Hunt most certainly did. His appearance the following evening in the S.U. stopped conversations between the female undergraduates in their tracks. Then, as he moved around chatting to different groups, talk resumed, with the girls keeping a watchful eye to see if they might be next on his list. Auriol was amused and slightly irritated. He was doing a sort of royal progress, how very patronising. Determined not to be a part of it, she made her farewells and left.

In the empty house, she scolded herself for being as silly as Jo. *So, he's good looking. Very. Has umpteen letters after his name and is an Oxford Blue. He probably talks about nothing but cricket and is boring, boring.*

But this wasn't the case, as she soon found out. Meeting him inside the entrance to the Bodleian Library, the next morning, he stopped and introduced himself.

"I'm Neil Hunt. Saw you in the pub the other night, but by the time I'd worked my way in your direction, you'd gone. I won't say it was to get your beauty sleep, because you obviously don't need that."

A smooth talking charmer . . . but those overtones of Canadian accent were very attractive.

"Auriol Hatton." They shook hands. "Here to take my Master's in English Lit."

"And, Miss Auriol Hatton, if I'm not mistaken, don't I recall seeing your name in last year's very select list of Firsts?" Auriol blushed.

"So, where's home?" And before she could answer, "No, on second thoughts, if you're not tied up this evening, perhaps we could meet for a drink, or better still, dinner. Then we can fill in each other's backgrounds and you can tell me all the things about life at Oxford I need to know, and what the older members of my profession, might not tell me."

Auriol laughed, "I am free this evening," then anxious not to sound too keen to accept, "or I can make myself so. And I'll happily tell you about myself, although with regard to the latter, I might not prove very helpful, a) it's too early in the year for gossip and b) what tittle tattle comes in my direction, is thin on the ground at any time."

She knew from the beginning, it was a special relationship. Never had she felt this way in Colin's presence. Neil was her intellectual equal and in many areas her superior. This was a challenge and one she enjoyed. He rarely talked about cricket, but by the time Diane arrived, Auriol had decided she might grow to like the stupid game after all! Neil, she liked very much indeed.

The girls were quickly immersed in their studies, with Diane soon realising that Auriol had a new relationship, which was important to her. Inevitably, Neil's work prevented him from a great deal of socialising and Auriol was careful, however reluctantly, to limit their meetings, to ensure that Diane did not feel 'out on a limb'. All three returned home for the Christmas break, and returned full of the joie de vivre and ready to get back to work again.

It was about the middle of February, that Auriol started to notice that, on several occasions when Diane's mobile rang, she jumped up and left the room, saying she'd take it outside. Assuming she wanted a conversation with her parents, Auriol thought little of it, until one day, when Diane was taking a shower and her phone rang in the living room. Without thinking, Auriol picked it up and clicked it on. The name PAUL leaped out at her, and in a flash Auriol had closed the phone down again. A few days later, Diane again went outside to take a call on her mobile, and on her return, Auriol decided to take the bull by the horns. "You're talking to Paul Rule again, aren't you?"

Diane looked taken aback, then said rather sheepishly, "Well yes, I am."

"For heaven's sake, Diane, are you out of your tiny mind? After all he put you through. You must be mad."

"Alright, so I'm mad. I can't help it. He's changed." A chortle from Auriol.

"You can laugh as much as you like. He served his time in prison, five months, and he's cut off all contact with his former life. He's determined to make a fresh start."

"Born again! How very convenient for him. What about the woman you thought might be his wife, Bryony?"

"Well she wasn't, she'd just been with him for quite a while."

"I see, so she's conveniently disappeared into the sunset. It couldn't be that she's just had enough of the Rev. Rule and his antics, I suppose?"

"Don't be so cruel."

"Cruel? He dragged you down to a state of utter despair and now you're chatting to him as if everything in the garden's lovely."

"There's no way I could ever make you understand Auriol. He was for me the first . . . and I loved him for so gently introducing me to . . . you know what I mean.

Whilst in prison, he's been studying accountancy and he's now in Reading in a flat, and working towards his exams."

"And just where is all this leading?"

"He'd like to see me again."

"Now I know you're stark raving bonkers."

"It's *my* life Auriol, I don't think there'll ever be anyone else to whom I can relate, as I related to Paul." Auriol tried to interrupt, "I know what you're about to say. He lied to me and cheated his way into my life, but I do believe he has changed and that with my help, he'll continue to change."

"And just how many stupid women do you think have gone into a relationship thinking just that, and then fallen flat on their faces, when it all came to a grinding halt?"

"Sorry, Auriol, on this, we will just have to agree to differ." And on that sour note, each departed to her own room.

After several more prickly weeks, Auriol came to a decision. Diane's parents would never forgive her if this current episode led to a second debacle, without their knowledge. Shocked at what Auriol had to tell them, they immediately telephoned Diane.

"How dare you ring my parents, Auriol? My contact with Paul was a private matter between you and me, and you were well aware I didn't want it go any further at this stage. Now I've had to put up with Mum and Dad bending my ear for almost an hour, telling me what a stupid fool I am."

"Well, they obviously agree with me on that."

"Whatever the lot of you agree on, will not make any difference to me. I shall plough my own furrow and if, as you no doubt expect, I make a mess of my life, then I shall only have myself to blame."

"And Paul . . ."

"You see. You won't even consider the possibility that he's trying to sort out his life, or that he still cares about me."

"The fact that you have some money and he presumably hasn't, doesn't come into this equation, I take it?"

"Oh, it's impossible to have a sensible conversation with you . . ." And Diane flounced out of the room. The next day she was gone. Whilst Auriol was in a tutorial, Diane had removed all her personal belongings from the house and left an envelope containing sufficient money to cover her share of the rental, up to the end of the academic year. There was also a note.

I think this should cover my share, so that you won't have the inconvenience of moving before your exams., etc. I have to do this, and I'm sorry that you can't understand why. My parents have an address, if you should ever want to make contact again, which I doubt. Sorry, our friendship had to end in this way. We've had good times together. Remember that. Diane

Auriol not prone to crying, wept a great deal that evening. She thought long and hard about Colin, Diane and herself, who had started this university journey with such enthusiasm, their initial happy go lucky relationship, and the fact that somehow each facet of it had now been soured. Had they just been unlucky, or was much of it inevitable on leaving home, becoming free agents with few constraints socially or morally? How many, she wondered, returned home wiser but sadder, as a result of their experiences?

Pull yourself together girl, she eventually reprimanded herself, *your studies are up to date and the future's looking good. Neil is a darling and I think, like me, he's happy to take things steadily, instead of rushing into something we'd both regret in a short time.*

And Auriol's future was looking good. A play she had written as part of her course work had been much acclaimed by her tutor, who had suggested it should be forwarded to the BBC. The reply was not only complimentary, but proposed that she meet one of the drama directors to discuss the play's structure and possible production. Diane had made it clear that she had her own life to live and the same thing applied to Auriol. If, the BBC was to take up her play and use it, then it could mean for her the beginning of a very exciting career. One of the dons had already suggested that following her Master's, she should stay in Oxford for a time, working with drama groups and assisting with university productions.

"I know you've done some drama here, but you need as much as possible to see a play develop from script to final production. It would assist your own script writing."

Auriol could see the logic of that and it would also mean some more precious time with Neil. Life was wonderful.

Neil had been delighted for her. Whilst he insisted that the journey from Oxford to London was negligible, he had also hinted that, if that proved to be where Auriol's future lay, he might have to rethink his own plans and consider a move. They now knew a great deal about each other. On her part, the loss of her father, the liaison with Colin and the feeling that her own, as she had suspected, dysfunctional family, was now less so, perhaps, she suspected, because they were no longer living in each other's pockets. From Neil, she learned that he had been born in Toronto, where his parents and young brother still lived. There had been several girls, first of all at Oxford, and then whilst in Europe, but like Auriol, he was no longer seeking a quick affair. This time he wanted to be certain that he and his partner could stay the course and look forward to a future together.

Neil was of course bilingual, French being almost a necessity in so many aspects of Canadian life. His father was a bank manager in Toronto, but due to retire very soon, his mother was an accountant who worked from home and brother James was learning his trade in business management. Weekends and some holidays were spent in a small house just outside Niagara on the Lake, a few miles from the Falls.

"No problem about keeping accounts in your home then," Auriol laughed, "although your mother could have, if so wished, been quite adept at fiddling the housekeeping!"

They were comfortable together and returning early from the Christmas break so that they might be on their own, Auriol at last found that the explosion of joy she had expected and never experienced during her sexual encounters with Colin, were at last hers to enjoy and savour. Following these wonderful few days alone, they each knew that this was not something transient, but that they both loved and were loved in return. Together they began to plan for the future.

CHAPTER 19

The Voices were giving Gemma a hard time. Why, they asked, did she sit there so docilely, listening to her mother's fulsome praise of Auriol and her success? Yes, her first play had been accepted and televised, and the TV companies were immediately beating a path to her door, asking her for more. Following her Master's Degree, and after several months observing drama at Oxford, Auriol was now comfortably ensconced in Simon's London flat, with his permission to stay there for an indeterminate period. All the problems which might have come her way neatly ironed out.

There was something else, about which the Voices grumbled and muttered. The new boy friend. A different kettle of fish this, from that humble chap from the North. This one was, by all accounts, a dishy intellectual at the peak of his own career, devoted to Auriol and prepared to move heaven and earth to spend as much time as possible with her. Can you believe that? One Voice asked loud and clear. This was Auriol, who was no raving beauty and certainly not noted for ready wit and success, socially. And this, another Voice pointed out, was the girl who had commandeered their father's attention, together they had read books, gone for walks and never, ever, asked Gemma to join them.

Now, another Voice added, just when Susan should have been enthusing about Gemma's success, she seemed overwhelmed by excitement every time Auriol phoned, or wrote. Do something, the Voices chorused, do something now.

But what? Gemma asked, annoyed with herself and them. How to burst the bubble? How to put a stop to this eulogy in praise of Auriol?

A night's sleep in which the Voices were silenced, and at last Gemma knew what she must do. Carefully she typed out her letter.

I think you should be aware that your lady friend, Auriol Hatton, is not quite the model of sweetness and light presented in her self-portrait. During her three student years at Oxford she had numerous lovers, taking people back to her rented home, whenever she knew the other residents were absent. The one man who really cared for her, left with a broken heart, when she refused to accompany him after they graduated. She said she didn't care enough for him, but in fact she knew that the liaison would mean assisting him with a terminally ill sister. Something she was not prepared to do. Her former room-mate will confirm that she was spied on with regard to her own relationship. She eventually left the house because of Miss Hatton's interference. Whilst Auriol Hatton is the niece of her London flat's owner, questions have been raised about their relationship, on the occasions he returns from his duties at sea.

That should put the cat amongst the pigeons! Nothing there that could be proved, or disproved. Almost all Auriol's associates during those first three years would have left, Colin was somewhere in Yorkshire, and Diane, well, no-one knew where Diane was. Enough surely, to sow some substantial seeds in Lover Boy's mind.

Carefully, Gemma typed the address on the envelope, addressing it to Professor Neil Hunt at the Central Office of the University of Oxford. She then placed that inside another envelope and wrote a short note to a male singer she had met on the concert recital circuit, asking him to be good enough to post it in Oxford, as she was not sure of the address and wanted to ensure it reached its destination.

A few days later, Gemma listened to Susan on the end of the phone to Auriol, but a very different Susan now. "What is it darling? Try and compose yourself. Are you ill?"

At last the phone was put down and Susan explained that Neil had said he and Auriol should cool their relationship, because of some unfortunate gossip he had heard.

"Gossip? About Auriol? Never, she's as straight as a die and thinks the world of him." Gemma was all innocence.

"*I* know it and *you* know it, but whatever has been said, has clearly upset Neil very much indeed. I can't remember Auriol ever being so distressed, well, certainly not since her father died. Clearly, she had thought that Neil was going to be an important part of her future. He seemed so proud of her, and rightly so. I don't know what to make of it."

"If he's the sort of person who listens to gossip and believes it, then perhaps it's for the best."

"I doubt if Auriol sees it that way, at the moment."

The Voices were pleased, they made soothing noises and Gemma knew she had done the right thing. Phone calls from Auriol, now produced a very different reaction from Susan.

Auriol's plans for living comfortably in London with Neil, were shattered. He had retracted his intention of applying for work closer to the capital, and Auriol's attempts to find out who her accusers were, had proved fruitless. Colin's young sister in Yorkshire *was* dying of cancer, Auriol had not cared enough for him to leave Oxford and live in the North, that part of it was true enough. She had no way of disproving the allegations about other men. As Gemma had anticipated, those who might possibly have known, had gone their separate ways and yes, Auriol accepted she had in a way, spied on Diane, because she was afraid for her and felt her parents should be informed. Just where Diane was now, no-one knew. The one accusation which left Auriol blazing, was that relating to her Uncle Simon. How dare anyone suggest that she and he . . . ? It was unforgivable, and Neil was told in no uncertain terms, that it was totally untrue. To add to her argument, she pointed out that Simon had been home on leave only once, since she was in London, when he'd had a week in the flat before rejoining his ship. Yes, they had gone out to the theatre then, and on another occasion had dinner together.

"But", as Auriol pointed out, furiously, "he's my uncle, for goodness' sake." It was no use, the magic had gone, the relationship soured.

In a few short weeks, it was all over, and Susan was fielding more and more distressed calls from Auriol, whose work was now starting to suffer. Susan's suggestions that she should come home for a while, met with a negative response, and eventually in sheer desperation, Susan phoned Auriol's boss at the BBC.

"I do apologise for troubling you, but I'm becoming increasingly concerned about my daughter and wondered if there's anything you think I should do."

"Mrs. Hatton, I'm glad you phoned me. We've been so pleased with Auriol's work and wondered if it was something we were doing wrong. I agree she seems in a very depressed state at the moment, I think she's suffering from the London Sickness."

"What on earth is that?"

"Well, it's when someone lives alone in London and really only ever communicates with people at work, about work. Writing is in itself a solitary occupation and unless Auriol has a reasonably active social life, she will find living in this city a very lonely life. I know she and her boy friend have separated and this is probably part of the trouble. There's only one suggestion I can make."

"Yes, what? I'll try anything, within reason."

"I think she needs to focus on something in the future, a good holiday perhaps. What about Christmas? If she can look forward to a really special break, away from the city and her work, I think she will perhaps concentrate on that, rather than her current problems. And after a complete break, hopefully she'll return all the more refreshed and ready to start again."

"Yes," Susan hesitated, "thank you. I think that sounds a really good idea. I'll give it some thought, see what can be arranged."

"Meanwhile, Mrs. Hatton, we'll do what we can at this end, see that she has company at lunch or dinner now and again. Leave it with me."

For a time, Susan had considered whether Gemma could have played a part in Auriol's break with Neil, then dismissed the idea as ridiculous. Gemma had never shown interest in her sister's activities in Oxford and therefore knew relatively little about Auriol's private life. She could not possibly have been a party to gossip related to what had happened. Yet . . . there was one niggling doubt. How many of Auriol's acquaintances would have been aware that when Auriol went to London she would be staying in Simon's flat? Auriol was essentially a very private person, and did not discuss her business with all and sundry. It was not until some weeks later, when Auriol mentioned the 'letter', that the suspicion once again gnawed at her.

"What letter?" Susan asked, suddenly knowing and dreading the answer.

"The letter Neil received, of course. It was vitriolic . . . all that business about Uncle Simon, absolutely sickening." So, this whole sequence of events was not based, as Susan had thought, on hearsay, but on something written and ostensibly factual.

Now once again, things started to fall into place. Susan's own absorption with Auriol's burgeoning career, and Gemma's carefully disguised jealousy, could well be at the root of this. If Gemma had merely transferred her hatred from Leo to Auriol, then Susan herself, was at the heart of it and to blame in some way. It did seem that if she showed affection or real interest in the activities of either of her other children, some nasty event always followed.

Bitterly she regretted the past. She knew that when Giles was alive, her own devotion to Leo and his to Auriol, had left Gemma very much alone. But she had tried so hard to make amends for that period of her life. Always now, she tried to ensure Gemma's safety and wellbeing. She had made a point of assisting hugely with her training for a singing career, a career which seemed, on the surface, to be both successful and rewarding. What more did the girl want? And what now, was the way forward?

After much heart-searching, Susan decided that her plans to take Auriol away must go ahead. Once Auriol was fit again, then Susan knew, she would make sure that Gemma was her absolute priority. She would try and persuade her to see a doctor. They could holiday together and she would endeavour to see that Gemma again felt she was the most important person in her mother's life.

Gemma had not been impressed with all the talk about London Sickness. Once again, it seemed that Susan was absorbed with what Auriol was doing, or should be doing. The Voices agreed. It's time she thought about you, and only you, Gemma.

It was not until the end of November, that matters came to a head. Gemma knew they had planned it, of course. Deliberately plotted to exclude her. Her Voices agreed. Susan and Auriol had been hatching this for some time, waited until all Gemma's engagements for the Christmas period were contracted, and in place.

Susan had been embarrassed naturally. Led up to it, with all that business again about London Sickness. "She's very unwell, Gemma. Her boss says it's definitely the Sickness, although obviously the business with Neil has been devastating for her."

"So?" Gemma's voice was icy.

"Mr. Symonds is suggesting that she has a complete break over the holiday, goes away somewhere. It could well provide material for her writing of course, but more importantly, he thinks she'll come back fit and well again. He's concerned that she's a workaholic and must learn to pace herself, and suggests she now needs an agent to advise on contracts, and generally take the pressure off her. So what we're going to do . . ."

"We?"

"Auriol and me, we knew you were already committed for the Christmas break, so I'm afraid, it has to be just the two of us."

Angry mutters from the Voices.

"And just where is this wonderful cure-all break going to take place?"

"Sri Lanka."

"Sri Lanka? It's the other side of the world! Why there, for heaven's sake?"

"Auriol has plans for writing something about the Far East, and this would give her some first-hand knowledge of the people, and the area.

It's also very quiet and peaceful and she'd be able to get lots of fresh air and enjoy the sunshine."

"Good! And while you're both enjoying the sunshine and the fresh air, has anyone, anyone at all, given any thought about me, as to how I would be spending Christmas, all alone in this big house? Or perhaps I should move into a hotel and also have a holiday . . . on my own."

Susan sighed, she had known this would be very difficult. "It has to be then because it's the only time Auriol is free, and for that matter the only time I'm free of Council meetings and duties. I'll miss a couple of receptions, but they're immaterial."

"And what about me? Am I also immaterial? I can't believe you would do this to me. How long is this holiday going to last? When are you leaving?"

"A few days before Christmas, December 18th, and returning a few days after Boxing Day, on the 28th. But Gemma, of *course* we have considered you." Jeers from the Voices.

"I've given it a great deal of thought, and this is what I'm suggesting. I've had a word with your Italian tutor. I know you always get on so well with Carlotta and her daughter, the whole family, in fact. They'll be delighted to have you stay with them over the period that I'm away. Wouldn't dream of taking any money from us, so I thought I could order something special, like a Fortnum and Mason hamper and a crate of wine. What do you think?"

It was obvious what the Voices thought, grumbling and groaning in the background, and Gemma scowled,

"I think you've pretty well got it all sorted, without bothering to consult me." Then, as something occurred to her, she smiled, "Don't worry Mummy, I'll fall in with your plans, but next time you and me get to holiday together. Understood?"

Susan sighed with relief, "Of course, darling, I promise, and what's more you can choose where, and when. We could do the States, or Canada . . ."

If she thinks that's the end of it, she'd better think again. When Leo's around, I play second fiddle to him, and now, when Auriol is away working in London, I still have to take second place to her requirements. They needn't think they'll get rid of me that easily, I'll make my own Christmas arrangements and surprise the pair of them. Ripples of approval from the Voices. *Now, there's quite a lot to do, so I'd better make a list. My agent first, I think.*

CHAPTER 20

By the time Susan and Auriol arrived in Sri Lanka, Gemma had already cancelled most of her Christmas bookings, pleading damaged vocal chords. Informing Carlotta that there had been a change of plan and she would be joining her mother and sister in Sri Lanka after all, Gemma had booked the hotel, and her flight out there, arriving on Christmas Day.

Gemma reached the hotel as guests were starting their cocktail party, prior to the evening's celebratory dinner. A word with the Maitre d' Hotel ensured that a place would be set for Gemma next to her mother and sister. 'A surprise for them,' she informed him. To her room for a quick shower, where Gemma slipped into her favourite and most stunning performance dress of palest gold.

Her entrance, and their faces, were everything she could have hoped for.

"Gemma darling, what on earth . . . ?"

And from Auriol, concealing her own surprise, behind a smiling exterior, "How lovely, Gemma. Were your concerts cancelled?"

"I'll explain later," Gemma replied, then enthusing over the décor and the food and drink being served by charming attendants,

"What a lovely place, and whilst all this looks far too pretty to eat, I'm going to have to do just that. I'm ravenous after that ghastly in-flight food."

The excuse Gemma had given at home about damaged vocal chords was aired once again and if Susan was slightly suspicious, that this had not revealed itself in minor ways earlier, there was little she could say or do, to refute what Gemma said.

To Gemma's surprise, of the three of them it was Auriol who seemed the more relaxed throughout their meal.

"You look so well, Auriol and your holiday's hardly started." Gemma wanted to ask what all the fuss had been about Auriol's ill-health, when she now appeared to be positively blooming. As coffee was served, Gemma received her answer.

"I'm glad we're all here together because I have some news. Some lovely, lovely news." Auriol beamed at them both.

Susan and Gemma looked at her in astonishment. Auriol was radiant, glowing with happiness. From her evening purse, she extracted some folded sheets of paper.

"Yesterday evening I received an e-mail," then, looking at Susan, "I know you thought it was something to do with work, but I wanted to wait and tell you this evening. Now, with Gemma here to share it with us, it's even more extra special."

Her smile at her sister was warm and sincere and Gemma, unusually, felt a pang of remorse. Auriol was always so good! All sweetness and light. Surely it was unnatural to be like that for so much of the time? Unless of course you wanted something out of the situation. Now, carefully, she painted a smile on her own face,

"Don't keep us in suspense any longer, we're all ears."

"The letter was from Neil, apologising for believing all those months ago the contents of that wicked letter. He said he should have relied on his own instincts from the start. Several people have now put him in the picture, as to the truth about what was said, all of it."

"But . . . ?" Gemma not knowing what to make of this, hesitated, fearing she might unwittingly reveal herself as the guilty party, "What has changed his mind?"

"One of the dons, Julian Conway, was Neil's mentor in his early days in the U.K. He's been away for a time both doing research and taking a sabbatical and just returned to Oxford to pick up the threads. Fortunately Julian knew me well. There were several occasions when he was kind enough to listen to my troubles. He knew that I repeatedly tried to make sure Colin understood our relationship was never going to be a permanent one and that yes, I did inform Diane's parents when Paul resurfaced in her life, because I was genuinely worried about her and knew they would be too. As to that nasty business regarding Uncle Simon–well Julian knew me well enough not to give any credence to that."

Gemma forced another smile, "And so . . . ?"

"And so . . . Neil says he loves me, knows we're meant to be together and, wait for it, he'll be joining us here tomorrow. Well, not quite here, this hotel was fully booked, so he'll be just a few hundred yards away at The Colonnade Hotel."

Later as she undressed, Gemma fumed at this new turn of events. She had been convinced that during Auriol's last year at Oxford and those later months when she was working in London, there would be very few left at the university who had any knowledge of the events detailed in the letter. Certainly no-one whom dear Neil would regard as a reliable informant. For him to have met an old friend, a respectable don, who was able to not only dispute everything, but praise Auriol's integrity, was something Gemma hadn't bargained on. It was not often that her meticulous attention to detail went adrift but, she thought ruefully, this was one such occasion.

Lying in bed she decided it had been worth that small hiccup, to have surprised her mother and Auriol with her arrival. She smiled, recalling the startled looks on their faces, as she walked into the dining room. *Why do people think they can mess me around and get away with it? I'll show them who's in charge, if it's the last thing I do.*

As yet, she had formulated no plan, but was confident that an opportune moment would soon present itself and she would get her own back, for their deliberate exclusion of her from this Christmas break. Until then, she was prepared to wait. Her voices were silent, apparently unaware that such a moment would arrive much earlier than she, or anyone could have could have predicted.

Once again Susan found that thoughts of Gemma kept her awake. If Gemma was responsible for that wicked letter, she must now be furious that Auriol and Neil were to be reunited. For two hours she tossed and turned, then went into the bathroom. Auriol, also awake but for very different reasons, sat up immediately. "Are you alright?"

"Yes Darling, just having difficulty sleeping. Too much excitement I guess. I'm going to take a pill, that will do the trick."

Then, without warning, it happened. Susan bust into tears and with Auriol's arms around her, started to talk. Childhood memories of her mother's violent mood swings, the horror of her parents' deaths and the revelations at the inquest and, most important of all, her fears for Gemma's health, all came spilling out. The suspicion she had had about the 'accidents' which had befallen Leo as a small child, the drowning of Fran, Mark's death, her fears for the future . . . Until, exhausted, she stopped.

"And Daddy, you don't think she was responsible for that . . . ?" Auriol's expression registered her horror.

"No, not for one moment. Everything for which I *suspect* Gemma has been responsible, has been carefully planned down to the last detail. She would never have attempted such a thing when she knew we were all coming up the hill behind her. No, the police said the skid marks where Daddy slid on wet grass were plain to see. I do think in view of what had gone before, Leo might have been suddenly afraid that she would attempt something and in moving away, made things worse."

"And that was why Leo was so furious with her afterwards?"

"Yes, he felt Gemma had frightened him so much in the past that his reactions might have contributed to his father's death."

"But why Mark? She seemed fond of him." In spite of her shock at these amazing revelations, Auriol was desperately trying to think logically.

"I think now, that what Gemma 'seemed' on many occasions, we have to discount as not being fact. I don't think she intended to kill Mark, although she resented his presence in my life. Leo was her target, but with only Leo in the pool and just one pair of shoes in the changing room, I think, very unusually for her, she made a mistake."

"But Mummy, if you have worked this out, why haven't others? Daddy for instance?"

"Only I knew of what had gone before. Daddy was unaware of how my parents' died, or what was said at the inquest. Imagine if I'd had to tell him that his mother-in-law was a murderess and I suspected that one of his children had inherited her genes. No, I couldn't ever bring myself to do it. Finding out that she was years ahead of her age group in intelligence came as a shock, as it meant I was not only having to consider schizophrenia, but genius bordering on a sort of madness."

"And no-one else knew? You never saw a doctor?"

"I daren't. Somehow it would have leaked out into the village and we would all have been ruined. There *was* someone else who suspected Gemma's behaviour was abnormal and thought she might need treatment… Eileen Biggs. She wrote to me and I was so shocked by seeing written down what I feared in my own mind, I burned the letter and never replied. I dreaded that she might confide in her sister and that gradually the story would be passed from mouth to mouth. But it didn't happen."

"Of course not. Eileen Biggs is as straight as a die. I'd never question her integrity."

"I realise that now . . . now it's too late."

"Did Leo know?"

"He didn't know anything about my background or my fears, but when he was old enough he soon worked out that Gemma was determined to hurt him." Susan shook her head, pulling a face. "With hindsight I realise now, that that was why he was so insistent about wanting to become a boarder at school and why, eventually, he joined the Navy. All Leo ever wanted to do was to get away from Gemma."

"Oh, my God! But what now? She needs treatment, medication. You can't let this go on."

"No, Auriol, *I* can't. That is why, I confess, I'm telling *you*. I can't do this alone, but I wonder if together, we might find a solution. There's something else, something which might persuade you to help me . . ."

"Surely, no more horrors . . . this is all . . . well, almost beyond belief."

"Neil's letter . . . the one which put an end to your friendship for so many months . . . I believe Gemma sent it."

Auriol eyes widened. Then, hesitating, she said "Of course . . . who else had access to all that information about my private life? But why? She didn't know Neil, couldn't possibly have taken a dislike to him. Why would she want to split us up?"

"Because you were happy, doing well at Oxford, with the possibility of a good job in the pipeline and . . . this is the point, because you were centre stage, the focus of attention. I've now worked out that this is what Gemma hates most of all. She must always be in the limelight. You remember when you were with me and the leading lady fell down the stairs . . . ?"

"Oh no, not that as well?"

"I just don't know. For so many of these incidents I've no proof. Gemma is expert at covering her tracks, nothing was ever proved, or even referred to, at Mark's and Fran's inquests. But yes, I think that was another incident and I wonder how many others there were, about which we know nothing."

"And she came here tonight because . . . ?"

"Because you and I were going to be together and she was excluded."

Stunned now into silence, Auriol sat, her arms around her mother.

Then suddenly, "Neil will help us. He's strong in body and spirit. He's kind too and," a wry smile, "forgiving. He'll know what we must do. We'll talk to him tomorrow. Now it's time you took that pill and got some sleep. Forget about all this, we really will help to get it sorted." And with that Auriol produced sleeping pill and water and once her mother was settled in, climbed into her own bed.

The blissful state Auriol had been in earlier was shattered. Her sister was ill and all too often, dangerous to others. How would her kind, generous-spirited Neil react to the fact that her sister had not only ruined their friendship, but carried disturbingly menacing genes? Waking at irregular intervals, she was at last relieved to see sunlight bordering the curtains. A new day had begun.

Waking early on Boxing Day, Gemma decided to examine her new surroundings in the daylight. From the front of the hotel, the view was stunning and the beach so much closer than she had imagined. The hotel formed three sides of a square facing the sea, with the open section containing gardens and a swimming pool. Gemma had learned on arrival that Susan and Auriol were sharing a room in the right-hand wing section, and asked if there was any possibility of being near them. The hotel was full and her original booking could not be changed. Her room, she found, was in the same block, but a floor above them.

Although it was early, people were already swimming and children running around excitedly. Then, as she watched, something amazing started to happen. The sea was receding. Not, as one might expect from an ebb tide, gently, little by little. The sea here was drawing back into itself, leaving swimmers and even fish, rather startled, the latter floundering in a new environment devoid of water.

It was then that Gemma saw and heard the girl. She was pulling her mother by the hand and dragging her towards the hotel, calling to other people, as she went. "It's a tsunami, I've learned about it in school. Get off the beach quickly. A big wave will come." In spite of her disbelief, Gemma followed her and in the entrance to the hotel the child repeated over and over again, 'It's a tsunami.' The concierge understood at once, snapped out instructions and vehicles started to appear at the front of the hotel. Bells were ringing, people rushing around and during the melee, no-one showed the slightest interest as Gemma leaned over the reception desk and snatched from the board, the spare key to Susan's room.

There were no sounds from inside the room, and Gemma carefully locked the door, leaving the key in the lock, so that it would be impossible to insert and turn a key from the inside. Hurrying down stairs, she saw that people still sleepy, were emerging from their rooms, puzzled as to what was happening. In the foyer the concierge, without any ceremony, told people to get into the waiting cars as quickly as possible and they would be taken to higher ground. No one argued, and Gemma smiled to herself, as she looked back at the windows of the hotel's right wing. The Voices were now aroused, and chuckling their approval.

In the last car packed with guests, Gemma waited until they had pulled away from the hotel and started their upward drive, then cried out, as if in anguish, "My mother and sister . . . I can't see them . . . I can't see them." Sympathetic silence, but as she had anticipated, no suggestion of a return. They were just in time. The massive wave was already making its move, and by the time the line of cars reached ground high above the beach, the wave was towering some twenty feet high, sweeping before it everything in its path. The shocked hotel guests saw from their vantage point its impact on the two wings of the hotel, which shuddered and then imploded with the force of tons of water. An hour later, the scene of devastation was beyond belief, with only the fragments of where the hotel guests had slept the previous night, remaining. Traumatised, they comforted each other, said how lucky they were to be alive and congratulated the ten year old, who had learned enough in her lessons, to save so many of them.

Only Gemma remained isolated. She had done it, or at least God had. Now she knew that her father had been right. God was watching over everyone and knew how unhappy she had been and how badly she had been treated. Now, God had helped her to restore the balance and put things right.

*They should have realised I was not prepared to be pushed to one side, as if I was of no importance. I am important. People love my singing, or they wouldn't ask me back over and over again. They will have learned now, that my singing is of more importance than mother's stupid committee meetings and Auriol's puerile scribblings about life. This **is** life. On second thoughts,* she giggled, *for them this was death.*

One of the drivers spoke to a woman in the group, "That girl is in shock, look she's laughing, yet I believe she might have lost her mother and sister. Could you please stay with her, until we've decided where we should make for next? I think she's badly traumatised and needs medical help, as soon as possible." And the kindly elderly lady put her arm round Gemma's shoulders, as others came forward to see if they could help in any way.

Gemma was once again where she always wanted to be, the centre of attention.

Auriol's day, like Gemma's had started early. Quietly, she went into the bathroom and prepared herself for the meeting to which she had so looked forward. . Only her bikini and a cover-up sarong, she decided. Nothing else necessary. She and Neil would certainly be swimming and anything more would be an encumbrance. Susan, as she'd anticipated, was sound asleep and likely to be so for several hours. One key was on their dressing table and the other she would leave with the concierge downstairs, ready for her own return. Breakfast could wait until she met Neil. He should have arrived at about 1.0 a.m. and, her head still reeling from the impact of her mother's revelations, she set out for his hotel, about a quarter of a mile inland from their own.

Her wonderful reunion with Neil, would now be sullied by this serious family problem. She thought back over the years and suddenly was aware of her own guilt in all this. As her elder, sister why hadn't she realised just how isolated Gemma must have felt after Leo's birth? Yes, she herself was only a child, but why hadn't she made more of an effort to make time to talk to Gemma, play with her? She knew the answer. Her father's dominant role in her life had left little room for anything else. How clearly she recalled that evening when Gemma's delighted laughter at beating her father at chess, had burst out and echoed through the lofty vicarage rooms. That laughter was a rare occasion and for that they were all guilty. The question remained, whatever they had done, would it have been enough? Gemma's fixation on Leo had eventually spread its poison to everyone who, as her mother had said, stole Gemma's limelight. Clearly she would go to any lengths to achieve her ends. It was imperative that they acquired medical help and soon.

Neil's hotel in sight, she determined that her troubles must wait until they were once again together and earlier problems resolved. Reception there had been warned Neil was expecting a visitor and she was quickly taken to his room. Before the key could be turned, the door was flung open and she was in his arms.

The bliss of being encircled once again by his strong arms, his breath on her cheeks, the warmth of his flesh, reduced her to a flood of tears. But, as she explained through her sobs, they were tears of happiness. Together they talked, made love, talked again and finally went downstairs to drink coffee and eat croissants in the sunshine. At last, hand in hand, they walked through the hotel gardens in the direction of the beach and it was then that the world suddenly went mad.

Hearing distant shouts and screams they turned to each other, puzzled. Then they heard another sound, a steady roar with an undercurrent of cracking and crashing. Something was moving towards them. Neil grabbed Auriol's hand and shouting, "Run!" dragged her back towards the hotel. Within seconds the water was on them, tearing them apart. Auriol, tossed into the mainstream of flotsam, now a dangerous threat, was carried for hundreds of yards before she was unceremoniously dumped onto the flat roof of an outhouse. In the space of two minutes in the water she had been struck in the side by a heavy table and her left arm sliced open by a piece of glass. She knew that she must try to stop the bleeding. Dragging at the sarong, now plastered to her body she at last managed to release it and one handed, awkwardly wrapped it round her upper arm. Trying to tighten it using the weight of the arm itself, she finally clenched the ends of the sarong in her teeth and sank back exhausted. Where was Neil? *Please, please God don't let him die, I've only just found him again.* And with these thoughts in her mind, she lost consciousness.

Neil was very close to death. His several attempts to clutch at trees, balconies, anything, as he was swept along, had torn his shoulder almost from its socket. But it was the blow to his head as the tsunami, in its own dying throes, flung him towards a low wall, which sent him spiralling into the blackest of depths. No longer could he hear or see, as he too, lost touch with reality.

As volunteers speedily rushed to remove hotel debris, Susan's body was soon found, still in the bed in which she had slept for the last time.

It was recorded that her daughter's body was not in the bedroom area and the theory, that on hearing the noise, the young woman might have gone onto their bedroom balcony and from there been swept away, was accepted as a possibility. Also was recorded that, unusually, the door to what could have been Mrs. and Miss Hatton's bedroom was found with keys still in the lock, but on the outside.

Whilst the checking of bodies, items of identification, such as watches, rings, dental records etc., would continue for many weeks, Gemma was told that there was little likelihood of ever finding out what had happened to her sister and that she should return home. But before that . . . the niceties of a proper funeral had to be dispensed with and immediate cremation take place. Several of those who had fled from the tsunami with Gemma insisted on staying with her during these difficult hours. It was only after the insistence of the officials there, and encouraging comments from those around her, that she handed over contact addresses for Leo and her uncles, Simon and Charles. As her Voices told her, she was quite capable of managing this situation without family help and certainly not from Leo.

But it was Charles's name and the nature of his office which ensured that Gemma's journey home was effected swiftly and smoothly. Clothes arrived for her at the Tsunami holding centre for those whose accommodation had been destroyed and their belongings lost. Declining his suggestion that she be taken to the Athens Embassy, she found, once in England, that Charles had organised transport to take her to Chichester. There a policeman and a locksmith were waiting to let her into her home, groceries had been delivered to a neighbour and were handed over immediately. Charles had thought of everything.

It was after their departure, safely ensconced in familiar surroundings in the empty house, that Gemma, to her own surprise, burst into tears.

The phone rang, startling her back to reality. It was her Charles, with, as he said, "Wonderful news! They've found her." Gemma's tears dried as if by magic.

"She's been badly hurt, but I've managed to get her to hospital here in Athens. The medical facilities over there are swamped, as you well know. No possibility of the surgery she urgently needs there, but now I can keep an eye on things and keep things moving."

Gemma tried to speak, but Charles attributing her silence to emotion continued,

"They seem to think the boyfriend could be alive too. Someone found a record that he was in a coma and had been transferred to Colombo where Intensive Care treatment would be available." Still no reply.

"Gemma, darling, are you alright? This has been such a dreadful ordeal for you and I know you're grieving for your mother. Would you like me to arrange for you to come to me, here in Athens? You'd be able to see Auriol and be looked after in the Embassy."

"Thanks, Uncle, but . . ." a sob, "It's all been so terrible, I think I need to be here where it's quiet for a time. I know you'll keep me posted about Auriol . . . and her boyfriend. I just don't think I can bear to leave home again just yet. Besides . . . there are a lot of people I must contact and tell them about Mum . . . and Auriol. I don't mind being on my own, really. I'm sure Leo will come and see me, as soon as his duties allow."

"I do understand, darling, but if you need help with paperwork, I could organise that for you, anything legal. Don't forget you only have to ask. And by the way, isn't it time you stopped calling me Uncle? It makes me feel quite ancient."

"You've already done so much . . . . Charles. Thank you for organising the police and locksmith and the food which arrived at the same time. You've thought of everything and I'm grateful. Now, all I want to do is go to bed and try to forget the events of the last few days."

"Do just that. On top of everything you've had a long flight. I'll ring you again at 4.0 p.m. tomorrow. By then I might have more definite news about Auriol and you'll be feeling more rested. Goodnight, darling."

As Gemma replaced the phone, she heard dimly the Voices. They, like her, seemed stunned at this latest development. Perhaps God wasn't on her side after all. Auriol and this 'meant for each other boyfriend' were both alive and if not exactly kicking, there was every possibility they'd recover. Picking up her case, she wearily climbed the stairs.

In Sri Lanka, Leo was doing his own investigating. His mother's cremation and Gemma' departure had taken place before he could get a flight into a country devastated by the effects of the tsunami. The knowledge that Gemma had been there with his mother and sister had been surprising. That had certainly not been the original plan. He was told that two days had passed before Auriol was identified and that, with her uncle's assistance, she had been short-listed and flown out to Athens for major surgery. When a Neil Hunt's name was registered and displayed, found on the salvaged hotel register, he recognised it, and guessed that Neil and Auriol had been together at the time of the wave's onslaught. At last he managed to piece together some of what had happened. Gemma, he learned, had been taken to the high ground in one of the hotel cars. Bells had been rung in the hotel to alert people of the danger and, surprisingly, his mother had slept through the noise and the turmoil. But the note against the record of her death stated that peculiarly, keys had been found on the outside of her room. Had she attempted to get out, it would have been impossible without help. He need look no further for the architect of that incident. Gemma had escaped. No doubt the scenario she had planned was that Susan and Auriol would both be trapped in their room, but her plans had once again gone awry. Now she was in her lovely Chichester home wondering what further misery she could inflict on family and friends.

Only Charles's phone calls roused Gemma from her apathy. She felt drained. The excitement of the past days was now over. And yes, she admitted, much of it had been exciting, as people fussed over her and tried to satisfy her whims. Now alone, whatever happened, there was no-one else to blame.

Charles refrained from commenting on his surprise that Leo had not made contact with Gemma and a week had elapsed before he was able to tell her that Auriol's condition had stabilised sufficiently to withstand major surgery on her ruptured spleen. From him, Gemma also learned that Mr. and Mrs. Hunt had located their son Neil, and that he was still comatose, but Charles added,

"I know it's devastating for them, but at least he's alive and his condition being monitored daily."

In spite of everything which had gone before, Gemma too, was surprised at the lack of contact from Leo. After all, their mother had died and Gemma herself had experienced the horror of the tsunami. One surprising contact she did have was from Neil's mother.

"Am I speaking to Gemma Hatton?"

"You are . . ."

"Gemma, sorry to be so familiar, but I'm Marie Hunt, Neil's mother. How are you my dear, after your dreadful ordeal?"

"I'm well, thank you. Trying to get back on an even keel," then hastily, "missing my mother of course and worried about my sister. But how is Neil? Is there any change?"

"Sadly, no. One glimmer of hope is that the scans have revealed no damage to the brain itself, but the surgeons are still concerned about abnormal pressure inside the skull and are working to reduce that. They're anxious of course to avoid any clotting."

"So what happens now?"

"Nothing, I'm afraid, my dear. We just have to sit it out and wait. They say I must keep talking to him about anything which might stimulate the brain, playing favourite music – the usual things. Then, hopefully, he will one day just wake up."

"Are you on your own out there, Mrs. Hunt?"

"Yes, I am now. My husband's gone back to Canada. There was little point in our both staying here, so it seemed logical. Your uncle tells me Auriol's had her operation. Has it gone well?"

"I think so. The next two or three weeks are fairly critical, but Charles says everyone's very positive that the outcome will be good."

"Well, that's a relief. It's a pleasure to have some heartening news for a change. So many have died and been injured. I feel it's going to take years before Sri Lanka fully recovers."

It was obvious that Marie Hunt wanted to talk and it was some time before Gemma was able to replace the phone. Reflecting on this latest news, she thought what a different scenario this was from the one she had planned. Her Voices were strangely silent, as if to register their own disapproval. Still, with so many people anxious to play Florence Nightingale to the happy couple, she had no doubt that they would eventually emerge smiling from this fiasco and once again their love would blossom and be sickeningly obvious for all to see. Time to get on with her own life, she would ring her agent.

At last came the call from Leo, which Gemma had been awaiting and half dreading. Leo knew too much about her. He was dangerous.

"Sister dear, back home safe and sound. Someone must have been watching over you."

Gemma, non-committal. "Someone was. But now that you've at last taken the trouble to phone, Leo, what do you want?"

"I want to know, Gemma dear, if you've found the will?"

"The will? What will?"

"For heaven's sake girl, get a grip. Mother's will of course. After all, we do have a vested interest in that, don't we?"

"No . . . I never thought of it. It's just been nice to be at home and quiet, after everything that's happened."

"But the point is Gemma, is it your home? It might be mine or Auriol's. Who's to know, until we find out just what Mum wanted? My guess is she'll have hidden the will somewhere, it's not the sort of thing you leave lying around."

"I see . . . I'll start looking straight away."

"Do that. And Gemma?"

"Yes?"

"Be warned. Mum was sufficiently organised to have left a copy with her solicitor.

So, no funny business, O.K.?"

"Get off the phone, Leo!" And with that, Gemma slammed the phone down on its stand.

Logically, she had thought the will would be in Susan's office, but after sifting through a multitude of files relating to Council work, household bills etc., without success, Gemma moved upstairs to her mother's bedroom. She already knew the name of her mother's solicitor and was not, as Leo had seemed, desperately anxious to learn the will's contents.

Since returning home Gemma had avoided Susan's room. Now, she caught her breath at the familiar perfume, the neatly arranged items on the dressing table, the dressing gown hanging behind the bathroom door, all somehow disarming. The dressing table drawers contained lingerie and Gemma remembered how thrilled her mother had been at being able to purchase satins and silks previously unaffordable. Underneath these she found the box containing her mother's jewellery. The few decent pieces given to her by Mark were missing and had obviously been packed with Susan's clothing for Sri Lanka. Gemma was just about to replace the lid of the box when she saw a gap between the layer of felt holding the jewellery and the base of the box. Emptying it, she found several old newspaper cuttings and some newer looking pieces of paper.

At first, she was slightly puzzled by the report on the accident, then Gemma suddenly remembered hearing Susan telling a woman in the village that she had been orphaned as a child, when her parents died in a car crash. Why then would the newspaper headline it as a murder mystery?

The second paper explained all. It was a detailed account of the Inquest's findings and her grandmother's part in her grandfather's death. The articles about Evil, Genius and Madness, she quickly discarded. It was one of the new pages, a copy of an analysis of paranoia and schizophrenia from which extracts seemed to leap out at her.

'Fixation of hatred on one person', 'Feelings of invincibility and grandiosity', 'extreme mood swings', 'bouts of rapid speech', 'the belief that God has personally handed out instructions', 'Voices'!

The paper fell from her hand. This was how she had so often felt, confident that no-one could beat her, that she was ultra important and no-one appreciated it. Certain in the knowledge that God had personally given her instructions to behave the way she did. Her hatred of Leo, from the day he was born. It all fitted. This was a picture of herself. The picture of a monster.

Suddenly the preservation of these cuttings made sense. Her mother, victim of her own mother's abnormality had carefully watched her children to ensure the sickness had not skipped a generation. Only after Leo was born had Gemma started to show those signs.

And the other cuttings about research into being evil from birth, the fine line between Genius and Madness. Now she read those too. It became suddenly clear why her mother had looked upset when her father had enthused about how quickly Gemma had mastered chess. He'd even said "Only a genius does that in such a short time."

What was also now apparent was that her father hadn't known about her maternal grandmother! That would explain why the cuttings were carefully hidden. The story everyone had accepted about Susan's childhood had been deliberately fictitious so that no-one would know of her parentage.

Now Gemma paced the room. *Oh my God! What have I done? Leo . . . the number of times I've tried . . . No wonder he hates me. Fran, Mark and now my mother . . . . I'm a killer. When they find out, they'll lock me up and throw away the key. It says here medication can help. So why haven't I been treated? Why didn't my mother do something before it was too late? Gemma knew the answer to that. Just as Susan had kept, even from her husband, the story of her own childhood, so she would not, could not divulge to anyone, that she suspected Gemma was ill and worst of all, mentally ill. Oh my God! My God! Don't desert me now.*

Falling onto the bed she drew to her, her mother's pillow, with its delicate, distinctive aroma. Cradling it in her arms, she rocked backwards and forwards, until at last, exhausted, she slept.

Aroused later that evening by the phone, she heard Charles's excited voice telling her he had excellent news.

"Neil is out of his coma. He's recognised, and talked to his mother and the prognosis is now good. Plenty of rest and a gradual build up of strength and the medics are confident he'll be fine. As you can imagine, Auriol wept buckets when I told her. She'll need another couple of weeks here in Athens, then she can leave hospital. I suggested she came here to the Embassy, but, Gemma, she has stressed that she wants to be with you in Chichester. How do you feel about that? She won't need nursing. Just a lot of rest. I could always arrange some assistance for you. In fact, Auriol says the one person she felt would be ideal would be the lady you all called Nanny Biggs. I don't want to rush you. Give it some thought and I'll ring you again later."

A few minutes elapsed before Auriol herself was on the phone.

"Gemma, darling, I'm better and I want to come home. I want to spend some time with you, talk to you."

"Why? What about?"

"We've never spent much time together and now, after what happened to Mum, well, I am your big sister after all, I should be looking after you."

"You know . . ."

Auriol hesitated, "What do you mean Gemma . . . I know?"

Gemma's words came spilling out, "You know that I'm sick and everyone hates me and that I've done wicked things. Are you the one that's going to do it?"

"What do you mean? Do what?"

"You're going to section me aren't you? Have me put away, where I can't do anything else wicked . . . ."

"Whoa . . . whoa Gemma, slow down. Just what do you know?"

"I found papers yesterday amongst Mum's things, describing just how I sometimes feel and how I act . . . it was as if they were writing about me personally. Why didn't anyone do anything to help me? Why didn't Mummy take me to a doctor and have me cured when I was little?" She was crying.

"Gemma, the only reason I know about this is that Mummy told me the night before . . . the night before she died. It was almost as if she might have had some sort of premonition and needed to tell someone." And, as Gemma started to speak, "No, darling, hear me out. We agreed that she and I would persuade you to have some treatment. These days it can be controlled. I'm going to help and I know Neil will too, when he's quite better. We can get over this together."

"Last night when I found the cuttings, it sounded as if I was a monster. If they find out what I've done, they'll put me in prison, or somewhere like Broadmoor."

"Never! Darling, it's an illness, for which there is a cure, or at least, medical assistance and we'll find it together. Yes, Mummy should have done something before, but Daddy didn't know about our maternal grandmother and Mum felt if the story got out, there'd be a lot of gossip and we might have to move house . . . I know that sounds trivial, but it would have meant Daddy's job, changing our schools, it would have been so complicated. Gemma, this is why I'm determined to come to Chichester and why I think we should get Eileen Biggs to come and stay with us. She once wrote to Mum, saying you needed some help, but nothing was done. Eileen's a kind lady who doesn't gossip. She's also a good cook and housekeeper, just the sort of treasure we need now. Do agree to my getting in touch with her . . ."

"She was always kind to me, in spite of what she must have known . . ." Gemma, trying desperately to calm down.

"Of course, because Eileen understood. I'll contact her. And Gemma, there's something else we must do now. We need to organise a service. And another thing, darling, Mum would have wanted you to sing. Think about it."

CHAPTER 21

As was to be expected, in the village of Moordean and in Chichester itself, there were sympathetic murmurings about the misfortunes of the Hatton family. The Vicar's death, his younger daughter finding her friend drowned, the youngest child almost being lost to the swamp and now three members of the family caught up in the horrors of the tsunami. Only Eileen Biggs made any connection between some, if not all, of these events. Auriol's call from Athens brought the memories flooding back. But it was not a time for sentimentality, and quickly she asked the nursery if they would accept her notice with effect immediately. They regretted losing her. But learning the circumstances, two sisters having lost their mother and one badly injured in the tsunami, now both requiring assistance and comfort from someone they knew, Eileen left with their blessing.

Nothing had been said about Gemma's health, but Eileen was shocked on her arrival to find the girl ashen faced, tearful and obviously very vulnerable. Everything unpleasant which had gone before was wiped out in that first embrace as Gemma clung to Eileen as to a supportive lifeline. Once those early moments were over, it was Eileen who made her way to the kitchen and quickly located what she needed. Soon they were seated in the calming atmosphere of the sitting room, a tray of tea in front of them.

"When does Auriol arrive, Gemma?"

"Tomorrow, in the afternoon. Charles . . . Uncle Charles, that is, has organised transport from Gatwick. She was travelling first class, so that a steward could keep an eye on her, but Charles says now she really only needs peace and rest."

"Well, she'll certainly get this here. What a beautiful house this is, Gemma, the furnishing is delightful. I'm sure your mother loved it. What a kind man her friend must have been to leave it to her." No comment from Gemma, "He must have loved her very much."

Eileen saw the girl's eyes had filled with tears. "I know it must be difficult to talk about your Mum, but it's better if you make yourself do so, it will help in the end."

"You don't understand . . . It's Mum and Mark . . . and what I've done . . . Oh God!"

Moving quickly across Eileen put her arms round the girl, rocking her gently until at last the tearing sobs subsided and she was quiet.

"I think I understand more than you imagine, Gemma. A long time ago I wrote to your mother, saying I was concerned about you and that I thought you needed to see a doctor. Sadly, she didn't respond. I couldn't understand why, but you might possibly know the answer to that."

"Yes . . . I . . ."

"You can explain later, we've all the time in the world. When Auriol asked me to come here, I felt there was something more than just her recuperation at stake. I'm here to help both of you in any way I can, not to be judgemental about anything which has gone before. What's done is done. Now our aim is to make you well and whole again." And, as Gemma at last started to dry her eyes, "The next question is, what's in the fridge and the freezer? We have a homecoming to plan for your sister."

And, in spite of everything, in the midst of the tears, there *was* some laughter and a deep-seated relief on the part of Gemma that here were two people who really cared about her and believed that she could, and would, be made well.

Eileen's examinations in children's emotional development and Auriol's brief encounter with psychological studies all started to prove helpful. Before enlisting medical help, they decided they must do their own research and find out as much as possible about the type of drugs available and their side effects, if any. Gemma's confessions to Auriol were only partially relayed to Eileen. As Auriol said to Gemma,

"I trust her implicitly, but it's in her own best interests not to know the details about Fran and Mark. If she had to be questioned at any time, she can say with all honesty that she was unaware of what happened. She's already aware of the incidents with Leo, let's leave it at that."

The biggest shock of all for Auriol was learning that Gemma had anticipated she and her mother would die together in the hotel bedroom and that Gemma had locked the door from the outside. Steeling herself not to show that she was reeling under the impact of this, Auriol said, "Gemma, you can't blame yourself for Mum's death. She'd taken a strong sleeping pill during the night and I didn't expect her to wake much before mid-day. There was no way she would have been roused by the bells and the noise outside her room and let's face it, the tsunami hit us all quickly and unexpectedly . . . as I know, to my cost."

"Auriol, I'm so, so sorry."

"We agreed not to do sorry . . . Have you decided on something to sing at Mum's service?"

"I thought, 'I dreamed that I dwelt in marble halls'.

"Any special reason why?"

"Well, Mum liked to hear me sing that and she loved beautiful places, that's why she was so thrilled to have this elegant house . . ."

"Then that sounds just right. We'll have to ask Leo. Are you alright with that?"

"*I'm* alright with it. I think it's him you should be asking that."

"Of course he'll come. He should also read one of the lessons and we must select some hymns. You know he came to see me in Athens?"

"No, I didn't. Was he staying with Charles?"

"No . . . I felt that something had gone wrong there. Couldn't quite put my finger on it, but there was definitely a frisson when Charles's name was mentioned. You know Leo's very friendly with a young Greek Cypriot?"

"No, but then I'm not familiar with anything he does nowadays."

"It was quite interesting talking to him about Jason, the Cypriot. I got the impression they were *very* close friends and I mean that in every sense of the word. The thing is, Leo seems so infatuated that he's totally convinced that everything Jason tells him is gospel. Apparently the boy's family, along with quite a few others from what I'm told, hate us Brits for what happened way back in the 50's when we agreed to letting the Turks have the Northern part of Cyprus. They'd been a Greek island and then a British protectorate and felt we'd let them down."

"And this Jason is still smarting from something which happened so long ago?"

"I gather his family won't let him forget. His grandfather was in a resistance group called EOKA and they went underground to fight the Turks . . . . it's all complicated. Jason apparently kept saying that his grandfather was killed in the fighting and all the women in his family had always worn black. Clearly his own father was indoctrinated to carry on the British hate campaign and Jason seems determined to pass on that hatred to everyone close to him."

"And Leo comes into that category?"

"Without a doubt. I've wondered before about Leo, and now hearing him talk so lovingly about Jason, I know I was right. He's definitely gay."

As expected, Susan's fellow councillors turned out in force at the Service of Thanksgiving. Members of the administration staff from County Hall were well represented, as were villagers from Moordean and many of the teachers who had known Auriol, Leo and Gemma.

The choir sang some of Susan's favourite pieces and Leo read from "And death shall have no dominion". Gemma's contribution left the congregation stunned by the clarity and sweetness of her voice. Only Auriol, sensible, unflappable Auriol, came to grief during her reading of the Rossetti poem 'Remember'. The breaking of her voice twice during the first verse was the forerunner of a sob and then a complete halt. It was Gemma, seated two yards away, who was quickly at her side, took the paper from her and completed the reading.

If, for the family and others, there was a feeling of déja vue as they left the Cathedral, no-one mentioned it. Leo, having declined the invitation to stay overnight or to partake of the tea and biscuits served in the Church Hall, left with almost indecent haste. The uncles had of course added their own quiet dignity to the occasion and if there seemed little or no contact between Leo and Charles, only Auriol appeared aware of it. The uncles had to leave promptly for London, Simon due to attend a meeting at the Naval Department the next day and Charles to visit the Foreign Office before returning to Athens.

As Charles said ruefully, "I keep hoping they're going to offer me somewhere really great, like Paris or Ottawa, but it never happens. Still, my congratulations to you both, you've handled this splendidly and I'm proud of you, as your parents and grandparents would have been."

And from Simon, "I hope you both know, that whilst we might be some distance away, if you need help of any sort, you're to let us know and we'll do all we can. Thankfully, you won't have any financial worries, your mother has more than seen to that." Then, kisses and fond farewells and they were gone.

Auriol was well aware the uncles were right about the money. The will had been finally located in Susan's office and stated that the house was to be passed jointly to the three children, with the proviso that if one wanted to sell, the other two must be given the first option to purchase. Auriol was to receive her father's desk and all his books, whilst Gemma had Susan's baby grand piano and her now considerable library of music. In lieu of these bequests, Leo was to receive £5,000 from the estate. The remainder of the considerable estate together with its valuable land, was to be split between the three of them again with the proviso that if land was to be sold by any one of them, then the others should have the first option to purchase.

Later that evening Auriol, with Gemma at her side, thanked Eileen for the tower of strength she had been throughout the planning of the service, well aware that its smooth running had been due in no small part to her constant, helpful, promptings. "Have you seen a printer yet about the Order of Service?" "Has the choirmaster got your music?"

"Have you told the Cathedral staff how many places to reserve?" "Did you find out if the Council dignitaries precede or follow the Church procession?"

Although unspoken, Auriol was grateful for the ease with which Eileen calmed any situation and ensured there was always time to sit quietly and discuss events in detail, so that Gemma did not become agitated or feel excluded in any way. From the ashen-faced young woman, still reeling from the shock of what she had discovered, Gemma now seemed relatively composed.

Trying to sleep, Auriol compared the different vibes she had felt whilst talking to people after the service. It was like looking at her mother from three different angles. Clearly the village ladies remembered the Susan they had known during those difficult years at the Vicarage when money was short, and, fearful of getting too close to anyone in case they learned of her past, she had been regarded by them as cold and aloof. Out of courtesy, they had attended the service to pay their respects.

The change in circumstances which brought Susan financial security and her lovely home in Chichester, had led to her successes there, where, by these newer contacts, she was known as an authoritative and capable councillor and very well respected. All were full of praise for her charm and efficiency. The typists, receptionists and cleaners saw Susan in a different light, a warm hearted and understanding boss, who was always considerate and concerned for their well-being. In her relatively short life her mother had experienced a great deal of light and shadow and this had certainly been reflected in her behaviour towards others. There was no doubt that Susan had loved and been loved by Mark, the pity was . . . but . . . she must not go down that road.

Whilst he was at her bedside in Athens, Auriol had considered telling Charles about Gemma.and eventually decided against it. In the future it might well prove necessary, but until they could get Gemma to an expert in that particular field of medicine, it was unclear just what they were dealing with. Then, the guilt feeling took over. Was she doing just what her mother had done? Putting off the dreaded moment of having to confess to an abnormality within the family? After her own operation the doctors had said she must rest. Some chance!

Tomorrow there would be other problems to solve. Neil was now walking each day and his mother had been told he could return to his home in a month's time, whilst advising another month before resuming work. Auriol's own boss at the BBC had been making noises about when she might be able to start working again. Soon she must make some decisions, start to . . . what was that ugly new word all the vogue, prioritise? Gemma must certainly be at the very top of that list. But when oh when, could she and Neil ever be together again, enjoying life?

Her pillow was damp before sleep finally came.

Auriol's first task the next day was to advise Gemma to inform her agent that she would be unable to work for some weeks more. Whilst appreciating what she and Eileen had learned, that music was often helpful for psychotic conditions, it was too dangerous now for Gemma to be travelling to different venues, meeting different people and, most importantly, run the risk of her feeling in any way unimportant. Auriol had not forgotten the leading lady's fall down the stairs some months ago!

The next decision was to select, from the short list of three physicians they had drawn up, the one Gemma should see. One man was based in Guildford and two others, a male and a female, in London. Whilst Guildford was closer, it was felt the journey to London would be more direct. Auriol, accustomed to the bustle of Oxford's traffic, was an experienced driver, but felt with Gemma as a passenger, it would be an easier journey to travel by rail and take a cab to their venue.

Professor James Hutchinson was their final choice. At fifty eight, they felt he would have considerable experience and having presented papers to the British Medical Association on different aspects of psychosis, he was obviously well respected. Auriol and Gemma would travel together on the first occasion, with Eileen taking over when it was thought to be the right time. Auriol had compiled her own file of papers, including one alarming report that pharmacists had noted a sharp rise in the number of children being treated with anti-psychotic drugs, such as Risperdal and Zyprexa, normally only used to treat adult psychosis and schizophrenia. She felt reassured that she now knew at least a little about what they were dealing with.

Gemma did not appear nervous. Included in all their discussions and decisions, she seemed, on the contrary, anxious for things to happen.

Meeting James Hutchinson, Auriol felt they had chosen wisely. He greeted them courteously, then asked Auriol to wait in reception whilst he talked to Gemma. With Gemma's medical history in front of him, he started to speak.

"You do know Gemma, that everything you tell me is in the strictest confidence?"

"Yes."

"Under the law of patient confidentiality, I am not allowed to pass information you give me to anyone else. Your sister, I understand, already knows much of what has happened. Even so, I cannot stress strongly enough, that if there is any information to which you do not wish your sister to be privy, you must tell me."

"So, if you can't tell anyone, it would not be possible for you to put me in prison?"

"Absolutely not. What you have is a sickness, which I'm going to help you to deal with."

"But there are places?" . . . Her question hung in mid-air.

"Of course but those are for the insane, incurables. Those who no longer have any control over their own behaviour. That does not apply to you. We are now, at this moment, having a perfectly sensible conversation. You have just made a fairly lengthy journey with your sister. I assume that you did not attract attention to yourself on the train, or in the taxi, or whilst waiting in my reception room?"

"Well, no . . ."

"Then you must see the difference. For the majority, in the homes you have mentioned, even one segment of your journey today, or what I've just mentioned, would be an impossibility. Now, having ruled out the things which will *not* happen, let's start work. Who was the first person you can remember disliking?"

"My brother, Leo."

"And you were how old?"

"Four, almost five . . ."

"Why didn't you like him?"

"Because, when he was born, he'd taken my place."

"What place?"

"In Mummy's love."

"She surely still loved you?"

"Yes, but she was always so busy . . . busy with the baby. I used to be her Little Princess, but then Leo came and he was her Little Prince."

"But surely you had a big sister to play with?"

"She was at school and anyway when Auriol came home, she and Daddy were always looking at books. I was too little to join in with them and Mummy couldn't take me, when she took Leo for a walk."

"Why, was that?"

"I was too slow . . . my legs were so little."

James Hutchinson noted that when referring back to her childhood, Gemma's speech seemed to revert to more childish expressions.

"So, from being quite small, you wanted Leo out of your life? Tell me how you set about that."

And so it unfolded . . . the pinching, the attempt to stop Leo breathing, the riding incident, the poisoned berries and the swamp . . .

"That must have been difficult to organise." James Hutchinson commented.

"Oh, I'm quite good at organising things" . . . Gemma hesitated . . ."I shouldn't say that should I? It's part of my problem, thinking I'm clever."

"You must say anything you wish to me. And you *are* clever, there's no doubt about that. What I need to know is every *part* of the problem. You've never been tested on the Mensa scale?"

"No."

"But from what your teachers have said, you are extremely intelligent . . . Did you, when you were hurting Leo, think at any point you were doing wrong?"

"When I was quite small, I knew I was being naughty. But in the infants' class there was a naughty chair and sometimes you had to sit in that for a while, then it was all forgotten. Sometimes in church Daddy talked about people doing wicked things and having to be punished, but I always thought that was only for grown-ups. Daddy always said God watched over us and would sometimes tell us what to do, so when the Voices started, I knew it was him sending me messages."

"And that was when?"

"When my periods started. I was fourteen."

"And your Voices encouraged you?"

"Oh yes. They were always on my side you see. Annoyed when people didn't give me my fair share of attention. Delighted when they did. They laughed and clapped when I got things right."

"When you got things right?"

"Well, the business with Fran, my friend. At least she wasn't much of a friend really, but she was going to be Head Girl and she'd just beaten me in school, so the Voices said I should get rid of her, then I could be Head Girl."

"And?"

"Well, she was a swimmer . . . ." Gemma was starting to get excited, "I gave it a lot of thought and planned it down to the last detail, I'm good at that. I was able to keep her under the water until . . . I know now it was very wrong."

"Why do you know now? What has changed?"

"Well, at first I was shocked when I saw how upset her parents were, then when I wasn't seeing them any more and there was the excitement of being made Head Girl, I seemed to forget all that. But just a few weeks ago, I read about my grandmother, my mother's mother. She had schizophrenia and she killed my grandfather whilst he was driving. They were both killed. When I read the description of her illness, it made me realise there was something wrong with me."

"But your grandmother didn't have any treatment?"

"No, she refused, although her doctor offered it."

"Then *your* case is going to be completely different Gemma. I know you have a great deal more to tell me, but some of that can wait until next time. Today, I want you to have a brain scan so that I can see if that shows any reason why you have such exceptional intelligence. I'm going to give you a drug which will help you *always* to ignore any intervention by your Voices – they will be silenced. And Gemma, I see from your record that you are a singer, a very good singer. I think we will soon be able to arrange for you to restart your career. Now," he rose and shook her hand, "I need to speak to your sister and tell her what I plan to do and when I can see you next. Will you wait in reception please?"

James Hutchinson's diagnosis was as they had feared. A supreme intelligence, paranoia which had found its roots in the hatred of her brother and then gradually spread to others, and early signs of schizophrenia. However, he was convinced that now Gemma herself was aware of the problems, she would co-operate. She should be allowed to sing, but must always be escorted to her venues, because the tension involved before going on stage might counteract the effects of the drugs.

There was one unexpected recommendation.

"There is one thing I'm going to suggest Miss Hatton. Do you know a masseuse, or anyone capable of learning one of their simpler techniques?"

Immediately, Eileen Biggs sprang to mind, "Why yes, a friend who lives with us. She used to be our nanny and has since then worked in child care and qualified as a nursery attendant. Eileen's fascinated by all things medical and, she knows a great deal about Gemma. In fact it was she who when Gemma was little, recognised a problem and tried to persuade our mother to do something about it."

"Sounds ideal. Try to arrange as soon as possible for her to take a course in Indian Head Massage. This, you understand, is in no way a cure, but regular sessions of this, particularly if Gemma is about to sing, or has sung, in public, would dramatically reduce her tension levels and prevent her getting agitated. That is to be avoided at all costs. In a calm, stable atmosphere, with the drugs I prescribe, Gemma will be able to lead a happy, and I hope, a fulfilled life. I will of course, see her at regular intervals and check on her progress by telephone."

"Thank you." Auriol got up to leave.

"There's one other important matter. Does Gemma have a gentleman friend?"

"No . . . why do you ask?"

"I'm afraid that should she enter a serious relationship of a sexual nature her partner should be made aware of her problem and of the family history. Only then can they together decide whether to start a family. If they do so, the same watchfulness your mother had to exercise will be necessary. Sadly, we have not yet learned how to eliminate the gene responsible."

Alarm bells rang in Auriol's head, "And me? What about me? Supposing I have children? What then?"

James Hutchinson hesitated, "I think, my dear, you also, being aware of the problem, should be watchful. Who knows, in a few months, we might have identified the root cause of the trouble and be able to eradicate it for all time? Please don't upset yourself about it. Now, take your sister home, ensure she takes her medication and ask your Eileen friend to embark on her massage training as soon as it can be arranged."

Their lives were soon amended to a new routine. Together Auriol and Gemma decided that Eileen could not be expected take on further duties in addition to running the house efficiently. It was then that Eileen suggested her niece, Sophie. Having witnessed at first hand Sophie's expertise in the kitchen, Eileen knew she could adequately cope with preparing their food and with a little tuition, was more than capable of dealing with laundry and cleaning, whenever necessary. Auriol's relief was tremendous, the fact that the girl had just left school and could start straight away was a bonus. By all accounts Sophie was a good cook and a pleasant girl and Auriol had no doubt that Eileen would very soon have her schooled in whatever else was required. One of the smaller rooms they now allocated as a sitting room for Sophie and Eileen, whilst making it clear that the latter was welcome to join them at all times.

Setting up the massage course also proved quicker and easier than they had hoped. At the first beauty salon they visited, the masseur, pleased at the prospect of earning extra cash, said she would be pleased to give Eileen lessons and was prepared to start the next day!

CHAPTER 22

Gemma sat down gingerly. The sheath-like cocktail dress, whilst showing her figure to maximum advantage, allowed very little room for manoeuvre. Definitely a case of standing room only. But oh, the bliss of being off her feet, if only for a while. The gorgeous shoes with their three inch heels, were crippling after standing for half an hour.

What on earth had possessed her to attend this stuffy Embassy 'do'? It couldn't be further removed from the 'clubbing' atmosphere to which she had in the past, been accustomed. Accustomed, but not always satisfied. Bright young things all living 'on the edge'. Funny that, the edge of what, she had never been quite sure. Here there seemed to be an equal mix of near geriatrics, desperate-to-climb-the-social-ladder Hooray Henrys, and the inevitable lounge lizards.

Only her own desperation to get back into some semblance of normality and her uncle's charm could have persuaded her. "Gemma darling, please say you'll join us. There will be other young people there, and I'm sure you'll find plenty to talk about."

"But it's awkward, with Auriol going off to meet Neil."

"On the contrary, that should make it a great deal easier. You'll be able to travel for most of the journey together, then you can go straight to the hotel, which I'll book for you. You might want to have a rest before you get yourself all glammed up, then when you're ready, reception will call you a cab to take you to join me in Whitehall."

"Well, I know Auriol's meeting Neil at Heathrow and they're going straight to Simon's flat for a few days, before they come down to Chichester. But I'm not sure, it doesn't seem quite my thing . . ."

"Look, I'll make it even easier for you. Supposing I send a car to Chichester to collect you and take you straight to your hotel?" Obviously Charles was anxious to ensure she was not still, after several months, grieving for her mother. Would he be quite so helpful, if he knew the whole story?

Finally, she had accepted Charles' invitation. It seemed churlish to do otherwise and she might well need to make use of his good nature in the future. Now she watched him, his charm currently at full stretch, as he clearly tried to extricate himself from the attentions of a formidable puce-clad matriarch.

A ripple of activity at the room's entrance. Now, this was more like it. The young man entering, slim, darkly handsome and obviously a workaholic, briefcase in hand as he greets the Ambassador, and accepts a glass of champagne. He turns away and with a 'silly me to have forgotten' type of shrug, deposits his briefcase and champagne and exits.

In that moment Gemma knows. Opens her mouth to shout and no sound emerges. Rises and gestures. People turn and stare, raise eyebrows, resume their conversations. Stumbling, she moves towards the brief case. Hears in another world, someone say, "Too much wine . . . how disgusting!" Seizing the case she pushes her way back towards the French doors, glasses are knocked from hands and distantly she hears squeals and protests, the tinkling of glass hitting the floor. At last the open doors and she hurls the case with such momentum that losing her balance, she herself staggers and rolls down the steps. A moment's silence, a loud crump and then the Embassy garden erupts in a burst of flame, showering in its aftermath, shrubs, seats and stone ornaments.

At the bottom of the steps Gemma rolls herself into a ball as windows shatter spraying glass in her direction. Her ankle, she thinks, is sprained or broken, but otherwise she feels in one piece. Yes, there are probably numerous cuts, in some she can feel glass still embedded, but otherwise she's O.K. Someone has been watching over her!

Within seconds people rush down the steps, peer at her as she uncurls, debate whether she should be moved, until at last Charles appears, outwardly calm and efficient, as always.

"The ambulance will be here in a few minutes. Don't attempt to move, Gemma, until we know what the damage is. Gemma, my darling, you are the bravest of girls. But how did you know?"

"There was something . . . something about the way he put the case down and looked around . . . then left the room so quickly."

"Well, sweetheart, I'd say you've saved a good many people from serious injury, or worse." There was a spatter of applause and murmurs of agreement from those around her. Now others started to emerge, surveying the wrecked garden with horror.

At last they heard the wailing of the ambulance's approach. Charles was, in fact, deeply shocked and afraid that Gemma might be seriously injured, but determinedly kept his feelings under control, until professional help arrived. Speedily Gemma was taken to hospital, the glass removed from her cuts and her ankle, which proved to be only sprained, was strapped. Charles hovered at her side as all this was accomplished, leaving only to make vital phone calls.

As he'd expected, Auriol and Neil said they would leave straight away for St. Thomas's Hospital, but Charles finally persuaded them that the doctor had suggested Gemma should rest now, as he was worried about delayed shock. He would be giving her a sedative and preferred that no-one visited her that evening as she must certainly stay overnight. Auriol knew that her uncle must now be put in the picture with regard to Gemma's health. As briefly as was possible, she told Charles about their maternal grandmother and that Gemma had seen a specialist. Charles, trying to come to terms with this second shock, agreed that this information must be relayed to the doctor treating Gemma, so that he could ensure drugs were not conflicting and that she had no extreme reaction to the events of the day.

And so, at last, Gemma drifted into a blessed sleep where Voices, explosions and shattering glass were not allowed to venture. Charles, weighed down with this new knowledge, returned wearily to the scene of the explosion and talked at some length to the police. Auriol and Neil, as their second, longed for, loving reunion, was once again disrupted in a violent way, wondered what next life would throw at them. And in Chichester, Eileen Biggs wept tears of pride for Gemma, who had this evening, been brave and strong and saved many lives.

Another day. Still confused, Gemma tries to orientate herself. Hospital and nurses. Of course, the explosion. She cries a little.

A figure at her bedside moves forward. "Now, now Sister dear, what was it you used to say, 'Don't be such a cry baby, Leo, nothing to be alarmed about'."

"You . . . ? What on earth? How did you know . . . about me, about the bomb?"

"Gemma, you're obviously not yet abreast with communications in our hi-tech modern age. Bad news travels fast. As of course, for some of us, so does good news."

"Go away, I don't want you here." A note of fear in Gemma's voice.

"Sorry Sis, you're stuck with me and my friend. Oh dear, how remiss of me, I haven't yet introduced you. Jason, this is my dearly beloved sister, Gemma."

A young man steps forward into Gemma's line of vision. *My brain is still muddled, it can't be . . . . But it is. The young man, who so conveniently left behind his brief case. The young man, who, she had guessed, was responsible for the explosion. Surely he wouldn't dare risk . . . ? And why with Leo? Then she remembered . . . Jason. Of course, the young man Auriol had told her about, the one Leo was devoted to.*

"You . . . ? What on earth are you doing here?"

"Jason, Gemma dear, is my friend, my best friend, in fact the love of my life. Oh, and he's also a descendant of a member of EOKA, you know the ones that were not at all happy about what happened to their beloved Cyprus. And are still not happy. It may be past history to the Brits but it isn't to those who lost members of their family."

"Terrorists!"

"Well, of course, that depends which side of the fence you're on. Not at all pleased with our dear Uncle's lot and the way the politicians brush on one side what happened, as if it's of no importance. Just as I wasn't too pleased with your treatment of me over the years, or with our dear uncle's inability to move with the times. So Jason and I decided to return one or two compliments to you and Uncle Charles, and kill two birds with one stone, as it were. Except of course, we didn't quite achieve that, in the same way you didn't quite achieve all your targets. Sometimes hitting the wrong ones as I recall."

Gemma groaned.

"Oh dear, it's not been a very good couple of days for you has it?"

"Go away, you and your nasty little friend."

"Oh, we're going alright, as far away from you as possible. All those years of making me suffer, blighting my life, you owe me, Gemma, and now I'm calling in my debts. I thought we might have reached a conclusion, but on second thoughts this way might be best, you've now got to live with what you've done over the years.

"You see, I unravelled your movements during the tsunami, and now know exactly what happened. I was always suspicious when I learned you'd gone out there, knew that wasn't planned. When the police said they couldn't work out why Mother and Auriol didn't get the message to evacuate the hotel and get to higher ground, it all started to look very murky. Then they added that someone had remarked on the fact that amongst the debris it was noted that their room keys were, amazingly, still in the door, but on the outside. Well, it didn't take a Sherlock Holmes to guess whose hand was evident in that. When I learned that you had conveniently escaped in one of the cars provided, minutes before the hotel was hit, it all started to make sense. Auriol's absence was puzzling at first and I've no doubt you thought she was still in the room when you made certain they were locked in. Can't lay the blame on you for the tsunami though. Clever you may be, but I don't think you've acquired those sort of powers . . . yet!"

"Call the nurse, I'm in pain!"

"Don't tell me you expect sympathy . . . from *me*? You, who have led lambs to the slaughter, without turning a hair. You, dear sister, who have been a thorn in my flesh since I was born, and witnessed me in agony, more times than I care to remember. You have orphaned me; first my father, then my mother. Somewhere along the way, Mark Fleming and your innocent school friend came to grief, and there may of course have been others, about whom we know nothing. As far as I'm concerned, you can rot in hell and I hope you live a very long and miserable life."

He turned away, "Oh there's just one other thing . . . I've left the Navy and Jason and I are going away, a long way away. So that's it, Sister dear. Retribution for me and for Jason, with a capital R. Don't attempt to persuade anyone else that Jason and I were responsible for last night's little episode. You see, Gemma, people don't really believe anything you say. They might go through the motions, but they're always smiling behind their hands. And that's what you must do, keep smiling, even when it hurts."

Leo paused, bending down over the figure on the bed, as if to embrace her, "Let's say this one is for old times' sake, Gemma," and with that, he pinched her arm and as she squirmed, added, "You should be more careful, Sister dear, Little Princesses shouldn't have nasty black marks."

Turning to the doorway, Leo found it blocked by a tall young man, who was glowering at him, "Leo, I think you've done and said quite enough. So last night was your idea of retribution was it? Something which involved killing about fifty people. Hardly puts you and your bigoted friend in the realms of the saints, does it? You must be very disappointed this morning."

Leo and Jason exchanged surprised glances.

"Ah . . . it's obvious you haven't seen the morning papers. You see, it didn't quite work out as you'd planned, and you have Gemma to thank for that. By throwing your bomb into the garden, she saved a lot of people from serious injury and perhaps death. Brave of her wasn't it? And don't be under any illusions about the police being fooled. I doubt if Jason will get through security at the airport, but if you do want to give it a go, you'd better make tracks now."

The young men moved forward, barred once again by the stranger's hand.

"I'm Neil Hunt by the way and just before you leave there's something else your *other* sister thinks you should know."

Suddenly Auriol was there amongst them, thrusting a piece of paper into Leo's hand, then moving quickly to the far side of Gemma's bed.

"I think you'd better read that Leo . . . it affects you, personally." And as he, scowling, scanned the report of the inquest, she added, "That article refers to our maternal grandmother Leo. She killed our grandfather. And her story is the reason why Gemma has been struggling for years to overcome something not of her own making, an hereditary gene – *your* grandmother's gene, Leo."

"Don't fob me off with this nonsense." Leo threw the paper on the bed. "Gemma was just plain jealous, from the time I was born. The irony was that none of you realised how much I hated all that lovey dovey stuff I had to endure and was only too glad to get right away from home and the lot of you."

Neil Hunt now intervened. "By all means dismiss it as nonsense if you so wish. But it's just as well you're not planning to be a father, Leo . . . ever." Leo's head came up sharply as he waited to hear what was coming next. "You see the physician Gemma has seen, is quite certain that she inherited an abnormal gene. Nor did he rule out the fact that it might be inherent in other members of the family and not show itself for some time." Clearly Leo was now hanging on Neil's words as he continued, "I can't help feeling he would be very interested in last night's incident and the fact that you were so easily swayed in joining your bigoted friend here, in an attempt to wipe out members of the British Government because of something which happened fifty odd years ago. Sounds pretty abnormal to me."

Leo had turned pale during Neil's comments. He started to move again towards the door.

Neil continued, "We now know the problem and Auriol and I are gong to make sure that Gemma's helped to overcome it and that, contrary to what you were wishing, Gemma becomes an important part of a loving family, *our* family.

"I don't suppose for one moment we've heard the last of you, Leo. After all, there's money involved somewhere along the line and I imagine you and young Jason here will not want to miss out on that. Could be difficult though, if you daren't come back to U.K. to collect it."

Neil raised his arm and the two young men scuttled away. Auriol moved quickly over to her sister's bedside, wrapping her arms around Gemma and rocking her backwards and forwards. At last tears were dried and Gemma sufficiently composed to smile at Neil and say, "What an amazing performance! I wondered for a moment who the handsome stranger was who'd come to rescue me from Leo. I think, Mr. Hunt, you've missed your vocation; surely with an entrance like that you should be on the stage."

Delighted that Gemma had so quickly recovered from both the shock of the explosion and Leo's diatribe, a smiling Auriol now sat on the edge of the bed, one arm round her sister's shoulders.

"We've got some news, Gemma, and a query. If you have no objections, we'd like to stay with you in Chichester." Gemma looked at her questioningly, "I mean, permanently."

"Neil's going to Canada for a few weeks to be with his parents and get really fit, but he's applying for a post at Lancing College as Deputy to the Principal there. Fingers crossed of course, but with his qualifications we're very hopeful. I can always work from home and commute to London as necessary. We'll keep Eileen and Sophie, as there'll be more work. What do you think? Will you miss your privacy?"

"Auriol, Neil, I'd love it and no, I wouldn't miss my privacy. But, what about you two? You must have had so many plans about having a place of your own."

"*If*, we really feel the need, there's plenty of room for expansion, another annexe, that sort of thing. We can meet those problems as we come to them. Mr. Hutchinson says that you, my love, are to resume your singing career, so it will soon be all systems go."

"Neil, you don't know me, but you obviously know my history?"

"I do, and I know there's nothing that a supportive family can't overcome, we're all in this together." And with that he came and sat on the other side of her bed, linking his arm with Auriol's around her shoulders.

"I've been thinking . . ." Neil was smiling at both sisters, "I've got a feeling that this young lady," pointing at Gemma, "could well be in for some sort of award for her actions last night. Promise me, that if that happens I get to accompany you to Buckingham Palace."

Relaxed at last, they laughed together.

EPILOGUE

Chichester 2008

Three year old Ryan skipped along the corridor, turning his head now and again to make sure Auntie Gemma was keeping up with him. Approaching his parents' room, the door was flung open and a beaming Neil drew them in.

At the edge of her vision Gemma was just aware of Eileen standing near the window, but for she and her nephew the focus of their attention was on the bed. A pale, but smiling Auriol sat against a bank of pillows, cradling a baby in each arm. Gemma's heart lurched, recalling another such encounter all those years ago. Now she heard Auriol,

"Ryan Darling, come over here, Daddy will help you on to the bed. There . . . now you can see your new brother and sister." The little boy's eyes widened as she continued, "I wonder if you'd help me look after them? Would you like that?" Ryan nodded his head enthusiastically and reached out his own small hand.

"That's right, put your finger in your brother's hand and see if he'll say hello by squeezing it." The small child's face said it all. "Now Daddy will help you to come and sit on this side and meet your sister." Bubbling with delight, the child did as directed. "Now that you all know each other, Daddy's going to put the babies back in their cots, so that I can give my big boy here, a lovely hug."

And, in the midst of this,

"Gemma?" Auriol looked at her sister.

Too full for words, Gemma was crying with joy. Not because of the babies, wonderful as that was, not because of Ryan's infectious delight, not even because of Auriol and Neil's evident enthusiasm. Rather she was suffused with happiness at the love and warmth almost tangible in the room and, as the tears rolled unchecked down her cheeks, she felt herself enveloped in Eileen Biggs' comfortable and reassuring embrace.

A tap on the bedroom door. The voice of Sophie, Eileen's niece.

"Excuse me, Mrs. Hatton. May I see Eileen in the kitchen for a few minutes please? I need her advice."

As Auriol murmured her assent, Eileen carefully moved so that she was holding Gemma at arms' length. In that moment she saw the flash of anger in Gemma's eyes, the tightening of her lips and felt her body tauten. They were danger signals Eileen had learned to recognise.

"This will only take a short while, Gemma. Would you like to come with me?"

The girl nodded, moving towards the door. Eileen followed, conscious that she and the others must remain vigilant. There were now three vulnerable children in the house. Children who would be fussed over and admired. Gemma's illness might be for the most part dormant, but it had not gone away.

There must be no complacency here. It was not over.

. . .

Lightning Source UK Ltd.
Milton Keynes UK
18 November 2010